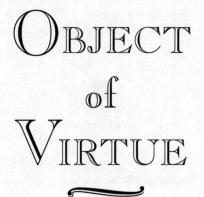

OBJECT of VIRTUE

A Novel

NICHOLAS B. A. NICHOLSON

A TOUCHSTONE BOOK
PUBLISHED BY SIMON & SCHUSTER
New York   London   Toronto   Sydney

This book is a work of fiction. The characters, conversations, and events in the novel are the product of my imagination, and no resemblance to any actual conduct of real-life persons, or to the actual events, is intended. Although, for the sake of verisimilitude, certain public figures do make incidental appearances or are briefly referred to in the novel, their interactions with the characters I have invented are wholly my creation and are not intended to be understood as descriptions of real or actual events, or to reflect in any way upon the actual conduct or character of these public figures.

TOUCHSTONE
Rockefeller Center
1230 Avenue of the Americas
New York, NY 10020

Copyright © 2004 by Nicholas B. A. Nicholson

TOUCHSTONE and colophon are registered trademarks of Simon & Schuster, Inc.
For information about special discounts for bulk purchases,
please contact Simon & Schuster Special Sales at
1-800-456-6798 or business@simonandschuster.com.

Designed by Jan Pisciotta

Manufactured in the United States of America

1   3   5   7   9   10   8   6   4   2

Library of Congress Cataloging-in-Publication Data
Nicholson, Nicholas B. A.
Object of virtue : a novel / Nicholas B. A. Nicholson.
p.   cm.
"A Touchstone book."
1. Art—Collectors and collecting—Fiction. 2. Saint Petersburg (Russia)—Fiction.
3. Americans—Russia—Fiction. 4. New York (N.Y.)—Fiction. 5. Rich people—Fiction.
6. Art dealers—Fiction. I. Title.
PS3564.I1985O23 2004
813'.54—dc22   2003070354
ISBN 0-7432-5783-9

For MFD, always #5.

In memory of Lisa Turnure Oldenburg.

*"I have left a glittering position in a glittering world,
but from it I go to a far greater place. . . ."*

ST. ELIZABETH OF RUSSIA,
GRAND DUCHESS AND HOLY NEW MARTYR (1864–1918)

*"In wit, as nature, what affects our hearts,
Is not th' exactness of peculiar parts;
'Tis not a lip or eye we beauty call,
But the joint force, and full result of all . . .*

*. . . Whoever thinks a faultless piece to see,
Thinks what ne'er was, nor is, nor e'er shall be."*

ALEXANDER POPE,
ESSAYS ON CRITICISM, PART II, LINES 43, 53

London, 1976

Princess Nina Ozerovsky pulled her brown suede trench coat tighter around herself, and grabbed Sasha's hand a little more firmly as they crossed Albemarle Street.

England's chill always bothered Nina, and though she had grown up in Paris where the damp was nearly as bad, there was something about the granite, marble, and brick facades of London buildings that made it seem unbearably frigid.

Sasha sniffed, and Nina looked down at her son.

"Sashenka, I promise, only one shop," she said in Russian. *"Only one shop, where we'll have a little tea, and then I'll take you wherever you like."*

"Madame Tussaud's?" he asked hopefully in English.

Nina sighed. He was only seven.

"If we must," she replied.

Sasha grinned, picked up his pace a little, and asked her the three hundredth question of the day.

"Where are we going?"

"We're visiting an old friend of Mama's, Mrs. Crane," she said.

The two walked along Albemarle Street past the jewelry shops and the worn facade of Brown's Hotel until they came upon a tiny lane that spun off it. Nina approached a small shop whose front was lacquered a deep cobalt blue and had a large plate-glass window filled with jewelry and silver. Nina remembered the first time she had come to Palais Newski Antiques with her mother, many years before, to sell an emerald ring. It was something they had had to do a lot, after the war.

"I can't see," Sasha whined, breaking her train of thought.

"Well, let's go inside," she said cheerfully, opening the door. "There is plenty to see."

Sasha walked in ahead of her. Nina gazed at her son as he approached the glass counter, his hands behind his back. He would be such a handsome man when he grew up—he reminded her so much of her own father.

God, I'm tired, Nina thought. She hoped she could get through the appointment without appearing as exhausted as she felt.

"Lydia, darling," Nina said, holding out her slender, gloved hands to the proprietress of Palais Newski.

"Nina," Lydia replied, smiling, "I'm so glad you called. I was afraid that I would miss you while you were in London."

"We just got in, but we're on our way to Paris for Easter with Sasha's grandparents," Nina said, pulling the silk scarf from her hair with a graceful, one-handed gesture.

"This *can't* be Sasha," Lydia said, looking at him. "But, Nina, he's just a baby!"

"I'm seven," Sasha said, with a sigh of irritation that made both women laugh.

"Sasha, why don't you look around a bit, while I speak with Mrs. Crane," Nina said.

Sasha nodded and moved away from the two women.

"Mama won't be long," she added as she watched him walk toward a large porcelain vase and then move to investigate a Russian inlaid table, the surface of which had a view of the Kremlin peopled with tiny marquetry Muscovites going about their eighteenth-century business.

"What luck you've come today. Come, come see," Lydia said, taking Nina's hand and drawing her back to the jewelry counter. "Really, what I've found *is* extraordinary, and I have something else—only you could possibly tell me who it belonged to. I need to establish the provenance."

The women walked to the back of the tiny shop, and Lydia took a felt bag from below the counter and set it carefully on the glass.

Nina opened the bag and smiled with pure pleasure—it was a Fabergé figurine of a Russian peasant girl, carved from quartz, purpurine, and other precious stones. Nina's eyes moved over the tiniest details; from the rumpled and gathered headscarf to the tiny woven *lapti* or bark shoes. The girl had a slightly weary expression, and Nina thought that if she had to wear shoes made of bark, she would probably look a little grumpy, too.

"Sasha, darling, come here," she called out to her son. "Mama wants to show you just one thing."

Sasha wandered over reluctantly. Mama had wanted to show him "just one thing" all day.

"Look," she said. "What is that?"

"It's a doll," he said without interest.

"No, sweetheart, not a doll, but a figurine. She's not to play with, she's to look at. Do you recognize anything?"

Sasha stared at the figurine and looked back and forth between it and his mother's face.

"She's the same color as your egg," he said.

"Good for you!" Nina said. "That's right—she's made of something called purpurine, and so is my egg." Nina fingered the small egg-shaped pendant that hung from the chain around her neck. "Would you like to know something else about purpurine?" Sasha nodded. "It's not really a stone at all. It's a special kind of glass." This piqued Sasha's curiosity.

"I can't see through it," he said.

"That's true, but it is glass just the same. People can't make stones, but we can make glass that looks like a stone, and that's what Monsieur Fabergé did. You know what else? Monsieur Fabergé was the only man who knew how to make purpurine, and now no one can."

"Really?" Sasha asked.

"Really," she replied. "So you know what that means? If you see something that has purpurine—"

"It was made by Fabergé," Sasha finished.

"Well, part of it might have been," Lydia said.

"Easy lessons first, Lydia," Nina said, interrupting her. "Mineralogical analysis perhaps when he's ten." The women laughed together as Sasha looked more closely at the figurine. Nina smiled and continued her lesson.

"When you look at a figurine, Sasha, you should always look at the stones—they are always chosen because each resembles the thing it is supposed to represent—you see? The pink quartz for her skin looks like skin, the purpurine dress looks like red linen. All of the surfaces are specially chosen to look as real as possible."

"You know what, Mama?" he asked. "Her shoes are made of twigs all woven together. And they're made of eosite."

Nina blinked. "What did you say?"

"Eosite. It's a stone. A real one."

"Where on earth did you learn that?"

"The museum today. That box you liked was made of eosite. I read the label."

"He's absolutely right," Lydia said. "The shoes are eosite, Nina. The boy has your eye, no doubt about that."

Nina thought for a moment, tilting her head to the side as she always did when she was concentrating. Suddenly she felt dizzy and she reached for the counter to steady herself. Smiling, she forced herself to go on.

"You know what else we call this type of piece, Sasha?" she said, breathing steadily. "We call it an object of virtue." Sasha stared blankly at her.

"The word *virtue* can mean that which is pure or perfect, but it also refers to the word *virtuosity*, meaning how well a person does something. When we call something an object of virtue, it means two things: that each piece of the whole object is perfect; the gold work, here . . . ," she said pointing, "and the stonework, here . . ." She pointed again. "And it means that the piece was made so that the person who made it could show their ability in a variety of skills in one object. So, can you show me another object of virtue?"

Sasha looked at the pieces in the display case, and Nina could see him thinking. He paused at a small sculpture, and again at a porcelain cup, before settling on a three-color gold Fabergé cigarette case with translucent oyster enamel and diamonds.

"That one," he said, pointing.

"Why?" she asked.

"Well, there is gold and enamel, and diamonds. It all looks perfect to me. Did one person make it?"

"No, Sasha, one person didn't. In the eighteenth century, one person would have, to show his skills. But with Monsieur Fabergé, always more than one person was involved. That's why the pieces are so beautiful. Each person who helped did the very best he could. The best goldsmith, the best enameler, the best stonecutters and setters; and so the finished result is still called an object of virtue." Nina gave her son a big kiss as he tried to wriggle away in embarrassment. Shaky, Nina sat in a small gilt chair nearby.

"He's you all over," Lydia said, and suddenly noticed Nina's exhaustion. "Oh, I'm sorry. I should have asked you to sit down the minute you walked in. Let me get you some tea and show you the reason you're here. I have a beautiful Fabergé frame, and it's covered with initials, but I can't make any connections. I don't recognize the people in the picture, but I'm sure that if I did, I could make sense of the monograms and establish the provenance. Can you help?"

"I'll try," Nina said absently, staring fondly at Sasha, who was pretending to shoot a gun at a statue of a Cossack, which fired back from its pedestal. "But pictures are so frequently changed in Fabergé frames, one really can never be completely sure," Nina said, returning her attention to Lydia.

Lydia brought Nina a cup of tea, and then pulled a large frame from beneath the counter, setting it up where Nina could admire it from her chair.

Nina's eyes ran over the heavy rectangular frame.

"Viatka birch," she said, "with lovely silver mounts in the

Napoleonic taste, cartouches with the Russian letter *sh*, and a count's coronet. And the people . . ." She looked down at the sepia photograph. "Why, it's Gaga and Bibi!" she exclaimed.

"Who?" asked Lydia.

"My maternal grandparents: Prince and Princess Ivan of Russia. How odd that they should be in this frame—the monogram doesn't—" Nina went rigid with anger.

"Nina, are you all right? You look as if you'll have a fit right here."

"Lydia, where did you buy this frame?"

"From a dealer in Paris. Why?"

"This frame belonged to my sister's husband's family, the Counts Shoutine."

"Do you think your sister sold this frame?"

"I'm certain she did," Nina said, turning away from the photograph and drinking some of the tea to fight her building nausea.

Lydia looked at her friend with sorrow. Nina and her sister, Tatiana, hadn't spoken for years.

"Nina, here." Lydia carefully opened the frame and removed the picture. "I have dozens of pictures of Empress Alexandra that I can slip in here. Just because your sister is selling her husband's things doesn't mean she can get away with putting her grandparents in a shop window." She handed the picture to Nina, who took it solemnly.

"Tatiana just doesn't think," Nina said softly. "She never thinks." Nina put the picture in her bag. "Lydia, you must let me pay you."

"Nonsense. I should pay you for giving me the provenance."

"Then we're even. Thank you again."

"Are we going?" Sasha asked.

"Yes, darling, we're off. Say good-bye to Mrs. Crane."

They made their farewells and were soon back on the street.

"Madame Tussaud's?" Sasha asked.

"Madame Tussaud's," Nina replied, helping him into a taxi. She closed her eyes and leaned back while Sasha clambered happily onto the enormous jump seat and looked out of the rain-dappled window.

One

⁓

EARLY ONE JANUARY MORNING, Alexander Ozerovsky drew on his brown suede gloves as he stood near a crowded bus stop. He stared up the stretch of Fifth Avenue north of Ninety-sixth Street and paid no attention to the other New Yorkers who looked at him with interest as they waited for their bus. He stood with them, and yet apart from them at the curb: aloof and impeccably dressed.

Though Sasha (as everyone called him in the Russian manner) was not unusually handsome, he had a physical presence that attracted attention. His clear grey eyes, aquiline features, and perfect posture (the result of years of childhood riding lessons) suggested he was one of New York's elite.

The trees in Central Park had turned brown early that fall, yet some leaves still clung tenaciously to the icy branches. Buses and cars streamed down the avenue, narrowly missing the lake of slush that separated the curb from the middle of the street. Mindful of a fast-approaching car, Sasha stepped back in time to avoid being splashed. The others were not so lucky. Clutching their newspapers and coffee, they jumped back too late, cursing and wet.

As the others grumbled, Sasha continued to look up the avenue, hoping to catch a taxi with its light on. If one came, he would take it, but he would certainly rather walk than ride a crowded bus with damp and unhappy people. He glanced over toward the park again and noticed a homeless man leaning up against a wall. He wore a large tinfoil crown and had a sign that read: "Deposed. Will reign for food." *This city is insane*, Sasha thought, and emptying his pockets, he walked over to the man and dropped the last of his change into a can placed on the sidewalk.

Checking the rose-gold tank watch that had been a twenty-first birthday present from his grandparents, Sasha realized he was running late. He gave up all hope of finding a cab this grey morning and began to walk. With the long stride that his friends often complained about, he began the mile-long trek to his office, leaving the soaked commuters and the deposed monarch behind.

❖   ❖   ❖

Upper Fifth Avenue was familiar to Sasha. He had lived in New York all his life, and his current apartment on East Ninety-seventh Street was only six blocks from the house where he had lived as a child before his mother's death. This morning, however, the walk down Fifth Avenue was a trial. Looking at the buildings he passed, all Sasha could see were the homes of people he could not convince to consign objects for sale at Leighton's Fine Art Auctioneers.

Our sale isn't so bad, Sasha reassured himself as he walked. *We have the Fabergé silver tea service and table with silver fittings, which belonged to Grand Duchess Marie, and the silver-gilt fish service. We have the paintings by Serov and Levitan, but we need something else. Something to compete with that damned necklace at Christie's.*

Sasha glanced up at the buildings as he passed. *1003 Fifth*, he thought. *The Travises have that Fabergé salmon pink enameled clock in the form of an egg, but they won't sell. What did Mr. Travis say? He was "waiting for the market to stabilize?" Nonsense. His wife wants to join the board of the Metropolitan Opera, and everyone on that board is a Sotheby's client. She's probably dangling the clock in front of Sotheby's to wriggle her way into the golden horseshoe.*

980 Fifth. Not much better there. Madame Joubert kept teasing him with her necklace of miniature Fabergé eggs, but the price she was asking was too high for Sasha—it involved a weekend he would have to spend alone with her at her villa on the Riviera.

Sasha didn't even bother to look up at 925. Mrs. Lloyd Winthrop had a Fabergé silver service made for Nicholas II's sister Xenia, but every year she decided at the last minute not to sell, wasting everyone's time.

If only he could find something better than that diamond necklace at Christie's—the necklace that everyone said had belonged to the last Empress of Russia, Alexandra. The press had been fascinated by the enormous glittering stones since it had been announced for sale by Christie's. So fascinated, that it was impossible for Sotheby's or Leighton's to get any attention for their own pieces. It didn't seem to bother anyone in the press that Christie's couldn't actually prove the provenance of the necklace, at this point. It didn't matter. The tragic ghost of Empress Alexandra circled the piece anyway, wringing her imperial hands. The only people who might have any information about the necklace were the Romanov family themselves, and they remained elegantly and conspicuously silent on the entire matter.

For the last seven years Sasha had worked for Leighton's—New York's premier small auction house—in the Russian Works of Art department. Despite his youth, he was an acknowledged specialist in the icons, silver, porcelain, jewelry, and ephemera of the Russian Empire. It was, however, his expertise in the works of the imperial court jeweler Karl Fabergé that brought him the respect he craved from his colleagues, and earned his department the millions of dollars it needed every season to stay open.

Sasha looked up at the limestone curtain of buildings along Fifth Avenue. He knew and was related to many of the people who lived behind those windows, but this season his connections had come to nothing. Despite his blood relation to half the aristocratic families of Europe and the few remaining families of old New York, Sasha was failing Leighton's. For the first time, he couldn't bring in anything to compete with Christie's.

From where he stood, Sasha could see a familiar building ten blocks away. The tall, solid 1920s tower known as 839 Fifth stood as it had since he was a child, filled with socialites, philanthropists, and a smattering of the very rich who had popped up like mushrooms in the New York of the 1980s.

Before 839 was built, on its site had stood the last mansion of *the* Mrs. Astor. The newest of New Yorkers didn't realize they were living at Mrs. Astor's old address, but Sasha's grandparents certainly did when they were accepted into the building in 1937, and Sasha and his father knew it when they took over the apartment after his mother's death and his grandparents decided to move to Greenwich. Sasha wondered if his father was in the city at all. *I haven't spoken to him in a month,* Sasha thought. *I've been too busy even to call my own father.*

Sasha had to admit it to himself—despite his connections and his bloodlines—his usual sources for Fabergé had completely dried up. The Russian dealers he knew had already been lured to Christie's and Sotheby's with promises of commission reductions he could not afford to offer. Many said they had nothing left to sell. This was the first time the head of his department was counting on him alone to find something incredible, and he wasn't sure he could do it. *This is the first sale I won't be able to pull off,* Sasha thought, dashing across Fifth Avenue at Seventy-third Street, and walking east toward his office.

❖   ❖   ❖

Sasha never ceased to be impressed by the beautiful building that housed Leighton's Fine Art Auctioneers. Designed by McKim, Mead, and White, and built at the turn of the twentieth century for a publishing magnate, the mansion was a copy of a Venetian *palazzo*. Leighton's galleried and columned facade was one of the greatest in New York, and Sasha glanced up at it, steeling himself for his day.

Inside his department the phones were ringing, and Sasha could see and hear through the glass window into her office that Anne was on the phone, having an agitated conversation with a client and tapping on a silver tureen lid for emphasis.

Dr. Anne Holton was one of the world's most respected experts on Russian works of art. She was universally admired within the field for her thorough knowledge of Russian language and culture, which she had acquired through years of studying at the NYU institute, teaching at Bard, and working for the Forbes Collection. Anne was attractive, her face unworn by thirty years in the field. This season, however, her patrician features remained permanently distorted by stress, and to enter a room where Anne was working was to leave exhausted, her palpable anxiety rubbing off on anyone near.

"*Ce n'est pas possible!*" she said firmly into the phone in her Farmington-accented French. "*Cette couronne est completement incorrecte—les Princes Wolkonsky n'etaient pas . . . Shit!*" She slammed down the phone into its receiver, and slammed the lid down onto its tureen.

"You're lucky that tureen isn't porcelain," Sasha said, leaning against the doorjamb of her office.

"Madame Safiyeh is lucky I don't fly to Geneva and tell her how better to occupy her days than by showing me again and again that she knows nothing," Anne said sharply while lighting an illegal Gauloise. "This tureen is making me crazy. She insists it belonged to the Princes Wolkonsky, and it does have a Latin 'W,' but it has a count's coronet. She has Wolkonsky documentation, but whose cipher is it? To top it off, it's an English silver tureen from the 1830s by Storr, and I can't even sell it in our sale."

Sasha thought for a minute, and his eyes brightened.

"One of the Counts Woronzoff was the Russian ambassador to Britain in the early nineteenth century—there's a great portrait of him by Lawrence in the Hermitage. Maybe his daughter or a niece married a Wolkonsky, and it was wedding silver with *her* coronet and cipher?"

Anne began to beam.

"That's why I keep you around, Sasha; you are just too good to be true!" Anne patted him on the shoulder and left to announce the discovery to the silver department.

Relieved, Sasha went to his desk. Praise from Anne was increasingly rare, and he was happy for any little bit that came his way. Anne had been a pupil of his mother's, and what Sasha hadn't learned from his mother, he had learned from Anne. In the absence of his mother's approval, Sasha had actively sought Anne's during the years he had been at Leighton's, and they had developed a rapport that was extremely important to him.

He weeded through his mail, glancing at the photographs sent to him for evaluation. The pictures of icons, porcelain, jewelry, and other trappings of the Russian Empire fluttered from their envelopes to his desk like brittle leaves.

The phone rang. It was Anne calling from the silver department.

"Sasha, listen—Silver is thrilled. Your idea means they can raise the estimate, and now it's off our plate entirely. I told them there's no way to complete the research in time for their catalogue deadline. They need everything by the end of the week."

"Don't be silly, I can do it," Sasha said and immediately regretted it. He was always trying to impress Anne with the amount of work he was capable of doing, and invariably ended up buried under it.

"Good work, Sasha, really," Anne said, and he could hear the smile in her voice. She continued, "Oh, we have a new client coming in at ten. He says that he has something so important, that he'll only show it to us in the boardroom. He's a Russian, but his English is excellent. Also, he specifically asked that you be there."

"Why me?" Sasha asked with interest. "You're head of the department."

"He said to make certain that His Highness Prince Ozerovsky would be at the meeting. The piece has something to do with your family. It's Fabergé."

"What is it?" Sasha asked.

"Sasha, who cares? At this point, we need to pull in some spectacular things to compete with the Sotheby's and Christie's sales in May. A great piece of Fabergé jewelry would really save us this sale."

"Well, I hope whatever this Russian brings in isn't some Brooklyn fake."

"He'll be in at ten. His name is Dimitri Durakov. We'll meet him in the boardroom. Will you arrange for coffee and pastries?"

"Sure. But he'll want tea. I have some good Kousmichoff tea in my desk—he won't drink that boardroom stuff, that's for sure."

Anne said good-bye and added, "Don't be late, Your Highness."

Sasha called catering to have the coffee and hot water for tea ready in the boardroom. As soon as he hung up, he turned his attention back to the evaluation requests on his desk, and busied himself in appraisals and identifications. Sasha was concerned, however, that even if he could find a good strong piece for the sale in the pile, he still couldn't be sure it would do them any good. Christie's necklace, "by repute" belonging to the Empress, had pulled all the attention away from the good pieces that they did have. Sasha and Anne were in trouble. Soon, the phone rang again. It was Lucile at the front counter.

"Sasha, your nine o'clock is here. She seems painless. Chanel suit, good jewelry." Sasha glanced at the clock. Had an hour gone by already?

"Does she look like a storyteller?" he asked. "I only have an hour for her."

"No, darling," Lucile said, "she looks like the real thing."

If this client didn't have an insanely long story about her object, he would be fine. The length of Sasha's appointments had become a joke around the office.

Descending the staircase, Sasha could see his client waiting; he could sum her up in a minute. She knew exactly what her piece was worth, and she had probably already shown it to Christie's and Sotheby's and was weighing her offers.

Lucile stood by the woman's side. Noting Sasha's arrival, she flashed him the broad and beautiful smile that was her signature and continued chatting animatedly with his client. Lucile introduced clients to specialists with the consummate skill of a hostess, immediately placing them at ease. She was one of Leighton's greatest assets. Lucile made incoming clients feel as if they were about to become members of an exclusive club, rather than about to be divested of a treasure that had been in their family for generations.

"Mrs. Dean, this is Alexander Ozerovsky, a specialist in the Russian Works of Art Department," Lucile said.

Sasha turned on as much charm as he thought she might want to receive. He was a good judge of those clients who wanted icy reserve, friendly professionalism, or flirtation.

"Mrs. Dean, it's a pleasure," he said, shaking her hand and smiling warmly.

"How nice to meet you," she replied. "When I lived in Paris years ago, I knew your mother, the Princess Nina."

"How kind of you to remember her," Sasha said, deciding to switch to icy reserve. "If you'll follow me, we can go into a viewing room. For privacy."

The two slipped into a small room lined in fawn-colored baize. Mrs. Dean settled into one of the two small French chairs separated by a desk that held a black velvet–covered tray and the tools for examining jewelry.

"The piece I want to show you belonged to my mother," Mrs. Dean began. "She was French, and married a Russian during the Great War. Not from an illustrious Russian family, but quite rich . . ."

Sasha's eyes began to glaze over. He could see the story would be ripe with nostalgia. Obviously, she had told it many times, and Sasha wondered how much of it would be accurate.

"My mother and father met in 1916. They were married in the Russian Church at Nice in May, and then went to Saint Petersburg. He called her his 'little lovebird,' and Mother adored it." Mrs. Dean sighed at the memory. "The winter season nearly killed her, however. She said wartime Russia was cold and dark, and the society at Petersburg a bore. When the season was over, she said, there was no way she would ever spend another winter in Russia. She never wanted to see the color grey again, and would hardly be his love-bird if she had to sit through another winter in Saint Petersburg."

How much longer will she go on? Sasha wondered.

"Well, when they had their one-year anniversary in Nice the fol-lowing May, Father gave her this." Mrs. Dean reached into her croc-odile Kelly bag. Sasha's heart skipped a beat. In her hand was one of the instantly recognizable boxes of the House of Fabergé. Made of pale holly wood, it was square with the rounded corners and care-fully beveled edges he knew so well. Mrs. Dean placed the box on the table and gently pushed it toward him.

Sasha opened it carefully.

Inside was a necklace that took his breath away. It was unlike anything he had ever seen by Fabergé.

Three graduated strands of perfectly matched grey pearls looped around the interior of the box and met at an exquisite clasp meant to be worn at the side. The clasp, a neoclassical wreath made of diamonds, was pierced by two arrows, on which sat two tiny kissing lovebirds. The stones were exceptionally white, and were set in brilliantly chased platinum, exquisitely contrasting with the soft grey pearls. It was a masterpiece.

Sasha lifted the necklace in his hands. The pearls were heavy. The Jewelry Department would fight to sell this piece—these nat-ural pearls would fetch a fortune—their sheer size and perfection made them far more valuable than diamonds.

"Mrs. Dean, I don't know what to say," Sasha said, gently placing the necklace back in the box. "I'm afraid I must be honest. I have no idea what this is worth. There are no surviving works by Fabergé like it that I know of, and, as I believe you already know, the pearls are worth a ransom. I can show this to the Jewelry Department, and they can let me know what the actual stones and pearls are worth. Then, of course, with research in the archives in Saint Petersburg, we may be able to come up with more on the piece that would greatly increase its value—the designs, bills, and other such things."

Mrs. Dean smiled.

"But," Sasha continued, "may I ask you a personal question?"

"I may not answer," she said, still smiling, "but please."

"Do you need the money?"

Mrs. Dean looked at him carefully. "No," she said. "I don't. But it lives in safe deposit. I wear it only on Easter and New Year's, and only at home. People just don't have the lifestyle for this sort of jewelry anymore. I'm terrified even to have it out for now."

Anne's voice rang in his head: *A great piece of Fabergé jewelry would really save us this sale.*

"Mrs. Dean," Sasha said slowly, getting the better of his need for an important piece, "this really goes against everything I am trained to do here, but if I were you, I wouldn't sell this necklace."

"And why?" she asked.

"Mrs. Dean, none of the families for whom these jewels were made has them any more. Even rarer than the necklace itself is the fact that your family still has it. I can sell this piece for you, and you will make a great deal of money, but it will go to someone who I am certain will not get as much pleasure from it as you do. It will only get more valuable as time goes on, and perhaps your children will need the money. If that turns out not to be the case, it will make more people happy in a museum, where it can be seen. I'd hate to see it vanish into the private collection of some Saudi princess, or be cut up by a jeweler for the sheer value of the three separate strands of pearls and the Fabergé clasp that can be reconfigured as a brooch."

Mrs. Dean sat silent for minute, and then she softly closed the lid of the box and slipped it back into her cognac-colored bag. "How funny," she said.

"What is?" Sasha asked.

"That is the same advice your mother gave me twenty-five years ago. You're very much like her, you know. You have the same smile." Mrs. Dean rose from her seat and extended her hand.

"Alexander, it has been a pleasure. Perhaps I'll wear this at the Russian Nobility Ball in the spring."

"I'll see you there," Sasha said. "I go every year."

"I'll look forward to it, then," Mrs. Dean said, and the two rose and walked back to the front counter.

And there, once again, was Sasha's biggest problem. He had been hired by Leighton's to cajole, seduce, and convince clients to sell their things, but one time in every ten he was unable to do so. Every transaction felt as if he had conscience on one shoulder and commerce on the other. He had no problem with his conscience when getting dealers or nouveau riche collectors to part with a piece of Fabergé they had acquired with the intention of making a profit or impressing others; they were all fair game as far as he was concerned. But when Sasha came across a piece of history still in the hands of a Russian family, he was incapable of the mercenary behavior required by his profession. He felt obligated not to break apart collections that had survived over generations, intact through revolution and war. How many pieces had he let slip through Leighton's hands over the past seven years? He couldn't count them anymore—and how long would it be before they found out? Sasha didn't know and didn't care. Even this season, when they were so strapped for a brilliant piece, blind need hadn't changed his behavior.

"Any good?" Lucile asked, stepping to his side as he watched Mrs. Dean walk down Leighton's front steps and into a waiting black sedan.

"Beautiful," Sasha replied, "but sadly, not for sale."

"That's too bad, darling. Better luck next time, yes?"

Sasha nodded and turned to leave when Lucile tapped him on the shoulder.

"Oh, by the way, that Russian client of yours just went up to the boardroom. He's very good looking, but . . ." Her voice trailed off.

"But what?" Sasha asked.

"But he's wearing one of those dreadful leather coats all the new Russians seem to wear."

"Oh, dear," Sasha said. "Thanks, Lucile. I feel a fake coming on."

Two

~

IN THE MEN'S ROOM, Sasha ran his hands under the water and glanced in the mirror. He was still young looking, though he noticed the first signs of age in the coarsening of his skin. He looked at himself in the mirror with slight regret. He was sorry he hadn't inherited any of his mother's dark beauty. Sasha wondered what his mother might have known about the piece he was to see. The piece that had once belonged to the Ozerovsky family. Sasha pulled a look of composure across his face. Funny that Mrs. Dean had mentioned that he had his mother's smile. It gave him comfort. Sasha turned and went into the boardroom, where Anne and Mr. Durakov were waiting. He had let one truly important piece go today because of his principles—there was no way he could relinquish another.

"Sasha, please meet Dimitri Durakov. He is representing the consignor, who wishes to remain anonymous," said Anne.

"*Mr. Durakov, I am very pleased to make your acquaintance. I trust that everything is to your taste. We have real tea, as you may have noticed.*" Sasha spoke a Russian no longer heard inside the former Soviet Union. Since the Revolution the "clear" Russian preserved by the émigrés had been replaced by a coarsened and simplified version of the language. Though Russia and the Russian tongue had changed, Sasha still spoke the language as learned by his grandfather in Saint Petersburg schoolrooms at the turn of the century. A language marked by an elegant grammar and a clarity of diction now lost, reviled as "elitist" by the Soviet educational system.

"*Yes. Your tea is good. A surprise in New York. Nice to meet you, too, Highness,*" he replied, extending his hand. His Russian was brusque and Soviet, but educated. He was good-looking, in a Slavic way, with dark hair, regular features, and the slightly Asiatic eyes that were common in Moscow. Lucile had been wrong about the leather coat—it was Gucci, and had probably cost a small fortune in Russia. In fact, there seemed to be nothing very suspicious about Dimitri at all. Sasha was relieved. Many of the new Russian consignors were so agitated you could feel their worry that they would be caught for something illegal. They often desperately needed to sell a piece, or were peddling something stolen. Dimitri exuded an ease that Sasha had always associated with two types of people: those from a background of privilege, and those who felt they were above the law.

"Well, Sasha and I were very interested to hear that you had something to show us. May I ask what it is?" Anne gestured to them both to sit down at the long boardroom table.

"It is a figurine," Dimitri said. "And an important one. It seems to be unrecorded."

"There are no unrecorded figurines," Sasha said with confidence, "and I don't know that my family ever had one."

"Well, I'll let the piece speak for itself." Dimitri said, smiling, and he pulled out the unmistakable Fabergé box.

Sasha was surprised to see that the box was covered in white velvet, aged now to a soft cream by hands and time. Usually the *objets de fantaisie* produced by Fabergé were contained in the pale holly wood boxes, while the silver and heavy objects were in sturdier oak. Only boxes for the Imperial Easter eggs, some jewelry, and other specially commissioned pieces were covered in velvet.

Sasha reached for the tall rectangular box and unlatched the small hook in the front. It opened in two sections, the top flipped back, and the figurine was revealed, standing on a white satin-covered pedestal sunk into the velvet-lined bottom of the case.

Sasha swallowed and looked at the piece.

The figure was of a young girl in Russian costume, her arms delicately raised in the gestures of Russian folk dance. Her smiling quartz face was upturned, framed by soft jasper curls and an enameled *kokoshnik*, or headdress. Her Russian dress, the *sarafan*, swirled around her as she turned, the beautiful diamonds set into the dress twinkling as Sasha lifted her from the box.

It was heartbreakingly beautiful, ravishing.

She seemed to move on her own: the light reflecting off the carefully cut and set stones, the face of the dancing maiden seemingly aglow from within due to the carefully selected quartz. Her *sarafan* was made of brushed rock crystal covered with a diamond-set platinum mesh, giving the appearance that her dress was embroidered with snowflakes. She wore a purpurine caftan underneath. He suddenly remembered seeing a figurine with his mother in London as a little boy. Sasha noted this figurine was not wearing eosite shoes. He smiled at the memory. Then whispered, *"Snegurochka."*

"What?" said Anne.

"Snegurochka. The Snow Maiden. It's a Russian fairy tale about an old couple who prays to God to grant them a child in their old age, and when one is not forthcoming, they build a daughter of snow, and their kiss brings her to life. She stays with them and helps them when they are sick, takes care of the house, and dances and sings for them in the long nights of the winter. When the spring comes, all the young men in the village want to marry her, but she refuses to make a match, growing sadder and sadder as the snow begins to melt. Finally, she calls her parents outside and shows them the last clump of snow left on the grass. She dances for them a final time, and suddenly melts into the ground, leaving nothing behind but a wisp of steam and a clump of snowdrops, the first flower of the spring in Russia," Sasha concluded.

"See the snowdrops at her feet? In seed pearls no less—and look at the style of the embroidery; it's typical of Ryazan. And look, all the frost motifs on the piece are consistent with the Winter Egg,

and the frost pieces that Alma Theresia Phil made for the Nobels."
Sasha sighed heavily. The figurine was extraordinary. It was unique.

"How interesting," Anne commented. "The Ozerovsky family
was originally from the Ryazan region, which would be just the type
of reference Fabergé would have incorporated into a special commission. Also, these frost motifs Sasha noted would date the piece to
around 1913, when the Winter Egg and Nobel pieces were completed. They were both designed by Alma Phil, so there is a good
chance we can identify her as the designer of this piece as well."

Dimitri looked at Sasha with interest. "I don't remember. What
happens to the old couple?" he asked.

"What old couple?" Sasha asked, pulled from his reverie.

"Snegurochka's parents. What happens after she vanishes?"

"I don't know," Sasha responded. "They're peasants—I guess
they eventually show up in a Gogol short story drinking themselves
to death."

Dimitri laughed. "You are probably right about that. Seriously
though, what do you think of the piece?"

"It's exquisite." Anne said.

"Besides what Anne has already pointed out, what makes you
think it once belonged to my family?" Sasha asked.

Dimitri pulled a folder from the black leather portfolio he carried with him, and set it on the table. Sasha opened it and removed
a photograph. It was of the Empress Alexandra looking sadly at a
small tea table, while a group of women sat with her, smiling and
looking at the camera with polite curiosity. Sitting on the tea table
was an object that indeed resembled the figurine.

"If you scan this at a really high resolution on a scanner in the
art department, you might be able to see it more clearly," Sasha
said, "but it really looks like it—"

"Sasha, look at the woman pouring the tea," Anne interrupted
him gently.

Sasha refocused his attention, and saw familiar eyes looking
back at him.

It was his great-grandmother.

Suddenly the whole photograph was repositioned for him, and he noticed other objects suspended in the sepia photograph like insects trapped in amber. The beautiful Serov portrait of his great-grandmother, which now hung at his grandparents'; a diamond and sapphire brooch that his father had given to his aunt Tatiana when she got married; photographs whose Fabergé frames he could just make out on every table; and finally, the silver samovar by Nicholls and Plinke, which now sat in his own apartment on Ninety-seventh Street.

"I believe that this piece belonged to your family for two reasons. Obviously, the fact that your great-grandmother is sitting in the picture with the figurine is one, but the mantel in the background of the photograph is identical to one in the reception room of the Ozerovsky Palace in Saint Petersburg. The Empress was obviously visiting your great-grandmother at home, so I am certain that this was an Ozerovsky piece, maybe even a gift from the Empress Alexandra."

Anne spoke quickly. "Of course, if the piece is consigned to Leighton's, we would have complete access to the Ozerovsky family records. Christie's and Sotheby's certainly can't promise you that."

"I thought not. That is why I am offering the piece to you first. May I ask what you think it might sell for?"

"I wouldn't put an estimate on it. We would have to say estimate on request, meaning that we aren't sure what it will fetch, but that the price is too high to mention without appearing vulgar," Anne replied. "The last figurine that came on the market was sold for around a quarter of a million, but this is much more beautiful than any of Fabergé's other hard-stone pieces, and it is totally unknown. It will certainly set the record for a figurine, of that I am certain."

"There has never been anything like it—it is, quite frankly, the best figurine I have ever seen," Sasha said. "The others are mostly male. Except for a tiny one of a nursemaid; and a large figurine of Varya Panina, the gypsy singer; and one of a peasant girl, none of the figurines is of a female figure. I might also add that none of those three figurines is of a lovely young female. The hard-stone figurines were generally caricatures of Russian types. This is a revolution for Fabergé—she is enchanting."

"Well," said Dimitri, "This all looks very promising. I will leave the figurine here to be put in your vault. Let us see what kind of research you can come up with before we sign anything." Dimitri held out his hand to Anne.

"I can guarantee you that Sasha will uncover more information about Snegurochka for you in a week's time," Anne said, smiling as she walked him to the door. "Let's take care of the initial paperwork for you, and we'll send a copy on to wherever you are staying."

"I'm at the Mark Hotel," he replied. "You can send it to me there."

"I'm very pleased," Anne said. "I look forward to a very successful sale for you."

"I hope so," Dimitri said.

Anne and Dimitri left the room, and Sasha was alone with the figurine.

For a minute, he felt a pang of jealousy that Snegurochka was not his, and the feeling was strange and uncomfortable for him. Taking his time, he carefully put her back in the box; then, carrying the box in both hands, he left the boardroom and headed for the new-property storage area next to the front counter, where incoming pieces were registered and held until they could be transferred to the departmental vault in the basement.

When Sasha reached the front counter, Dimitri was still standing with Anne, finishing the paperwork.

"Mr. Durakov, if you would sign here, and here, we will acknowledge receipt of the figurine, and it will be covered under our house insurance. When we finalize your consignment of the piece, we'll discuss the contract terms."

Dimitri signed the forms where Anne indicated. "It has been my pleasure. I look forward to talking with you soon. Perhaps we can all get together for a drink. I hope we do good business." With a smile, he shook their hands and left.

❖   ❖   ❖

Back in her office, Anne paced back and forth, smoking furiously.

"Sasha, this is it. We are going to blow away the necklace at Christie's with this. I want you to drop everything. Call your family, go to the library, send a fax to Gennady Antropin in Saint Petersburg to get right onto this. We need this piece fully researched and catalogued immediately. We have to look like we've been sitting on this for a long time. Oh, Sasha, this is going to be brilliant!"

Sasha looked at her with some concern. The amount of work would be staggering, and on top of the silver research he had offered to do that morning. Anne had said to drop everything, but Sasha knew he couldn't.

"Okay, boy wonder. I'm off to press and marketing to talk about strategy and sales plans. You can get that info by, say, Friday?" She smiled and left the office.

Sure, Sasha thought. *No problem. Friday.* He sighed and returned to his desk. Time to make a list.

He ran through the holes in the piece's history. Why had the figurine been commissioned? Where had it been? How could he get more information? He would have to call Tatiana Fabergé to see if she had anything in her private papers. He needed to check with Wartski in London to see if they had sketches. Did he have photographs at home? Might his grandparents even still have the bill or any other information? Might there be something in the Slavic and Baltic division at the library? Sasha scribbled furiously on a pad. He checked his list to see if he had missed anything; something was gnawing at him.

I'm starving, he realized. *I need lunch.*

As Sasha got up from his desk to head to the cafeteria, he noticed that the message light on his phone was blinking. He punched in the seemingly endless series of voice-mail codes to access what would no doubt be unimportant.

"You have one new message!" bleated the computerized voice with excitement.

The message began, and Sasha was at first mesmerized, then stunned. The voice on the phone was soft and low, speaking exquisite Russian with the barest hint of a French accent. It was of a particular timbre, expressive and sweet.

It was his mother's voice. Or a voice exactly like hers.

The message ended with an electronic tone, jolting Sasha back from the sudden flood of emotions and memories.

"To hear this message again, press one!" said the computerized voice with urgency. Sasha took a deep breath, and did so.

"Good afternoon. I was hoping to reach Alexander Kirillovitch Ozerovsky. This is a bit strange, I know, but I am his cousin, Marina Grigoriievna Shoutine from Paris. Our mothers, Nina and Tatiana, were sisters. We've never met, but I am in New York, and I had hoped that I might have the chance to see Alexander while I am here. I'll be at the Mark Hotel for the next week or so. Again, this is his cousin, Marina."

Sasha blinked, then saved the message. Mechanically, he wrote on his pad: Cousin Marina. Mark Hotel. He couldn't call her now; he'd call after lunch. No, wait. He'd call his father first. His father needed to know that he had heard from Tatiana's daughter.

❖   ❖   ❖

In the basement cafeteria, Sasha found himself standing next to Delilah Ma, whose Chinese parents still lived in splendor in Hong Kong, surrounded by their Kangxi porcelain, snuff bottles, and

Swiss-educated children, despite the return of the island to China. Sasha had known Delilah for years—they had started at Leighton's front counter together, and Sasha's father was a big client for her department.

Like her parents' art collection, Delilah was extremely valuable to Leighton's. She was beautiful, smart, multilingual, and in the center of the social life of the young employees at the auction house. She had access to members of every major Chinese family, and entrée to their collections of Chinese paintings, jadeite jewelry, Ming furniture, porcelain, and Shang dynasty bronzes. She was a fixture in New York society; as a result, she constantly brought to Leighton's new clients whom she had met recently at lunch or dinner. She also had what seemed to be an unending succession of very rich and badly behaved beaux. Their antics never fazed Delilah, however. She simply shrugged and moved on, knowing full well that her parents would eventually choose a Chinese industrialist for her.

She was currently dating a Venetian named Paolo, who was Conte di something, and whose secret extracurricular activities with men were the talk of their circle. She referred to him as "Paolo *nuovo*" to distinguish him from "Paolo *vecchio*," who had been the Genoese shipping heir boyfriend of four months earlier. Paolo *nuovo* collected snuff bottles. Paolo *vecchio* had collected bronzes. Delilah, everyone knew, collected Italians.

"Darling!" Delilah exclaimed in her British Hong Kong accent, and then let the excitement of the insincere greeting fall from her face, rendering her expressionless. She gnawed her lip distractedly and poked at the salad bar without interest.

"Hi, Delilah," Sasha responded. "You look wonderful."

"Liar," Delilah said. "I adore you."

"You seem distracted."

Delilah sighed and replied, "We're having a drama in Chinese. There is a major piece of Ming porcelain in Hong Kong, and we just submitted our proposal for it to the owners, who are in town for the I. M. Pei dinner on Thursday. We have a hitch, however."

Sasha raised his eyebrows.

"The consignor arrived with his *new* wife." Delilah rolled her eyes. "Twenty-six, from Shanghai, and with a body that would stop a supermodel in her tracks. She is apparently a former Miss China or something, but I mean nobody has heard of her in Hong Kong or Taipei—"

"The problem?" Sasha interrupted.

"Oh, right. The consignor's ex-wife is the newest Sotheby's representative in Hong Kong. We will get that piece of Ming porcelain, which is one point five to two million."

"That's great," Sasha said.

"Sure. But guess what—the ex-wife is selling *her* collection of jadeite jewelry, which is worth three to five million—through her new employers, Sotheby's. Thank you very much." Delilah looked heavenward and sighed. "So we have Gaston de Miron-La Tour in jewelry on our asses all day about it. He can't get over losing the jewelry."

"Tell him to calm down. Sooner or later the consignor will have to buy new jewelry for his new *t'ai-t'ai*, and if the Ming thing sells well, he'll shop for it here. He won't want his former wife aware of his new buying habits, right?"

"True." Delilah smiled, selected an apple, then put it back. "You look a bit worn down also. Are the Empress's jewels ruining your season?" She resumed her halfhearted poking at the salad bar as they moved forward in the line.

"They will if I can't find something better," he said. "I might have today, but . . ." his voice trailed off. He couldn't count on the figurine quite yet. "Well, I'm worried about Christie's and Sotheby's. Our clients are so picky, but theirs seem willing to buy almost anything."

Delilah looked at him with concern and affection, but said nothing. She knew his season was turning out disastrously. She smiled supportively, but shrugged her shoulders. She knew that without a knockout piece this season, Sasha could find himself among the legions who had been fired from Leighton's.

"Sasha, are you going to the Museum of the City of New York's winter dance next week?" Delilah asked, changing the subject.

"I hadn't planned on it," Sasha admitted.

"You have to go, darling," Delilah purred. "The theme is snowflakes and diamonds—very Russian, don't you think? And besides, there might be someone nice there. Isn't there a Miller girl left for you?"

"I don't think so," Sasha laughed. He thought carefully, *Snowflakes and diamonds. There is no way that Anne won't find out about this—I'm going to have to end up going anyway. Perhaps it would be best to beat her to it.*

"Well, maybe I'll have a little dinner beforehand. Could you make it?" he asked hopefully.

"I can't, Sasha. Paolo *nuovo* is throwing one of the dinners before the dance, and has invited all his boyfriends." She smiled. "I think I'm finally getting tired of these Italian men. I may have to just give up and let my parents marry me off to a Chinese billionaire." She kissed him on the cheek, then walked off with her final choice for lunch: a cup of tea.

New York City, 1982

Cyril Ozerovsky looked around the sanctuary, which was filled with mourners. Even he was taken aback by the sheer number of people who had arrived at the tiny Cathedral of Our Lady of the Sign on East Ninety-third Street. The open coffin sat in the center of the nave. Priests in jeweled brocades and readers dressed in black surrounded it, chanting the gospel, as the Divine Liturgy for the dead was performed by a hidden choir.

Nina lay in the open casket, emaciated and pale despite the best efforts of the undertaker. Around her forehead were tied the scripture-decorated bands that were always placed on the deceased, and candles on tall stands burned around the bier. The cathedral was hot and crowded, and the oppressive fragrance of the incense and the flowers settled over the mourners as heavily as their grief. Cyril looked around and saw Sasha wandering dutifully through the crowd, greeting the people he knew. *I know I should be doing the same*, Cyril thought. *But I just can't bear it. I can't listen to their pity. If I just stay here with my parents, it will all be fine. Watch Sasha. How can he be so calm?*

"Look at Sasha," his mother said. "He looks just like you, but he's really Nina's son, isn't he?"

Cyril looked and saw Sasha talking to a group of the Romanovs. Carefully he watched his son's face. As Sasha listened to what Prince Constantine said, he cocked his head slightly to the side—Nina's gesture.

The room was hot, and the lengthy service made standing difficult for some of the guests. Cyril recognized some people, but he didn't realize that Nina had ever met them—how had she known George Balanchine?

Of the many guests, however, there was one notable absence. If he hadn't been so unhappy, he would have been enraged. Even now, with Nina dead, her sister, Tatiana, refused to come to the funeral. After all these years. Cyril sighed—he had called, after all.

After an hour or so, right before the service ended, Cyril decided to leave the sanctuary to stand in the courtyard. It was too hot, the air too thick. Touching his son lightly on the shoulder, he indicated that he was going out. Sasha nodded, and grasped his grandmother's hand, indicating that he would stay.

Outside, Cyril took in the air with convulsive breaths. With his back to the entrance of the cathedral, he wiped his eyes.

How on earth can I explain this to Sasha? he asked himself. *He wasn't aware that she was ill for so long. It's amazing he didn't know—that Nina's death has been such a shock to him. She wanted me to keep it from him, but I was never sure it was the right thing to do. Both of us were so worried about him. I'm afraid Sasha even thought we were angry at each other.*

Cyril looked back into the cathedral through the tall French doors. Cyril saw the priest read the final prayer for the dead, roll it into a scroll, and place it in Nina's coffin; the service was breaking up. The family was moving toward where he stood to form a reception line. There was so much to do: bid the guests good-bye, go to the burial, arrange for the *pannakhida* memorial services to be performed on the ninth and the fortieth days after the funeral.

"Thank you so much for coming; we so appreciate it," he said a hundred times as people and relatives shook his hand and kissed him on both cheeks.

Standing next to his father, Sasha did the same. Cyril couldn't help eavesdropping.

"*Thank you for coming, Marie-Thérèse,*" Sasha said in French to a friend of his mother's.

"*Thank you for being here, Cousin Leonid,*" Sasha said in Russian to a third cousin.

"Mother would be so pleased that you came all this way," Sasha said in German to friends of Cyril's from Vienna.

"Thank you for your note," Sasha said in Polish to their house-keeper, Magda, who was weeping as if she had lost a member of her own family.

When did Sasha learn Polish? Cyril thought to himself. *Did Nina teach him?* He looked down at his son, and Sasha looked back up at him, helplessly.

"There are a lot of people here," he said.

"Everyone loved your mother very much," Cyril responded simply.

"I want to go home," Sasha said to his father.

"I do, too, but we have the burial and then the reception at the club," Cyril said. "What if we go out for dinner after the reception, just you and me and your grandparents? Anyplace you like."

Sasha thought for a minute. "The Carlyle," he said firmly.

"Why the Carlyle?" Cyril asked. "The food isn't very good."

"Mama liked the Carlyle. She said that she always felt calm in a good hotel."

Cyril gazed at his son. He hadn't realized just how much time Sasha had spent with his mother. "The Carlyle it is," he said then. "We just have to get through this, kiddo."

Sasha smiled at him, and went back to shaking hands.

Cyril made a promise to himself. He would make sure that he would give Sasha everything that Nina would have wanted him to have. Sasha would end up the man Nina had wanted him to become—a better one than Cyril felt he was.

Cyril followed his son's example, and turned back to the line, where he greeted old Princess Barinovsky, who couldn't hear and was in a wheelchair, being pushed by Prince Batushin, head of the Nobility Association in America. *"Dolly, thank you for coming. Nina would be so grateful,"* he shouted in Russian, clasping his hands behind his back as he bowed toward the old woman's ear, in unconscious imitation of his son.

Three

~

SASHA CALLED HIS FATHER for the first time in a month. Not casually, as he had hoped he might, but for the dual purpose of giving him the news about Marina's call, and to ask if he could hold a small dinner at 839 the following week. Since he was going to have to attend the dance, he might as well make it bearable with a small and private dinner beforehand.

The large Ozerovsky apartment at 839 Fifth had originally belonged to Sasha's grandparents, and had been decorated in the 1930s by Boudin. Formal, French, and a bit too grand for Cyril's taste, Cyril redecorated when he and Sasha moved after his parents left for Connecticut. It was no more casual after Mrs. Parish and Mr. Hadley had finished with it. Mrs. Parish had insisted on keeping the French paneling ordered by Boudin (too expensive to have made anymore, she said, and *such* good quality!), and had glazed the walls in transparent layers of ivory and taupe (worth every penny), picking out the moldings in gilt to offset the beauty of the ormolu-mounted Chinese celadon porcelain that Cyril collected. An eighteenth-century Axminster carpet covered the floor, and the room was filled with soft Scalamandré upholstered sofas and chairs, as well as some beautiful giltwood French armchairs that had belonged to Nina. Autographed photographs of deceased relatives and exiled monarchs filled the rest of the room, which was dominated by a large Aaron Shikler portrait of Sasha's mother, looking over her shoulder and twisting a long string of pearls between her elegant fingers. It was a perfect apartment for entertaining; large and impressive, yet comfortable.

"Hullo!" hollered Sasha's father, picking up the phone.

"Hello, Father, glad that you are in town," Sasha responded, smiling.

"Just passing through, though—I'm on my way with Diane to visit the Pages in Aspen for a bit of skiing. How are you, Sasha?"

"I'm fine. Things are very busy." The jury was still out on Diane Denning, Cyril's girlfriend. Diane was a decorator, specializing in getting herself onto newyorksocialdiary.com, rather than in getting design jobs. Sasha couldn't tell if he liked her or not, but he did know he didn't like the idea of Diane as his stepmother. "Say hello to Diane," Sasha said as sincerely as possible. "Actually, I called to tell you a few things, and to ask a favor of you. May I have a few people over for drinks and a small dinner before a dance uptown next week?"

"Who's having the dance?"

"The Museum of the City of New York."

"Oh, a charity thing," Cyril said dismissively. "When I was your age, people still had *private* dances in New York. I guess some people still do, but I don't know any of them, certainly. Well, of course you may, and you can ring Derek to see if he can help you. Tell him I said it was all right. You may have any of the wine that is here, but please don't go into that crate of Rothschild-whatever-it-is that the Davieses gave me. Apparently it's worth so bloody much I owe them more than a thank-you note. What other news do you have?"

Sasha decided to be blunt. "I got a call today from Marina Shoutine."

"I see," said Sasha's father, obviously taken aback.

"I don't know what to do. She said that she was in town." Sasha paused to let that sink in.

After a moment, Cyril replied, "I think you should invite her to this dinner you're giving. Just because your mothers had a feud doesn't mean that the two of you should. You have few enough relatives, let alone people who are your own age. Why not make it a little party for your own generation. Invite Betsy Romanov and

some other cousins—I'm sure Marina has been as lonely growing
up as you have. Tatiana Shoutine wouldn't come to her own sister's
funeral, but I want her to know that we rolled out the carpet for
Marina here in New York, no matter how stupid a cow I think your
aunt has been all these years."

"Thank you very much, Father," Sasha replied. Suddenly he
heard static and shuffling sounds.

"I'm in the library so Diane can't hear me," Cyril said quietly.
"Do you need any money? Of course you do; they don't pay you a
dime in that snake's nest you work in. I'll leave an envelope in my
letter tray for you—this dinner's on me. Don't tell Diane, or she'll
want me to start having parties again—can you imagine?" His voice
boomed suddenly as he passed back into Diane's earshot. "And
don't make a mess of the dining room. Diane's redone the whole
thing beautifully since you last saw it. The cost of the glazing nearly
killed me. Even Mrs. Parish got a paint job done cheaper. Bye-bye,
Sasha. See you when we get back."

❖   ❖   ❖

That evening, Sasha entered his father's apartment with trepida-
tion, terrified that the dining room would be a nightmare. The air
in the apartment was still full of Fracas, Diane's expensive perfume,
and so Sasha opened the windows to drive her out.

He walked into the dining room and looked around. The walls
had been glazed a hundred different shades of gold and amber, and
all of the plaster decoration similarly painted. In place of the old
Louis XV chandelier, an absolutely beautiful Russian neoclassical
one with a central stem and base plate of amber-colored glass had
been suspended. The windows had been hung with miles of
Georges Le Manach brocade and passementerie, spilling into pools
of fabric on the floor, which was now stenciled and stained in imitation of the floors of the Catherine Palace. The furniture had been
replaced by an expensive set of ten Russian neoclassical side chairs

around a table of softly figured Karelian birch. Sasha put his face in his hands. He knew exactly which dealers had sold her the furniture and the chandelier. If his father thought the paint job had nearly killed him, he obviously hadn't seen the bills for the furniture.

The room, though it used all the elements of a Russian salon, had none of its charm. It looked like a hard Soviet-era re-creation, everything too bright, too new, and too sterile. Sasha could see that Diane's goal had been to create a neoclassical version of the Amber Room at Tsarskoye Selo, the Tsar's summer palace outside of Saint Petersburg. No doubt she also hoped one day to sit at that table's head as the second Princess Cyril, entertaining her new husband's important relatives and friends. Relatives and friends, he thought to himself, who had been perfectly comfortable in Mrs. Parish's gently painted French dining room with the worn sand-colored satin curtains that had existed before the advent of Diane.

"Not sure if it's taste with a capital T, are you?"

Sasha turned quickly to find Derek, his father's butler, standing behind him. Sasha had known Derek all his life.

"Subtle. Does she think that it is still 1986?"

"She must. She's still telling people she's forty." Derek smiled. "Don't worry, Sasha, by candlelight, it's actually very beautiful. The light through that chandelier is amazing. Takes years off a face. Even Diane's."

Sasha laughed.

"I hope so, because my father will cut off her head when he gets these bills."

"I don't think he ever will see the bills," Derek added. "They were never submitted to the accountant."

Sasha was taken aback. "You couldn't actually mean that she paid for all of this herself?"

"Exactly. A first for your father, I might add—a woman of means."

Sasha looked at Derek. "I still can't say I like her."

"You're far too hard on her. Really, she's a lady. And she does make your father very happy."

"Well, Derek, I don't know if my father told you, but I'm having a few people over for dinner before the Museum of the City of New York party next week," Sasha said. "It'll probably be a dozen or so, no more. Something simple. Russian *zakouski*: three hot, four cold. For dinner a consommé, and then some chicken and mushy stuff. Nursery food." Sasha rattled it off automatically. It was the kind of meal his mother would have served.

Derek smiled. "What will you serve to drink?"

"Oh, I don't know. Let's see. . . . A nice white burgundy to go with the chicken—and during the *zakouski*, we need to serve that special rose-flavored vodka. My cousin Marina Shoutine will be in town, and the dinner is for her."

Derek raised an eyebrow. Sasha realized that Derek probably knew more about what had happened between Nina and Tatiana than he did.

Deciding the conversation was over, Derek inclined his head respectfully and left Sasha looking out the window of the dining room at the dusk settling over Central Park.

Saint Petersburg, 1913

Alma Theresia Phil, artistic designer for the House of Fabergé, put her hands over her eyes and wondered why, of all days, today would be the one to dissolve into disorder and chaos.

The telephone was ringing constantly, jangling her nerves. The *dvornik* who opened the doors of the shop on the Bolshaya Morskaya had appeared for work drunk and vomited in front of Madame Kalinin. Madame had been considering a set of pearls, but after this morning's performance, she would no doubt go to Monsieur Cartier's to make her purchase. One of the kilns in the enameling workshop had overheated and formed a fissure in its interior lining, which would have to be replaced—and soon—before the Easter production rush began. All of this on the very day that she had to give final approval on the figurine that Prince Ozerovsky had ordered as a gift for his daughter-in-law, who was, after all, a German, and known to be a perfectionist.

Alma stubbed out the cigarette she had been smoking and reached into her desk for the small bottle of Coty Lilas perfume, which she reserved to calm herself in just such moments of agitation.

"Alma Oskarevna?" asked one of the runners, whose business it was to carry messages from one department to the other.

"Yes?" she replied.

"Agathon Karlovitch waits for you in the third-floor workroom."

"I received no message that he expected me there."

"Nevertheless, miss, he waits," replied the boy, uneasily shifting his weight from one foot to the other while wringing his cap.

Alma stood up, brushing the wrinkles from her grey serge dress with black braiding. She checked her hair in the mirror of her pink enamel compact, then grabbed both a pad and a mechanical pencil from her desk. There would no doubt be instructions—Agathon Karlovitch always had instructions.

Hurrying down the hall, Alma stepped into the elevator, and the gate was closed behind her by the old man who ran it. A newspaper lay on the stool where he rested when no one else could see him. It was touching that the paper was there every day. Alma knew the old man could not read.

The headline screamed news of yet another possible strike. Alma's eyes ran over it to make sure that it was nothing that might affect their production—the last coal strike had been paralyzing. The enameling furnaces had been down for a week, and the trains had stopped between Saint Petersburg and Moscow, making it impossible to transport stock. Alma sighed heavily and wondered if Mr. Cartier had these problems. In America, she wondered, did Mr. Tiffany also have to deal with coal strikes, bad trains, and drunken doormen? Probably. America, as it was represented by the cinema, was a place where Indians regularly invaded cities and set fire to the shops. Though many Americans shopped at Fabergé, and had married members of the highest Russian aristocracy, Alma had little time or patience for them. They were uncultured, they spoke too loudly, and they smiled too much—but at least they spent money.

The elevator stopped, and Alma walked down the long hall to the workroom. The large room was very hot, and it smelled of the sulfur, chlorine, and formaldehyde used in enameling. By the windows were several circular workbenches, where teams of jewelers worked on the objects that were sold in the cases downstairs. Alma glanced across the room, where she could see the imposing figure of Agathon Fabergé addressing a small group of miserable-looking workers. Alma waited patiently until he was finished.

"Ah, Miss Phil!" he said, his face lighting up with pleasure when he spotted her. "Come here!"

Alma heaved a sigh of relief. There was no crisis. Not yet, anyway.

"Agathon Karlovitch, good morning," she said, walking past the benches and noticing that while some workers were absorbed in their projects, others eavesdropped openly. She would have to ask the foreman to make certain that the workmen at least pretended to be busy when one of the Fabergés was in the workshops.

"I have come from Wigström's workshop."

Alma shuddered. The figurine was there—she hoped it met with his approval.

"I have never seen anything like Snegurochka," he continued. "She is exquisite, and you are to be commended. In fact, everything you designed this year is coming along extremely well in the workshops, though I am worried about the Easter egg for His Majesty."

Alma winced. The egg was running over projected costs.

"In principle, we have an unlimited budget, Miss Phil, but this egg is very expensive—much higher than last year."

"It is the topaz that has been the problem," Alma demurred. "We had no idea it would take so long to find two flawless pieces of white topaz in that size."

"Did they come from Siberia?"

"No, we had to buy them from Idar-Oberstein in Germany."

"That alone cannot justify the enormous price."

Alma sighed. "No. Our agent in Germany made the mistake of telling the stone merchant that the pieces were intended for the Emperor, which suddenly caused the market price of German white topaz to double."

"I hate those stone merchants. It is distasteful the way they cheat His Majesty."

Alma nodded in agreement, but she knew that the Emperor would suffer an even greater markup. She looked down at the jet buckles on her black calf shoes, which were already covered with dust from the workroom. Of course, the prices Fabergé's clients paid weren't confiscatory. People valued the brilliant craftsmanship. Alma did wonder what the Tsar would say if he knew how much was added onto his bill, though.

"At any rate, I asked for you to come because my father wanted me to thank you personally for your work this season. The egg for the Nobels has been finished, and it is beautiful, as are the numerous pieces of jewelry you designed for them. His Majesty's egg will be one of the best we've ever done, and thanks to the Germans, certainly one of the most expensive."

Alma smiled slightly, and looked up.

"Finally, Snegurochka is truly a masterpiece. I don't think that anyone thought it could be so beautiful—the stone carvers have outdone themselves."

Alma warmed with pleasure at his praise.

"However did you get the idea?" he asked, seating himself and gesturing for her to sit across from him at a large desk at the end of the workroom.

Alma sat down. "Well, as you remember, it was quite a winter," she began.

Fabergé nodded.

"It was so cold that there was a thick layer of frost on the windowpane, and as I was speaking to one of the diamond dealers I was given a price. I couldn't find a pencil . . ."

Fabergé nodded, wondering just where the story was going.

". . . and so I took my fingernail and scratched the sum into the frost on the windowpane. The light came streaming in through the frost, and it gave me an idea—what if we used white topaz to represent ice, and engraved a layer of frost crystals onto it? That led to my thinking about snowflakes, and before I knew it, everything I was working on was full of snowflakes. In the Imperial Egg, I set a mesh of platinum-set diamonds over the engraved base, and in the egg we made for the Nobels, I let the enamelers try their hand at the same look—I think it very successful."

"As do I," replied Fabergé.

"Well, as the jewelers were working on the mesh for Snegurochka and the Imperial Egg, there were beautiful sections of the settings that were being cast off, and it occurred to me to hang them as pendants, and make bracelets, and cuff-links as well."

"Very clever."

"Thank you, sir."

"But how did you get the idea for the figurine?"

"Oh, that was Prince Ozerovsky himself, sir. Princess Ozerovsky translated the story of Snegurochka as an exercise while she was learning Russian."

"How charming," Fabergé said. "Miss Phil, my father and I would like you to join us in presenting the piece to Prince Ozerovsky this afternoon. Would you be available around five o'clock? We will serve him some tea, and my wife has arranged for some strawberry cake from that *pâtissier* on the Liteniy Prospect."

"Oh, I am not dressed properly," she said, running her hands over her hair, "and I have been in the workrooms all morning, I must smell of sulfur and silver polish."

Fabergé laughed, rising from the desk.

"Miss Phil, feel free to take the afternoon off. I can't tell you how pleased I am with Snegurochka. Would you like to see her?"

"Isn't she still in the workroom?"

"No. She was perfect, and so I brought her back myself. She is in Monsieur Fabergé's office. Please come and see me in five minutes." He walked through the workroom and out the door.

Alma exhaled as she stood, and felt a tap on her shoulder. It was Henrik Wigström, the workmaster for the figurine.

"I heard that," he said, smiling and kissing her on both cheeks. "The egg, I believe he said, was one of the best we've ever done."

"I'm so embarrassed," Alma said, looking down.

"Better than that. You're talented. You have a great future here, my dear. You have style in your blood. Your father will be very proud, indeed."

"Thank you, sir."

Wigström turned to his jewelers. "Men, according to Agathon Karlovitch, the Winter Egg is the best we've ever made. A cheer for Miss Phil!"

"*Ura!*" cried the men, clapping boisterously and pounding on their worktables.

"Thank you, thank you." Alma said, blushing a bit. "I'm off, gentlemen. Keep working." She smiled at Wigström and left to go to old Fabergé's office.

✤ ✤ ✤

Alma knocked on the heavy oak door.

"Come in," called Agathon Karlovitch.

Alma opened the door and entered, glancing around the wood-paneled room. The walls above the paneling were a deep green with Art Nouveau gold stenciling. The electric lights were covered with soft pink silk shades, which cast circles of light onto the green baize-covered table in the center of the room. Agathon Karlovitch was behind his father's desk, and Alma could see the holly wood box on a table by the window.

"Come in, come in," he said cheerfully. "Let me show you."

He moved to the window and opened the box, removing the figurine and placing it on the desk in the light, gesturing for Alma to sit down where she could see the figurine better.

Alma sat on a nearby chair, and pulled out her jeweler's loupe. Her eyes ran over the seams where the carved stone pieces had been carefully fitted together. They were perfect, she noted with pleasure. The stones were joined together so tightly, not even a razor's edge could fit between them. The sapphire eyes were tiny rounded cabochon stones, and they had been fitted into the tiny sockets with wax—they appeared to be held in by magic. Her eyes took in the skillful carving of the hair; the twisted tresses in brown jasper had honey-colored striations that looked incredibly natural. Drilled into the hair were gold mounts, filled with opaque flat red enamel. It appeared that a red ribbon was woven through her hair, and ended in a bow at the bottom of her plait. Alma had agonized over that ribbon, and her arguments with the workshops had become legendary—she had known they could do it, but they had balked because it would be technically demanding to create a convincing illusion of plaiting with the different media. She had won in the end, and the ribbon was delightful.

The face was charming. The stone had been chosen to appear as if she were blushing, and the delicate smile was budlike—the lips had been stained with carmine before polishing. Her traditional head-dress, or *kokoshnik*, was in purpurine, and mounted with platinum snowflakes. Her overdress, the *sarafan*, was exquisite. In brushed white topaz, etched with hoarfrost, it was also mounted with the dazzling platinum and diamond snowflakes. The whole costume swirled around the figurine as she turned, her arms lifted into the air.

Alma set the figure down and looked at Agathon Fabergé.

"It didn't turn out badly at all," she said, folding her loupe and tucking it back in her shirtwaist.

He laughed. "No, my dear, not badly at all. Congratulations, and we'll see you at five."

Alma stood, shook his hand, and turned to leave the room. She looked at the small watch hanging from her necklace, and realized it was two. She would go out, have her hair coiffed, and buy a more becoming hat. It would be just enough time.

Returning to her office, Alma donned her serviceable brown velvet toque with osprey feathers, fastening it into her dark hair with a hatpin tipped with a small Easter egg in sable-colored enamel. She was proud of the color, having invented it last year with the enamelers—it had been last season's sensation, and the first color she had developed herself. This year's color was a nacreous turquoise. She found that it lacked subtlety, but then, as her father had reminded her, so did most of their clients. Pulling on her fur-trimmed coat, she decided to pass through the store on her way out.

The shop was full of people buying gifts for Easter, still two months hence. Behind the handsome glass-mounted cases, salesmen in black frock coats gently removed the velvet trays to show Fabergé's glittering and exquisite offerings to Saint Petersburg's most discriminating clientèle. As she passed, several of the salesmen inclined their heads, acknowledging her without stopping their French narratives to their clients.

All seemed well, and Alma sailed out the door in a cloud of pride and well-deserved pleasure.

Four

~

THE NEXT MORNING, Sasha and Anne sat down with the figurine and began cataloguing with the small amount of information they already had. Anne identified the different hard stones that had been used to create Snegurochka, and tested all the diamonds to make certain that they were real and hadn't been replaced. She paid particular attention to the purpurine; recently there had been a rash of fake purpurine pieces made of epoxy. Sasha went through every reference book they had in the department to see if there was any mention at all of Snegurochka. As he did so, he compiled a list of all of the known figurines. Fabergé had made even fewer portrait figurines than he had Imperial Eggs. There were hard-stone portraits of gypsy singers and lemonade vendors, religious pilgrims and imperial guards, but none of fairy-tale characters. Snegurochka was indeed unique, just as Sasha had expected.

Sasha then gathered up information which showed that Snegurochka was related artistically to other pieces made by Fabergé. *Anne had been right yesterday*, Sasha thought. There was little doubt that Snegurochka had been designed by Alma Phil in the period around 1913. The similarities between the Winter Egg, the snowflake jewelry made for the Swedish industrialist Nobel, and other pieces now in the Forbes Collection were too close to ignore.

The box was evidently original. It had signs of wear, and it fitted the piece perfectly. The stamp inside on the silk had the appropriate Fabergé logo for the year 1913. Sasha and Anne were satisfied.

Anne wrote a fax to Gennady Antropin, their researcher in

Saint Petersburg, telling him of the figurine's discovery and asking him to go directly to the Fabergé archives in Saint Petersburg to determine whether he could find an original bill, or any of the design sketches. Sasha spoke to several New York and London dealers who owned a number of the Fabergé workshops' sketchbooks to see if they would let him come and look at them, while simultaneously trying to conceal exactly what object Leighton's had found.

As Sasha pulled together the information they had, he wrote an initial catalogue entry for the piece. The notes were fairly well thought out, but he still had nagging doubts: Who had originally commissioned the piece? Had it really belonged to his family? Most important, where had the piece been since the Ozerovskys had left it behind in 1918? They needed this additional information that they could find only in Russia, or in Sasha's own family's archives. If they could only find that lost proof of the figurine's authenticity and provenance, they could get the press to stop their unrelenting focus on Christie's and the diamond necklace, forcing them to share the season's spotlight with Leighton's.

PROVENANCE:

Possibly commissioned for Princess Ozerovsky, née Countess Cecile von Streichen, ca. 1913–14. In the family's possession until 1918. Private collection since 1919.

NOTES:

This lost and highly important piece is undoubtedly one of the greatest hard-stone figurines produced by the workshops of Fabergé, yet one of only four in the female form known to have been produced (cf. Varya Panina, private collection, New York; Peasant Girl, Metropolitan Museum of Art, New York; and a small figurine of a Nursemaid, private collection). Only three of these were known until the recent rediscovery of the present piece.

The offered lot is related to a number of other Fabergé pieces, most notably the Imperial Winter Egg of 1913 (sold Christie's Geneva 1994, Christie's New York 2001). Designed by Alma Theresia Phil, the Winter Egg is related to a number of unique and important designs for the Nobel family, which include various pieces of jewelry (cf. Forbes Collection) and an important Easter egg containing a watch, known as the Nobel Ice Egg (sold Christie's, now Forbes Collection, New York). Due to the similarity of the offered lot to the Winter Egg and the frost pieces, it is probable that Snegurochka was also designed by Alma Phil.

"Not bad for a morning's work," Anne said, smiling. "But we really need to establish the provenance more clearly. We know your great-grandmother had it at this tea because it is in the photograph, but that really means nothing. What if the Empress brought it with her? What if it was borrowed for the visit to amuse her? There are plenty of holes here that need to be filled, and only you and Gennady can do it. Aren't you rushing off to Connecticut this afternoon?"

"Exactly right," he said. "I'm off."

"Good hunting!" Anne said, waving him away with her hand. "Remember, any scrap of information you can uncover will give Gennady more information to narrow his search."

Sasha nodded. "I'm just going to go home to change out of my suit," he said. "For all I know, I'll end up in my grandparents' basement or attic looking through mildewed photographs and moldering dance cards."

❖   ❖   ❖

Sasha walked into his apartment still sailing with energy from the morning's work. Moving to the windows, he drew back the curtains, letting the northern light flood the small space. If Sasha's father's apartment was a Petersburg palace, Sasha's was a Moscow *dacha*. Cozy and comfortable, Sasha's nest was full of oversized furniture that belied the small space. A Russian Bessarabian carpet covered the floor, its chocolate brown background rich and well worn. The walls were painted a soft nile green, and were covered with gilt-framed photographs and prints. A few family icons hung in the corner, and in the center of the living room stood a round mahogany library table, covered with books and the small niello boxes he collected.

Through the window, Sasha could see the Russian Orthodox Cathedral of St. Nicholas. Built in 1903, it was a strange building for New York, topped with golden onion domes and decorated in the florid style of seventeenth-century Moscow. Sasha had bought the apartment just for that view, which more than compensated for his lack of space. On a winter night, in the snow, with the candles burning and the lamps on their dimmest setting, Sasha felt that he was in Moscow's Arbat, or near the Griboyedov Canal in Saint Petersburg. Sasha liked the idea that he and the building were both Russian émigrés who found themselves neighbors on Ninety-seventh Street.

Sasha looked around and tried to remember where to find his family albums in the compulsively tidy space in which he lived. He took a deep breath and focused on finding them, finally locating them in a closet, the front of the box marked "Cici's things" in his mother's Russian hand.

Sasha's great-grandmother Cecile, or Cici, as she was known in the family, had been born in Germany and raised at the Hessian court, where she was a childhood friend of the little princess who would eventually become the Empress Alexandra of Russia. After the turn of the century, she had traveled to Russia, was presented at court, and fell in love with Prince Oleg Ozerovsky, an aide-de-camp to the Tsar. They were married at Nice with both families in attendance, and there was very little more about her that Sasha knew. Cici had been active in charities, and in the arts, and was known for her beautiful and extremely artistic entertainments. Bakst and Diaghilev had called her the "Northern Light." She remained friends and *dame d'honneur* to the Empress until 1916, when, without warning, the Empress refused to see her and she was dismissed.

Sasha examined the photographs but saw no trace of the figurine in any of them. There weren't many taken in Russia anyway. Most of them were from after the Revolution in Frankfurt and Paris.

Preparing to leave, Sasha pulled on jeans, a cashmere turtleneck sweater, and a houndstooth jacket. He was ready to go, but he still had one important thing left to do: he had to return Marina's call. Picking up the phone, he called information for the number of the Mark, and allowed his call to be placed through.

"Thank you for calling the Mark, New York. How may I direct your call?" asked an indifferent voice.

"I'd like to speak with Marina Shoutine, she's a—"

"One moment and I'll connect you."

Suddenly, Sasha was listening to Vivaldi.

"Hello?" answered a breathy young voice, not like his mother's at all.

"Is this Marina?" Sasha asked carefully.

"Speaking," the young woman said, with the accent of a Parisian who had studied English in London.

"Marina, this is Sasha." He paused, "Your cousin."

"Ah!" Marina exclaimed. "Sasha! I may call you Sasha and not Alexander, then? I am so pleased you have rung me back; I so hoped you would."

"When I got your message, I was so surprised. Actually, you sounded so much like my mother—"

"Oh, I know. How funny you should say so. Whenever my mother was annoyed with me, she would always say, 'Marina, do stop, you sound just like Nina.'" Marina's voice caught a little.

"How is your mother, Marina?" Sasha asked.

"Well, I am sorry to tell you this, but she died of breast cancer this past autumn. My father is quite lost without her."

"We hadn't heard. I am so sorry. My mother died of cancer, too," Sasha said, surprised by the unexpected news.

"So, once again we have something sad in common. Well," she said, her voice brightening a bit, "I hope now we will be able to become friends—*real* family. I have always wanted to know you, but my mother was so . . . well, you understand. It has made me terribly sad to know I had a cousin in America I could not know. Please let me take you to dinner while I am here."

"I know what you mean," Sasha said. "But take *me* to dinner? Never," Sasha said firmly. "I am sorry that my father is away this weekend and won't be able to meet you, but there is a dance at one of the museums here, and I am giving a dinner before it. Several of our cousins are coming, and I know that everyone would like to meet you. Is it too soon after your mother's death?"

"For dancing, yes. But we had the forty-day *pannakhida* over a month ago. And so I won't dance, but I'll come to dinner and your benefit. Sasha, that is so kind of you, and I accept with pleasure. When is it, and what is the *costume*?"

Sasha told her that the dinner and the dance were formal, gave her the information (seven-thirty, long dress), and assured her that a written invitation would be delivered to her hotel.

"This is wonderful, and I don't want to impose on you already, Sasha, but I am traveling with a friend, and I hate to—"

"Nonsense," Sasha said. "Feel free to bring anyone you like. It will be strange enough for you as it is. It will be easier to have someone you know. Come a bit early, though, so we have time to chat."

"I will. I'm looking forward to the evening. Thank you, Sasha. It means a great deal to me that you called. Good-bye," Marina said, and hung up softly.

Sasha hung up his phone, grabbed his things, and hurried out the door to catch his train.

❖ ❖ ❖

Sasha's train pulled into the Greenwich station, which was larger and more modern than he remembered it, as was Greenwich itself. When had all these shops arrived? It had been too long since Sasha had been to Connecticut.

Sasha caught a cab and gave the driver his grandparents' address. The short drive to Belle Haven seemed like an eternity, with snow in large banks everywhere. Soon, however, the driver turned into the lane and drove along the banks of boxwood, wrapped in burlap bags for what appeared would be a long winter. Sasha paid the driver, got out of the cab, and hopped up onto the front steps of the columned stone Georgian revival house and rang the bell. Sasha's grandmother answered the door.

Tall and blonde, Princess Ozerovsky had been born a de Witt and was every inch the old New Yorker of Mrs. Wharton's novels. She had a cool and impeccable sense of what was appropriate, and gave no quarter to Sasha's grandfather when he was in one of his Russian moods. She pulled Sasha inside with her athletic arms and gave him a resounding kiss.

"You're freezing," she announced. "Put your coat on the rack, and throw your things in the corner." She looked at him critically. "What? No briefcase and no suit on a workday? What on earth has happened at Leighton's?"

"This is only a semi-official visit. I went home to change," Sasha said, kissing his grandmother back. "I wanted to ask Grandfather about Cici and some other things, and I wanted to see you."

"Well, we're happy to see you anytime," she said. "You'll stay for dinner and overnight, and I'll get you on the earliest train in the morning. You'll have plenty of time to go home, get ready, and get to work before nine." It was a statement of fact, and though Sasha doubted it was possible, he couldn't say no to his grandmother. Taking him by the arm, she led him into the library where his grandfather sat, reading.

Sasha loved his grandparents' house, particularly their library. The room was glazed a wonderful warm tamarind color, and the softly waxed pine shelves were laden with beautiful Russian, French, and English books with fine bindings, all well worn. *Toile Indienne* curtains patterned in sandalwood, pumpkin, and turquoise hung at the windows, and the well-worn Turkish Oushak carpet was stained by dogs that now existed only in the silver frames scattered on the small tables around the room.

It was a cheerful room and a comfortable one. Somehow in it, Sasha had always thought that flowers looked better in their vases, tea steamed warmer in its china pot, and problems seemed less important in the face of his grandparents' happiness.

"Hello, *Dedushka*—don't get up," Sasha said, leaning over and giving his grandfather a kiss. Sasha's grandfather was in his nineties, and though increasingly frail, still had about him an air of authority and a military demeanor. His most distinguishing characteristic, however, were his changeable grey eyes, which Sasha had inherited.

"Sashenka," he replied. "Good to see you! What are you doing here?"

"Oh, stupid business," he said, hesitating. "I'm just glad to see you two. How are things out here?" Sasha began moving around the room, looking at photographs. Signed pictures of Nicholas and Alexandra, family picnics before and after the Revolution, exteriors of palaces no longer extant, interiors in styles long deemed unfashionable. In contrast to the Russian pictures were photos from Sasha's grandmother's family: nineteenth-century archery matches at Newport, pictures taken in Palm Beach in the 1920s, banquettes filled at the Stork Club; all of them full of the relentlessly cheerful faces of the thoroughly American de Witts.

Sasha's grandfather smiled expectantly, waiting for the young man to stop fidgeting and to ask the questions he had come to ask.

"Well," Sasha said, "something very funny has happened at the office. A young Russian—"

"A *new* Russian, I should expect," his grandfather interrupted, making the word *new* sound as if it had four letters rather than three.

"Well, yes," Sasha said, "but educated, and nice. He brought with him a photograph. A photograph of Cici."

"Really?" said his grandfather. "I would have thought all those things would be gone by now. How funny."

"A photograph of Cici with Alexandra Feodorovna at the house in Petrograd," Sasha replied.

"Saint Petersburg," his grandfather corrected sharply. "It is a tea party, yes? That was taken in 1913, and the city was still Saint Petersburg then. It didn't become Petrograd until after the war was declared."

"How did you know which photo it was?" Sasha asked incredulously.

"I took it," Sasha's grandfather responded. "And it was the only photograph ever taken of my mother and the Empress together."

"Then you remember the day?" Sasha asked.

"As if it were yesterday," replied Sasha's grandfather.

"I have questions about the photograph itself," Sasha said.

"What?" said his grandfather, jolted from his memory.

"I noticed in the picture a lot of things that belong to us even now—the painting you have here, Aunt Tatiana's brooch—even my samovar."

"Yes, yes, all true," confirmed his grandfather.

"Well, this is the reason I am here. It is the figurine on the table. Can you remember what it was?" He held his breath.

"Sasha, I may be ninety-odd years old, but I am not *dead* in this chair. Of course I remember it. That figurine was by Fabergé—and it was of Snegurochka—the Snow Maiden."

Sasha sighed. So it was true. The figurine had been theirs in Russia, and his own grandfather remembered it. In fact, it was he who had taken the photo. He could not dream of any better proof of the figurine's provenance.

"How did it come to belong to us?" Sasha asked.

"My father—your great-grandfather—his parents, and his brother gave it as a gift to your great-grandmother for her tenth wedding anniversary. It was terribly expensive, of course."

Sasha's brain raced. That meant the bill had gone to his great-great-grandfather; now Gennady would know where to look in the Fabergé archives for more documentation.

"Why was the Snow Maiden chosen as the subject?" Sasha asked.

"When Mother moved to Saint Petersburg, it was the winter of 1902, and she decided to learn Russian—her first exercise was to translate the story of Snegurochka. She did it perfectly, and it was then that Father proposed—before she also vanished with the last snow. It seemed a fine subject. She loved that little figurine very much, even though she always said she found Fabergé vulgar. I'll come into the city to see it when it goes on view. I'm glad to hear it has turned up in one piece. It makes me happy to know those Bolsheviks didn't hack it up the same way they did poor Uncle Dima."

Saint Petersburg, 1913

Cici Ozerovsky sat in the blue salon of the Ozerovsky Palace on the Moika Canal, and delicately tied off a French knot on the embroidered silk panel at which she had been working on and off over the past few weeks. She hated embroidery, and would have far preferred to be reading one of the new Moscow plays, or even the newspaper, but on the days of her "at home," Princess Ozerovsky always sat with an embroidery frame by the window. Though no one in Saint Petersburg, particularly among her circle of friends, cared whether she could embroider as a lady-in-waiting to Her Majesty the Empress, she had to set a slightly more genteel tone than was generally evidenced in the salons of the first capital.

Lady-in-waiting. *That is a bit of a joke*, she thought, poking herself in the thumb with the needle and quickly withdrawing her left hand for fear of staining the pale silk with blood. The Empress was always at the Alexander Palace, outside the capital. Last month's tercentenary celebrations were the first major court functions in years, and they had come too late to stem the tide of disapproval of the Empress. Since 1905, Empress Alexandra and her whole family had withdrawn into an imperial mist. What, people were beginning to ask, was the point of having an imperial family if they showed themselves so rarely and so grudgingly?

Cici looked around the formal room with its brocade curtains and important Sèvres porcelain collection. It would be so much more fun to have ten or fifteen good friends in the charming Gothic library upstairs, rather than fifty to seventy-five in this cavernous and infrequently used room. Cici wondered idly if her husband would let her have a small *vernissage* for a female artist she had recently met in Moscow. She admired her work for the stage, and had seen some of her modern paintings. They were so unusual—but Oleg would probably not allow it. She would have to wait until Moscow to indulge her interest in contemporary art—Saint Petersburg frowned on such things. It was a city that thought it was Venice, Vienna, and Paris combined. *Beautiful it is*, she thought, *but Moscow!* Now *there* was a city—new theater, new music, new art. The merchant money made the city restless, and the harsh government forced the people and artists to yearn for new things: Berlin and Vienna had a touch of the same energy, but nothing was like Moscow to her.

In the distance, Cici could hear the tinkling sound of the telephone, and she winced in anticipation. The phone had been installed for years, but the staff, still distrustful of the instrument, continued to shout into it, deafening whoever had the misfortune to call the Ozerovsky family at home.

"Your Highness?" shouted Karpov, the butler.

Cici rose in a rage. How many times had she asked them not to shout? She couldn't seem to control their yelling into the telephone, but she could certainly stop them from shouting through the halls.

Cici moved slowly out the door of the salon onto the landing, knowing that in her ecru silk tea gown, pearls, and the magnificent brooch given to her by Grand Duchess Elizabeth, she would cut a threatening and intimidating presence at the top of the stairs, where he would first see her.

"Karpov, there is really no need for you to—"

"Your Highness, it is the Empress!" he interrupted, setting the receiver down on the small marquetry table where the telephone sat.

Cici lost all semblance of hauteur and ran down the stairs, her laces fluttering and her swans' down boa falling behind her onto the marble stair.

Grabbing the telephone off the small table, she took a deep breath and said in her clearest French, *"Hello, this is the Princess Ozerovsky speaking."*

"Your Highness? Her Imperial Majesty the Empress," announced the Tsarskoye Selo operator in Russian.

Cici swallowed, waiting for the Empress to take the line.

"Cecile?" asked the Empress in her light, cool English.

"Yes, Your Majesty," she replied, also in English, trying to be heard without shouting, as Karpov did.

"How are the children?" the Empress asked cordially.

"Your Majesty is kind to ask. Both are very well and growing every day. I hope the Tsarevitch and their Imperial Highnesses are equally well." Cici wondered when the chitchat would come to an end and Alix would reach her point. The Empress had been this way since they were children.

"Ah, poor Tatiana Nikolaevna is still ill with the typhoid, and we pray constantly. She is feeling stronger, however, and so we are thankful."

"Bless her," Cecile responded awkwardly, made uncomfortable by the Empress's piety.

"As you may or may not know, the wedding of Marie-Louise, daughter of Kaiser Wilhelm, to Ernest-August, Prince of Cumberland, Duke of Brunswick, is in April. The Emperor and I are presenting a state gift of some importance, but I would like to give her something very personal as a private gift. I was speaking with Lili the other day ..."

Cici stifled a yawn so the Empress wouldn't hear. Lili Dehn, another member of the Empress's entourage, was a lovely woman, but she was prone to chatter and fashion.

The Empress continued, ". . . and she mentioned that at your last 'at home,' she had seen a beautiful figurine by dear old Monsieur Fabergé."

Does she want the figurine? Cici thought.

"We are thinking of ordering something like it for the Princess Marie-Louise. Would it be possible . . . ?"

"I will have it made ready immediately to send to Tsarskoye Selo. Your Majesty does us an honor—"

"No, no, no!" protested the Empress, and Cici was startled by the graceful and musical sound of laughter that erupted from the

Empress so rarely. "I know that you are at home today, and I wanted to let you know that I would be coming. I hope to see the figurine when I am there."

Cici sat down on the hall bench with an ungraceful thud.

"We welcome Your Imperial Majesty, and wait to attend you," she said automatically.

"Well, Cici, until then." The Empress hung up the phone with a solid click, and Cici heard the other clicks as the palace operator, the Saint Petersburg operator, and, no doubt, the secret police's operator hung up their lines as well.

It was worse than she ever could have imagined. The Empress was coming—she was joining Cici and her ladies at tea. That very afternoon.

Cici's hand rose to her mouth, and her heart began to race.

There was no time to prepare. She stood up slowly, and turned to the assembled staff, who waited. Karpov, the butler, was standing there with Ivan, a footman, and Nastasiya, the housekeeper.

"The Empress comes here this afternoon. We have no time to prepare," Cici said. "We shall have to make do. Ivan, send a footman to Eliseev's—get more cakes, more of everything. There's no time to bake. We have only a few hours."

"Yes, Princess," he said, running down the hall to the servants' stair and to the kitchens.

"Nastasiya, I must telephone the others who are invited to let them know the Empress is coming. I will have to call the Grand Duchesses as well—they will all have to be invited now. Also, make up my bedchamber for Her Majesty, and make sure the bath is spotless—my guests will have to suffer the inconvenience—my bathroom must be reserved for the Empress's personal use."

"Yes, Princess," she replied, racing off to find the upstairs maids.

"Karpov, come with me," Cici said, walking down the hall. "We will greet Her Majesty in the vestibule, and receive her with bread and salt in the gallery. We will then have tea in the Blue Salon. Which linens are on the tables?"

"The plain linen, Your Highness."

"Replace them with the embroidered damask with coronets."

"Yes, Your Highness."

"Her Majesty prefers spring flowers. Place these orchids in other rooms, and please have lilacs, white peonies, and pink roses substituted for them."

"And if they have none at the florist?"

"Then, Karpov, go down to the Neva in front of the Winter Palace."

"Why, Your Highness?"

"Because I want to make sure the Empress sees me when I jump in and kill myself, and I will need you to fish out my cold and lifeless body." Cici smiled to let him know she was joking. "Now, run— we have no time. Send up the housekeeping staff."

Karpov ran out, and soon the maids were shuffling into the Blue Salon, many of them weeping and crossing themselves over the thought that the Empress would be there.

"Now, I know you are all excited, and so am I, but we have very little time. I don't want the Empress to think even for a second that we have been disturbed in any way, but I need you to clean this room as if we were expecting, well, as if we were expecting the Empress, because we are."

The maids set about polishing the floor with beeswax collected on the estate at Poltava, slightly thinned with turpentine and spirits of antimony. On their knees, the girls buffed the floor to a high shine with lambskins. Soon, Karpov returned, trailed by a footman brandishing a heated copper pan on a long handle. Periodically a footman would pour into the hot pan scented "court water," an alcohol-based perfume that evaporated on contact with the heated copper, filling the air with orange, bergamot, and spices.

The flowers arrived, and were sent down to the kitchen to be arranged. The linens came up from the linen storeroom, ironed and carried in flat, each by four maids, so that there would be no wrinkles. When the flowers had been arranged, they were placed on the small round tables and tall *guéridons* that filled the room; soon, Princess Ozerovsky was placing on the tables beautiful objects to amuse her guests: small hard-stone animals, eighteenth-century jeweled boxes, bowls of uncut precious stones (counted carefully). Finally on the table where she would sit with the Empress, she placed her magnificent eighteenth-century French silver tea service by Meissonier, and her figurine of Snegurochka.

There was a clamor of voices from the vestibule, and Cici went down to investigate. There she found Karpov and the doorman struggling with a group of uniformed men trying to get into the house. It was His Majesty's Security Service, headed by Spiridovitch. Cici knew that this was only the beginning. They would search the house, and leave a detachment of men hidden in the palace throughout the Empress's visit. Cossacks would be posted outdoors as well. She would have to offer them all something to eat, but none of them would partake while they were on duty. What a waste. At least as a noblewoman she was spared the detachment of dogs.

"It's all right, Karpov; it's all right. They need to come in." Cici sighed as the men began their search of the house, tracking mud all over the recently polished floors. She had exactly two hours until the Empress would arrive.

❖   ❖   ❖

The Blue Salon was filled.

At every table, the most fashionable women of the capital sat dressed in the latest finery of Callot Soeurs, Patou, Lanvin, and Madame Olga. Almost all of them wore white, but some wore the palest rose, cream, *eau de nil*, or mint. Their necks glowed with pearls, and their ears were heavy with low-hanging drops. Their hats were magnificent confections of tulle and taffeta, silk flowers and rare feathers. The women chatted quietly in French and English. The food had not been served, the tea not poured. *It is a party in no regular sense of the word*, Cici thought. When the Empress was expected, everything existed in a state of suspended animation until her arrival.

Karpov entered and bowed deeply over Cici's shoulder, whispering: "Her Majesty's motorcar is leaving the Tsarskoye Selo station."

Sitting at the table of honor was the Empress's aunt, Grand Duchess Maria Pavlovna, and the Empress's sisters-in-law, Grand Duchesses Olga and Xenia. Cici stood, turned to her guests, and announced the Empress's arrival. Rising as one, the women formed lines near the doors to wait while the Grand Duchesses went down the stairs with Cici to receive the Empress.

"Lord, I hope she doesn't sit through this like a stone," Cici heard Grand Duchess Maria Pavlovna whisper to Grand Duchess Olga.

"Aunt Miechen, that she comes at all is a miracle," whispered Olga.

The four women moved down the stairs and lined up on the red carpet that had been laid across the floor from the vestibule through the hall and up the stairs.

There was a heavy knock at the door, and it opened wide to the canal, where the glossy dark red French-made Delaunay-Belleville phaeton with the golden double-headed eagle on the door was visible. It opened to reveal the Empress in a white hat trimmed in tulle and tall egret feathers, and a cashmere coat trimmed in chinchilla. With effort the Empress stepped slowly from the automobile, and she stretched out a kid-glove encased hand for assistance.

The chauffeur, looking very smart in his khaki cashmere uniform and black patent-leather knee boots, handed her a palisander walking stick with a mauve-enameled handle. With effort, the Empress walked across the carpet, nodding left and right to the small crowd who had been alerted that she would be arriving.

She entered the palace and climbed the stairs of the vestibule on the arm of her Cossack guard. With a fleeting glance at her hostess and family, the Empress lifted her veils and turned to reverence the icons that hung in the hall, crossing herself repeatedly. Cici glanced over and saw the Grand Duchess Maria Pavlovna stare ahead rigidly. Cici could tell that the Empress's religious observance annoyed her.

Cici curtseyed deeply, offering up the traditional tray of bread and salt, an ancient symbol of Russian hospitality, which the Empress touched lightly and which was then whisked away by Karpov. Cici kissed the Empress's hand, then rose, waiting to be addressed.

"Such a charming old custom, Cecile," the Empress said, removing her chinchilla-trimmed coat and handing it to her Cossack guard. "It is a pity more of our Russian ladies do not adopt these wonderful usages." The Empress looked pointedly at the cosmopolitan Grand Duchess Maria Pavlovna, who kissed the Empress's hand and rose from her curtsey with barely concealed rage in her eyes. Finally, turning to her sisters-in-law, the Empress offered each of them her cheek, murmuring their names as she did so.

Turning back to Cici, the Empress smiled, revealing her perfect teeth.

"I suppose it couldn't just be the five of us, could it?" she said hopefully, and a bit sadly.

"I am afraid not, Your Majesty," Cici said, leading the Empress toward the stairs. "Several of the princesses of the blood, and most of your ladies are here, as well as some visitors to the capital recently presented at court."

As they climbed the stairs, Cici pointed out portraits and other objects of interest, many of which had been given to the Ozerovskys by the imperial family. As she did so, Cici watched the Empress's breathing become more labored, and a blotchy red spread across the surface of her skin. She seemed panicked, and more than a little distraught.

As they reached the mezzanine, Cici, concerned, broke etiquette and asked the Empress a direct question, offering her a glass of water. The Empress smiled and refused, gesturing for them to continue into the Blue Salon.

A pair of liveried footmen opened the vast twin doors, revealing all of the guests who sank into deep curtseys.

"Her Majesty the Empress!" shouted Karpov, pounding the floor with the long baton reserved for the announcement of important guests.

Alexandra Feodorovna entered, and as she passed the ladies, acknowledging them with her nodding egret plumes, they rose and stared at her in frank curiosity. The Empress had not been seen privately in the capital for some time, and she looked older than many of them remembered her.

The Empress sat down, visibly exhausted from the climb up the stairs. She began an amiable train of conversation, touching lightly on the weather, the completion of the church built at Tsarskoye Selo the previous summer, and the health of the imperial children, studiously avoiding anything controversial.

Cici poured the tea, and the Empress drank it gratefully.

"Ah," she said. "Real English tea. I love our Russian teas, but the taste of this takes me back to my childhood." The Empress smiled sadly at Cici over her cup, knowing full well that without even mentioning her, she had summoned up the spirit of her grandmother, Queen Victoria, the memory of whom brought a mournful pall over the conversation. Cici hoped that the Empress enjoyed her tea. Her guards had stood over the poor terrified servant in charge of its preparation, to foil any attempt at poisoning. It was a miracle it was still hot.

Sensing the awkward moment she had created, the Empress changed the subject, picking up Snegurochka.

"Oh, how charming!" she exclaimed, turning the figurine in her well-manicured hands.

Cici glanced at the door and saw that her children had been brought in by their governess for public inspection. Olga looked sweet with the enormous bow perched in her hair like a butterfly, and Oleg was adorable in his sailor suit, his new camera around his neck. Cici gestured to the governess, who guided the children over to their table.

"Are these your little ones?" said the Empress, putting the figurine at the edge of the table and smiling at the children, who bowed and curtsied very nicely, much to Cici's relief.

"*This is my camera,*" Oleg said in Russian, holding it out to the Empress.

"*Well,*" the Empress replied in English-accented Russian, "*the Tsarevitch has a Kodak just like it. Can you take a picture?*"

He nodded and raised the camera.

Cici smiled at her young son, and noticed that the Empress had adopted a mournful expression.

The shutter clicked.

Five

~

Sasha arrived at work the following morning on the late side, after a tiresome commute from Greenwich to his apartment then back down to Leighton's, to find a note on his desk: *Any new info? Don't forget the marketing meeting in the boardroom at 9:30—A.*

New info indeed. Sasha couldn't wait to tell her everything he had learned at his grandparents'.

Sasha looked at the clock, grabbed a pen and a pad, and made for the boardroom.

Entering the same room where he had seen the figurine for the first time only days before, Sasha looked around. Most department heads, the directors of marketing, finance, business development, and the president of Leighton's himself, John Burnham. Sasha immediately dreaded the high-level meeting. John was often horrible to the young people at Leighton's, partially because he knew only 2 percent of them would still be there the following season, and partially because he resented the energy and determination they had that his own children lacked.

As he was the last person to enter the room, Sasha took a chair in the corner. He looked at Anne and mouthed, *I have more information.* Anne smiled in response, and gestured for him to move to a seat at the larger conference table.

"Are we all here, now?" John asked with evident impatience, opening his files and looking at no one. The assembled murmured their assent, and the meeting began as it always did—with the obituaries.

"Did anyone have any dealings with Jacob Goldberg, the judge who died day before yesterday?" John asked.

Jane Stoke in customer service spoke up.

"I went to Barnard with his daughter Cindy. She's married to David Fine, who works at some big law firm downtown."

"White and Case," murmured Lena Martin, house counsel.

"Right, whatever," Jane continued. "I was invited for Thanksgiving once. Lots of nineteenth-century Louis XV-style furniture, but if I remember correctly some very good Barbizon paintings."

"Sold in 1990 at Sotheby's," Greg Shaw of Nineteenth-Century Paintings noted with regret. "They should have waited—the market was better a few years ago when the Japanese were interested."

John sighed. "Anything else? Jewelry?"

"She collects David Webb," offered Gaston de Miron-LaTour. "Small things—maybe eighty thousand a year."

"Okay, okay," interrupted John. "Let's move on—any more dead prospects? No? Fine. Anne from Russian has a new consignment that may be major. Anne?"

Anne got up and pulled out color photographs in poster size of the figurine, and began setting them up on easels around the room as she began.

"The year is 1913," she said dramatically. "War is about to break out in Europe, and the Russian Revolution of 1917 is on its way. At Fabergé, Prince Ozerovsky commissions for his wife an amazing figurine of a Russian fairy-tale character called 'Snegurochka,' the Snow Maiden, and gives it to her. It was lost in the Revolution, and unknown until it reappeared earlier this week—here at Leighton's."

The room burst into excited murmurs. Sasha had to hand it to Anne; she sure knew how to work a jaded crowd.

"This is the most important Fabergé discovery of the last ten years," Anne continued. "It is the best figurine ever made. It has never been illustrated, never been sold on the open market, never been exhibited, but we have a photo that proves it existed in the collections of the Ozerovsky family before the Revolution, and who is sitting in the picture? The last Empress." Anne smiled. "It's fresh to the market, unique. Once our researcher finds the bill in Saint Petersburg, we will have undoubted proof of its authenticity. It is a star lot—its own catalogue, media hoopla, et cetera."

"Estimate?" asked John.

"Now, I'm being conservative, but I think that the figurine could bring between three hundred and five hundred thousand—maybe even more. I would hope for as high as a million. I know it's not a lot, but it will bring us publicity we couldn't get otherwise—and with all of our documentation we can really undermine Christie's tenuous provenance for those jewels," she finished.

"Why am I more interested in this figurine's documentation than in the mystery of the jewels?" John asked irritably. "We sell magic here, not museum bullshit."

"We have a trump card. The Romanovs will never say if those jewels are a family piece or not, and there is no evidence outside of Russia to corroborate the claim that they are. We, on the other hand, have something better." She smiled at the room. "We have Sasha."

Sasha froze as everyone in the room looked at him. He felt as if he were a puppy caught wetting a chair.

"Why is Sasha our trump card?" asked Jane.

"Sasha?" Anne said, gesturing to him to give his news. He hoped he could emulate Anne's confident and authoritative tone.

"I went to see my grandparents last night, and I showed my grandfather the photograph. He remembered the piece in detail. He told me that it was ordered by my great-great-grandfather as a family gift to my great-grandmother Cecile. In fact, he took the photograph."

"Really?" asked John, his interest piqued. "He remembers the piece from that long ago? How amazing to have a primary source for it. Who are you again, son?"

"My name is Alexander Ozerovsky," he said simply. He knew John knew exactly who he was.

"*Prince* Ozerovsky," Anne said, emphasizing his title. "He's a young and very promising scholar. This piece will make his reputation, and burnish ours," Anne added.

"Ooooh, not the *last* prince, I hope—do you know Lydia Digger, dear? She's available, and looking for a nice title. Hundreds of millions down in Houston, I hear . . ." added Mary Pratt from Special Events.

"And amazing Gauguins at the house in Fort Worth—three, I think," added someone from Impressionist Modern. Their chatter turned to the desirable properties of the Diggers until John focused the conversation once more.

"Well, the figurine sounds fine—set up a marketing and publicity meeting for it, and get it out there as quickly as possible. Some special event maybe. Good—now on to the lecture series on Jayne Wrightsman's collections. . . ."

The meeting continued, while Sasha, Anne, and Irene, the marketing coordinator, all left the room.

"Can you meet now?" Irene asked. "I have a lunch with Chinese I can't break."

"I'm free," Anne said, her cheeks flushed with triumph. Anne seemed like her old self for the first time in weeks. Sasha was pleased. "Come on, Sasha. Let's go."

Sasha and the two women walked down the stairs to the saleroom, where an auction of carpets was under way. The room was almost empty, save for the regular group of Middle Eastern dealers, sitting in a cluster and talking loudly, and a small squadron of dealers from Paris, there to bid on the chief lot, a late eighteenth-century Aubusson carpet, rejected for use at Versailles, but sent to the Palace of St. Cloud. The three slowed instinctively to watch the star lot go.

"And we have lot number two forty-five showing at the front, then," called Andrea Laurence from the podium. Sasha smiled. Andrea was his favorite auctioneer: cool, elegant, and mercifully quick.

"Lot two forty-five, a highly important French royal carpet made for Queen Marie-Antoinette at the Palace of St. Cloud, and we can open the bidding at—" She paused dramatically. "We can open the bidding then at five hundred thousand dollars. I have an advance bid of five hundred fifty. Do I have another bid?"

A New York dealer in the room raised her paddle.

"And I have five hundred sixty for the carpet, and the bid is with me, still with my advance bidder at five hundred seventy."

The New York dealer raised her paddle again.

"In the room five hundred eighty, and still with me at five hundred ninety. Another bid, madam?"

The woman hesitated, then made the gesture for a half bid of $595,000.

"I'm sorry, madam, I will not take half increments, and the bid is in the book at five hundred ninety. The next bid will be—"

"Six hundred thousand!" called a new bidder in the corner.

The auction went on for several very quick minutes, until the bidding began to slow at $850,000.

Andrea looked around the room with a confidence Sasha could tell she didn't really have. Her bids in the book had run out, and it was obvious to him that the carpet must have a reserve price of somewhere over $850,000, meaning Leighton's could not sell the piece because their contract with the consignor guaranteed it would sell for more.

"And any further bids? Any further bidding on lot two forty-five? Do I hear any further bids on lot two forty-five?"

Breaking the tension, a young woman on the phone raised her hand. Smiling jubilantly, Andrea announced, "And eight hundred sixty thousand. I have eight hundred sixty thousand dollars for the carpet, selling, then, at eight hundred sixty thousand—"

Suddenly the bidding went crazy. Dealers, realizing that there would be no opportunity to buy the unsold carpet cheaply after the sale, began bidding in earnest. The numbers jumped higher and higher—phone bidders catching the excitement. Soon, the dealers were no longer involved in the bidding—it was between two anonymous phone bidders and an academic-looking woman in the front row. Finally, at $2.2 million, one of the phone bidders gave up, and it was between the woman in the front row and the remaining phone bidder.

"Who is she?" Sasha asked Anne, who stood mesmerized by the sight of the sale, already surpassing its high estimate.

"No idea," said Anne. "But she's got to be French. Look at that scarf and bag."

Finally, with a dazzling and grateful smile, Andrea knocked down the sale: "And sold, to paddle number twelve eighty-five, for two point five million dollars!" There was applause in the room, people expressing their admiration for anyone who would spend $2.5 million on a carpet. The woman approached the podium, and Andrea covered the microphone with her hand, leaning over to listen to the woman. Smiling, she turned back to the microphone and spoke: "It is my pleasure to announce that the last lot, number two forty-five, made for Marie-Antoinette at St.-Cloud, has been purchased by the French government, and will be restored and subsequently placed on exhibition at the Palace of Versailles, for which it was intended."

Sasha found himself applauding again with everyone else. This was a rare auction house moment. A wonderful object returning to its original home was one of Sasha's greatest pleasures.

"We're going to get a price like that for the figurine," Anne said, poking him in the ribs and ruining his mood. "Let's have that meeting."

❖   ❖   ❖

The three walked to the marketing department. Entering the area, Sasha took in the other side of business at Leighton's—the frantic ringing of phones, the elaborate planning calendars, piles of invitations on the floor, and posters of past top lots on all the walls. The three sat in the midst of the chaos and ordered coffee from an intern.

"So, we have a blockbuster on our hands?" asked Dorothy Sanders of marketing and publicity in her smoke-colored voice.

"We hope so," said Anne.

"We need a splashy debut for Snegurochka. It has to burst onto the scene, and soon. Christie's has had months to butter up the press about this necklace, and we have only a few weeks. Forgive me, Anne," Dorothy added, "it's a nice angle that it was made for Sasha's family, but we can't focus on that too much. It will look like we're pushing it because it belongs to Sasha—that's conflict of interest, and nasty fodder for the press."

Sasha sighed with relief.

"Laura!" yelled Dorothy to her associate, who appeared at the door. "What is the next big public event in town?"

"Um, let me see," said Laura, a tall and elegant brunette in coffee-colored suede rifling through a scheduling book that looked more like the original manuscript of *War and Peace* than a Filofax.

"Benefit dinner at the library, a DAR designer showhouse, and the Museum of the City of New York's winter dance."

Just as I expected, Sasha thought. *Just my luck—I get to work the night of my dinner.*

"What is that—a junior thing?" Dorothy asked.

"The very best of them," Laura confirmed. "The *Social Register, Avenue,* and *Town and Country* crowd."

"What's the theme this year?" asked Anne.

"Snowflakes and diamonds," replied Laura and Sasha in stereo.

Anne and Dorothy looked at each other and smiled.

Six

⁓

THE GUEST LIST FOR DINNER had been reduced to eleven. Sasha himself. Grace Winning, an academic, and her friend David Speed, a porcelain collector. Sasha had invited the Grant twins, Sarah and Becky, because they were young and lively, and Douglas McKee and Grady Wilton because he was matchmaking for Mr. and Mrs. Grant. Finally, he invited his cousins, Betsy Romanov and Katia Kurassov. Finally, Marina and her unknown friend. Sasha had tried to get his cousin Victoria de Witt, but she had canceled at the last minute, saying that she would see him at the dance. Victoria was always busy, and now she had left him with eleven guests instead of twelve.

Sasha moved slowly around his father's apartment, checking everything one last time before the guests arrived. He knew no one smoked anymore, but somehow he still felt that the small silver cups had to be filled with fresh cigarettes, and the silver match holders and table lighters needed to be replenished as well. Nut dishes held the same boring mélange that his parents had served, and the passed hors d'oeuvres included water chestnuts wrapped in bacon and puff pastry stuffed with chopped mushrooms. No wasabi-marinated tuna rolls with garlic aioli or prosciutto-wrapped peach sections for this crowd. The guests at this party were not interested in having the best dinner they'd ever had; they wanted the *same* dinner they'd always had. As a final touch, Sasha had Derek draw the curtains. No one in New York seemed to draw their curtains anymore, but Sasha's mother always had, and Sasha got a perverse pleasure in shutting out the multimillion-dollar view.

Derek entered the drawing room and walked over to the bar, where he arranged bottles of liquor and freshly cut limes and lemons.

"How many drinks shall I allow people before dinner?" he asked.

"Two, I think. If people want more, they can have it, but we'll have a vodka toast for Marina at the *zakouski* table before we eat, and it might do someone in if they have more than three before the meal. I don't think that this is a heavy drinking crowd though."

"Very good. Magda couldn't find any fresh herring, so I hope you don't mind that she bought the smoked herring in cream from Zabar's."

"Not at all. She goes to too much trouble making it from scratch anyway. The *zakouski* table looks beautiful, Derek, thank you," Sasha said. The traditional Russian cold and hot hors d'oeuvres table was magnificent. A large silver epergne stood at the round table's center, dripping with ivy and carefully arranged miniature sugared fruits. Positioned around it on small silver trays were bottles of homemade flavored vodkas: lemon, blood orange, vanilla, mint, rose, horseradish, and buffalo grass, each frozen in a block of ice with flowers, along with pieces of the essence that provided the flavoring. Often people who came to dinner at the Ozerovskys' didn't realize that the *zakouski* table wasn't dinner itself, and they stuffed themselves before the customary five course dinner was served.

When the building phone rang, Derek went off to answer it. In the absence of a hostess, Sasha lit the candles himself.

"It's the Princess Elizabeth," said Derek, returning. "They've called from downstairs."

Sasha glanced at the bracket clock. Betsy was always punctual. It was a pity that Marina had not arrived first, though, so that they might have had time to talk.

Derek showed Betsy into the drawing room.

"We welcome Your Imperial Highness, and are pleased to attend you," Sasha teased in Russian, bowing deeply from the waist.

"What? No bread and salt tray? Alexander, you're slipping."

Sasha took her arm and led her through the room, careful not to tread on her long, bottle-green velvet skirt.

He looked her over carefully. Betsy was, unlike her other sisters, tall and thin. Her eyes were wide-spaced and her nose a bit pug for conventional beauty's current taste, but she was what had once been called a handsome woman. Betsy Romanov, though only thirty, filled a room with her presence—her posture alone was enough to silence people. It was, however, the slight familiarity of her face that was striking. She looked very much like her great-grandmother, the Grand Duchess Xenia, Nicholas II's sister.

"Betsy, I'm glad that you're here first, so that we have a chance to talk before everyone arrives. How have you been?" he asked.

"Oh, fine. I'm painting a lot. It's nice and quiet out in Water Mill now. Except for the random bit of mail from some oddball monarchist group in Russia, I'm left fairly undisturbed. You'll have to come out one weekend, though during the week is really far nicer. How are you?"

"Busy. A sale I thought would be a disaster is suddenly turning out to be one of the most exciting in years. Lots of work to do, and no time to do it."

"It sounds stressful. I've taken up yoga. It makes me feel wonderful. You should try it." Betsy laughed lightly and accepted the glass of Champagne that Derek had brought her. She took a sip.

"Mm. It is nice to be back in town, though, for a treat like this. So," she said conspiratorially, "it's all over New York that Marina Shoutine is here. Sasha, what on earth is she like?"

"I don't know, Betsy. I haven't met her yet. How is it 'all over' New York? I haven't told anyone."

"Well, Katia, who'll be here in a minute, by the way, was at John Barrett getting her hair done, and she was in the chair next to Belinda Davis, who works at Sotheby's. Belinda said that she heard Victoria de Witt say that she sat next to Marina at the collections in Paris, and that Marina told her that her mother had just died, and that she was planning a business trip to New York. Victoria suggested that Marina call you, and gave her your number at Leighton's. I *am* sorry about your aunt, by the way," she finished.

Sasha took it all in. How funny that it involved his cousin Victoria. He and Victoria had been friends since their teens, and Victoria had a successful career as a fashion designer, though she always referred to herself as a "dressmaker." What she really did was copy one of the hundreds of pieces of couture that she had inherited from her grandmother. Her grandmother Ellen had been a legendary beauty, and she had raised Victoria when her parents insisted on moving to an ashram in the 1980s. Victoria cultivated the air of an eccentric, but she was one of the shrewdest and most honest women he knew, and he valued her friendship.

"Well, it would be like Victoria to help along an olive branch."

Betsy sniffed. "Your cousin Victoria is a busybody. I would never get involved in someone else's family business that way."

"Perfect segue," Sasha said, changing the subject. "On the topic of family business, what do you think of the stray jewels wandering around at Christie's? They've ruined my season."

"I'm sorry, Sasha. I heard there were some things of Alix's that had come up."

"Are they really Alexandra Feodorovna's diamonds?"

"Sasha, you're the expert, not I. We really have no idea. If we kept track of everything with a double-headed eagle on it that hit the market, we would go insane. It's family policy not to comment on these things."

"So you *do* know! Were they hers?"

"No comment," Betsy said, smiling over the rim of her glass and taking a sip of her Champagne. "Mm, heaven." The doorbell rang again. "Saved by the bell, no?" she said, laughing.

"Mr. Speed and Madam Winning," Derek announced as they came into the room.

"Hello there, Sasha," said Grace, kissing Sasha on both cheeks. "Now you do remember David, don't you?"

"Of course I do, hello there, David. Welcome—I'm so glad you could make it for dinner. Do you know my cousin, Elizabeth Romanov?"

"Elizabeth and I have met a few times, actually," said Grace. "How nice to see you again." There was a sudden rush as Sarah and Becky Grant arrived, trailed by Katia, Douglas McKee, and Grady Wilton. After a few moments, Sasha sensed a frisson of activity at the other end of the room.

Marina had arrived.

Sasha walked slowly through his guests, smiling automatically and making certain they were comfortable, all the while trying to see Marina through the thicket of lamps and flowers that he suddenly realized blocked his view to the hall. Finally, he could see her clearly.

She stood framed in the doorway, the soft light of the drawing room falling across her face. She was beautiful; there was no doubt of that. Much to Sasha's relief, he saw she didn't look too much like his mother, Nina, though the family resemblance was still striking. She had the same coloring, inherited from their mothers' family, the Shchermanovs, but she was far more seductive-looking than he ever remembered his mother being. Marina was tall and thin, her skin was unbelievably pale, and her delicate head sat on a long and elegant neck. Her eyes, Sasha could see, were a brilliant pale aquamarine and tilted delicately beneath high arched brows. She wore her black hair twisted into a low bun at the nape of her neck. Marina was truly beautiful, and she knew it. A long, bias-cut black satin gown set off her lean silhouette to perfection, and she wore no jewelry other than a thin platinum chain from which, Sasha could tell even from this distance, dangled the diamond and sapphire brooch that had been a gift to her mother from his family.

Marina turned her head, and, as she caught sight of him, there was a glimmer of recognition in her eyes. Sasha watched as she slowly crossed the room. Every conversation in the room gradually came to a halt. Sasha had the feeling that everything Marina did was this slow, this deliberate, and this mesmerizing.

Marina walked right up to him and stopped, meeting his gaze.
"Sasha," she said. "I'm Marina."

Reflexively, the two reached for each other and exchanged
kisses.

"It is good to have you here at last," Sasha said, and meant it.

"I wore this so you would recognize me," Marina said, lightly
fingering the jewel at her throat and smiling.

"I would have recognized you anyway," Sasha said, gesturing to
the portrait of his mother over the mantel. Marina's eyes ran over
the portrait, and Sasha could see that she recognized the resemblance. He also had the impression that she was pleased to be
prettier.

"I'm sorry I wasn't able to be here earlier, but my friend was
delayed at a meeting. Here, Sasha, come meet him, please." Marina
turned and held out her hand to the man crossing the room.
Sasha's eyes focused. It was Dimitri Durakov.

*"Dimitri, I recommend to you the acquaintance of my cousin Prince
Ozerovsky. Sasha, please meet Dimitri Durakov, a dear friend."* She
used a very formal and old-fashioned Russian, which Sasha believed had been last employed by the better-born characters of Tolstoy.

Sasha waited for Dimitri to say something. He wasn't sure that
Dimitri wanted Marina to know that he was already a client.

"Actually," Dimitri replied in Russian, *"the Prince and I have
already met. When you asked me to join you, Marina, I didn't realize
your cousin would be Alexander Kirillovitch."*

Marina smiled. *"Well, this is a nice surprise, then!"*

"I'm pleased to have you both here," Sasha said. Turning to his
left, he grabbed Becky Grant.

"Becky, this is Dimitri Durakov, a client of mine, and a friend of
my cousin Marina's. You'll keep him entertained while I have a few
words with my cousin, won't you?" Becky nodded, and gestured for
Dimitri to join her on the marquise.

"Marina, may I show you around?" he said.

"I'd love a little tour."

The two walked around the drawing room, Sasha pointing out the few things of family interest, such as the photographs in their Fabergé frames, the bust of his great-grandfather by Troubetskoy, and some of the more important pieces of Chinese porcelain his father had collected. When Marina asked him a question about one of the Fabergé frames, she spoke so softly that he was forced to lean in close to hear. The intimacy was heady and frankly seductive—all the more disturbing given their close relationship.

"Marina," Sasha said crisply, pulling back and removing himself from the subtle jasmine scent of her perfume. "I don't even know what it is that you do."

"What I do?" Marina asked, raising her eyebrows. "Ah, I forget. Just because we are both Russians doesn't mean we were raised the same way. All you Americans want to know is what people 'do.'" She smiled, indicating she was teasing him. "I make introductions for Condé Nast. I am a contributing editor at large." She smiled. "Europe," she added for his clarification.

"What does that mean?" Sasha asked with curiosity.

"Oh, an editor calls me and says, 'I hear Lady Townsend's Esmond Court in Sussex is beautiful. Can you get us inside to photograph it.' Well, generally I don't know who they are talking about, so I bluff, and say that of course I can, but that the Principessa di L'Amacchi has a lovely villa in Casole d'Elsa, which is much prettier, and that they should see that instead. They pay me a little; they pay her a little; they get their pictures; we all get by." She shrugged and looked around the apartment. "It seems that whatever it is you 'do' does you far better than introductions do me."

"This is my father's apartment, Marina. Mine is more modest."

"I'm teasing you, Sasha. I am a tease," she said. "Well, sometimes I do well. This trip to New York was courtesy of an introduction. I made a little meeting. Say," she said mischievously, "this apartment would be wonderful for the luxury issue of *House and Garden*, no?" She laughed, knowing he would never say yes.

Sasha smiled. He liked her Gallic playfulness.

"Seriously, I had a wonderful trip to Moscow, thanks to *House and Garden*. They asked me because of the name, Shoutine, you know." She made a dismissive gesture with her hand. "Well, we photographed a house for a couple called the Dikarinskys. Vulgar, vulgar. New rich, *uncultured*." She used the Russian word. "The house is Slavic revival, very dramatic. I met Dimitri through them. He is their adviser on Fabergé. They have a huge collection. The wife is quite nice. Anyway, we became very friendly. They had a party for me—all of the hand kissing, you can't imagine." She took his arm, and they moved closer to the *zakouski* table.

"Dimitri arranged for me to go to a warehouse outside of Moscow. You'll never believe what was there. All of the furniture from Olenkovo, our old estate. Rooms of furniture, moldering. It made me sick." She stabbed angrily at a shrimp with a silver seafood fork. "The curators were all so desperate. 'Can you get us money to restore all of this?' they said." Marina scooped up an impossible amount of caviar onto a mother-of-pearl spoon and ate it in one swallow. "You know what I told them? 'It was in perfect condition when we left; fix it yourselves!'" She smiled, a flash of anger in her otherwise beautiful eyes.

Sasha didn't find the story funny at all. He knew those curators. They were desperately trying to fund a Museum of the Russian Country Estate so that they could save the suites of furniture, precious documents, and historical pieces that were in such danger of being lost forever through neglect. The curators worked day and night, virtually without pay. They didn't need émigré derision; they needed help. Sasha felt keenly that these objects needed to be preserved so that people could enjoy them and learn from them, while Marina saw them only as things stolen from her family. Her speech had upset him, and he needed to get away from her for a minute.

He glanced across the room and spotted Derek in the doorway holding a tray. Sasha sighed with relief at the timing, and cleared his throat to speak. "May I invite all of you to join me in a toast in honor of my cousin, Marina, from whose friendship I have been kept too long. May we all grow to love her as if she had grown up here with us." As Sasha spoke, Derek moved through the room, urging everyone to take from his tray decorated with small roses a small glass filled with vodka.

"In our family, this rose-flavored vodka is served only on very special occasions such as weddings or christenings, but I thought Marina's debut in New York merited it. To Marina, welcome," he said raising his glass.

"To Marina!" replied the other guests in unison.

"I don't know what to say," Marina said, lowering her eyes and blushing a becoming shade of rose. "Except to thank you all so much. This is very moving for me. To all of you." The glasses were raised, the vodka consumed, and the difficult moment passed. Sasha guided Marina over to where Betsy sat.

"I would recognize you anywhere," Marina said, dropping to sit next to her on the sofa. "You must be Volodya Romanov's cousin. I know him well." Betsy was in fact Volodya's cousin, and the two began to chat amiably.

Sasha made his way about the room, urging people to eat. He stopped to press another vodka on the rapidly loosening Grant twins.

"Sasha!" trilled Grace. "I have to stop eating those hors d'oeuvres before I gain a hundred pounds. I sense that Russian cuisine's foundation is built upon heavy servings of sour cream and butter." She laughed loudly, and Sasha glanced around the room. Dimitri was talking with Katia Kurassova, who looked bored. It was time to rescue her, and Sasha excused himself, leaving Grace with Betsy and Marina.

"Dimitri, you can't monopolize Katia, no matter how pretty she is. Katia, Betsy wants you to meet Marina." Katia kissed him on the cheek and gave him a grateful look.

"So," Sasha said to Dimitri, "it appears you know more about me than I would have thought."

Dimitri smiled and lit a cigarette without asking. "I hope you don't mind. It seemed inappropriate to let you know that I knew Marina when I saw you at Leighton's."

"Did Marina suggest that you contact me?"

"I told her in Paris that I had a piece I wanted to sell at Leighton's in New York, and she said that introducing me to you would be no problem."

Introductions, Sasha thought. *Marina's business of introductions.* Sasha wondered idly if Marina and Dimitri had had an even more intimate introduction to each other.

"I see. Well, how lucky for both of us. Now I have the figurine and a new cousin to thank you for. It seems I owe you a great deal."

"Perhaps we will figure out a way for you to repay me someday," Dimitri said, blowing smoke.

"Perhaps. But now, it's time for dinner." Sasha smiled, and touched a bell push to summon Derek.

Derek entered, opened the doors to the dining room, and everyone began to file in. Sasha showed people to their seats, and chattered amiably. The dining room, Sasha hated to admit, was magnificent by candlelight. He would have to write Diane a note tomorrow.

❖   ❖   ❖

Instead of lingering at the table, Sasha decided to serve coffee and after-dinner drinks in the library so as to speed up their departure for the museum.

"Tell us about this lot that is going to be on view at the dance, Sasha," Marina pleaded charmingly. "I'm just dying to know. Dimitri is cruel, and he refuses to tell me what it is."

"If Dimitri wants it a secret, you will just have to see it when we get there," Sasha responded. Marina pouted and leaned into Douglas. Sasha could see that Douglas was as caught by her as he had been.

"I think my new cousin is being hateful, don't you?" Marina said into his shoulder, where she had decided to nestle attractively.

"I reserve judgment until I see what it is. That is, if I can still see after all of the flavored vodkas that have been foisted on me," Douglas replied.

"Do you think we should be getting along soon, Sasha?" asked Grace, glancing quickly toward the Grant girls, who were looking a little tipsy.

"The sooner the better. I'll ring the doorman and have him round up a couple of taxis," Sasha replied.

"Never mind that," said Dimitri. "I have two cars waiting downstairs for all of us."

There was a flurry of "thank yous" and "you really shouldn't haves," then everyone rose up, worked their way to the door, and bundled into coats, anticipating the icy February winds. Down the elevator in two batches, and into the waiting cars that smelled (appropriately, as Princess Betsy remarked) new, the group was at the museum in a matter of minutes.

Entering the Federal-style Museum of the City of New York, Sasha was overwhelmed by the decoration of the entry hall. It seemed as if the room were a small forest of silver birches, their branches laden with small silver ornaments shaped like snowflakes. Sasha assumed that upstairs the café tables would be decorated similarly. In the middle of the lobby, past the crowds of people waiting to present their invitations to the volunteers seated at the reception tables, a group of people huddled. When someone eventually moved aside, Sasha caught a glimpse of the figurine's diamonds sparkling in the light.

Once they all had checked their coats, Marina grabbed Sasha's arm and pulled him toward the crowd. Smiling, Marina approached the group gathered around the case, with Betsy and Katia close behind her, until the figurine was finally visible.

Sasha noted that Leighton's had created a wonderful display. The security case in which the figurine sat was lit from within by fiber-optic cables. The multiple light sources gave maximum play to the diamonds' facets. The piece was also set on a small revolving platform, so the smiling figure of Snegurochka revolved endlessly, sparkling like frozen fireworks.

"Oh, Sasha!" exclaimed Marina. "It's magnificent! How could you keep this a secret? Was it imperial? It must have been—Betsy come and look."

Sasha smiled. "Actually, Marina, you'll like it even better in a minute. Read the text." Sasha watched Marina's glowing face as she read the text he and Anne had written earlier:

> The present lot was designed as a gift for Princess Cecile Ozerovsky for her tenth wedding anniversary. The subject was chosen because in learning the language of her new country, her first exercise in translation was that of the Russian folk tale "Snegurochka, or, The Snow Maiden." The offered lot was commissioned probably in the winter of 1912, during the creation of the Winter Egg, which obviously served as an inspiration for the offered lot. (Leighton's wishes to thank Pce. and Pcss. Serge Ozerovsky for their kind assistance in compiling this entry.)

As Sasha watched, Marina's beautiful smile grew tense, tightened, and finally dropped away. Trembling with anger, she turned toward Sasha and Dimitri.

"How *could* you? Dimitri, why didn't you tell me? This is so humiliating. And Sasha—selling a family treasure like this? We have so little—my mother and I had nothing from the Shoutines, nothing from the Shchermanovs when I was growing up. Only this brooch, and even that a borrowed heirloom from your family. We émigrés have nothing of our past—don't you understand? This piece is who you *are*. How could you work to help sell this piece which is rightfully *ours*? Sasha, I will do everything to stop this sale. I am calling a lawyer in the morning. *Good-bye*."

She said the Russian farewell with intensity, and the word she chose indicated she would not see him again.

Dancing Class, the Seventh Regiment Armory. New York, 1983

Sasha dropped his backpack onto the heavily carpeted floor of the Park Avenue armory, loathing its familiar smell of dust, old wood, and cleaning detergent. He pulled off his Walkman's earphones and stuffed it all into his backpack, which was already full of his summer reading list for Groton.

He looked around for the other kids but didn't see anyone. Soon a tall soldier in camouflage fatigues stepped out of a side room and saw him.

"Hey, kid!" the soldier said in an aggressive voice. "What's up? Why are you here?"

"Uh, Knickerbocker Dancing School?" Sasha asked

The soldier rolled his eyes. "Down the hall," he said disgustedly, and went back into the room where he sat guarding the silver trophies and paintings of dead generals.

Sasha wandered the dark wood-paneled hall under the dim and buzzing glow of the Tiffany light fixtures until he heard the sound of an out-of-tune piano playing a warped version of the "Tennessee Waltz."

Ugh, he thought. *This is going to be the worst.*

Sasha walked into the square room with flaking salmon-colored paint and saw a motley group of kids. Most of the boys were older than he, but, fortunately, none seemed to be markedly taller. All of them were bigger, though. *Why am I so skinny?* he asked himself. Many of the boys were in the uniform of the Knickerbocker Greys, an elite cadet group, and others wore the blazers of the city's private schools: Trinity, Collegiate, and Browning.

Looking around, he didn't see any of his classmates. Most of them were also going off to boarding school, but apparently none of them had grandmothers who insisted on dancing lessons.

"Where else will you learn, darling?" she had asked. "Wouldn't you rather learn here with your friends instead of having to tread on some poor girl's toes at a dance?"

Frankly, Sasha didn't care. He just wanted out. The boys made him nervous with their floppy blond hair and casually rumpled oxford-cloth shirts and rep ties. The fact that they were all rough-housing to get the girls' attention made it worse.

The girls were even more terrifying to him. Long-haired, icy, and seemingly years older than the boys present, they were morti-fied and excited in equal measure to be in male company. The boys and girls sat on opposite sides of the room in cliques. The wallflow-ers of both sexes waited not only to be asked to dance, but to par-ticipate in the life around them from which they were unfairly and unreasonably excluded by their looks.

In one corner a girl caught Sasha's eye. She was tall. Too tall. Her long, mousy hair was held back by barrettes trailing thin silk ribbons. Pale but pretty, she was engrossed in a well-worn copy of *Lace*. She wore a pink sweater with a low neckline, and her uni-form's kilt had been hemmed high on her thigh. Her jeans jacket, covered with buttons and pins advertising Canal Jean and Elvis Costello, lay crumpled on the floor next to a chocolate brown can-vas schoolbag, its shoulder strap fashionably frayed. Sasha heaved a sigh of relief and approached her. "Hi." He hesitated. "Victoria?"

The girl looked up. She had amber-colored eyes, one of which was oddly flecked with green. She looked at him blankly.

"I'm Sasha Ozerovsky, your cousin." She gave no indication of recognizing him, so he tried again. "We met at your grandmother's last week. At the tea? For your homecoming?"

"New York isn't my home," she said firmly, shoving the book into her schoolbag. "Oh, right," she said after a moment. "The little prince. I remem-ber you. How are we related again?" she asked with only mild interest.

Sasha smiled at the opening in the conversation. He wouldn't be abandoned in the room after all.

"Your grandfather and my grandmother were brother and sister.

My dad and your dad are first cousins; you and I are second cousins. You're Victoria de Witt, and my grandmother is a de Witt. Well, was a de Witt. Now she's Ozerovsky."

"Whatever," Victoria said without interest. "How did you get stuck here?"

"My grandmother made me," Sasha replied.

"Mine, too," she said. "Oh-oh. Here we go."

Just then, Mr. and Mrs. Caine, the dancing teachers, came into the room.

"All right, all right, young ladies and gentlemen!" called Mrs. Caine in a singsong voice. "Line up according to height."

They all did so, and Sasha saw with regret that he and Victoria, though the same height, were not paired together. Victoria was with Trey Calvert, whom Sasha had disliked his whole life. Sasha looked into the blinking and unfamiliar eyes of his partner, who seemed terrified.

"All right," called Mr. Caine. "The first dance is a fox-trot—"

Trey Calvert raised his hand. "Can I dance with someone else?" he interrupted.

"No," said Mr. Caine, "you are matched by height."

"I can't dance with her," he insisted.

"Why on earth not?" asked Mrs. Caine.

"Because her parents are hippie drug addicts. My parents said so," interrupted Serena Holton, the tallest and most beautiful of the girls.

A stunned silence fell over the class.

His face turning red, Mr. Caine walked deliberately over to Serena, took her by the arm, and left the room. Flustered, Mrs. Caine realigned the students, and this time Sasha found himself across from Victoria.

"Don't listen to her," he said calmly. "Serena Holton is a bitch."

Victoria smiled weakly.

"Fox-trot!" shouted Mr. Caine, reentering the room. "Take your partner."

The accompanist started, and from the piano came "Tea for Two." Sasha took Victoria in his arms awkwardly, and as they stumbled into the "slow, slow, quick, quick" of the box step, Victoria put her head into the shoulder of his blazer, and he could feel her trying to steady her breathing so she would not cry.

Seven

THE REST OF THE EVENING PASSED in a blur for Sasha. After Marina left, he could not reconcile his feelings of guilt and anger. He was forcing himself to behave as if nothing had happened. He wished he could have told the guests from his dinner that Marina had fallen ill and gone home, but everyone had seen her outburst. Sasha was grateful only that the ever present social photographer from the *Times* hadn't caught it for next week's paper. Dimitri left to follow her back to the hotel to see if he could calm her down, and so now Sasha and Betsy climbed the curving staircase, trailed by Katia, the Grant twins, and the rest of the dinner party. They began to move slowly through the young and well-dressed crowd.

"I used to hate these things, but as I get older, I really enjoy the chance to come into the city and dress up a little. Thanks for talking me into this," Betsy said, swatting at a brunette with a vagrant cigarette. "But how can everyone here stand this crowd?"

"Court Easter receptions were worse," Sasha said.

"We had the Cossacks to hold them back. Let's get out of this crush," she replied.

Sasha squeezed her arm. "Look," he said, pointing to a tall blonde in a Schiaparelli pink beaded jacket and gray sheath, "it's my busybody cousin Victoria—you like her."

"Do we have to?" Betsy asked. "I'm not sure I'm up for her, um, *energy*."

"You called her a busybody—you now pay the price," he said cheerfully.

"Well, I just hope she doesn't start telling us about how she feels. She's *always* wanting to tell us how she *feels*. I don't care about how Victoria feels; I care whether or not she shows up for dinner—Victoria de Witt! Don't you look wonderful."

"I've been in Istanbul."

"Well, you look spectacular."

"I *feel* wonderful," Victoria responded.

Betsy dug her nails into Sasha's wrist. "How lucky you've come, Victoria. I was just about to invoke female prerogative and go home. I thought this would all be great fun, but the crowd is terrifying, and I don't know a soul here. Sasha, sweetheart, dinner was wonderful, and please, please, please, come out to Water Mill sometime this winter." With that, Betsy disappeared into the throng of people.

Victoria looked at Sasha with an appraising glance. "You don't look so well yourself, Sash. Are you okay?"

"Well, by missing my dinner, you missed Marina Shoutine's introduction to New York, which you so kindly set up."

"Oh, did it work out? I'm so happy."

"Well, it depends what you mean by 'work out.' She came, bringing one of my clients in tow, and it turns out they seem to have been using each other to get to me to sell that piece that's whirling around downstairs."

"Wow. Sorry, I was in Paris—"

"I know. For the collections. You sat next to her and gave her my card."

"No, where did you hear that?"

"Betsy heard it from Katia, who was getting her hair done, and she was in the chair with some gal from Sotheby's—"

"Stop! Stop! Stop!" Victoria raised her black-gloved hands. "This is like a horrible game of telephone. I was at the collections. On the seat next to mine was a card that said Countess Shoutine, Condé Nast. So, I'm expecting some sixty-year-old fashionista in a Chanel suit. Well, you saw her. She's no sixty-year-old, and the suit was Galliano for Dior. Fabulous, by the way."

Sasha nodded.

"Anyway, we start talking, and I mention that my cousin in New York is Prince Ozerovsky, and so we discover that we're all cousins," she finished brightly.

"So that's it?"

"That's it. I was happy to meet her because I thought she might do my business some good—I gave her *my* card, not yours. Did I do something wrong?"

He smiled. "No—not at all. Let's change the subject. That's a great dress. It could almost be Schiaparelli."

"It *is* Schiaparelli, and thank you for noticing. It was Gran's. I know I should give them to the Costume Institute at the Met, but she never let me try them on when I was a little girl, so now I'm wearing them all, one by one, and copying and selling them to anyone who'll buy them. My business, p.s., is booming."

"That's great."

"I keep telling everyone how great I feel. I may fire my therapist, I'm doing so well—for now. You never know. I come to events like this, though, and I look around, and it depresses me."

"Why?" Sasha asked.

"Well, the things I know about these people and their parents would knock out your teeth . . . and theirs, if they knew what I do."

"Like what?"

"Like . . ." Victoria looked around and smiled. "Like that bitch Serena Holton and Andrew Colt."

Sasha looked at them. "They seem perfectly happy. Aren't they getting married?"

"Yes, but their parents tried to stop them—remember?"

"I guess I did hear something about it a year ago, why?"

"Oh, just that Serena's mother, your boss's sister-in-law, and Andrew's father have had an affair that has lasted over thirty-five years, and there might possibly be some confusion about whether or not Andrew and Serena are half siblings."

"Victoria, no!" Sasha's eyes widened.

"I, for one, am holding my breath until the blood tests in June."

"Victoria, how do you know this?"

"Unlike you, or any other of the well-bred idiots in this museum, I made the mistake of listening to my grandmother's drinks chatter as a child. Unfortunately, I also have a photographic memory. I know where all of the dirt is on all of these people, and I see nothing but doom for everyone here." Victoria picked up her drink: a large glass of vodka, neat. "You are looking, Sasha, at the Cassandra of East Sixty-third, and I am screaming from the walls of Troy."

"What happened to Cassandra?" Sasha asked. "I can never remember."

"She went mad," Victoria said pointedly. *"Santé."*

"Forgive me," Sasha said. "I don't quite know how to follow that."

"How about . . . 'You look depressed, Victoria, though still ravishingly beautiful, and it is only now that I dare confess the love I have had for you since dancing lessons at the Park Avenue armory in 1983. Run away with me to Paris, and I'll make you a princess and shower you with jewels from my dead ancestors, which will go beautifully with the gowns of your dead grandmother.'"

Sasha laughed. "I think marriages between second cousins are still illegal in New York, Victoria. How about lunch at Doubles instead?"

"Done!" she replied, and kissed him on both cheeks. "Call me. I've read *The Rules,* both books. I'm never supposed to call a man."

"It will be my pleasure."

Victoria smiled and moved into the crowd, her pink jacket blazing. Sasha turned and spotted Betsy still trying to make her way toward the stairs. He felt terrible for having brought her, and decided to leave with her.

"Betsy!" he called. "Over here!"

Betsy turned and forced her way back over to the top of the staircase.

"Thank God," she said. "I went the wrong way and ended up in a discotheque. I turned to come back, and ran into Adam Witherspoon. He's been trying to marry me off to that senile Bragança for years. Isn't it time he stopped being on the Junior Committee?"

"He does it very well. Even if he is forty."

"I suppose that counts as 'Junior,' considering how old the people on the board are—I think the average age is eighty."

Sasha smiled. He took her arm, and the two of them began to make their way down the stairs.

"Isn't that your boss?" Betsy asked.

Sasha looked. At the foot of the stairs, Anne stood talking to a man, gesturing to the figurine of Snegurochka. She caught sight of them on the stairs and waved excitedly.

"Shall we?" Sasha asked Betsy.

"Do we have a choice?" Betsy asked, smiling brightly. "Hello, Anne, nice to see you," Betsy said, extending her hand as she reached the bottom step.

"Elizabeth. Sasha. This party makes me feel so old! I haven't been to one of these in years." Anne looked around at the crowd. "I think the figurine looks wonderful, though. Don't you?"

"It does, Anne. The press seems to have gone wild for it. Congratulations. If you'll excuse us, Betsy and I were just on our way out."

"Oh, you can't possibly leave!" Anne exclaimed. "I've invited a group of potential clients to come see the figurine. You really should stay here."

Sasha sighed. "Let me put Betsy into a cab," he said. "I'll be right back." He and Betsy moved toward the coat check.

"I am *so* sorry for you," Betsy said, allowing Sasha to help her on with her coat.

"Don't you worry, I'll be out of here soon enough. You're not going back to Water Mill tonight, are you?"

"No, I'm staying with Katia, and I have my own key. Don't worry about me. Thank you again for dinner. Call me, I'm deadly serious about a week in Water Mill—that is, if those *Los Angeles* people don't suddenly decide to come and ruin the place like they do during the summer. Good night, Sasha. Talk to you soon." With that, Betsy ran lightly down the front steps of the museum and into a waiting cab.

Sasha took a deep breath and returned to Anne. She chattered about plans to tour the figurine around the world, but Sasha was distracted. He found himself looking up toward the balcony, hoping to catch a glimpse of someone he knew who could rescue him from talk of work. All he could think about was Marina. Suddenly, he felt a hand on the small of his back. It was Victoria.

"I know we said good night, but you looked as if you needed saving," she said. "Screw *The Rules*. Let's blow this mausoleum and have a drink somewhere else."

Sasha looked around. He saw the Grant girls, who had finally found male companionship to their liking, and noticed Adam Witherspoon trying to foist his Bragança on Grace Winning.

"Come on," Victoria urged. "Let's dance."

"Now there's an idea. Shall we?" he excused himself from Anne, and held out his hand to his cousin.

The two crossed the room and stepped onto the dance floor, which was crowded with couples. As the orchestra struck up a Peabody, most of the dancers cleared the floor, not knowing what to do.

"Should we?" Victoria asked wickedly.

Sasha smiled. "Well, we sure didn't spend all that time at the armory for nothing."

The two moved out into the middle of the floor. The Peabody, a quick step from the early twentieth century, was fun to dance and even more fun to watch. Named after a New York City police lieutenant who was so fat, he had to dance with his partner to his side, the dance took up a lot of floor space. The couple skipped and ran across the floor, spinning as they did so; when they reached the end of the parquet, they whirled around, dangerously close to the edge, hanging in the air for a second before racing back to the opposite end of the ballroom. The trick of the Peabody was to avoid hitting another couple, but Sasha and Victoria didn't need to worry, for as soon as they started to dance, they were alone on the floor.

The two danced beautifully together, thanks to years of practice, and soon a crowd had gathered to watch them. The jazzy music, the drinks, the soft lights, and the sight of Sasha and Victoria flashing across the polished floor, a whirling column of hot pink and black and white, made for an exciting picture. For a minute, for those watching, everyone felt that they were actually as sophisticated as they pretended to be, that New York was still a small town filled with an intimate circle of friends and family, and that no one had a care in the world.

They danced up to the edge of the floor, and the crowd scattered, laughing. The music got faster, and Sasha began to tire.

"Shall we stop?" he asked.

"Are you kidding?" she replied. "Look at Serena Holton's face!"

"Well," Sasha said, "if she hadn't gotten expelled from dancing class, she might be dancing now, instead of being about to marry her own brother in an episode of the Carnegie Hill Hillbillies." The two of them laughed, the song finished, and those watching burst into applause.

"Get us," Victoria said, stepping back into the crowd, "the teenaged Duke and Duchess of Windsor."

Eight

⁓

At eight-thirty the next morning, the phones were already ringing madly. The Arts section of the *Times* was on his desk with a Post-it attached from Anne: *Great news in the* Times. *Can't wait for the press conference.*

"Leighton's Sparkles with Russian Treasure," the headline read. Sasha skimmed the short article, which showed Anne giving a lecture to a group assembled around the case at the party the night before, along with an inset close-up of the figurine. Next to it, there was a photo of the collet necklace at Christie's in front of a studio portrait of Empress Alexandra wearing a necklace that looked similar, though not identical.

The article came out favorably for Leighton's. The figurine was a wonderful piece of Fabergé, all the more remarkable in that it had never been seen before. Anne was quoted in the article as saying she was confident that the bill would shortly be found, but that would be icing on the cake as far as Leighton's was concerned. The memories of Sasha's grandfather were more than enough to set them on their way to recovering the original bill and authenticating the piece. The jury was still out, the article remarked, on what experts around the world would believe. Christie's, on the other hand, had little supporting documentation, only provenance "by repute." The attempt to link these impressive stones with the Empress by speculation was tenuous at best. All in all, it was good news, but there was still the issue of Marina's upset. Sasha sighed. It was going to be a long day. At least the *Times* hadn't asked what was, for Sasha, the most important question yet unanswered: Where had Snegurochka been since the Revolution?

Sasha headed to the vault. He signed in at the security desk, ran his magnetic ID card through the security monitor, and stepped through the door into the secure section. The freight elevator clanked and rattled as Sasha made the trek down to the area where the figurine was stored beneath Leighton's. Once in the subbasement, he dialed his code into the keypad and entered the monitored storage area. Pulling out a key, he opened the door to the Russian vault.

Unlike the quarters of the other departments, the Russian vault was clean, comfortable, and well organized. Sasha had a knack for controlling clutter, and he had made the space look lived in instead. In one corner hung the better icons for the upcoming sale, their silver and gold covers set with precious stones glittering in the light, their painted eyes gazing peacefully over the room. A pair of pretty Russian Empire chairs sat on either side of the brass-mounted mahogany desk he and Anne shared. In the corner, Sasha had placed the silver-mounted Fabergé tea table and service. Behind it on shelves stood an impressive amount of Russian Imperial porcelain, neatly displayed. Another wall held banks of felt-lined drawers containing the jewelry and other pieces of Fabergé that would compose the larger part of the sale. The vault smelled comfortably musty, a mixture of books, dust, and the solution used to clean the pieces of silver and silver-gilt decorated with shaded enamel.

Next to the drawers of Fabergé stood an old-fashioned safe, which held the figurine. Sasha gently turned the dials and opened it, then pulled out the velvet box. Closing the safe again, Sasha left the vault, taking the box, and returned to the area near the front counter where the figurine would be displayed for one week before its tour around the world: New York, London, Moscow, Hong Kong, Los Angeles, and back to New York.

The front counter was already humming with activity. French furniture was about to be on view, and members of that department were dashing around, filling out condition reports on many of the pieces. Lucile was busy replenishing the stock of new catalogues on the front counter, and refreshing the flowers for the weekend ahead.

"What's that, Sasha? Something for me?" she called.

Sasha smiled and walked over, setting the box on the counter.

"Only if you have about half a million," he said, smiling. Lucile's face shone as he opened the box. Sasha loved showing things to Lucile—she was interested in everything.

"I'll take that over Twentieth Century's Warhol urine painting any day," she said cheerfully. "Is that what all the fuss was about in the paper?"

Sasha nodded. "Do you know where it goes?" he asked.

Lucile pointed behind Sasha to the front window. He turned.

An enormous piece of blown-up photography printed on transparent vinyl had been applied to the window facing Seventy-third Street. The whole front window now appeared to be covered in hoarfrost—the same as on the figurine's skirt. Behind ropes sat the display case from the party the night before. Next to it was a blown-up reproduction of the photograph taken by Sasha's grandfather. Banks of flowers completed the display. Sasha opened the display case carefully, then gently added the figurine, placing it in the center of the revolving platform. He closed the case and set the security system by tapping a code onto the touchpad.

The lights glowed softly, and the pedestal began to turn slowly. Snegurochka danced, the lights in the case making her *sarafan* sparkle and the green-gold grass shimmer. Sasha turned as everyone at the front counter burst into applause.

"And now for the *coup de grâce*," remarked one of the young men on tenure at the front counter as he flipped a switch. From nowhere came the rich sound of an orchestra.

"What is that?" Sasha asked.

"Rimsky-Korsakov," the young man responded. "It's the overture to his opera—*The Snow Maiden*. We'll all be singing it in our sleep by the time the sale rolls around."

Sasha shrugged apologetically and went back to his office.

Anne was on the phone when Sasha reached his desk. His message light was flashing. Two collectors. The director of the Forbes Collection. *Town and Country.* Wartski. A La Vieille Russie. A woman claiming to have the same figurine. Press and information stating that there was to be a press conference that afternoon at four in the main salesroom. Finally, a message from an elderly woman who said that her name was Anastasia, and that she wanted her doll back. Sasha rolled his eyes.

There were also two notes on his desk in Anne's handwriting. One read: *Phone call from Victoria—please call her at home.* The other read: *Call Dimitri ASAP. He wants to see you for dinner. P.S. It is important that you keep him happy, Sasha. —A.* Sasha blinked.

"Thank God you're here. The phones have been ringing off the hook. Where have you been?" Anne stood in the doorway to her office, arms akimbo.

"I was putting the figurine on view downstairs; I got here at eight-thirty."

"Oh, sorry. Thank heavens one of us remembered. I swear I left my head at home today, and I sure need it. This place is a madhouse." Anne smiled. "You'll never guess what."

"What?" he asked.

Anne walked over and put a piece of paper in front of him. Sasha's eyes ran over it quickly, deciphering the elegant Russian hand. It was the bill for Snegurochka—the final receipt for the piece. Sasha was thrilled.

"Anne, this is amazing. With the order number we might be able to find the internal Fabergé bills as well—the ones that list individually all of the artists who worked on Snegurochka, and the breakdown of the costs for the materials. What an incredible job of research we can do now!"

"I know," said Anne. "And you, my dear, are going to Russia to do it. Gennady specifically asked that you join him to get this done. Congratulations—I know you can do it." Anne smiled fondly at him. "Until then, drudge work. Can you call back all those people? I need to go handle the press release."

Sasha smiled and nodded. Russia. He hadn't been in over a year, and he was thrilled to get to go. He sat down and began returning calls to the various dealers who wanted to see the piece. He dreaded the meeting with the Schaffers from A La Vieille Russie. They were tough, but the best in the business. In fact, they had been dealing in Fabergé longer than the master had himself. Finally, taking a deep breath, he called Dimitri.

"The Mark, New York. How may I direct your call," a voice answered in a rush.

"Dimitri Durakov, please." Sasha was immediately transferred to Vivaldi.

"I'm sorry, Mr. Durakov is out. May I take a message?"

"Please tell him that Sasha Ozerovsky called, and that he can reach me at—"

"Leighton's Russian department. Yes, sir, he was expecting your call. You might try him on his cell phone. He said you would have his number."

"I see. Thank you." Sasha was a bit taken aback.

"Not at all, thank you for calling the Mark."

Sasha hung up.

Anne stuck her head into the office. "Sasha? I have Palais Newski Antiques downstairs from London. Would you go down and talk to them? I've got a phone interview with *Connaissance des Arts*."

Sasha nodded and headed downstairs.

Lydia Crane waited by the front counter and beamed when she saw Sasha. "Oh, Sasha! What a treat—I was expecting Anne," Lydia said with a smile.

"That's the nicest thing I've heard all day," Sasha replied. "Would you like to go into a private room to look at the piece?"

"Thanks so much," Lydia replied. "Yes, please. I am thrilled about this piece. I had to come to see it myself, even before it gets to London next week on tour. By the way, I have something for you. Normally, we wouldn't do this, but since this piece belonged to your family, I thought you'd be interested in something we have."

Sasha escorted Lydia into one of the small viewing rooms, and then he went to take the figurine out of its case. He had to go through the whole process of turning the alarm off, and putting the small LEIGHTON'S REGRETS THAT THIS LOT HAS BEEN TEMPORARILY REMOVED FROM VIEW sign in the case. He sighed. He was going to have to do this over and over today. Finally, he was able to bring the figurine into the viewing room.

Lydia's eyes sparkled as she picked Snegurochka up. She lifted her loupe and examined the enamel, the metalwork, the careful detailing of the face and hands. After admiring the stone setting, she heaved a sigh.

"Just remarkable," she said, putting it back on the table. "I never thought I'd see it again."

"See it *again*?" Sasha asked.

"My father bought this from the Soviets in 1921 when he was doing his early deals with the state antiques division Antikvariat, which sold nationalized valuables to the West. He bought the Danish Jubilee Egg, the Wheelbarrow Egg, and this."

"But those two eggs are lost—no one has seen them since the Revolution," Sasha said.

"Exactly. My father sold all three objects to a German family. After the war, they told my father that all three pieces had been in the safe of their apartment in Berlin—"

The blood drained from Sasha's face. *Sold all three objects to a German family.* The piece might not belong to Dimitri's client after all. Sasha tried to remain unfazed. "Do they still have the two Imperial Eggs?" Sasha asked quickly, trying to sound calm.

"—their apartment in Berlin, which was razed by Allied bombing in 1945."

"I see," Sasha said, his head lowered. "So the eggs were destroyed?"

"We thought so. When we called the heirs to find out if they were selling the piece, they were fairly surprised to hear the figurine still existed. They also thought all three pieces were destroyed in the bombing—they said they never even bothered to file a claim, they were so sure it was a victim of the war. I last saw this when I was thirteen years old, in 1938. I'm very pleased to see it again. Only one problem with it."

"What is that?" Sasha asked.

"The hair bow has been reenameled. When I last saw it, it was matte red opaque enamel; my father's notes comment on it. Very unusual. Not *guilloche* like this. It must have been replaced."

"The enamel is beautifully oxidized," Sasha protested.

Lydia smiled patiently. "Sasha, you're still learning. A Q-tip and some Windex can oxidize enamel like that. Now—here is a copy of the bill from Antikvariat that was made when my father purchased it. You go public with this at your press conference this afternoon, and make sure that you give us credit for providing you with this additional information. The piece is lovely—it will fetch a fortune. I bet you anything the Forbes Collection will buy it. Too rich for my blood. Ah, well, at least we owned it once."

Sasha smiled and thanked Lydia as she departed.

There was only one problem. Lydia's information explained where Snegurochka had been since 1918; now there was a question about the legal title of the piece. Whoever Dimitri was selling Snegurochka for might not legally own her.

Placing the figurine back on display, Sasha looked at the bill from the Soviet government. He was certain Anne would be livid.

Anne was quietly studying press releases when Sasha returned to their office. He showed her the Antikvariat bill.

"Well, goddamn me straight to hell," Anne said under her breath, understanding the problem immediately.

"Anne, what do we do?" Sasha asked.

Anne turned to Sasha slowly. "Well, the piece was obviously in Berlin during the war. This may ruin everything. Those Germans may still have a claim on her, and Dimitri's client may have acquired it after it was stolen during the war."

Sasha was stunned. "What should we do?"

"Nothing. I don't think that we should mention this at the press conference, but I'm going straight to legal. Lena Martin will know what to do." Anne stood up and walked out of the office. The phone rang.

"Leighton's Russian department."

"Sasha! Glad I caught you. Can you hear me? I'm in the car." It was Dimitri.

"Hi, Dimitri. I tried to reach you at the Mark. I had a note from Anne that you called."

"Listen. I know we'd decided to have a drink, but I've been invited to a dinner party uptown. Will you come along with me? You'll know people there, I'm sure, and Mrs. Greer would love to meet you. I told her all about you."

Sasha was annoyed. He had not actually made plans with Dimitri, and he didn't really want to. But Gloria Greer was one of New York's most important hostesses, and Sasha knew she had one of the better private collections of Fabergé—a collection that had never been photographed. Sasha was torn. Taking a deep breath, he heard a voice that he barely recognized as his own accepting.

"Great. We dress for dinner, and she's in Hampshire House. Shall we meet at the Carlyle for a drink before?"

"Fine. I'll see you there. What time?"

"Let's say six? We're expected at seven-thirty."

"Fine. Bemelman's at six, then. See you."

"I'm looking forward to it." Dimitri signed off in a haze of static. Sasha had just decided to get lunch when the phone rang again.

"Hello, Russian department."

"Sasha? It's your father."

"Well, hi there! How's Aspen?"

"Well, fine, but that's not why I'm calling. I'm in the airport, and I'm coming back on the ten A.M. plane."

"Why on earth are you coming back so soon? Nothing is wrong, is it?"

"I should think of all people, you would know that something is *very* wrong. Sasha, I had a very disturbing message from Marina late last night. When we got in last evening there was a message for me from Derek to call her no matter what time it was, and I did. What she told me is very upsetting."

"I could see that she was upset, but I think she was really overreacting."

"Frankly, Sasha, I can't figure out why *you* are not reacting to this."

Sasha was surprised by the tone in his father's voice. He sounded angry, and Sasha had never heard his father moved to anything stronger than a bit of aggravation.

"Father, there is no reason to be upset. We have no legal claim—"

"This is not about a legal claim—this is about what is right."

"What do you mean?"

"What would be right would be for us to have something that is a symbol of everything we lost."

"Father, what do you mean? We have everything we need here in New York. We're financially secure; we have our family here, our language, our religion—we don't need pieces of Fabergé."

"I'm disappointed in you, Sasha. I would like to explain how I feel to you, but not over the phone. It is important that I speak with you today. I should be back late this afternoon. We'll have a drink at the Knick."

"I can't meet then, Father. We have a press conference at four— I'm swamped."

"Dinner then. Dinner at that place around the corner from me. The one with the nicely papered walls."

"Swifty's. But I can't, Father, I'm having dinner with Gloria Greer."

Sasha's father sighed. Dinner with Gloria Greer was nothing to be taken lightly.

"All right. Tomorrow. We'll discuss how to take care of this. I'm sorry if anything inconveniences you today. I'll see you at Swifty's tomorrow at eight." He hung up.

Sasha wondered what on earth his father could mean, then headed to the cafeteria for a sandwich.

❖   ❖   ❖

Anne returned from lunch with a new hairstyle and a Manolo Blahnik shopping bag.

"Did everything work out with legal?" Sasha asked. "Nice hair, by the way."

"Thank you. Yes, everything did work out—we don't have to worry because they're not Jews."

"What?" Sasha asked.

"It's true. If they were to make a claim against us and were Jewish, and the piece had been confiscated by the Nazis, or stolen by the Soviets, it would be horrible—we'd have the Commission for Art Recovery all over us. It would be terrible press—Leighton's sells Holocaust treasure, blah, blah, blah. But since they're Gentiles, and German, we don't have to worry. They didn't file a claim for it after the war, and so acts of war, booty, and all that. It will look bad for them to show up and say, 'Hello! We were rich Germans with Fabergé eggs during the war, and we were complicitous with the Nazis, and now we're still rich Germans, and we want our Fabergé back.' We're clear."

Sasha smiled at her, but he was upset both by her casual anti-

Semitism and how base the auction business could be. He also couldn't dismiss the claim as easily as Anne. A claim on the piece could mean that they would have to stop or postpone the sale, no matter what.

Slipping on her new shoes, Anne glanced in the brass-trimmed mahogany mirror in their office.

"Ready for television?" she asked, turning to Sasha.

He nodded. "You need a brooch. One minute." He went back to his work area and took a Fabergé pin out of the small safe near his desk, a Catherine II gold ruble with the background enameled in red and surrounded by diamonds. He returned and pinned it to her dark jacket.

"Nice touch," she said. "Thanks. Come down whenever you can. It starts in twenty minutes." With that, Anne left. A few minutes later, Sasha followed her.

The main lobby was crowded with reporters. Sasha marveled at the press department's ability to pull in the media. No matter what happened, Christie's would have to share the spotlight now.

Sasha watched the women from special client services race around, plying the reporters with coffee and Champagne, asking them about their families, trying to get them excited about the piece. Lynn Terfel, head of press, surveyed the scene. At four, after an introduction by John Burnham, Anne stepped up to the podium.

"Thank you all for coming. Leighton's is pleased to announce that on May twelfth, we will be offering as the star lot in our sale of Russian works of art the heretofore unknown hard-stone figurine of Snegurochka—the Snow Maiden. You will find in your press packet transparencies of the piece, as well as black-and-white glossies for publication. You will also find copies of the original Fabergé bill discovered in the Russian archives by our researcher Gennady Antropin. This makes the piece the first completely documented Fabergé figurine ever to come on the market."

Sasha winced. Anne's exclusion of the Palais Newski bill from 1921 would come back to haunt them, he was certain.

Flashbulbs popped, and lights for the TV cameras focused on the glittering figurine, which was revolving in its case. Sasha looked at his watch and then glanced around the room, his eyes coming to rest on a distinguished older man in an English suit. Without warning, the man got up and approached the podium.

"My name is Craig Tippett, and I am the attorney representing the von Kemp family trust. This figurine, which belonged to the von Kemps before the war, was believed destroyed in the Allied attack on Berlin. Evidently, the piece was not destroyed, just stolen, and it is now being sold without clear title. We have just presented papers to Leighton's house counsel. We've asked for an injunction to block the sale of this important property, and to restore it to its rightful owners."

Suddenly the activity in the room doubled. Cameras flashed repeatedly, capturing Anne's paralyzed expression.

Taking the situation in hand, Lynn stepped to the podium. "Ladies and gentlemen, until the legal department can address this issue more fully, Leighton's has no further comment except to say that the sale of Snegurochka will take place as scheduled on May twelfth. The piece will be going on tour next week, and it will be exhibited in New York, London, Moscow, Hong Kong, and Los Angeles, before its return to New York. We have no further comments at this time. All inquiries may be directed to the legal and press offices. Thank you all for coming." With that, she whisked Anne out of the room.

Sasha stood there for a minute, not quite knowing what to do, when the man noticed him and approached.

"You work in the department, don't you? I'm Craig Tippett."

"Forgive me if I seem rude, but I'm still in shock over what you just said."

"Aha, I see. Well, don't worry. Oh, by the way—I've known your father for years. Let him know I hope this blows over soon. Bad luck for you, really." The man turned and left.

Sasha went back to his department, where he found Anne, Lynn

Terfel, Lena Martin from the legal department, and John Burnham. Anne was calm but furious.

"That was *unbelievably* humiliating. How did he get in? Lena, what does this mean?"

"Well, the sale will go on as planned, but we'll have to go to court to prove that the consignor has proper claim and title."

"Will that be difficult?" John asked, his fingers strumming the desk.

"I don't think so. We'll need to know who the consignor is now, naturally; and if they are Russian, we'll need the export papers, et cetera."

"I'm having dinner with Dimitri tonight," Sasha said. "I'll get the consignor information so you can get started first thing."

"Well, that will be a help, Sasha, but we have more concerns than just that. This has been a busy day in legal."

"Why?" John asked.

"Well, we had two other claims filed today; both are fairly serious."

"Who else has a claim on Snegurochka?" Sasha asked.

"Sasha," Lena began, "one of the claims was filed by your cousin, a Countess Marina Shoutine of London—and, well, the other was filed by your father."

Nine

SASHA WALKED INTO BEMELMAN'S BAR and smiled at the pianist, who began, as he always did, to play "Lara's Theme." Several years earlier, Sasha had mentioned to him that he dealt with Russian antiques, and so "Lara's Theme" it was. Sasha wondered idly if he could choose a new song, and toyed with the idea of composing the "I Can't Believe I May Lose My Job Because My Father Is Suing My Company Blues." He ordered a Gibson and sat down to wait for Dimitri, thinking that there was no place in the world he would rather be than in the Bemelman's Bar. Sasha and his mother had had a lot of tea in the lobby of the Carlyle. It felt like nothing in the world could happen to him in the safety of that dimly lit room. Though George, the legendary waiter with whom he had grown up, had retired, the small room off the Carlyle lobby still afforded Sasha a sense of security and well-being. He was about to address the disturbing thought that the only place he felt safe was a bar when Dimitri arrived.

"I'm sorry I'm running late—but I heard the news." He sat down and ordered a vodka, neat.

"I'm surprised you came at all."

"I am worried about the von Kemp suit. But it's Marina and your father who bother me most. I was hoping you might give me some reassurance about those claims."

"How did you hear?"

"I got a call from John Burnham."

"Don't worry about Marina. That's just silliness. I'm having dinner with my father tomorrow. I think Marina has him riled up. He's not a litigious sort, really. I bet I can talk them both out of it." Sasha spoke with a confidence he did not feel.

"I hope so."

"Me, too. If my father goes through with it, I'm certain to end up fired."

"Could it really come to that?"

"I can't imagine Leighton's would keep me on with my father suing them for your property."

"At least you agree that the figurine is ours. *To your health*," Dimitri said in Russian.

"Dimitri, I do have to ask you. Who owns the piece?"

Dimitri paused, trying to make a decision. He looked Sasha in the eyes. "Actually, I do."

"Why didn't you just tell us that?"

Dimitri sighed. "Sasha, this is complicated. Did Marina ever tell you who I work with in Russia?"

"The Dikarinskys. They're new oligarchs. I've heard of them."

"Exactly. I found Snegurochka in Finland in a private collection. I wanted to sell it to them, but I couldn't."

"Why not?"

"All I had to go on was that photograph. I figured out it was your great-grandmother in the picture, but I was stumped after that. I haven't been dealing long, and my earliest pieces were far from thoroughly reputable. I made a fortune selling them but now I know better, and still, none of the Russian researchers will have much to do with me. I'm no academic, and they are envious of my success. They're happy when I can sell one of their pieces to one of the new rich they don't know, but other than that, they're no help to me."

"So when you found out the piece belonged to my family, you sought me out?"

"No. You came to me. Marina arrived in Moscow to do the *Architectural Digest* story, and we met. When I found out that you two were cousins, I told her that I had a piece to sell that had belonged to your family. She said she could introduce us. She talked me into flying her to New York with me, and so I did. I had no idea that to meet you all I had to do was call and make an appointment. Marina is very convincing." Dimitri laughed sadly.

Sasha felt badly—it seemed that Marina had taken Dimitri for quite a ride. "Did you know that the piece was ever in Germany?"

Dimitri put down his glass. "The woman I bought it from said it had passed down in her family. I had no reason not to believe her."

"Well, we'll do what we can." Sasha raised his glass.

The two chatted agreeably, but inside, Sasha seethed. Dimitri had been careless. After finishing their drinks, they left through the lobby of the hotel, and Dimitri gestured to the white limousine at the curb.

"I always use a car—so much easier in the city," he said.

The chauffeur opened the door, and Sasha took a deep breath then got in. The car was deeply vulgar.

The ride to Central Park South was quick. Dimitri gazed appreciatively at the building, which was so familiar to Sasha. Hampshire House was a New York landmark.

They pulled up to the curb and got out of the car, entering the warm and highly polished lobby of the Hampshire House. "Well, here we are. I know you're going to love Gloria."

"How do you know Mrs. Greer?"

"She was on an American Friends of the Hermitage tour. I met her in Saint Petersburg. She became a client of mine."

The elevator took them up and let them out into a private vestibule decorated with a small Louis XV giltwood console and a Degas pastel. The door to the apartment opened, and they were ushered into an oak-paneled reception room by a maid who took their coats, and then showed them into the drawing room, where several other guests were sitting around their hostess. As she saw them enter, Mrs. Greer rose and came to meet them.

Gloria Greer was probably in her seventies, but she looked years younger. She was tall, lithe, and surprisingly sexy, wearing a Givenchy gown that looked better on her than on the anemic nineteen-year-old model who had worn it in *Vogue*. Around her neck was an impressive Indian emerald-and-diamond necklace. She came with her hands outstretched to Dimitri.

"Well, Dimitri, how great to see you!"

"Thank you, Gloria. It's wonderful to see you, too. May I introduce my good friend, Prince Alexander Ozerovsky?" Sasha winced. He hated it when people used his title. Mrs. Greer smiled and took his arm.

"You know, you don't remember this, but I met you when you were very young. I was an old friend of your mother's—I miss her terribly, you know."

"That's very kind of you. Thank you, Mrs. Greer."

"Gloria. I'll kill you if you call me Mrs. Greer."

She led them into the living room to meet the other guests.

Sasha looked around. The room had Louis XV-style plasterwork and was painted all white. A very large suite of Louis XV giltwood furniture dominated the room, upholstered in a soft rose-colored satin. Small marquetry tables were everywhere, littered with Verdura objects and silver bowls full of flowers. Candles flickered in the rock crystal and ormolu wall sconces, and the matching chandelier shed a soft and flattering light. The windows were framed with cascades of silk brocade, and outside, Sasha saw the spectacle of Central Park banked by glittering Fifth Avenue and Central Park West.

"Everyone, this is Dimitri Durakov, a young friend who sold me a divine piece of Fabergé, and this is Sasha Ozerovsky—Nina's little boy. Can you imagine?" Sasha barely took in all the names as everyone piled him with effusive praise for his mother. She had been so chic, so clever, and so beautiful. They had loved her.

The crowd was older, and it was quite obvious that he and Dimitri had been invited to perk things up a bit. Mrs. Greer showed him to the drinks table, and let him pour himself a vodka and tonic before she took his arm again.

"Dimitri tells me that you're a specialist in Fabergé, like your mother. Would you like to see my collection?" She smiled.

"I had hoped you would ask me," Sasha said, and the two walked to the far end of the room, where two glass vitrines held her extraordinary objects.

Sasha's eyes widened as he looked into the cases. So many pieces he had never even seen before—she had a beautiful selection with examples of all of the types of work for which the House of Fabergé was justly famous. Sasha's eyes wandered over the cigarette cases, bonbonnières, opera glasses, and miniature animals. In the center of the case stood the piece that impressed him most—a hard-stone flower study of purple and white lilacs, with each flower carved from an amethyst or rock crystal. The tiny blossoms were individually attached to the golden stem with wire pistils, each set with a small diamond. The nephrite leaves were carved so thin, the lights in the display case shone through them, causing the delicate striations within the stone to appear as if they made up the structure of the leaf itself. The spray was so lifelike, he could practically smell them.

In another corner of the case, he saw Atlas holding a silver table clock on his back, as if it were the world. Sasha recognized it as having been on a table in the mauve boudoir of the Empress Alexandra at the Alexander Palace.

"Where on earth did you come by Alexandra Feodorovna's bedside clock?" Sasha asked, turning to Mrs. Greer.

"My late husband went on a trip to Moscow in the 1950s with Marjorie Merriweather Post and her husband, Ambassador Davies. She gave it to him as a gift," she replied. "Oh, here's the piece I bought from Dimitri. Isn't it lovely?" She handed him a lapis lazuli box.

Sasha turned it over in his hands. It was a round hinged compact, the gold mounts shaped like a serpent coiled around the lapis, which was well flecked with gold and looked like a night sky. Seven tiny diamonds had been set into the surface of the lapis to form the constellation Ursa Minor—the little bear.

"Isn't it wonderful? That's what I love about Fabergé. Behind every piece there is such a wonderful story. Who could it have been made for? What is the story behind the constellation? Isn't it romantic?" she said.

"I could ask our researcher in Saint Petersburg to look it up for you," he said, opening the box and raising it to the light to see if an inventory number had been scratched into the gold.

"Don't you dare. I'd rather make up my own stories. Who needs the truth? At my age, all I want is the romantic mystery—far more satisfying to imagine a story than to know that some old dip bought it for twenty-five roubles in 1910," she said, smiling.

Sasha examined the box carefully, opening and closing it several times. The piece wasn't right. The hinge was stiff, and the box made a hollow clicking sound as it closed. The top and bottom pieces weren't flush. As he examined the tooling of the snake, he saw that it was very poorly finished. He closed his eyes and ran his fingertips over the hinge—he could feel where the two pieces were joined together. With real Fabergé he never could. It was a good fake, but a fake nonetheless. Deciding to say nothing, he handed the box back to Mrs. Greer.

"Isn't it beautiful?" she asked.

"It certainly is. Quite a piece of work, Mrs. Greer."

"Sasha, I told you. Call me Gloria. Oh, Dimitri, I didn't see you there."

Sasha turned and saw Dimitri right at his elbow.

"Nice little piece, isn't it?" he asked.

Sasha smiled, and turned his attention to a tiny rococo-style chair in rose-colored gold with an enameled seat cushion. Near it, a jeweled and enameled box drew his attention. Its lid featured an enamel plaque with a detailed miniature rendering of his mother's family palace in *grisaille*, and the sides were decorated with other Shchermanov residences.

"Your mother gave that to me," Gloria said. "I've always loved it. The whole collection grew because of it. My husband gave me the clock, and Nina gave me this. I remember, she was having a very difficult time with her health, and I got her into treatment with the best doctor in Switzerland. She was so Russian, your mother. So emotional. She brought this to me when she heard she was in remission. I knew nothing at all about Fabergé. She showed me the enamel plaque, pointed out the guilloche frame and the tiny diamonds set into the rim. She showed me how beautifully *heavy* it was, and introduced me to the gorgeous way Fabergé *feels*, as well as looks. 'This,' she said, 'is how you judge an object of virtue. Each facet of its execution is a tour de force of technique. Look at this: the artist who painted the enamel plaque was astonishing. The enamel artist who executed the guilloche created a perfect surface. The stone setter who mounted these tiny diamond chips did so perfectly. And the stone carver who cut this from one hunk of nephrite made the stone so thin that when you hold it to the light you can see right through it. Every facet of the piece is perfect,' she said, and then she said, 'Just like you, Gloria. Every bit of you is perfect. You're an object of virtue, too, and I want you to have this for being such a good friend to me.' Just so you know, when I die, it goes back to you. You'll have it back one day. In the end, we really all only have these things on loan, don't we?"

Sasha picked up the box.

"Why is this *so* heavy?" he asked. Gloria reached forward and opened the lid. From within, a light tinkling came, as the music box concealed inside burst into a sparkling version of the "Polonaise" from Eugene Onegin. Gloria's eyes filled, and she looked at the ceiling to conceal her emotion. The music played from the tiny mechanism, and the three of them listened to the song until it finished. Gloria closed the lid and returned the box to the vitrine.

"Well, I can't cry at my own dinner; it's rude. Feel free to look at the rest—I daresay you don't need me to tell you what things are, and I'm ignoring my other guests. Amuse yourself, and come and join us when you're ready." With that, she flashed them an affectionate smile and moved back to the others.

"I had no idea your family knew Gloria so well," Dimitri said.

"Neither did I. My father never talks about my mother or her friends. It's nice to meet someone who knew her."

"I would think so. What do you think of the box I found her? It comes out of the Dikarinsky collection in Moscow—I had a bitch of a time convincing them to sell it. I knew that Gloria would love it."

"Actually, I'm not convinced by it. I'm sorry to say that I'm pretty sure it is not right."

"You can't be serious. Did you tell her that?" Dimitri bristled.

"Of course not. The fit of the lid is off, and the chasing on the snake is badly done."

"Oh that. The woman who owned it before had dropped it and had the hinge fixed. I think she also used to clean the gold with Brillo—I agree with you about the chasing. But did you look at the marks?"

"I never look at marks anymore. They're so easily faked. You have to look at the piece as a whole to judge if it's real or a forgery," he replied. "So you see what happens. Sorry if I gave you a start."

Dimitri smiled and patted him on the shoulder, then walked away.

It is a fake, Sasha thought to himself.

Picking up the drink that he had left on a small Venetian table, Sasha walked back and sat on the sofa, well away from Dimitri, and introduced himself to an Italian princess.

"Well, well, finally!" interrupted Gloria, getting up to welcome her last guest. Sasha turned to look. It was Craig Tippett.

This cannot be happening to me, thought Sasha.

Gloria walked through the room with Craig, introducing him to the others. Finally she arrived at Sasha.

"Craig, I'd like you to meet Sasha Ozerovsky, a young art type. Sasha, this is my great friend and attorney, Craig Tippett."

"Prince Ozerovsky and I have already had the pleasure, Gloria. We're old friends."

"Yes, indeed," Sasha replied. "Mr. Tippett came to Leighton's today to put a stop to our May sale."

"Hope you won't hold that against me. Just business." He grinned at Sasha's discomfort.

"Well, this should be a fun-filled evening, then," Gloria said cheerfully. "Shall we all go in to dinner?"

❖   ❖   ❖

Dinner wasn't nearly as terrible as Sasha had expected. The *Principessa* turned out to have been born in Florida, and over the past twenty years in Rome had managed to transform herself into an Italian of the first order. She didn't take herself seriously at all, and as they spoke to each other over dinner, Sasha realized that she cared deeply about music and had spent most of her year traveling to follow a baritone whose career she was supporting.

"He's going to be better than Samuel Ramey. His voice is just enormous, and he's only twenty-seven."

"He sounds wonderful, Princess."

"Oh, don't call me princess—I'm from Tallahassee. These people make me crazy. The only nice thing about having a title is holding it over the heads of people who don't and who want one badly. It makes people like that Dimitri over there nuts that an old broad like me is a princess. Call me Candy—everyone I like does." She winked.

"All right, then, Candy it is." Sasha winked back.

At the head of the table, Gloria was regaling her guests with a story of how she and an English duchess had once gotten locked in a guestroom at Blenheim. "And so I had to stand on Jane's shoulders—and this was in the 1950s, so I am in this simply enormous Dior, and Janey couldn't see, and she kept laughing—and this is *Blenheim*, so the transom over the door is, of course, fourteen feet high, and I had to throw cakes of soap through it until somebody outside noticed that we were inside!"

Everyone laughed.

"Did someone notice the soap falling into the hall?" Craig asked.

"Well, no," she continued. "Apparently I have very good aim, because I knocked the tiara right off the Duchess of Devonshire." The table erupted into laughter. "Fortunately, Debo is a great sport. Now, if you're all finished with your dessert, we can move into the library for coffee."

Everyone rose, and Craig managed to sidle over next to Sasha as they moved into the library to sit down.

"You really don't like me, do you?" he asked.

"Mr. Tippett, I don't even know you," Sasha said. "We've met twice now, and both times you've managed to shock me or put me on the spot. I'm perfectly happy to start over. Hello, I'm Sasha Ozerovsky."

"Craig Tippett. Nice to meet you." They shook hands.

"Do you really think you can get an injunction to stop the sale?"

"As the attorney for the von Kemp family trust, absolutely. As your new friend, I don't really know. It's a long shot, and I doubt any American court will feel that a rich German family deserves its Fabergé back sixty years later, even if it was stolen from them."

"It seems I've heard that once already today."

"Well, the von Kemps aren't my biggest clients. I do much more work for Gloria."

"Isn't that supposed to be confidential?"

"Maybe. Let's keep in touch during this legal situation; we could help each other."

"I'm afraid I must refer all requests to Leighton's legal department."

"Clever reply. Talk to you soon." With that, Craig gave his thanks and bid his good-bye to Gloria.

Dimitri moved over to sit next to Sasha. He was a bit drunk.

"Shall we say good night?" he asked.

"I think we should," Sasha replied, setting his coffee cup down and standing up. The two of them crossed over to where Gloria stood kissing Candy good-bye.

"Oh, are you two leaving? Dimitri, Sasha, thank you so much for coming." Gloria took Sasha by the shoulders. "It was a real treat to see you again, Sasha. You are so much like your mother—I hope we'll see each other soon."

"So do I, Gloria. Perhaps you can come to the boardroom lunch we're having at Leighton's next week for the figurine?"

"Call me tomorrow—I'd love to be there," she said, showing them to the door. The two men left and got into the elevator.

"Thank you for asking me," Sasha said to Dimitri. "I really enjoyed meeting Gloria and seeing her collection."

"Well, it was my pleasure to invite you," Dimitri replied as they reached the lobby and went outside to where the car waited.

"Let me drop you at your house," Dimitri said. "No trouble to swing up your way before I go to the hotel."

"That's good of you, thanks." Sasha got into the car, and Dimitri climbed in after him. He poured himself a drink, and Sasha gave the driver his address.

"I've wanted to ask you something," Dimitri said. Sasha was a bit worried.

"Fire away."

"How long have you been at Leighton's?"

"Seven years."

"That's a long time. Do they pay you well?"

"A personal question. I'd never discuss it."

"Ah. How genteel. Well, I have a business proposal for you. Mr. Dikarinsky is an important backer of mine, and he would like to see me in business in the United States. If we sell the figurine, what would you say about becoming partners? I can guarantee that I will provide you with pieces from Russia of the same caliber as Snegurochka, if you could provide me with a gallery here filled with old Russian class, culture, and clients like Gloria Greer. As a recent new Russian, I face a series of prejudices that are difficult to overcome. You would be invaluable and would be paid accordingly. Also commission."

Sasha smiled. "A tempting offer, and one that I will think about." Mercifully, the car pulled up in front of his house. "This is where I get off. Thank you for the drink, dinner, and lift. I'll see you at the boardroom lunch next week, if you choose to come."

"I'll be there," Dimitri said. He pulled the door of the limousine shut, leaving Sasha on the street.

Ten

After the dinner at Gloria's, Sasha had a tough time getting out of bed the next morning. He managed to pull himself together and made it to work only a few minutes late. Jogging up the steps to Leighton's, he entered the familiar and sumptuous lobby.

Passing the front desk, he noticed that Snegurochka wasn't yet in the window. He would have to go to the vault to get it. Lucile popped up from behind the counter where she had been putting supplies away.

"Hi, Lucile!" Sasha called cheerfully.

"Hi, sweetie," she said, without one of her trademark smiles, and she disappeared behind the counter again.

Sasha walked toward the vault door and swiped his magnetic card past the sensor.

ACCESS DENIED read the glowing red screen.

He tried again.

ACCESS DENIED read the screen again.

Delilah appeared, staggering under the weight of a small Shang bronze kettle.

"Darling, can you get the door for me?" she gasped. "This weighs a ton."

"My card isn't working. Where's yours?"

"Ugh. At my desk. I'll go to the front and borrow Lucile's, and let you in."

"Don't be silly," said Sasha. "You put that on a dolly and rest. I'll go get it."

Sasha walked back to the lobby and approached the front counter.

"Lucile," he said briskly, "may I borrow your card? Mine isn't working, and Delilah is sitting outside with a Shang bronze."

Lucile looked pained. "Sasha, darling, I'd love to, but I think you better go up to your office. Anne is waiting for you."

"Did something happen?" Sasha asked.

"Anne will tell you everything. Sweetheart, I'm sorry. I'll let Delilah in; don't worry."

Sasha's mind raced as he ran up the stairs. Perhaps legal had decided it was better to withdraw Snegurochka. Maybe Dimitri had pulled out. Was that possible?

Sasha walked into the Russian department. Anne and Lena Martin were deep in conversation when he arrived, and Anne looked miserable.

"What news of fresh disaster?" Sasha asked, throwing his coat over his chair. He looked around. Something was different. "Hey, where's my computer?" he asked.

"Sasha." Lena walked toward him, an insincere approximation of kindness on her face. "Why don't you come in and sit down for a minute."

Sasha walked into Anne's office and sat down. Anne looked at him with genuine sadness in her eyes.

Lena began. "Sasha, you've done such a wonderful job here at Leighton's over the years. Seven years, in fact. We've been so impressed with you—"

Oh my God, Sasha thought. *I'm getting sacked.*

"—so impressed that it is very hard for us to take this step. John is so sorry, he couldn't even bear to come give you the news himself."

I'll bet. The son of a bitch.

"Given the fact that Snegurochka used to belong to your family, and that we are now facing three lawsuits, two, incidentally, instigated by members of your family, it really seems in the best interests if we all take a little break from each other."

"Am I fired?" Sasha asked.

"No, Sasha, no," Anne jumped in. "It's a suspension. Well, a hiatus, really. Just until things blow over."

"That's right, Sasha, just consider it a paid vacation. We don't want you to come into the office to work, but we want you to remember that you are very much a member of the Leighton's team. We still consider you an important colleague." She smiled.

"An important colleague who never comes into the office."

"Right," Lena said, smiling. "Exactly."

"I'm so sorry, Sasha," Anne said, "but it seems the only thing we can do. Of course I still want you to come to the boardroom lunch—I mean, half the people who will be there are your relatives, and the rest are your clients—"

"And we would hate for things to look the least bit *uncomfortable*," Lena added.

"And the research?" Sasha asked. "Do you still want me to go to Russia?"

"Oh, no," Lena said. "Anne can handle that. Don't disturb yourself. After the lunch, you can go anywhere you like—your father has a place down in Palm Beach, doesn't he? I'd just kill to go down there for a week." She let out a sharp laugh. "Lucky you."

"Well," Sasha said. "So that's that." He stood up and walked to the door. He couldn't quite put his finger on how he felt. Now he wouldn't have the chance to do the research that would make the sale a success. Now he'd never learn, except secondhand, the *real* story of how Snegurochka had traveled from his family in Saint Petersburg, to Antikvariat and the Cranes, to the von Kemps, and then back to him in New York.

"Unless . . ." Lena said thoughtfully.

Sasha turned, his hopes lifting slightly.

"Well, if you could only get your cousin and your father to drop these suits, Sasha, everything could be just as it was. And we need you here, really we do. So. That's that. If you can get the lawsuits dropped, wonderful, if not—enjoy Palm Beach." She smiled at Anne and Sasha brightly, then turned and left the office to tell John Burnham she had successfully accomplished her mission.

Sasha turned to Anne.

"There was nothing I could do, Sasha. You know I had nothing to do with this. We can barely handle all this work together—there's no way I can do it alone. I need you, and I did everything I could, but you know John. Legal told him that there was no other way, and so that's that."

Sasha understood, but he had nothing to say. Silently he walked back to his desk to get his coat, and to gather his personal things.

Anne stood up and called from her office.

"Sasha, don't worry. Security did all of that already. Your things are in a box downstairs with Lucile. Keep in touch, won't you?" Anne closed the door to her office.

❖   ❖   ❖

Standing on the steps of Leighton's with a cardboard box in his hands, Sasha finally realized what he was feeling. He was furious, and he breathed heavily. He was going to the Carlyle Hotel, where he would have a big breakfast and read every paper he could buy to calm himself down. Then at noon, he was going to meet Victoria for lunch at Doubles; at seven he would meet his father at Swifty's. By the end of the day, he would have a plan on how to deal with everything—either that, or a ticket to Palm Beach and a sinking sense of failure.

❖   ❖   ❖

Sasha walked down the long narrow staircase that led to Doubles, the private, subterranean eating club at the Sherry-Netherland. Sasha had come here with his grandparents as a child, and had eaten innumerable meals within its red-velvet walls and at its crisply set tables. In recent years, the place had undergone a renaissance of sorts; the young women who had gone there as children now returned as young matrons and businesswomen. Chic and exclusive, Doubles was not as strait-laced as the Colony Club. Sasha sighed. He would probably be the only man in the room besides a waiter and a couple of decorators. Lunch was strictly female.

He checked his coat and looked around the room. Dozens of John Barrett and Kenneth-coiffed blondes in well-cut suits sat chatting, the soft light glinting off their diamond engagement rings. His eyes scanned the crowd. Victoria was in the corner; as usual, she stood out.

As Sasha approached, she rose and stepped out to hug him.

"You like?" she asked, turning slowly to show him her suit.

"I love," he replied. "*Quel élan*. Is it Dior?"

"Better. It's Sophie of Saks Fifth Avenue. Again, Gran's."

He admired the wasp-waisted midnight blue two-piece suit with an asymmetrical collar and peplum. The fabric was rich and luxurious—a silk jacquard with a harlequin pattern. The three-quarter-length sleeves revealed her delicate wrists clad in slender diamond and sapphire Art Deco cuffs.

"It's really a cocktail suit, but who the hell cares. I need a corset to get it on. I can barely breathe."

"Well, you look amazing," Sasha said as they both sidled into the banquette.

"I know. You, however, look distressed," Victoria said. "What gives?"

"I'm suspended from Leighton's. Indefinitely."

Victoria raised her hand and beckoned a waiter.

"An Absolut gibson, up, very dry. And an iced Absolut neat. Actually, forget that. Just bring the bottle and two glasses." The waiter slipped away, horrified. "I take it you are not going back to the office after this lunch?"

Sasha shook his head.

"Good," she said. "Let's get legless, and then we can go back to my apartment, watch *The Best of Everything*, count the Norman Norells, and figure out how Suzy Parker keeps her hair done so perfectly under those scarves."

"I can't," Sasha said. "I have dinner with my father at Swifty's. I need to talk to him about what's going on. The reason I'm suspended is that my father and Marina are each suing to block the sale of Snegurochka."

"Ugh!" Victoria said. "Sounds like *real* life to me. What are you going to do?"

"I'm not sure. I'm either going to buy a ticket to Palm Beach and hide until it's all over, or I'm coming out, guns blazing."

Victoria smiled. "It sounds like you've made your choice already, Sasha. I'm proud of you."

Sasha smiled. The drinks arrived. They raised their glasses, and Sasha began to talk. "I'm not sure who to shoot at though," Sasha admitted, sipping the icy drink.

"Let's break this down. Start with Leighton's." Victoria set down her vodka.

"Well, they want me at the boardroom lunch next week."

"They *suspended* you! Why?"

"They don't want anything to look awkward."

"Screw them," Victoria said.

"And they've canceled my trip to Moscow. I really wanted to go, too. I was so looking forward to doing the research—I just know if I could get into those archives with Gennady, I could figure out exactly what happened to the figurine. There is something about the chronology that sits badly with me. And that reenameled hair bow bothers me, too. I just wish they'd still let me go. I need to know what really happened."

"Well, sure. They don't want you to steal their thunder—after all, you're a Russian prince, and they're just a bunch of secondhand jewelry dealers trying to make a buck. Moscow. Hmm. I've been thinking of seeing if I should open a boutique there—there's tons of money now."

A slow smile spread over Sasha's face. He was going anyway. Screw them, Victoria had said, and she was right.

"Hey, Victoria," Sasha said. "You want to go to Moscow?"

❖   ❖   ❖

Lunch with Victoria had prepared Sasha for the dinner with his father. Fortunately, Sasha had Swifty's on his side. It was small, impossibly public, crowded, and very noisy—which Sasha knew his father hated. Dinner would be short, no matter what.

Sasha walked into Swifty's and looked around the cozy room. The tables were already occupied by well dressed New Yorkers. Many people were clients Sasha recognized from Leighton's. He saw his father and Diane sitting at a small table and moved to join them.

"I'm glad you made it, Sasha. Why don't you sit next to Diane, and we'll talk this all out."

Sasha shook his father's hand, and leaned over to lightly graze Diane's cheek. He looked at her as he pulled away. Her hair was fashionably golden, and she wore a well-tailored dark brown suit, covered with a light shawl in an autumnal russet. A citrine bound-heart brooch from Verdura glowed at her shoulder.

"Hello, Diane, aren't you looking smart. Is that a Shahtoosh? The color is wonderful on you."

"Silly, Shahtoosh is illegal now. It's pashmina. Much more correct, but now that everyone and their cleaning person wears pashmina, I may get rid of it. By the way, Sasha, I wanted to thank you for the wonderful note you wrote me about the dining room. It meant a lot to me that you approved. It's a daunting task to add to a classic Parish-Hadley apartment, but I thought that the dining room needed a bit more sparkle."

"Any room sparkles when you're in it, Diane," Sasha's father said, beaming at her.

Sasha smiled and looked at the two of them. His father really did seem happy.

"Something to drink, son?"

"I'll have some wine with dinner."

"Would you like a vodka?"

"No, thank you."

"Diane?"

"I'll have a Kir."

Sasha's father ordered for the two of them, and sat looking at Sasha expectantly. "How was dinner with Gloria?" he asked casually.

"Wonderful, Father, but let's be frank and get to the point. I was suspended today. Indefinitely. They packed my things for me and put me out on the street with a cardboard box. They canceled my trip to Russia next week. All because of the two suits against them. Against the place where I have struggled to gain respect and responsibility for seven years. Against the place where I am, was, succeeding *despite* my family background. You realize that everyone has always thought I was hired because of who my family is, don't you? That I have worked this hard to prove to *everyone* that I'm still here because of what I can *do*? Can you see how upsetting this is for me?"

"Well, I'm sorry about that. I hope you'll understand better once I have explained my point of view," his father said, as the drinks arrived.

"I'm going to Russia next week," Sasha replied, fiddling with his napkin.

"Not for work? Aren't you suspended?"

"I'm going anyway. Whether I am employed by Leighton's or not, I have work to do there. Before the sale."

"If the sale goes through, that is," Diane countered. "I would think that you would want to be here. The injunction will be going through either next week or the week after. Don't you want to be here when the whole family files?"

"What do you mean the whole family?" Sasha asked, confused.

"Marina and I have decided to join our suits," his father replied.

"I assure you, the *whole* family will not be filing," Sasha said coldly.

"I hope this dinner will change your mind, Sasha," Diane said, adjusting her shawl. "Your father and I feel very strongly about this."

Sasha's father looked at him carefully. "Sasha, this must be hard for you. I understand that. But I want to explain to you how I came to this difficult decision."

Sasha waited.

"Sasha, you and I aren't alike. We love each other deeply, and I know that you know that, but we are not alike. You are really a Shchermanov—dreamy, accomplished. Like your mother. Your mother gave you a love and appreciation of Russian culture before she died. You grew up feeling Russian *inside*. You know that I was born here, that my mother is an American. When I was growing up, in the 1950s, I was taunted for being Russian—at Groton they called me 'Commie Cyril' and the 'Red Prince' and other such nonsense—never mind that I was born here, just as they were. Never mind that my mother was as American as could be, and that through her I was related to half of them. I pulled away from things Russian as much as I could, and I became as American as the times would let me be. And then, I met your mother." He stopped, and took off his glasses.

"Your mother was like an exotic bird to me. She had grown up in Paris, with two Russian parents, and simply because I was an Ozerovsky, they welcomed me into their family and into a community that I had never known in the States. Your mother opened doors for me—the doors of Russian culture, Russian music, the church. I loved her so much for everything that she did, and when she moved to New York to be with me, I was so happy. For the very first time in my life, I felt that I had done something which made my father proud of me. By marrying a Shchermanov, I showed him that I had absorbed all of the lessons that he had tried to teach me while I was growing up, and that he felt I had rejected."

"And?" Sasha asked a bit testily. He had heard this before and saw no relevance. "Why sue for the figurine? My mother never would have done this," he said.

"Nonsense," his father said gruffly, clearing his throat. "Your mother studied these things and taught them to you because she felt they were important. I want that figurine back, and I want you to have it one day. When Marina called me and told me what you were doing with the piece, I knew that that damn Leighton's had too much influence over you. I hope you understand why we are doing this. It is for the honor of the Ozerovsky family. That figurine represents who we were, and who we are. Marina made it very clear to me."

So that was it—Marina was behind the whole thing. Sasha looked at Diane. She stared at his father, her eyes beginning to brim over. *She can't be all bad*, Sasha thought, *if she really seems to love him this much*.

"Father," Sasha said, "I understand, but really, I don't think Mother—"

"Cyril, you haven't said to Alexander about what we've planned with the lawyers?" Diane said.

"What on earth can you do that you haven't done already?" Sasha asked.

"Marina has formed a family association. We have a document signed by twenty-two members of the Ozerovsky, Shoutine, and Shchermanov families. The only person who hasn't signed it is you. I feel very strongly that you should. It may put an end to your job at Leighton's, but you can always go to one of the other houses. If we win, the association will donate the figurine to the Met. It should be in a public collection, unless . . ."

"Unless what?" Sasha asked.

"Unless, as Marina suggested, she can arrange for an introduction to a private collector she knows," replied Diane.

"Are you serious?" Sasha asked. "I can't believe you people. This isn't about anything but greed." It seemed pretty obvious to him that, having seen the figurine, Marina realized that if it were sold for her benefit, she'd get something out of it, but that if it were sold on Dimitri and Sasha's behalf, she would end up with nothing but a trip to New York and a public humiliation.

"Father, Diane, I'm sorry, but we will have to agree to disagree on this. I don't know how or why Marina has such a hold over you, but I hope that you can look beyond her convincing arguments, whatever they may be. The facts are these: We lost the piece during the Revolution and never made a claim on it. It belongs to someone else who purchased it in good faith and is selling it the same way. If you press your suit and win, Marina will be making money—money on a figurine, I might point out, that never belonged to her family. Does that seem fair to you?"

Sasha's father hesitated, then said, "I am only doing this for the family."

"But Father, I *am* your family, and *I* don't want this done!" he said too loudly, causing the people at nearby tables to look at them.

"Sasha, if you can't control yourself, you might as well leave."

"I'm leaving," Sasha said, getting up. "I love you, and I respect you—but this? I don't understand at all. Diane, I am sorry to put you through such an unpleasant conversation. Father, I'll call you when I get back from Russia. Maybe things will be better then."

Sasha walked out of the restaurant. Marina. Damn her. Why on earth had she shown up? What did she really want, and how could she have driven such a wedge between him and his father in such a short time? No wonder his mother never spoke to his aunt. *If things go unchanged*, Sasha thought, *I will cut Marina out of my life as thoroughly as Mama cut Tatiana out of hers*. Sasha only hoped he wouldn't lose his father in the process.

Russian New Year, an Evening Tea. Paris, January 14, 1962

Princess Marina Shchermanov looked over the round table carefully set with all the silver the family had left. New Year's Eve and two girls, engaged at once. And good matches, too. True, Tatiana was marrying a pauper, but he was well educated and a Shoutine. But Nina had indeed done very well for herself. Not only was her husband an Ozerovsky, but he also made money and stood to inherit millions from his American mother. Nina had always been such a good girl.

Princess Marina's eyes scanned the table. She wished for at least this night she might have engaged someone to serve, but there was no money. In fact, there was so little money, the Shchermanovs couldn't even serve a full dinner for the extended family, and so a Russian evening tea seemed a better idea, and more traditional at that. The food looked wonderful. Everything was the best the little money they had could buy, and the table glittered with the Romanov tea service she had inherited from her parents. The lovely eighteenth-century silver tureens with the Shchermanov coat of arms would soon be full of soups, both cold and hot. Bottles of vodka and Champagne were set out. Flowers were everywhere. The icon lamps shed soft light, and the scent of roses filled the room. Her husband entered.

"So, my dear," he said, smiling at her, "everything is ready?"

"Everything. Nothing could be better," she said. He took her hand and kissed her open palm.

"So, both girls married at once."

"In a double ceremony, thank God. Two weddings would have ruined us."

"It is a happy occasion, nonetheless." He smiled wearily, and moved toward the window, leaning out into the icy January night and looking down the rue Daru toward the Cathedral of Alexander Nevsky, which lay in the bend of the road like an exotic bird resting on a branch during its migration. The onion-domed building was incongruous in a block of Parisian limestone apartment buildings, but since the Revolution, it and the *quartier* in which it sat had served as the main center of the lives of Russian émigrés.

"Do you think, my dear," he asked, "that the girls will leave Paris?"

"Nina, certainly. Tatiana, I don't think so."

"At least one of them will stay with us." He smiled.

"Have you decided what to give them?" Marina Ivanovna asked her husband.

"For Tatiana, the last piece of Shchermanov jewelry, the black pearl earrings."

"And for Nina?"

"The Fabergé box with the palace on the lid."

"She has always loved it. I'm glad you are giving it to her."

Alexander smiled, and looked back down the street. Coming up the rue Daru was a young couple he could tell was Tatiana and her fiancé, Count Shoutine.

"They are coming, my dear," said Prince Alexander.

The bell soon rang, and the creaking wooden stairs announced the arrival of the young couple. Princess Shchermanov opened the doors of the apartment to receive them.

Tatiana appeared first, her beautiful face wreathed in smiles, and behind her, the slim and elegant Count Grigorii Shoutine, dressed in a worn overcoat over what was no doubt a threadbare suit.

"*Maman*, happy New Year," Tatiana said, kissing her mother on both cheeks. "Everything looks lovely. Thank you so much for doing all this for us."

"Well," Marina replied, "it's not every day that it is New Year's Eve, with both my daughters to be married the following week!"

Count Shoutine smiled bashfully at Tatiana's father. "I would have waited and saved a little more money if I had a bit more of a choice in the matter," he said. Alexander smiled knowingly. Tatiana's will was a powerful thing, and he was now certain that what he had felt was true: Tatiana had pressed her fiancé into an early engagement out of a sense of competition with her sister.

Alexander looked at his younger daughter. She sat in a small Louis XV chair, her back straight and her ankles crossed delicately. *She is so beautiful*, he thought, looking at her. Her slim ice blue satin dress and short jacket were the perfect foil for her black hair and exceptionally pale skin. Her eyes were a luminous green, and there was the barest tilt to the line of her lids. *Such a pity*, he thought. Had there been no Revolution and no war, what a different life she would have led.

The buzzer rang again, and with a final lingering glance at Tatiana's beauty, Prince Shchermanov went to let in his other daughter.

Moving to open the door, Ivan wondered what the Ozerovsky boy would be like. Of course he had known the father well—they had left Russia together in 1918. The American mother was an unknown quantity, however, and he hoped that his new son-in-law would not be too American.

Pulling herself away from her other daughter, Princess Marina walked to her husband's side. The couple looked down at Nina as she came up the stairs with her fiancé. She was not as beautiful as her sister—there was something a bit too strong in her features, too sharp in her coloring, but her chic was breathtaking.

This night, Nina was stunning. Her hair had been swept up into a chignon, and she was in a long evening dress in broad black-and-white horizontal stripes, with a matching evening coat.

Dear God, I hope he's not buying her clothes before the wedding, thought Marina Ivanovna. *It's so inappropriate.*

Too many teeth, thought Prince Alexander. *Why must Americans always have so many teeth?* Alexander looked with interest at the young man. *The mother must be huge*, he thought. He remembered young Cyril's father from pictures as a handsome and slim young man, but Cyril was well over six feet, with broad shoulders and a big square jaw. The face was aristocratic, but young Cyril looked more like an American movie star than anything else.

"Papa, happy New Year," said Nina, smiling. "Are we the first, or are Tatiana and Grisha here already?"

"You're right on time, but yes, your sister is here. Now, will you let me say hello to your fiancé?" he asked, standing as tall as he could to compensate for his inferior height.

Nina smiled bashfully. "Of course, I'm so sorry. Papa, *Maman*, this is Cyril Olegovitch Ozerovsky. Darling, my parents, Alexander and Marina Shchermanov."

"What a pleasure to see you again, Ninochka and I have been away too long," Cyril said in Russian, holding out his hand and smiling.

Prince Shchermanov let relief flow over him. Cyril's Russian was exquisite. When he spoke, Alexander couldn't even tell he wasn't Russian-born. *Perhaps I was hasty*, he thought. *His grandmother was a German, after all—perhaps that's where he gets the height and size.*

Kisses and handshakes were exchanged, and the young couple entered the small apartment. At the sight of her sister, Tatiana rose and crossed the room; the two girls tearfully gave each other hugs and kisses. It had been months since they had seen each other, with Nina in New York and Tatiana in Paris.

"How long are you here?" Tatiana asked, holding her sister at arm's length.

"Well, we were with Cyril's parents in London for New Year's Eve, arrived in Paris for Russian New Year's yesterday. The wedding, as you know, is next week, and we leave for New York again on the third of February."

"Oh, can't you stay longer?" said Tatiana, clutching her sister's hand.

"Are you flying?" asked Grisha.

"No," said Cyril. "We're sailing on the *France* from Le Havre. Hello, I'm Cyril Ozerovsky."

"Grigorii Shoutine. A pleasure," he said smiling and bowing slightly.

The family moved to the table and helped themselves to small plates of smoked fish and meat, handmade savory pastries, and glasses of tea from the beautiful silver-gilt samovar set.

"Well, I'm afraid the wedding will be quite simple," sighed Princess Shchermanov, sitting down and placing her glass of tea on a *guéridon* table.

"No matter, *Maman*. Nina and I would have had it no other way, even if there were all the money in the world," Tatiana said, patting her mother's hand.

"What a beautiful liar you are, darling," said Marina Ivanovna.

"I hope that it is not too forward of me," said Cyril, "but my parents have sent gifts from New York for each of the girls, and they hoped that they might be able to wear them at the wedding. They can represent something old or something new, depending on how you look at it." He smiled, and reached into his suit pockets, handing a velvet pouch to Nina and a red leather box to Tatiana.

Nina loosened the drawstring of the bag, and from it drew an incredible strand of pearls. Heavy, lustrous, and opera length, the pearls were magnificent.

"I don't know what to say," Nina said, kissing Cyril lightly on the lips.

"They are almost too good for a woman as young as you are," said Princess Shchermanov with a smile.

"I'll say," said Tatiana, with a look of frank envy.

"Please, Tatiana, open yours. This is a family piece, but you are family now, and we want you to have it." Cyril smiled.

Tatiana opened the box and let out a small gasp. She lifted from the satin lining a very large and very beautiful sapphire-and-diamond brooch.

"It's enormous," she said. "I can't accept it."

"You must. My parents will be offended if you don't. Please, Tatiana."

"It's far too valuable. I can't."

"It is valuable, yes, but the sapphire isn't perfect—the color is a bit pale. It is more valuable because of its associations in my family. My grandmother treasured it. We believe she received it in Hesse, before she went to Russia. She always called it the 'Hessian blue.'"

Tatiana looked at her fiancé helplessly. She would never receive anything like this from him, she knew. Grigorii looked down at the floor, embarrassed. Tatiana looked at her mother, who looked at her husband, who nodded imperceptibly.

"Well, it is a treasure, and I thank you," Tatiana said, getting up, and kissing him on both cheeks.

Cyril smiled, and turned to help Nina loop her pearls around her neck, where they lay in four impressive rows.

The six sat in quiet for a while. The gifts had spoiled something indefinable by underscoring the meager means of the Shchermanovs and Shoutines. There came a buzz from the street. The three men stood automatically, and the three women turned their faces to the door to receive the rest of their guests with smiles.

❖   ❖   ❖

The party was great fun. In the tiny apartment sat the cream of prerevolutionary Russian aristocracy and the *gratin* of the Faubourg. Young and fashionable friends of Marina's and Tatiana's peppered the rooms, their unconventional and modern clothes standing in contrast to the old-fashioned evening.

The guests brought even more food, and they drank bottle after bottle of Champagne. Some older Russians brought out *balalaiki*, and music filled the room. Several of the young couples danced in the tiny apartment, and others made plans to meet later at a fashionable discotheque near the Étoile.

Nina looked around the room. It was a wonderful party. She touched the pearls around her neck absentmindedly. She had had just a little too much Champagne and felt warm. Touching Cyril lightly on the arm, she gestured that she was going to get some air, and she slipped through the guests and went into her mother's room, closing the door behind her.

"I was wondering where you were," said Tatiana as she stood at their mother's large mirror, coaxing her hair back into place with a tortoiseshell comb.

"That crowd is something, isn't it?"

"I loathe all those people. We're in Paris, and the Revolution is over. It's like a village feast day in Smolensk in 1890 out there. *Balalaiki*? I've never seen anything so *gauche*." Tatiana turned back to the mirror and began repairing her eye makeup.

Nina smiled. "I think it's touching."

"I think your fiancé is great. How dear of him to give me this brooch."

"It is beautiful, isn't it? I'm a bit jealous," Nina said smiling, and began to address the issue of her own chignon.

"It will probably be the only good piece of jewelry I ever receive. Grisha will never have any money."

"Oh, he'll do fine, you can be sure. Once he's finished at the *Sciences Po* and begins practicing law, he'll do very well. Have faith."

"Perhaps," Tatiana said, looking at herself in the mirror and adjusting the brooch, which sparkled like a lake against the pale ice blue of her dress.

"I think the wedding will be lovely, don't you?" Nina said, finishing her hair and turning to her swiftly unsealing false eyelashes.

"As lovely as an endless orthodox service in that crumbling pile at the end of the street can be, surrounded by the remains of the imperial army. We deserve better, and you know it."

"Tatiana!" said Nina, turning to her sister, "you can't be serious. It's our family we're talking about here. It is precious to me that we can all be together, and the four of us get married together here, where we grew up. I'm surprised at you."

"You would feel that way, since you're the one who goes off to be Mrs. Fifth Avenue millionaire, and I'm left behind with the waxworks."

Nina sighed, and began to put her make-up back in her evening bag. Sometimes, when she had had a bit to drink, Tatiana's competitive nature went from silly to belligerent. Nina had learned simply to walk away.

"I'm sorry that's the way you feel," Nina said, turning to leave and drawing on her gloves again. "If you want to get away from these people so badly, Tatiana, why on earth are you marrying Grisha?"

"I'm pregnant, Nina," Tatiana said flatly, fingering the brooch at her shoulder and admiring her reflection. "I have to marry Grisha."

Nina turned back and looked at her sister in amazement.

"Oh, don't be such a prude, Nina. Grisha's the father."

"Well, of course he is . . ." Nina said in confusion.

"The brooch is beautiful. How old would you say it is? You're the expert."

"About 1870, the main stone must be at least twenty-five carats. The diamonds are quite fine as well," Nina said automatically, stepping into her role as art and jewelry specialist without even thinking.

"How much do you think it is worth?" Tatiana asked casually, glancing at Nina's reflection in the mirror.

Nina looked at her sister in horror.

"You can't be thinking of selling it, Tatiana?"

"Well, we have no money, and with a baby coming—"

"Tatiana, it was a gift from my husband's family! It is something important to them—"

"Honestly, Nina, I won't do it tomorrow. After the wedding—"

"I can't even listen to this nonsense anymore. Tatiana, you can't sell this piece; it would kill Cyril."

Tatiana turned to Nina wickedly.

"You'll look wonderful in black with those pearls then, won't you, Princess Ozerovsky?"

Nina swallowed and turned to the door.

"I will see you at the wedding. I hope you will reconsider. If you do choose to sell the piece, I hope you will let me buy it back from you. I would never want my husband to know." Nina left and walked back into the party, which was in full swing, Catching sight of her from across the room, Cyril went to her side.

"Are you all right?" he asked. "You look exhausted."

"I am tired. Cyril, after the wedding, may we leave Paris? We have a week before we sail, don't we?"

"I thought you wanted to spend time with your family," he said, tipping her chin up to his face so that he could look at her.

"I think I need a little sun," she said quietly.

"Fine," Cyril said, smiling. "I'll cancel our tickets on the *France*, we'll fly back and go straight to my parents' house in Palm Beach."

"That sounds like heaven."

"Anything for my girl," he said, kissing her on the forehead.

"A little sun is just what I need. Away from here," she said, and pressed her face into the soft cashmere of his jacket, which smelled comfortingly of tobacco, strong tea, and bay rum.

Eleven

❧

It FELT STRANGE to walk into Leighton's, yet not to be there to work. Lucile smiled at him as he passed, and pointed to the crowds around the figurine, which was to leave for London that afternoon after the luncheon. He smiled back and climbed the stairs to the boardroom.

Jewelry was on view on the second floor. Women in pearls clustered around the glass cases filled with diamonds and colored precious stones. As he approached the door to the boardroom, he took a deep breath. This was going to be tough.

Sasha entered. The group was just whom he had expected it would be. Anne, Dimitri, Gloria Greer, Betsy's parents, and some other people he didn't recognize. Sasha glanced at the place cards and realized that two of them were the famous Dikarinskys about whom he had heard so much.

Nadezhda Dikarinsky, the woman whom Marina had mentioned and whom Dimitri worked for was arresting. Not beautiful, and more than a bit matronly, she had the wide eyes of a child, and she was apparently enjoying her adventure as a billionairess with relish. Her clothes were Chanel, and sized far larger than Mr. Lagerfeld would have cared to see made; her jewelry was too large and too colorful for the afternoon in New York. Yet there was a slight edge to her, and Sasha could tell that, despite her riches and her new position in the new Russia, she was slightly scared—of what, Sasha could not tell, but he liked her.

Her husband was part of an Azerbaijani oil syndicate, and had made $1 billion through speculation on the Baku fields. He was red-faced and small, but Madame Dikarinsky looked at him with the affection and respect that came only from a long relationship of shared experiences and difficulties.

"Hi, Sasha. I'm glad that you could be here," Anne said, approaching him and patting him on the shoulder. Her eyes were steely, and Sasha recognized the hard look from before the discovery of Snegurochka in them. She made Sasha very nervous. He smiled at her, and moved away, toward Gloria Greer.

"Good afternoon, Gloria. I'm pleased to see you again."

"I wouldn't have missed this for the world. The figurine is just wonderful. If it weren't so expensive, I'd consider bidding on it myself—I don't have a figurine, as you know. I was just telling Anne that you have exquisite taste—I could tell as you looked at my collection."

"Kind of you to say so," Sasha replied.

Anne smiled. "Instead of talking about Sasha's taste, why don't we all sit down and start tasting lunch?" Sasha smiled back, but he thought that Anne was being a bit hard. The legal matters probably weren't going well, and this was her way of letting off steam. She was managing the department alone, and his father's suit was the reason she had no help.

They all walked around the two tables, looking for their places. Sasha had hoped he would be seated near Gloria Greer, but it looked as if he was seated between Madame Dikarinsky, and Betsy's mother. He was at the same table as Dimitri.

Nadezhda gave Sasha a wide smile as he moved toward her, and giggled like a schoolgirl when he kissed her hand, as he did all married Russian women. Sasha introduced her to Princess Constantine, who regarded her coldly.

"I'm sorry. My English is not so good," Madame Dikarinsky said, and smiled sadly.

"Would you prefer to speak in Russian?" Sasha asked, switching to Russian himself.

"I should practice English. You speak such good Russian. Where did you learn?"

"Sasha is Prince Ozerovsky. He spoke Russian growing up," Dimitri said from across the table.

"Really?" Nadezhda turned back to him, smiling. "When I was a small girl, I had ballet lessons in your family's palace on the Moika Canal."

Sasha smiled. The thought of the large Madame Dikarinsky *en pointe* was funny. "I'm glad at least that there are some happy memories there."

"Many. But now—so many changes there. They are restoring the palace, you know."

"I didn't know. I'm looking forward to visiting it when I am there."

Dimitri turned from his conversation.

"You're going to Russia? I thought that they canceled your trip."

"I'm going anyway, the tenth of March. First to Saint Petersburg, and then to Moscow," Sasha said loudly enough for Anne to hear at the other table.

"Good for you!" Dimitri said. "I'll take you to dinner at the Astoria."

"I'll be in Moscow, mostly."

"Then it will have to be Maxim's—you'll stay with Nadezhda in Moscow."

"We will have a dinner for you. I have the best chef in the capital," Nadezhda piped up.

Sasha realized he was trapped and raised his glass. "Until Moscow."

"Until Moscow!" Dimitri and Nadezhda responded.

Princess Constantine turned to Sasha. "So, you're off to Russia next Monday?"

"I am."

"Then we will see you at Synod on Sunday, won't we? It has been a long time since we saw you at the cathedral, Sasha."

Sasha smiled. She'd be looking for him at church on Sunday, as everyone knew that you couldn't travel without confessing and receiving absolution before you left.

"Of course I will be," he replied.

"I'll expect you!" she said, smiling and raising her glass.

At the other end of the room, Anne stood up and prepared to speak.

"I'd like to thank all of you for coming. It is very rare for us to have an object of such quality, and I'd like to say what a pleasure it is to have you here. To have the Romanovs here as representatives of the vanished court for whom Fabergé worked. To have Sasha here as a member of the family for whom she was created. To have so many of the great collectors and museum curators who have worked with Fabergé in this country. It is a privilege to be here with you all. It is moments like this that make all the troubles associated with the art world seem insignificant. To all of you, and to the future owners of Snegurochka!" She raised her glass and drank.

The room dissolved into applause. Betsy's mother turned to Sasha.

"Representative of a vanished court? That makes me feel like I was in Russia when the Revolution came. I'm not so old, am I?" Sasha smiled and squeezed her hand.

❖   ❖   ❖

The rest of the lunch passed quickly. Dimitri was exuberant, but Nadezhda was silent and hurt after Princess Constantine expressed her distaste for the vulgar new Russians, who, she maintained, were all associated with the mob and bleeding Russia dry. She had not meant to include Nadezhda in this group, but offense was taken, and Sasha was sorry for it.

As everyone stood up to go, Sasha approached Anne.

"Thank you for having me, Anne. I'm sorry about the situation, but what you and John have decided is probably best. I'm going to

Russia for a while. It's a private trip, but I'll be looking in the archives in Saint Petersburg and Moscow. I need to get away."

Anne looked at him coolly. "I hope you have a wonderful time. You needn't help Gennady. He can manage."

"Good-bye, Anne, and good luck. I'll see both Snegurochka and you in Moscow on the fifteenth, I guess."

"Sasha, how did dinner go with your father?" Anne suddenly asked as he turned to leave.

"Not well, I'm afraid," Sasha said.

"Pity," she replied. "See you in Moscow, Sasha."

❖   ❖   ❖

Arriving home, Sasha moved slowly to his kitchen and got a bottle of water out of the refrigerator. Even though it was afternoon, he felt dirty and exhausted.

He ran a hot shower and took off his clothes. The shower felt good, and after drying himself off and putting on a robe, he picked up the phone and dialed Saint Petersburg.

The phone rang once and was answered quickly.

"Slushayu!" I'm listening! The conversation proceeded in Russian.

"Gennady Alexeievitch? It's Sasha Ozerovsky calling from New York."

"Sasha! How are you? It has been too long. Why don't you ever call us? When are you coming back?"

Sasha smiled. Talking to Gennady was like talking to his grandfather.

"Well, I think that I will be coming back to Russia sooner rather than later."

"Hooray! Leonida! Sasha's coming to town. When do you arrive home in Saint Petersburg? I'll send someone to pick you up at Pulkovo. You will stay with us. I won't have it any other way."

"Don't make trouble for yourself and for Leonida. I'll make reservations at the Astoria. I want to take you two for dinner there."

"Ugh. Their blini are like rocks. You'll come to us for meals."

Sasha smiled. Gennady was like every Petersburger he had ever met—cultured, generous, vivacious, and deeply cynical—but with a wonderful sense of humor.

"When do you arrive?"

"The tenth. I should tell you, however, that there's been a lot of trouble at work. I've been suspended."

"I know. Anne and that lawyer lady from Leighton's sent us a fax this afternoon saying we were not to give you any information concerning clients in Russia who were interested in purchasing Snegurochka."

"Really? Are they that afraid of me?"

"They're afraid of everything. I'll tell you who's interested in Snegurochka—no one."

"Why is that?"

"When there's a chance that any day the president may declare a war or restore a palace or shut the banks, and the Cabinet opens and closes like a Swiss clock every hour, who's worried about Fabergé?"

"In 1918, lots of people were."

"Yes, and look what happened to them. Listen. You sound exhausted."

"I am. I miss you all."

"Of course you do. Why else would you decide to come to this desperate place? Your soul must need it. Come home, Sasha. You'll forget all this nonsense. I need help doing some research for the Russian Museum, and you're just the boy to help me. All the papers are in English and French. Then, we'll go to Moscow, and you can be my guest at the reception in the Kremlin for Snegurochka. How does that sound?"

"Wonderful. Gennady, thank you for being a friend."

"Nonsense. We take care of each other. You got me this job with Leighton's, remember? I can pay for food and send my children to school abroad because of you. I owe you my life. The least I can do is invite you back to where you belong. For an American, you're awfully Russian, Sasha. What is that line from Saint-Exupéry? 'You are responsible for those you tame'? I feel responsible for you. Come to Russia. We need you here."

Sasha felt his eyes begin to fill, and his chest tightened with emotion. Why didn't he have friends like this in New York? He decided to hang up before he bawled outright.

"I'd better be going now. It's late. I'll send you my itinerary by e-mail."

"That's the best way. You know how the phone service can be. We can put a man into space, but we can't keep the phones running even now." He laughed.

"See you in Peter. Good-bye. Don't let those bastards get to you."

"I won't. Thank you, Gennady." Sasha hung up the phone, rolled into bed, and fell sound asleep.

❖   ❖   ❖

The next morning, Sasha showered and pulled himself together. He needed to be at church by eleven. He dressed in a dark suit, and for once he wore a somber tie.

The weather was cold, but Sasha looked forward to the short walk to the Cathedral of Our Lady of the Sign. The cathedral and the synod of bishops were, in fact, contained within a large neo-Georgian mansion at the corner of Ninety-third Street.

Sasha entered the courtyard of the beautiful building and climbed the sweeping marble staircase that rose to the old ballroom, where the cathedral was installed. Entering through the tall French doors, Sasha took in the beauty of the sanctuary. Though converted from secular use, the room gave the impression that the parishioners were in the private chapel of a palace in Saint Petersburg.

The plaster moldings were rococo, and frivolous, but to Sasha the palms had only ever referred to Christ's entry into Jerusalem, and he was incapable of seeing the cathedral as anything but that— a sacred space, and a Russian one.

Within the walls of the cathedral, Sasha had had, as a little boy, his first taste of Russia. Surrounded by Russians of all the emigrations, Sasha had heard the language in all its forms, from the elegant clear Russian of his grandfather to the Soviet Russian of recent immigrants, to the ancient and melodious old church Slavonic of the liturgy—the language that was the vernacular when his first ancestor had accepted Christianity.

In church, Sasha had been introduced to Russian music, and had been exposed to the beauty and the soul of the Russia his mother had always hoped that he would come to know and appreciate. As a child he hadn't, but once he was grown and visited Russia for the first time, Sasha felt something special when he entered his first church there. He knew that, no matter where he was, if he entered a Russian Orthodox church, in some kind of strange spiritual extraterritoriality, Sasha was in Russia itself.

He entered the sanctuary and purchased candles from the woman behind the counter near the door. He moved around the room, venerating the feast day icons and the icons of his family's patron saints, listening to the murmuring voices of the readers as they chanted the texts. Sasha saw the line of parishioners approaching the priest to say their confession. Sasha joined the line, made his confession, and then retreated into the crowd, letting the service wash over him. Services often reminded him of his mother, but today, all he could think of was how much he wanted to return to Russia.

He looked around the room and made eye contact with Princess Constantine, who beamed at him. He recognized many people, most of whom nodded at him in acknowledgment and in pleasure at seeing someone young in church.

Though the service was long, it passed by in a flash. Leaving, he walked by Princess Constantine. They spoke in Russian.

"*I promised I would come.*"

"*I knew that you would. Before a trip away from home, one must worship with one's own people—who knows if you will be allowed to return?"* She smiled. *"Have a wonderful trip home. Come back safely."*

"I will, thank you," he replied.

Sasha walked home through the snow, which had begun falling at some point during the service. He thought about his father, and his trip. He hoped that he would be able to work things out. The service had given him a feeling of hope that he had not had before.

As he turned into his building, Sasha realized with a smile that he was thinking in Russian.

❖   ❖   ❖

That night, Sasha had an unusual dream. In it, he found himself standing on the street in Saint Petersburg before the palace where his mother's family had lived before the Russian Revolution. Alone in the street, Sasha looked up at the building and saw his mother standing in the window, where she gazed out over his head toward the Neva River behind him. Sasha's heart raced at the sight of her, but when he called to get her attention, he realized that he could make no sound. In the dream, he saw her pull away from the window, and he continued to stand, his mouth open but silent as the mists closed in, gradually obscuring the raspberry pink walls of the Shchermanov Palace on the English Embankment.

He awoke and prepared for his trip. After showering, he put on clothes comfortable enough for the long journey, and then, like a character out of Turgenev, he crossed himself, sat on his luggage in the front hall, and prayed for a safe trip home to Russia, then a safe return home to New York.

Leningrad, 1945

Gennady looked out the window of the filthy bus that crawled along the streets, reeking of diesel exhaust and dirty children. He pressed his face against the glass and looked ahead toward the Nevsky Prospect, hoping to catch a glimpse of the Moscow Gate, which indicated that he was nearing home in the central district. Instead, he saw a man sledding down the street, pulled by another man. Looking closer, he realized that the man wasn't sledding at all. He was dead, and he was being dragged down the street on a piece of carpet.

The air was smoky and full of a strange smell. At first, Gennady thought it was garbage burning, but when he looked around, bile rose in his throat. It wasn't garbage. They were throwing bodies on pyres set up off the Nevsky Prospect.

Gennady glanced around the bus. The other children returning to Leningrad were dazed and staring straight ahead, numb to what they saw. Many, he thought, had probably seen worse.

He thought of his family's apartment, and of how much he wanted to see his mother. It had been three years since he had been sent to relatives in Tomsk for safety. But as the bus got closer to the city, Gennady became concerned.

Leningrad was gone. Half the buildings were completely destroyed. The rest seemed damaged beyond repair. Blocks were vacant and full of rubble. Signs everywhere proclaimed in red: LENINGRAD, HERO-CITY IS AN EXAMPLE FOR THE MOTHERLAND! and STALIN SAYS WE SHALL REBUILD! But Gennady could not connect the pretty city he had left with the devastation he saw in front of his eyes.

The streets were torn up, old tram lines twisting out of the earth and reaching toward the skies. As the autobus pulled down the street toward the old market, Gennady could see that the spire of the Admiralty was intact, and he let out a sigh of relief. Something was the same, at least. Gennady hoped that what the newsreels said was true and that Berlin was now dust under the boots of the Red Guard. That nothing was left at all.

"Pioneers!" shouted the tired driver of the bus, "thanks to the fascists, the road is impassable from this point. We shall have to walk from here to the Kuibishev District headquarters." The exhausted children filed silently out of the bus and onto the street, which was filled with emaciated men and women who had formed silent chains, picking rubble out of the streets and passing the pieces back into the damaged buildings from which they came to provide material for reconstruction. Gennady looked at their faces and saw that they were hungry and exhausted.

They walked down the Nevsky, and their tired eyes widened at the destruction. They had heard that the city was heroically standing against the fascists, but for Gennady and the other children, that had meant that robust Leningraders were defending the city with arms, holding the fascists at bay—in fact, it was very different.

Arriving at the party district headquarters, they entered through the huge, scarred doors into the building. Even despite the neglect during the siege, Gennady was awed by the beauty of the building. A long graceful marble staircase swept up the far end of the hall, then separated into two staircases that looped up the walls to the parade chambers. Graceful arches divided the room; instead of being supported by columns, naiads and satyrs held up the arches with beautifully sculpted arms, their elegant torsos shifting into pilasters and ending in gilt bases on the marble floor. Large shattered mirrors reflected the available light.

Gennady tugged at the arm of the driver.

"Citizen?" he asked, "what was this building before?"

"Before what?" asked the driver ominously.

"I'm sorry," replied Gennady.

"Pioneers, wait here," the driver said. "I will find the person responsible for alerting your parents that you have returned."

Gennady sat against the wall with some other children, near an old woman who was darning a piece of fabric and watching over the room. She smiled at the children.

"You'll be home soon, and things will get better. Papa Stalin will take care of you." She patted a young girl on the head. Gennady looked at her, and she crooked a finger at him. He approached her slowly.

"Before," she whispered, "before, we called this place the Sergeievskii Palace. It was the home of Sergei Alexandrovitch, uncle of the Tsar, and his wife, Elizabeth, who was the sister of the Empress."

"How do you know?" he asked.

"I worked here," she said, "before the Grand Duchess moved to Moscow and took the veil."

"Why did she do that?" Gennady asked.

"So that she might help the poor without restrictions, and so that she might help Moscow in particular. They say," she whispered, "that she died a saint."

Gennady looked around. He was terrified that someone had overheard their conversation.

"I have to go, Grandmother," he said carefully.

"Pioneers!" shouted a matronly woman on the stairs. "Come with me."

The group rose and climbed the stairs. As they turned the corner, he could see the small crowd of parents who had come to pick up their children. Gennady scanned the small cluster for his parents, but he didn't see them. All around him, children were reunited in quiet tears with the women who had come for them. There were no men.

Slowly, Gennady focused on a woman across the room looking at him with curiosity. He realized that it was his aunt Larisa. He approached her slowly.

"*Tyotya* Lara?" he asked.

"Gennady," she said quietly, "you're so big."

Larisa took his hand and moved him toward the desk where bureaucrats were processing the arrivals.

"Name?" asked the woman behind the desk.

"Antropin, Gennady Alexeievitch," he replied.

"Are you the mother?" she asked Larisa.

"No," Larisa replied. "I am his aunt."

"Where are his parents?" asked the woman. Larisa squeezed his hand.

"Father, Alexei Efimovitch Antropin, and mother, Elena Niko-laevna Antropin, both dead."

Gennady looked down at his feet and fought tears. Pioneers didn't cry.

"Do you take responsibility for this child?" she asked.

"I do," replied his aunt.

"Your name?" she asked.

"Borodin, Larisa Nikolaevna," she replied.

The woman stamped his papers, and handed them to Larisa. The woman looked at Gennady's face, touched him on the cheek, and gave him a weak and sad smile. Then, she noticed one of the soldiers staring at her.

"The Motherland is aware of your sacrifice, and a grateful Soviet Union honors your heroism," she said brusquely. "Next!"

Larisa guided Gennady out of the building and into the street.

"I'm sorry you had to hear about your parents that way," she said. "I wish I could have told you first. Your father was among the first killed at Stalingrad. He is a hero, and thank God he didn't suffer through the worst of the battle. After the university closed, your mother was assigned to the Hermitage. They needed additional cataloguers, and people to help with the evacuation of objects in case the Germans invaded." Larisa spoke in an expressionless voice. "When the shelling began, your mother was among the curators and volunteers in the painting galleries. They had very little time.

They took knives and cut the paintings from the frames. Your mother helped save almost the whole gallery of Spanish paintings. She was rolling a painting up when a shell exploded outside of the window where she was working. The casement blew in, and she was killed. It was war, but we have won. We are all safe because of what they did for us. You are safe, and so, one day, will be your children."

Gennady began to cry, Pioneer or not.

They walked down the remaining stretch of the Nevsky Prospect. Gennady glanced up at a sign perched high on the building. CITIZENS! IN CASE OF SHELLING, THIS SIDE OF THE STREET IS SAFEST! He looked across the street at the rubble of the buildings that had stood opposite.

They turned the corner, passed the Admiralty, and headed back toward St. Isaac's Square.

"Wouldn't it have been faster to go another way?" Gennady asked.

"The streets are blocked with rubble," she replied. "We have to go the long way."

St. Isaac's Cathedral was scarred with marks from shelling. The Astoria had been scarred by fire, and all the glass on the first floor was destroyed. Gennady wondered what the lobby looked like. He looked at the dome of St. Isaac's, once blindingly gold; it had been painted to disguise it from attack. The cathedral was hung with camouflage netting. The sculpted angels at the corners were hidden with sandbags.

Gennady was angry. He was angry at his parents for dying; he was angry at the Germans; he was angry that his city was in such distress. When he grew up, he vowed, he would fix this city so that it would be as if it had never happened. His children would grow up in the same Leningrad that he had, where the Hermitage was full of treasures and the streets were beautiful. Each and every one of the city's bridges, palaces, gardens, and museums would be perfect again for all the people to enjoy.

They arrived at his aunt's apartment. It was small and as clean as she could manage, given the situation. There was no water and no electricity. The apartment was lit by candles that, Aunt Lara told him, were purchased for a fortune on the black market. His uncle Boris was there when they arrived.

"So you're still alive," his uncle said, patting him on the shoulder. "Good for you."

Gennady sat down on a small chair. Larisa showed him how they went to the bathroom, and where they stored the drinking water she went to get every morning. Gennady reached into his small bag and turned over the egg, the hard black bread, and the leeks he had been given when he got on the bus that morning.

"Thank God," Larisa said.

"Thank Stalin and the Soviet," Boris said. "God had nothing to do with it."

"What did you eat during the siege?" Gennady asked.

"Don't tell him, Boris," Larisa said quickly, but too late.

"Boy, don't you know?" he asked with cruelty. "We ate each other."

Twelve

~

SASHA WALKED OUT of the Pulkovo airport terminal and glanced back over his shoulder at the stolid fascist-looking facade. The light had started to drain from the sky, and the air was already damp and cold. Sasha saw a driver leaning up against a black Lada. There weren't many of them left these days. The other drivers all seemed to have European cars.

"To the Astoria?" Sasha asked in Russian.

"Why not?" the driver replied, tossing his cigarette onto the ground. Sasha got into the car, which turned left off the airport access road and headed toward the city of Saint Petersburg.

As the car rattled and groaned, Sasha looked absently at the sides of the road, lined with birches and pine trees. In the median, recently restored markers listed the number of *versts* between Saint Petersburg and the summer palaces of Tsarskoye Selo. Sasha listened to the news and pop music as the landscape began to change.

First, he saw a ruined convent and some churches in disrepair. Then a few small houses and modern apartment blocks from the 1960s followed. Finally, as they approached the monument to the Great Patriotic War, the city began in earnest. This was the center of the greater Leningrad, which Stalin had built right after the great victory against fascism. Huge buildings set shoulder to shoulder like a phalanx of soldiers, all in a style the Russians referred to wryly as *Stalinskii Ampir'*. Like Stalin's empire, Sasha noted, the buildings were decayed and crumbling.

Soon the car passed the Moscow Gate, and the old city of Saint

Petersburg began to unfold before them. The sky was now a pale and opalescent grey, shot through with bursts of pink and turquoise. Streetlights along the Nevsky Prospect went on one by one as the car sped toward the hotel.

Sasha noted the many buildings under restoration; yet many more were still neglected. Returning to Saint Petersburg was like seeing a former lover at a party. Older perhaps, a bit more tired-looking than one remembered, but still fascinating and deadly attractive.

The palaces began at the Fontanka. The Sergeievsky Palace glowing garnet red in the fading light, its atalantes supporting the baroque-style balconies designed in the nineteenth century. They crossed the Anitchkov Bridge, its horses rearing in the same tense salute as the last time he had visited. He saw the Cheremeteff, Shouvaloff, and Stroganoff Palaces, freshly painted, their windows glowing with light.

A crush of people hurried along the Nevsky, all of them moving toward the metro stations. There were quite a few elegantly dressed people as well, some holding bags that declared Estée Lauder, Chanel, and Versace, as if the city were Paris or New York.

But Saint Petersburg is not New York, Sasha thought as he caught sight of the floodlit Hermitage through the Rossi Arch. Scaffolding was everywhere, indicating the enormous amount of repair work that needed to be made to the venerable complex. As the cab passed the Admiralty, Saint Petersburg's most famous tower, lights illuminated the delicate spire, and the gilding blazed suddenly like a signal flare into a sky deepening to cobalt.

The cab rounded into St. Isaac's Square and pulled up to the Astoria Hotel. The building was one of Saint Petersburg's most res-onant. The last word in early twentieth-century glamour, the Asto-ria was to Petersburg hotels what the *Mauretania* had been to ocean liners. It was a symbol of all that was modern, beautiful, and luxurious in 1910. The glamour of the Astoria lingered on far after the fall of the empire. Hitler had planned to have his victory dinner there, but even though he printed the menus, he never got anywhere near the beautiful dining room of the Astoria.

Sasha stepped out of the car, and the smell of the Saint Petersburg winter hit him: cold, wet air, tinged with the specific and acrid scent of salt on granite. A chill seeped up from the ground, like fingers reaching through the soles of his English shoes. It struck him with a cold that he already knew could be dulled only by vodka or, perhaps, by brandy. Sasha paid the driver and entered the warm hotel.

The lobby looked like the stage set of a Merchant Ivory film. The long mahogany check-in desk gleamed, and the grand lobby was full of Russian neoclassical furniture in birch. Palms sat in Chinese pots on the mosaic-tiled floor, and flower arrangements adorned the tables. The sound of a harp echoed through the white halls, and guests sat in groups, drinking tea, coffee, and Champagne. Clusters of young waiters and waitresses hovered, smiling indulgently and conversing in dozens of languages. Sasha noted, however, that while in repose, the faces around him were more careworn than the management probably would have liked them to be. For despite the Astoria's worldly glamour and its veneer of Western European civility, Saint Petersburg was still a difficult place to live, and all the smiles in the world could not wipe that from the faces of the hotel's Russian employees.

Sasha approached the desk, where he was greeted in fluent English by an extraordinarily pretty young woman.

"Good evening, Mr. Ozerovsky."

Sasha smiled.

"We hope your stay will be a pleasant one. You are in suite six eighteen, facing the cathedral. We hope that you enjoy it."

"I'm afraid there must be some mistake. I didn't reserve a suite, and I certainly can't afford one."

The young woman scrolled through the information on her computer screen.

"Your reservations were changed by our office in Moscow. Last week, we were instructed to upgrade you to a suite and to disregard your credit information in favor of a corporate account from Mosdikoil. Do you work for this company?"

"I do not. There must be some mistake."

"Well, why don't we send you up to suite six eighteen, and we'll try to sort all of this out. My name is Yelena, and if you have any questions, please call me here. I will let you know what I discover. As far as the hotel is concerned, the room is yours and is already paid for. If there is some misunderstanding, we will adjust the rate to that of the single room you reserved."

"Thank you, I appreciate it." Sasha reached for his bag, and noticed that it was already on a cart ready to go upstairs. He followed the young bellhop to the sixth floor; at the end of a long hall stood the door to his suite.

The bellhop opened it, and Sasha peered around inside. The rooms were large and graceful. Despite recent redecoration, the suite still had the air of a turn-of-the-century hotel. The room was full of antiques, including a large painted grand piano that, Sasha suspected, was original to the hotel. There was a small dining area, large living room, powder room, small hall, and an enormous adjoining bedroom and bath. The bellhop stood expectantly by the door.

"Thank you for your trouble," Sasha said, handing him several thousand roubles. The boy looked shocked that Sasha spoke Russian, smiled uncomfortably, and left. There was a large bouquet of flowers on the center table. Sasha went to see if there was a card attached. There was. A heavy ivory envelope held an equally weighty card that read: *Until Moscow. Please allow us to make your stay in Saint Petersburg as comfortable as possible. Fondest regards, Nadezhda and Ivan Dikarinsky.*

Dikarinsky. Mosdikoil. Moscow Dikarinsky Oil. Of course. Perhaps somehow Dimitri had arranged this. Sasha sat down in an over-upholstered chair and sighed. He picked up the phone and called Yelena at the front counter. There was obviously no mistake.

❖   ❖   ❖

At about eight o'clock the phone rang.

"Hello?" Sasha asked.

"Sasha. This is Nadezhda Dikarinsky. How are you?"

"Very well, thank you, and very surprised. I can't allow you to—"

"Nonsense, nonsense. The suite is very inexpensive. My husband's company does great business with the Astoria. They were happy to do us the favor. The room isn't costing us a rouble, or you either. We are happy to take care of the rest for you. We arranged to have dinner delivered for you, and we're sending up some liquor so you may have people over. Those little bottles of vodka are for airplanes. Have a real drink, and get some sleep. When you arrive at the airport in Moscow, our driver will pick you up and bring you to the house. In Moscow, you are our guest."

"I'm actually taking the overnight train. Madame Dikarinsky, I simply don't know what to say."

"Please, call me Nadezhda. Don't even say thank you. Just tell all of your fancy relatives that Russian hospitality didn't die under communism. The train? They're terribly dangerous. I'll send bodyguards for you. See you on Friday next, then. Our driver will pick you up at the station."

Sasha tried to protest some more, but finally said good-bye and hung up the phone. The doorbell rang. He went to open it and before him stood another bellhop with a drinks cart laden with bottles. Vodka, scotch, rum, gin, Champagne, and red and white wines, all French. And brandy (Louis XIII, Sasha noted, and $3,000 a bottle on the room service menu) and grappa. There was no way he would ever open even half of these bottles. He tipped the bellhop who, he noticed, eyed the tray. Sasha had a feeling that what he didn't drink would be disseminated in short order on a secondary market.

As the bellhop left, the phone rang again. It was Gennady.

"Such luxury! In a suite, I hear."

"Please don't tease me. This is really embarrassing. It's all being paid for by Mosdikoil."

"They can pay for me to stay at the Astoria anytime they feel like it." Gennady laughed. "Listen. Why don't we meet tomorrow. You must be exhausted from your trip, and you need your wits about you tomorrow. We're going to the archives."

"Fine. I need to know, Gennady—just for myself, you understand, where Snegurochka was between 1918 and the day it showed up on my doorstep. There are too many things about what we've discovered that make me uneasy. I am tired. I think I will take a bath, have a drink, and go to bed early."

"Welcome home, Sasha. Good night."

Sasha hung up the phone and went to the bedroom. He turned on the TV and flipped from channel to channel. The Russian news was loudly trumpeting a massive defeat of Chechen rebels near Grozny. Victory over the breakaway republic was not certain, said the announcer, but was closer. No Russian lives had been lost.

Sasha changed channels.

CNN announced that the Russians had made an attack on Grozny, killing dozens of people in a public market that had opened for the first time in weeks. The attack had made no impact on the status of the conflict, asserted Christiane Amanpour. Sasha turned off the television and went to the bathroom to start a bath. The floor was heated. There was a basket of bubble bath near the tub. Sasha turned the water on and threw some in. Taking off his clothes, and pulling on the voluminous bathrobe he found behind the door, Sasha crossed the bedroom and opened the curtains.

St. Isaac's Square spilled out below him. An equestrian statue of Nicholas I faced the City Hall, which had been built as a palace for his daughter. The cathedral, floodlighted, sat to his right, its gilded domes glowing. The original gold had been paid for by the sale of Alaska to the United States. At each corner, sculptures of archangels bowed toward enormous censers, which had once blazed with fire fed by hidden gas tanks but now sat lifeless atop the building. Sasha looked at the city before him and worried. He worried about his job, his father, the figurine; he even worried about Victoria. Sasha opened the double windows to let in the freezing-cold air, and as he looked toward the cathedral, an old woman in the square began to sing a Russian folk song, brandishing a hat and urging passersby to give her some money. Sasha could just make out the words.

> *Homewards toward me quickly run*
> *My darling Kolya mine.*
> *Don't play or tarry, darling,*
> *I wait for you to come to me*
> *On those light-winged shoes of yours*
> *Those light-winged shoes that*
> *will bring you home to me.*

The song struck Sasha as sad, and suddenly, as he leaned on the window frame watching the old woman in the square, listening to her sing, Sasha wished someone was there with him. He wanted not to be alone with a longing so intense that it made him catch his breath. He closed his eyes and leaned his forehead against the cold glass of the windowpane.

Thirteen

SASHA RANG THE BUZZER of the archives in Saint Petersburg. The building was an unassuming one in a largely residential neighborhood off one of the smaller canals. The building's exterior was neoclassical, but as he walked in, he realized that it had been reconstructed after the war. The interior was low-ceilinged and punctuated with bare bulbs. The staircases were peppered with signs that read in Russian CAUTION! because of the dangling wires, dim lighting, and missing handrails. As Sasha climbed to the top floor he smelled the unmistakable scent of every Russian library he had ever entered: old paper, musty air, smoky tea.

"You're late," Gennady said in Russian as he rose to meet him, "Lyudmila Arkadyevna, could you find some tea for Sasha?" The smiling woman left the room to get him a glass.

"Am I late? I'm sorry. I got a little lost. I walked from the Astoria."

"You're crazy. A bus would have been easier."

"I've never figured out the buses in Saint Petersburg. They're too confusing."

"Tourist. We'll take care of that. Let me show you what I've been working on." Gennady brought Sasha over to a large table, where a number of piles of papers were arranged.

"After the Revolution, the files of Fabergé were all confiscated and broken up. Instead of being organized by inventory numbers, which would have made life easier for us, they were organized by purchaser."

"Why?"

"It made confiscation of jewelry and precious objects easier after the Revolution. The Bolsheviks already had inventories of what people owned."

"I see."

"However, when there were ancillary charges—for example, if a piece was sent out to be finished, or if stone was purchased outside the House of Fabergé—they went on an internal bill. These bills are very valuable to us, because they often lead us to unknown craftsmen, sketches that have been misfiled, and information we would not have otherwise. I found the bill that was sent to your great-great-grandfather for the figurine, but last week, right after I spoke to you, I found the internal bill. Here it is." He handed the sheet to Sasha.

Sasha looked at the paper in his hand:

> For the occasion of the anniversary of H.E. Prince Oleg Ozerovsky and his wife, Princess Cecile Ozerovsky, which takes place this December, the amount of 2,575 roubles has been paid by his Excellency's father in the form of the following expenses:
>
> Payment due to the artist Benois for the execution of the technical drawings.   roub.   250
>
> Payment due the studios of the workmaster Henrik Wigström for finishing of the stonework and metalwork.
>
> roub.   2,325
>
> Consequently, the total is 2,575 roubles. I urge payment to Benois and Wigström, as full payment was received from H.E. Prince Ozerovsky.

Sasha looked up at Gennady.

"So, what do we do with this information?" he asked.

"So, we go through these three piles and we look for sketches from those workshops to see if we can find anything related to the figurine. One is full of information from the Benois studios, one is what is left of the Wigström archives, and the last are bills from various German hard-stone suppliers. I'll go through the bills to find anything related to Snegurochka."

Lyudmila Arkadyevna returned with the two glasses of tea and set them beside the two men before returning to her desk, which, Sasha noted, was covered with scraps of paper written in an ancient ecclesiastical script he couldn't read.

"Here we go!" Sasha said, and pulled the pile of Benois information toward him.

Systematically, he went through the pile, separating the hundreds of documents. Soon, among the sketches, he saw dozens of brief sketches that he knew to be related to the figurine: sketches of hands, facial expressions, the swirl of her skirt. Whole pages with embroidery patterns of the Ryazan region. A blonde version of the figurine, half melted into a lump of snow made of rock crystal. They were ephemeral watercolors that would be materialized in stone. Many of them had written notes from Fabergé's son Agathon, or Fabergé himself: "No. AF." "Yes. KF."

Sasha moved through the stack with increasing speed. He noticed details from other pieces he had seen in his career at Leighton's. He began taking notes. Sketches for frames that clients he knew owned. He had had no idea that Benois had done so much work for Fabergé. He knew Benois as an architect, and soon, he began seeing sketches of a building he recognized. He placed them together in a separate pile once he realized what they were: preparatory studies for the enamel plaque on the nephrite box his mother had given Gloria Greer.

Then he came upon a series of plastic folders that were empty. He looked up at the clock. Had he really been sitting there for three hours? His tea was gone; six neat piles lay around him. His notebook was full of information he barely remembered writing. He was exhausted, and his head ached.

"Gennady. I have to stop. My head is splitting open."

"You made short work of that stack. There was a half an hour where you were working so fast, I couldn't believe you were actually seeing the papers in front of you."

"I get that way when I work. Gennady, why are all these folders empty?"

"I can answer that," said Lyudmila Arkadyevna. She joined them at the table where they worked. "About six months ago, we had a theft here. Several things went missing. Some of Benois's sketches, some Fabergé bills, and a huge, uncataloged file of photographs from the 1920s of objects confiscated from Saint Petersburg safe deposit boxes. We have no idea why they were taken. They also stole a copy of Audubon's *Birds of America*. A complete folio."

"But very valuable in the States," Sasha replied. "Seven to eight million dollars."

"But the Benois sketches were worthless to anyone but Russian art scholars. Some of them were ceiling treatments for palace renovations, some animal sketches probably for silver sculptures. A strange choice. The police will find them eventually, we hope. The loss was reported to Interpol."

Sasha sighed. These libraries were so vulnerable, and their resources were so precious.

"Do you have the catalogue entries for what was stolen?"

"No. Everything was in the head of the librarian for the division."

"May I speak to him?"

Lyudmila Arkadyevna crossed herself quickly.

"No. He was murdered in Moscow six months ago. It was a tragedy. Some bankers were killed in a restaurant. He just happened to be in the way."

Sasha closed his eyes and sighed. Moscow was still so dangerous. He didn't even want to go anymore.

"Is there anyone who remembers what the photographs were of?"

"I could ask Tatiana Yermolov. She was doing some research for an American in the files not too long ago. She might have seen them, and it's possible that she remembers."

"I hope so," Sasha replied. "She's our only chance of finding them if they come up for sale in the West."

She crossed herself again and returned back to her desk. Sasha followed her.

"What are you researching?" he asked.

"Akathists. These are eleventh century. I'm doing work for the synod of bishops."

"Anything new?"

"There are some beautiful prayers. It makes the work easier to complete them."

"What do you mean complete them?" he asked.

She looked at him blankly. "They're in pieces. The fascists destroyed them at Novgorod. The shreds were used to pack silver they were taking back to Germany. The silver was recovered in the 1940s, and the shreds were saved. I've been piecing them together for the past twelve years. Much is lost."

"What have you pieced together?"

"Today?" She smiled. "Forgive the wicked, for they are loved by God and his saints and will be redeemed. Forgive the merciless for they shall one day be powerless before the hand of God. Forgive the guilty . . ."

"Why should we forgive the guilty?" Sasha asked.

"Ask the Germans. They have the missing piece."

"I think we all know what the missing piece says," Gennady said gently. "Whether the Nazis destroyed it or not—it is not really lost. We all know that only God can judge the guilty. Remember the dedication of *Anna Karenina*? 'Vengeance is mine, saith the Lord, I shall repay.'"

"I do wish that we had the missing piece to this Fabergé puzzle," Sasha confided.

Gennady smiled. "Don't worry about that too much. You still have the archives to go through in Moscow. There is plenty there, and I know of a jeweler named Orlovsky in Moscow who has been buying Fabergé sketches in the West. He may have something."

"I hope so," Sasha said.

Several more hours passed as Sasha and Gennady went through other files. There was nothing else on Snegurochka.

Just as he was putting the file away, Lyudmila Arkadyevna approached them, leading a petite and scholarly-looking woman.

"Sasha, this is Tatiana Yermolov. She was the librarian in charge of the leaves that were lost."

"It was a tragedy for Fabergé scholars," Madame Yermolov said in a quiet voice. "There were a great many studies and sketches. Some of the pieces were identifiable; most were not. There were sketches of hard-stone flower arrangements predominantly, but also some figures for silver pieces, and some small *objets de vertu*."

"Anything you remember specifically?"

"A pretty lapis box with ropes for borders, maybe a naval gift. Also an arrangement of sweet peas done in enamel. There was only one page saved. Here it is." She handed him a sheet of paper that was covered in small watercolor sketches. One in particular struck his attention; it was a plait of hair tied with a red ribbon. He heard Lydia Crane's voice in his head *"The hair bow has been reenameled. When I last saw it, it was matte red opaque enamel. Very unusual. Not guilloche like this. It must have been replaced."*

Sasha looked carefully at the bow. This must have been the original sketch. Sasha looked closely at the illustration. It was different. Not just the enamel, but the whole shape of the bow and the plait itself. Whereas Snegurochka's hair hung straight down her back with the guilloche bow at the bottom, in this drawing the ribbon was woven into the braid itself, in the manner of Russian peasant women. Sasha began trying to justify the difference. There could be any number of possible reasons. It may have been technically difficult and thus abandoned. Then again, the whole plait may have been replaced at some point, though Sasha doubted it.

"Sashenka? Are you all right? You seem confused."

"I'm fine, Gennady. Madame Yermolov, may I have a photocopy of this corner?"

"It is against library administrative procedure to copy something like this for a foreigner without permission. I will have to receive written authority from the director."

"Tatiana," coaxed Lyudmila, "you can make a copy for any of your superiors, can you not?"

Tatiana nodded.

"Then, would you make me a copy? I'd like one for my report on the theft."

Tatiana smiled and went off to the photocopier.

"As you see, Sasha, we never break the rules. We simply must allow ourselves to be flexible. I'm so sorry that I am always asking Tatiana for copies. I just can never seem to remember where I put anything these days." Tatiana returned and gave the copy to Lyudmila, who ostentatiously left it on the corner of her desk.

"And now, we really must be going. I'm leaving for the day, and I know that poor Tatiana here has had too much excitement for one afternoon. Gennady, my dear, please let yourself out. Don't worry about the lights. They will shut off automatically after you lock the door." With that, the two women left.

Gennady began gathering his things. "Don't forget the copy," he said. "That was quite a gift she gave you just then. They could lose their positions over something like that."

Sasha picked up the dark copy and placed it in his notebook. There was much to think about before he had his dinner with Gennady and his wife.

"I think that I will go back to the Astoria and lie down," Sasha said to Gennady. "Would you like to come to the Astoria for dinner, or are you serious about having me over?"

"I'll kill you for doubting our hospitality. We will see you at the flat at eight o'clock."

❖   ❖   ❖

Gennady and his wife, Leonida, lived on Krestovsky Island, facing the Gulf of Finland. The island had once been the personal property of a prince's family, and the home of the Saint Petersburg Yacht Club. The palaces and clubhouses had been largely destroyed during the siege of Leningrad. After the war, an athletic stadium replaced the various buildings, and so the island had largely retained its recreational character. Though the small Chapel of St. John still stood where it had been erected by the exiled knights of Malta in the early nineteenth century, there were largely only blocks of flats where lucky academics and party members had lived until 1991. Gennady and Leonida had been able to keep the apartment where they lived with their son, Ivan, their daughter, Natalia, and their dog, Mutzi.

Sasha climbed the steps to the third floor, where Gennady and Leonida lived. Tucked under his arm were two bottles of French red wine and the expensive bottle of brandy from the bar in his room. *They have been paid for, after all,* he thought.

"Sasha! Welcome!" Leonida said, kissing him as he passed over the threshold of the apartment. "It has been so long since we saw you last. Two years? Can it be? Come in, come in, and give me those heavy bags." Sasha smiled at her. Leonida was from Tbilisi, and had all of the ebullience and hospitality associated with Georgians. She was quick to anger, yet equally quick to forgive and laugh. She was a physicist, and also played the harp at near concert level. Sasha gave her a warm embrace, walked in, and looked around.

The apartment was small, but very tidy and well maintained in comparison to so many others he had seen in Saint Petersburg. The room was wallpapered in a large brown-and-white pattern; the worn but good-looking Russian 1970s-style upholstered furniture was well placed. A few antique pieces were scattered here and there, and above the sofa was the prize piece: a large abstract painting by Yevgenii Rukhov, an important dissident painter of the 1970s. The painting was largely red, and stood out strongly against the bourgeois decoration.

"It takes the breath away, doesn't it?" Gennady said, stepping out of the kitchen and clapping him on the shoulder.

"Intense," Sasha agreed. "But where are Vanya and Natalia?"

"School in London still, thanks to God," said Leonida. "The money Leighton's paid Gennady was enough for us to send them over for one semester. They worked very hard while they were there, and now are each on full scholarship. Natalia just finished her examinations, and she got an amazing score, particularly since English is her third language, after Russian and Georgian. We expect her to end up at Cambridge, and then to come back home and do her graduate work in Moscow." Leonida spoke modestly, but Sasha could hear how proud she was of her daughter's hard work and success.

"She is also, I might add, even more beautiful than her mother was at that age," Gennady teased. Leonida threw a spoon at him from across the room, making them all laugh.

"I hate to admit it," she said, "but he's right. She looks just like my mother did before the war. She is ravishing—despite the fact that she's half Russian."

Gennady smiled at the gentle jibe.

"And Vanya?" Sasha asked. "Also a success?"

"The devil incarnate," Leonida responded. "I don't know how he makes his grades and still manages to do so well on the piano."

"He's his old man's son, that is for certain," Gennady said with a smile.

"Between the girls and the nights in London, I don't know how I'll keep from strangling him. He did win his school's piano competition, though, with a very difficult piece by Stravinsky. He'll be the death of me," she concluded with a smile of triumph. "Now all I have left is this lazy husband, and a starving dog. Woe is me!"

The three of them fell into the easy conversation, which had always been their pattern. They skipped quickly and passionately over many topics: recent advances in science, art, politics; tentative discussions of religion; scandalous and frankly libelous talk of politicians and public figures in Russia. The French red was opened, and soon the three were at dinner, enjoying Leonida's Georgian lamb, delicately seasoned with cinnamon, cumin, and a scattering of pomegranate seeds and lemon rind in the sauce. There were cold salads and spicy side dishes of vegetables. Sasha ate and ate until there was nothing left, mostly because it was delicious, but knowing as well that if he did not, Leonida would be deeply offended.

After dinner, Sasha opened the brandy, and they all sat together quietly, looking out the window at the streets below and the glittering gulf.

"So, tomorrow—Moscow," Gennady said. "Are you looking forward to it?"

"Not really. I have to stay with these horrible oligarchs called the Dikarinskys, and I'm worried about what will happen at the viewing of Snegurochka. The more I think about our time in the archives, the more I keep coming to one very frightening possibility."

"And what is that?"

"That there's some connection between the stolen drawings and the figurine."

"But, why on earth? How can you think so?"

"It's a feeling. There are too many coincidences."

"Sasha, don't be silly. You needn't find a snake in the grass, just because—"

Sasha went pale. That was it: the phrase "snake in the grass." Tatiana had mentioned it at the archives. In the stolen drawings, she had said, was the sketch of a lapis box, possibly a naval gift, its edges wrapped with ropes.

They weren't ropes; they were *snakes*.

The snakes that coiled around the lapis box that sat in Gloria Greer's apartment in Hampshire House. The box Dimitri had sold to her from the Dikarinskys' collection.

Sasha turned to Gennady and Leonida, his eyes widening as he continued to make the connections. The missing drawing was of the piece in Gloria's house. Someone was stealing the drawings to create forgeries.

"Sasha," Gennady said, "are you all right? You look like you have seen a ghost!"

Oh God, Sasha thought, putting a bit more of it together. *There were drawings of Snegurochka in the file that was stolen. One of the drawings of the figurine which was left behind was of the braid. The braid is the only part of the figurine that doesn't match Lydia's memory of the original. But the figurine is made of purpurine. Long ago, Mama said that only Fabergé could make purpurine, and now no one could. How on earth was it possible?* Sasha didn't know how, but deep inside, he knew it was so.

Sasha looked up—he was certain he was right. "Snegurochka is a forgery."

"You're mad. Why on earth?" said Leonida.

"No, seriously. I'm in terrible trouble, and I can't quite figure it out," Sasha said.

"Let's go for a walk," Gennady said. "You need some air."

The three left the building and walked toward the quay. Though it was cold, and they could hear the grating sound of the ice against the stone, the wind from the gulf was mild, and so the cold was not so biting.

"Sashenka," Leonida said. "What on earth makes you think the figurine is a forgery? Who could carry such a thing off?"

"There are just too many holes in this story. First, in the archives, the drawings are stolen. The librarian is murdered. Months later, I visit a collection in New York where they have recently acquired a piece from Russia that I think is a fake."

"So?" Gennady asked.

"So," Sasha continued, "one of the stolen drawings is of that same piece."

"I see," Leonida said.

"Second," Sasha continued, "in the same file are all of the original Benois sketches for Snegurochka, *except* rejected versions and one sketch left behind—the drawing of her braid. The braid is the one part of the figurine, the only part, that does not match Lydia Crane's memory of the piece when she saw it as a girl."

"Sasha," Gennady said, "I'm afraid that you may have something here."

"I know," Sasha said. "There is only one thing I can't reconcile. Snegurochka's caftan and Kokoshnik are made of purpurine. Only Fabergé could make purpurine, and now the secret is lost. How could the figurine be a fake?"

Gennady stopped walking. "What on earth makes you say that?"

Sasha turned to look at him. "My mother taught me that when I was a little boy. It's common knowledge."

Gennady shook his head. "Perhaps in the West, twenty years ago people thought that, but now we know that isn't true. Other people besides Fabergé used purpurine. Britzin, for one. And who knows if people can make it now? Sasha, think of the advances in chemistry in the last eighty years. Do you honestly think that the recipe for a colored glass is lost forever? What nonsense!"

Sasha closed his eyes. Gennady was absolutely right. "So, it is true. Someone stole the drawings and photographic references because somewhere there is a workshop of extraordinarily talented jewelers making copies of lost pieces from original documents. The forgeries appear, and when we search to authenticate them, we find real bills, we find real references to the pieces, and we congratulate ourselves as scholars for finding the ultimate treasure: a fully documented lost piece."

"But the piece is actually a fake," Leonida finished. "Sasha, who do you think is responsible?"

"Dimitri sold the compact to Gloria Greer in New York, but he's small time. There's no way he could create a forgery of that caliber. He doesn't know enough, and I doubt he has access to such highly trained artists. But the piece he sold to Gloria came from the Dikarinsky Collection. Dikarinsky, with his money and connections, could certainly manage it—he'd have access to international jewelers, precious metals and stones, and a top-notch lab that could whip up a batch of purpurine. Either Dikarinsky is backing a circle of forgers, or he's being used by them, and Dimitri and I are supposed to be unwitting accomplices. They got away with the lapis compact, and now they are trying their hand at something larger, more audacious, and more public: Snegurochka."

Leonida grabbed Gennady's hand. "Gennady, I think that Sasha's right. There are too many coincidences. We must be very careful in Moscow."

"Well, as far as we know, they don't give a fig for me. I've only done legitimate research on the piece, which has helped them. If Sasha begins making accusations, they will be very bothered indeed. Sasha, I think your best bet is to stay as close to the snake's head as possible, and to play dumb. Keep your head low, and when we are in Moscow, I will ask a friend at the archives to see if we can get a list of all of the drawings that have been stolen recently, as well as a list of lost pieces that they may know of. It just might end up being a list of things that will start appearing on the market. You will need to be aware of them."

"This could destroy the whole market for Fabergé in the West. This is a disaster. I'm not sure I'm up to this," he replied.

Leonida stopped and put her hands on Sasha's shoulders.

"Sasha, we have known you for a long time, and we have watched you become a better scholar and a more decent man than many in your field. Forgive me for bringing God into this, but God never gives us more than we may bear."

Gennady added, "It's only Fabergé, Sasha. This isn't about stopping a drug cartel or thermonuclear war. We'll help you."

Sasha looked at the couple with affection. "Let's go back to the apartment and have another brandy. Tomorrow night, I leave for Moscow."

Fourteen

~

SASHA HAD PACKED and checked out of the Astoria before noon. The train wasn't due to leave until nine that evening, and so he had visited the Hermitage to pass the time. A stroll on the Nevsky Prospect brought him without thinking to his family's former palace. Standing on the opposite side of the Moika Canal, Sasha admired the rhythmic facade. Long and low-slung, the canary yellow structure had a string of cream-colored ionic pilasters that created an illusion of height for the rather short three-story building. The capitals and ornamentation on the facade had been brightly gilded. It was a restoration error: Sasha knew that they had originally been painted to resemble bronze. The facade gave no hint of the palace's most interesting secret: There was an interior courtyard that passed uninterrupted through the entire block, resulting in long interior galleries and a massive private garden—the facade was merely the short end of an enormous rectangle. Sasha had seen photographs of the house over the years, and he decided to see if he could finally get inside.

Approaching the vestibule, the illusion of restoration began to crumble. Though freshly painted, the building's plaster face was badly cracked, and many of the wooden framed windows were rotting. On the second floor, whole panes of glass were missing and were blocked with plywood painted black. He pushed open the iron-and-glass front door grille and stepped inside.

Though the marble floors were cracked and filthy, and the treads were worn shallow from two centuries of use, the proportions of the twelve-sided hall were beautiful. The walls were a pale oyster grey, and the plaster decoration was picked out in white. Around the ceiling ran a carved marble frieze separated by paterae, each panel showing a scene of dancing naiads. Each wall was adorned with a different sign of the zodiac—a touch of his great-great-great-grandfather's, who had been a founder of the Imperial Society of Astronomers. Sasha climbed the stairs and passed into the stair hall, where a ticket seller sat waiting behind a flimsy card table.

"There are no more tours today," the old woman said with irritation. "You must return tomorrow, between eleven and four."

"I am sorry," Sasha said, "but I will not be in Saint Petersburg tomorrow. I leave for Moscow tonight. Is there any way I might look at the first floor?"

"Impossible," the woman said firmly, picking up her cashbox and standing to face him. Sasha turned up the charm and stretched his hands out to her, palms up.

"Grandmother, I have come all the way from the United States. I am a student of Russian culture, and I had hoped to see this building especially. It is so little known, and so much finer than so many other more famous buildings. . . ."

"Well, you're right about that," she said eagerly, taking Sasha's bait. Sasha knew that she spent most of the day giving tours to tourists who would have preferred to see the more famous Yusupoff or Stroganoff Palaces. "This building is a national treasure. I could show it to you if only I didn't need to go to the market right now. . . ." Sasha recognized the opportunity for a bribe immediately.

"Well, Grandmother, I wouldn't take too much of your time. I would be happy to make a donation for restoration, and, if you are going to the market, I'd be happy to give you a little extra to buy tea for the curators and staff of the house. . . ."

The bribe was very graceful. Sasha knew every penny he gave her would go directly into her pocket, and as far as he was concerned, the poor woman could have it.

"That's very kind of you, young man. I'm happy to show you the first floor—the third floor is ruined anyway. The fascists blew the roof off in the siege. You speak good clear Russian, by the way. You almost sound like a real Russian, if it weren't for that French accent." Pulling herself up to her full height of about five feet, she began the memorized tour in the declamatory style that marked all former Intourist guides. As she spoke, Sasha realized that though communism had fallen, the text of the tour remained intact.

"Welcome to the People's Artistic Center of the Central District. This building in the neoclassical style was built in 1825 by Sergei Ozerovsky, a general in the war of 1812, and a confidant of Alexander I. You are now standing in the stair hall. It is estimated that it took ten Russian laborers over a year to carve the marble-work friezes, and an estimated two tons of marble to finish the impressive staircase. Notice the ceiling, painted with portraits of the family, and notice the floors made with Siberian marble."

She was, of course, only partially correct, Sasha knew. The house had originally been built in 1780 to designs by Thomas de Thomon, a French architect who had been working for Catherine the Great. It had been substantially remodeled in 1820, and again in the 1850s. Sasha knew from his grandfather that his ancestor Sergei had bought the marble frieze of the naiads while on the grand tour in Italy. They had been created for an English lord who had gone bankrupt, and so Prince Sergei had acquired them from the frantic Italian sculptor at a fraction of the price. The stair hall had been completely remodeled in 1820 to accommodate them. The ceiling was an allegory of honor triumphant over time, and the marble was *Bleu Turquin*, purchased on the same trip to Italy.

"You will follow me into the Hall of War." The two of them walked through vast doors into an oblong room. The walls were divided into large rectangles by deep brown sienna marble pilasters with gilt bronze capitals. The room was lighted by large sconces, each with a masque of the goddess Athena.

"This is where the general planned his great attack on Napoleon before he joined the Russian army forces at Borodino. The walls once hung with large paintings of the battle, but they were taken and hidden during the Great Patriotic War, and were stolen by the fascists. The artists of the State Russian Museum will one day paint copies to take their place from documentary photographs that are in their possession. This is also the room in which Lenin signed the documents that made this and all other nationalized properties the possessions of the Russian people. Notice the ceiling, and notice the floor, which is made of over fifty exotic hardwoods."

Sasha looked at the room. Though the guide was quite correct about the lost paintings, she was mistaken about everything else. This was the first reception room where guests were received, and where, in addition to the paintings of Borodino, all the family portraits had hung. In this room had been portraits by Borovikovsky, Levitsky, Roslin, Vigée-Lebrun, and later portraits by Repin and Serov. Sergei had not planned the attack on Borodino in this room—he had done so in the field. This was merely the room that commemorated it, and in which the family had held receptions and received guests. It was here that Sasha's great-grandmother had shown the Empress their collections before the famous tea.

"You will now follow me to the Blue Salon. The Blue Salon was the main reception room and where much of the painting collection was hung, and where the famous Sèvres porcelain collection was displayed. Notice the ceiling; notice the floor."

Sasha was dismayed by the condition of the room. The walls were of Louis XVI boiseries, which had been partially ordered from Paris, then copied in Saint Petersburg to fill the room. A long wall was lined with windows onto the private garden, and the opposite wall had been lined with mirrors. Now, painted plywood filled the spaces where the glass had been. Originally, this room had been a marvel. On each mirror, a half chandelier had hung. When the mirrors reflected the opposite windows and the half chandelier, the illusion was that one was standing in an arcaded ballroom with a central colonnade. Recently put up, cheap sateen curtains in a vibrant blue hung from every window. The original damask, Sasha recalled, had been woven in Tours, and had been a pale turquoise, decorated with griffons and arabesques. It had been rewoven in the 1890s by the same firm that had made it originally. The firm was still open, and Sasha hoped one day to be able to afford even one yard for pillows. Sasha could imagine the day when his great-grandmother had entertained the Empress in this very hall, his young grandfather clicking his camera.

"The next hall is the Dining Hall. This is where lavish banquets and entertainments were held. Dozens of servants were required to serve the lavish meals. In an attempt to swell the rising tide of anger over the foreign pretensions of the nobles, in the 1880s the Dining Hall was rebuilt in the Russian folk style, to emphasize this family's origins in the province of Ryazan."

Sasha cringed as he entered the Slavic revival room. What beautiful French or Italian style room had been destroyed for this? The walls were rough planking, and the ceiling gave the appearance of a joined Russian *isba*, or peasant cottage. Hanging from the ceiling were three iron and gilded chandeliers so massive that Sasha could not believe the ceiling could support their weight.

"How do they stay up?" he asked. "They must each weigh a ton."

"They are made of papier-mâché. The family was running out of money," the guide said, smiling with glee.

A library, a Gothic ballroom, large salons, small salons, a room for samples of rare rocks and gems, a private theater, a private chapel, a music room, and finally, a tiny study, the walls of which were covered in tortoiseshell and Japanese lacquer, completed the tour of the palace.

"This is the last room of the tour, and in it, portraits of the last owners of the house. They are typical decadents."

Sasha looked at the pictures on the wall. There was a large portrait of his great-grandfather in his Life Guardsmen's uniform; and on the opposite wall was a painting of his great-grandmother

Cecile. On her lap, a Pekinese wrestled for space with Sasha's grandfather, perhaps a year old.

"I can't say I care much for the paintings," the guide said, "but I do like the looks of that baby—seems like a decent kid."

"Oh, he is still quite decent," Sasha replied. "He is my grandfather."

The guide's eyes widened in astonishment. Sasha handed her $50 in roubles, and she thanked him effusively as she showed him back through the stair hall and the vestibule again.

"Come again! You are always welcome, Your Excellency . . . Your Highness . . . Prince, or whatever you are now."

Sasha turned to leave, smiling. Whatever you are now. That was rich. Then he paused. "Would you mind terribly if I asked you for a favor?"

"Not at all, sir—what can I do?"

"Would you let me into the courtyard for a minute?"

"Certainly, sir. There are plans to restore the garden after they remove the car park."

Sasha walked out into the courtyard. In the center stood a tree stump, and the asphalt cut a wide swath around it.

"That was a beautiful tree when I was a girl," the woman said. "It was cut down during the siege for firewood. We cried when we did it. The tree was almost a hundred fifty years old, even then."

Sasha smiled, then knelt down. Pulling an envelope out of his pocket, he began scratching at the earth, and putting the soil into the envelope with his ungloved fingers.

"What are you doing?" the woman asked.

Sasha looked up at her. "Grandmother, my own grandfather left Russia when he was eight years old, and has lived away from here ever since. He is now ninety-six years old, and will not live forever. When he dies, I want to make sure that he is buried in Russian soil from his own home."

The woman looked at him in shock. "You wait right here. I will be right back," she said, disappearing quickly into the old palace. Soon she came back with several other ladies and an old man carrying a trowel. She explained to him quickly that they all worked at the palace together. One of the women had been on the restoration group who had reassembled that shattered entry hall after the siege. Another was a gilder who had been working at the palace since 1946, restoring the gilding on the ceilings. The old man, she explained, had been the foreman who oversaw the reconstruction of the floors. They had all lived in the palace and brought it back to life over the past sixty years. Sasha was very moved, and he greeted each one with kisses and an embrace.

The man pulled a large, empty tea tin out from his pocket; bending down, he used a small trowel to scoop some earth into the container. Handing the trowel to each of the women, they did as he had done. Finally he handed the trowel to Sasha, who did the same, filling the tin. He closed the lid and handed the trowel back.

"I cannot thank you enough. There was no need to disturb yourselves."

His guide smiled. "You come back, Your Highness. Next time, we will have more of the house restored. Bring your parents and your family. We need your help."

"You have my promise," Sasha said.

❖   ❖   ❖

As he walked back to the hotel to have a quick supper and pick up his bags before catching the train, Sasha realized that, moving though it was, the trip to the family house hadn't changed his problem: He was still going to Moscow and would have to try to behave normally.

Sasha walked to the hotel restaurant and let the maître d' know that he would be having an early dinner and would be catching the night train to Moscow. He stepped down into the white, barrel-vaulted glass-ceilinged room, and sat at a table for two set up by the tinkling fountain. In the corner, a Russian folk trio played quietly, their *balalaiki* buzzing like distant insects.

The menu came, and Sasha ordered *shchi*, fish consommé, followed by a roulade of veal with fresh cherries. Complimentary wine appeared, and as his eyes searched the restaurant for the giver, Sasha noted something odd: Two burly men stood by the door in dark suits. Obviously not hotel employees, the men seemed to be on easy terms with the staff of the restaurant, and they were brought glasses of tea as they stood in the reception area of the dining room. Had they sent the wine? Sasha couldn't tell, and he was losing his appetite. As he ate, Sasha became more and more anxious. The men were staring at him.

Forty minutes or so passed, and as he finished his meal, one of the men approached him quietly.

"Alexander Kirillovitch?" he asked politely.

"Yes, that is me," Sasha replied, standing up to greet the man. "May I help you?" Their exchange continued in Russian.

"Not at all. I will be helping you. I am Igor Vassilievitch, and my colleague is Mikhail Petrovitch. We work for the Dikarinsky family in Moscow as part of their security detail. Nadezhda Arkadyevna sent us instructions that we were to make certain that your travel to Moscow was both comfortable and safe. She was very concerned about your taking the train, and has sent the Mosdikoil car for your personal use. We will accompany you the entire way from the hotel to the Dikarinsky house in Moscow."

"That is very kind of Madame Dikarinsky, but certainly this is both expensive and unnecessary?"

"The security on the trains is not what it was under the Soviets. Foreigners have had trouble, and the trains are unreliable now. The Dikarinskys insist that you travel safely. The Mosdikoil car is bulletproof, and is separate from the common cars on the train. It is used when executives travel on business to the Siberian interior."

"They take a train into the interior?" Sasha asked, knowing that the journey to the oil fields could take weeks.

"Of course not. They fly, but the car is sent on ahead for them to live in—there are very rarely European-standard accommodations in Siberia." He smiled. "You will be safe and quite comfortable. We saw that you have checked out already—your luggage has been moved to the car, and we will escort you to the station and ride with you on the train."

Sasha found it all a bit disturbing. This was often the way people had once disappeared without a trace in Russia, but he knew he had to appear to trust the Dikarinskys completely.

"Well, thank you, Igor Vassilievitch. I am grateful to you and to the Dikarinskys. I leave myself in your hands."

With that, Igor put a hand lightly on Sasha's shoulder and guided him through the restaurant. As they approached the door, his partner fell into step with them. The two men began a graceful dance around him; Sasha noted that as they passed people in the corridor and the lobby, one of the men was always in front of him, preventing oncoming traffic from getting close to him, and the other was always just behind him, informing him of where he was going and reporting their progress to the waiting driver over a wireless headset. Strangely, it gave Sasha the illusion that he was moving through the crowd alone and of his own free will. He could tell the difference, though, by the alternately respectful and terrified looks of the people he passed as they registered the fact that he was accompanied by guards.

They left the hotel, and Sasha was guided to an unobtrusive black Mercedes. Not a stretch car, but larger than usual. He was hustled inside; Igor sat in the back with him, while Mikhail joined the driver. The car pulled away from the curb and began its journey to the train station.

The streets of Saint Petersburg were filled with people shopping on their way home from work. The buildings were brightly lit from inside, and Sasha kept looking back toward the Nevsky Prospect as the car approached the station.

"First time in Saint Petersburg?" Igor Vassilievitch asked.

"No," Sasha said, "I come often." He couldn't help looking though. Because of the way he had been brought up, every time he left a place he looked at it carefully and with great emotion, convinced that it might be the last time he saw it as it was. Given what he now knew about the Dikarinskys, it might well be his last trip to Peter's capital.

They pulled up to the station, and the dance began again. Sasha's bags were pushed ahead of them by an old porter. They approached the ticket and security check, and both Sasha and his entourage were whisked through. The weary-looking train sat on the platform, its pale blue paint worn and sad. The last car, however, was very different.

Though the shape of the car was similar, its windows were larger, darker, and the body was a shining deep cobalt blue. In the center of the car, a gold corporate monogram for Mosdikoil blazed out. The lights inside glowed softly from behind transparent curtains.

"Here you are, sir," Igor said smartly. "Step inside, and Masha will show you around. We are in a room at the opposite end of the car, if you need us." Sasha thanked him and stepped onto the train, where he was met by a remarkably beautiful young woman in a crisp uniform.

"Good evening, Your Highness. I am Maria Nikolaevna Varsanov, and I am the coordinator of travel for the Mosdikoil Corporation. I manage the security, plane, and ground travel arrangements for the executives and their families. If you would like, I am happy to show you around the Eagle, which is one of the nicest cars in our fleet. Madame Dikarinsky requested it especially for you."

Sasha looked around in awe. *Air Force One* had nothing on this, he was certain. The car was paneled in pale mahogany and lit by a series of sconces and chandeliers, most of them Lalique, Sasha noted. There was a small dining area, set for an evening tea with smoked meats, fish, and sweet pastries. The larger living area was fitted with banquettes, upholstered in a striped silk of garnet, sand, and gold. The windows were hung with the same fabric, and the walls were covered with Russian drawings and porcelain. A pair of doors at the far end of the room were closed.

"The doors at the end of the car lead to the three bedrooms, the bathroom, and the room in which the security guards and I will be during the journey. I am happy to get you anything you need at any point. You may stay back here alone, or if you like, I can remain with you to keep you company. I am completely able to make any arrangements you may require," she said in a voice heavy with suggestion. Sasha blushed and demurred.

"Thank you, no, Masha. I am quite self-sufficient. I might have a drink or some tea, but I will probably sleep early. It has been a long day, and I'm quite tired. I ate at the hotel. You needn't trouble yourself."

"Not at all," she said, smiling evenly. "A day in the Hermitage is tiring, and I am sure that your first visit to your family's home was emotional for you. I'll slip away then, and should you need anything, just hit any of the bell pushes, and I'll be right there." She turned and walked toward the far doors. As she reached them, she paused and turned again.

"Oh, and Prince, enjoy your stay on the Eagle. Everyone who travels on this car loves it. Sleep well." With that, she left the compartment. Sasha could hear her heels click down the passage, and then a door open, shut sharply, and lock with a snap.

Oh, God, Sasha thought. *I am a prisoner on this train, and the entire time I am in Moscow. I was followed every minute I was in Saint Petersburg—that is clear, since she knew that I was at the Hermitage, and at the old house. They will be monitoring all of my calls from this moment on, if they haven't been doing it all along. They know I went to the library, and they know whom I spoke to and what I saw there. They know I saw Gennady and Leonida. Everyone I met may be in danger, and I cannot call anyone with a warning. This trip to Moscow is going to have to be the performance of my life.*

Sasha walked calmly over to the tea table, knowing full well that he was probably also being watched on hidden security cameras. He picked up a small plate and piled it with smoked herring and a helping of *salat Olivier*. Moving to the table, he sat and picked at the fish, soaking up the cream sauce with a piece of black bread. He looked around for the bar. He needed a drink.

Sasha's eyes scanned the compartment. It was beautiful. He wondered who had built it for Dikarinsky and where the bar would be. There was a wall of cabinets, which, when opened, revealed books in every language, as well as periodicals. Moving back to the table, Sasha noticed a control panel. He touched one button, and the light levels lowered to a more romantic setting. He touched the same button, and they returned to normal. When he pressed another switch, a television set rose from an ottoman. Touching the last, he saw a cabinet on the other side of the car swing open, revealing glassware and neatly stacked bottles in individual silver plated holders. Sasha smiled despite himself. It was kind of like a James Bond movie, except that he really was in a lot of danger.

Sasha looked out the window. When had the train begun moving? He hadn't even noticed. He could see that snow had begun to fall quite heavily. He was exhausted. Sasha looked across the car toward the bar and decided against a drink. He pushed all the buttons and shut down the television, bar, and other accoutrements of the car, then went to his room.

The bedroom was every bit as beautiful as the rest of the car. The walls were paneled in birch, and highly varnished. The bed was large and comfortable looking. Sasha undressed and climbed into the bed, turning out the light. He fell asleep quickly, watching the city of Saint Petersburg recede into the distance.

❖   ❖   ❖

A clanging sound woke him. *Ching. Ching. Ching.*

Not a bell, but the sound of metal on metal. He sat up and peered out of the window. Snow was falling heavily, and it was impossible to see through the whirling white.

Lights glowed, and it was obvious the train had stopped. Sasha rang the bell push, and the voice of Masha floated into the cabin from a hidden speaker.

"Yes, Prince?"

"Is there a problem?"

"Not at all. We have stopped to de-ice the wheels. It is freezing weather outside, but we will be on our way again soon."

Sasha leaned back in bed. *Ching. Ching. Ching.* It was eerie, the sound. What made it worse was the fact that it was exactly what happened in *Anna Karenina*. In the book, of course, she throws herself under the train. Sasha put his head down on the pillow. No such drastic measures were required.

Not at this point, anyway.

Fifteen

IT WAS COLD AND BRIGHT when the train pulled into the Leningradsky Station in Moscow. Sasha had risen, showered in the small bathroom, and put on a suit and tie for his arrival at the Dikarinsky house. He walked into the salon, where Masha was waiting for him.

"I trust that you slept well," she said smiling.

"Yes, I did. Everything was quite comfortable."

"Well, under normal circumstances, we would give you breakfast here, and let you leave when you are ready, but it is nine and I know that Madame Dikarinsky has planned a luncheon reception for you at the house. You may have coffee or tea, but we really must get you going," she said brightly.

"I'm happy to go now, if you like. I'm certainly ready."

"Your bags are already in the car. May I show you there?"

"Fine. Let's go."

Sasha left the Eagle, and Masha followed him. As he stepped off the train onto the platform, he was overwhelmed by the number of people hurrying about the station. The Moscow station was large, yet it overflowed with people sprawling out from the platforms and descending into the metro stations for other points in the nation's capital.

The smell of Moscow was as different from Saint Petersburg as it could be: Moscow smelled of tobacco, diesel fuel, and a fierce cold that was not seasonal. Looking through the arches onto Komsomolskaya Ploshchad, Sasha could see that the snow was still falling from the night before. No one seemed to mind, though—Moscow refused to acknowledge any snow under a few inches.

Igor and Mikhail resumed their protective stance around Sasha and Masha, but Sasha recognized an acute difference this time. He felt very much at risk in the large open spaces of the Moscow station. There were too many groups of young people wandering around, too many drunks passed out in the corners, too many slick-looking types whom his grandfather would only have described as "hooligans."

They left the station, and Sasha followed Masha into a large, black Mercedes limousine. This stretch car accommodated not only Sasha and the Mosdikoil entourage, but also a television, large bar, and a small writing desk with laptop computer and telephone.

Sasha settled into the backseat. He had not been to Moscow since the late 1980s, and he was amazed to see how the city had changed.

Gorky Prospect was again Tverskaya, and the beautiful chapels of the Tverskaya Virgin destroyed by Stalin had been rebuilt. The Cathedral of the Virgin of Kazan on Red Square was reconstructed, and high on the hills over the River Moskva, the golden domes of the Cathedral of Christ the Redeemer rose over the city again, erasing the Stalinist swimming pool that had replaced it in the 1930s. An enormous and hideous sculpture of Peter the Great stood on the banks of the Moskva River, stretching his arm out over the city.

Over the doors of every government building, large double-headed eagles again stared down both sides of the street, their crowns precariously balanced. At the Kremlin, Sasha noticed the two things that surprised him most: the pre-revolutionary tricolor flew over the domes of the Great Kremlin Palace, despite the continued presence of red stars on all the towers. There was no line in front of Lenin's tomb.

The car moved slowly along the banks of the Moskva, and Sasha caught glimpses of children skating in the Alexander Gardens. Soon, the car wound toward the old south side of the Moskva River, toward the street known as the Bolshaya Ordynka.

The south side of Moscow had never been an aristocratic center of the city. It had been a home for the poor, and, in the late nineteenth century, for the upper bourgeoisie whose homes were largely in the Slavic Revival style, many of which had breathtaking views of the Kremlin for a century. Craftspeople and peasants sold their art and handcrafts along the sidewalks, but as the car slowly made its way through the pedestrian area, the crowds pulled back. The limo went deeper into the *pereuloki*, or lanes, that peppered the neighborhood, eventually exiting onto the Bolshaya Ordynka. On this broad street, there was a small and shuttered church, heavily covered with advertisements for nightclubs, a great convent that had been built by the Empress Alexandra's sister, Grand Duchess Elizabeth, and a series of Russian Art Nouveau– and Moderne-style apartment buildings. In the middle of the block, a pair of large gates, partially gilded.

"Is this it?" Sasha asked.

"Yes," replied Masha. "This is the Moscow House. It used to belong to a daughter of a famous sugar merchant. It was then a school for legal students. The Dikarinskys bought it two years ago. Its restoration is only just completed. It is widely considered the most beautiful of the private homes of Moscow."

Sasha looked up at the brick facade in the pan-Slavic style. The dark and dreary house was ornamented with stained glass, turrets, and majolica tiles in the style of ancient Moscow reinterpreted by the gilded age taste of 1880s Moscow. Half mansion, half ecclesiastical in appearance, it was a relic of commercial Moscow's golden age. Pulling up in front of the recently repaved forecourt, the great bronze-bound wooden doors opened, and Nadezhda Dikarinsky stepped out to greet Sasha.

"Sasha, my dear, welcome!" she said in English. "We are so pleased to have you in our home. We hope that your trip on the Eagle was comfortable—we tried to make certain that everything was up to your standards." She smiled pleasantly and held out her hand to him. "Come in, come in. It is freezing out here, and we have dozens of people coming for a luncheon in your honor. You'll want time to change and get ready."

Sasha followed her into the vast reception hall of the mansion. It was Alexandrine in taste—it was in the Gothic Revival style, and unlike the delicate eighteenth-century Gothic library at his family's former house in Saint Petersburg, this entry hall looked like one of King Ludwig of Bavaria's Wagnerian castles outside of Munich. Garnet-colored walls were stenciled with golden ciphers, which Sasha soon realized belonged to the Dikarinskys themselves.

"It cost millions to bring this all back, and to have all of the furniture restored and re-created. We are very proud. I'll give you a tour later. Now, please follow Irina; she will show you to your room."

Sasha followed the unhappy-looking maid, dressed in a black uniform with a wrinkled lace-bordered apron. She showed him to a grille that opened to reveal a walnut-paneled lift.

"Third floor," she said dejectedly. "I'll meet you there." The grille slammed shut, and Sasha began a slow and silent ascent. He noticed a camera in the corner. *I'll take the stairs from now on,* he thought.

The lift stopped, and a young man opened the door for him.

"You are in the English room, sir. I will show you to the door. Irina will be up with your bags shortly. As soon as you are comfortable, please just step into the hall, and I will take you down to Madame Dikarinsky, who waits for you in the reception room."

The two walked down the hallway, and the man opened a vast brass-inlaid rosewood door.

The room was beyond anything Sasha had expected. The walls were upholstered with bright yellow damask, which he knew came from the English firm Claremont, and on the floor was a brightly colored Axminster carpet. A large George III giltwood canopy bed dominated the room, dripping with new hangings of Claremont silk. The walls were decorated with blue-and-white Chinese porcelain on gessoed brackets, and a large lighted Romney portrait hung over a malachite mantel. George II giltwood sconces and a chandelier attempted to complete the illusion that he was in a stateroom of Chatsworth, Blenheim, or Castle Howard. Unlike those houses, however, the room had no charm, no refinement, and, it seemed, no place to sit down or write a letter.

"Is this to your satisfaction?" asked the young man.

"Oh, yes. Thank you. The Dikarinskys are too kind."

"Let me know when you are ready, and I will take you downstairs." He left the room, shutting the door with a slight slam.

Sasha looked around for the door to the bath. Spotting an ormolu handle in the endless expanse of the damask walls, Sasha opened the concealed door and walked into a bath with heated floors, pink marble whirlpool tub, steam room, and sauna. Two sinks, and mirrors everywhere. An empire chandelier hung from the ceiling. Sasha washed his hands, straightened his tie, and turned to leave the room when he noticed something on the windowsill.

Glowing in the light was a Fabergé flower study of a chrysanthemum, its petals carved from long wands of citrine, curving inward toward a center of keishi pearls, huge, luxurious nephrite petals framing the perfect blossom.

It was a fake. Cold and lifeless.

Sasha made a mental note to get to the archives. He had in his pocket the number Gennady had given him to call. He hoped he would have a chance to do it before the reception at the Kremlin. Perhaps one of the stolen documents featured a chrysanthemum?

Sasha looked around the room and noticed other pieces—picture frames with excessive metalwork and unsophisticated enamel colors, elephant-shaped bell pushes with upturned trunks and evidently of Asian construction. Inauthentic cigarette cases were scattered about the room. They all called out to him, their wrong notes mingling in discord. Real Fabergé, Sasha noted, was always perfectly charming. These objects were charmlessly perfect.

As worried as he was, it was time to go downstairs.

❖   ❖   ❖

Sasha walked through the ornate halls after the young man who had shown him to his room. The walls were covered with copies of second-tier paintings by major European painters. The copies were fine enough to be perceived as real, but they were such unimportant paintings, no one would ever look closely enough to check. It was, Sasha thought, a very clever decorating job. He looked up at the elaborately gilded ceiling. The greenish tone gave it away as Dutch metal rather than real gold, though layers of glaze skillfully tried to hide that fact.

Reaching the bottom of the stair, Sasha was shown into the reception room, which was actually quite attractive and full of comfortable upholstered furniture and a few French antiques. Madame Dikarinsky rose to greet him. Her smile, he noted, was real; her Fabergé brooch, he noted, was not.

"*Is everything fine? Do you like your room?*" she asked in Russian.

"It's charming," he said, replying in English. "I had no idea you collected so much Fabergé."

"Oh yes, it is my joy," she said, switching back to English. "Let me show you the entire collection. I have been buying here and abroad for several years, but the best pieces are the most recent ones. Dimitri helps us sell the less important pieces. I hope to be able to add Snegurochka to the list of things we have before too long. . . ."

Madame Dikarinsky walked with Sasha from room to room, telling him about how she began buying Fabergé. They finally came to an octagonal room, whose glass cases, originally lined with books, were now lined with works by Fabergé.

"When I was a small child, after the war, my parents would give me money for sweets. My father was in the government, and we were comfortable. I went to good schools in Leningr—, excuse me, Saint Petersburg. I would take this pocket money and save it, and on my way home from school, I would always look into the windows of the consignment shops that sold antiques to foreigners. And in one, near the Anitchkov Palace, I saw this." Madame Dikarinsky pulled from the first case a small carnelian doormouse, its tufted tail caught in its own mouth. The detailing was beautiful, and the tiny cabochon ruby eyes were invisibly set. Sasha smiled in pure pleasure—the mouse, at least, was the real thing.

"Of course, I wasn't allowed to buy it, and so I gave the money to a classmate whose father was in the Italian legation, and she had him buy it for me. I kept it hidden from my parents and continued to hide it until 1991, when the coup occurred. It was only then that I felt comfortable taking it out. My husband urged me to sell it at one point to help start Mosdikoil, but I never could. I sold my grandmother's emerald ring instead."

Sasha was incredulous. "You bought Mosdikoil with a ring?"

She smiled. "No. I sold the ring in Berlin for twenty-five thousand dollars after we were allowed to travel for the first time. When the state oil market was privatized, the workers got shares. I gave the twenty-five thousand to my husband, and he scoured the country for the workers. He would buy five to ten shares on the rouble. As you know, back then, there were officially five hundred roubles to the dollar, and unofficially twenty-five hundred. By 1992, we had over thirty million shares of the state oil company, and had made money in privatization of real estate the same way, buying apartments and vacant land. So, we became Mosdikoil. Now, with Western backing, we are worth billions. We were the first billionaires in Russia since the Revolution," she said proudly.

"Of course we are in danger all the time. If the government were to fall, what would we do? We'd lose everything. All our profits are sent abroad. We have become Irish citizens; we have houses in the Cayman Islands, et cetera. All the money, like our children, has been sent abroad. We do what we must to protect ourselves and our interests here. But I prefer the West these days. I have made so many friends, and I have the Fabergé to thank for it. That little mouse has done a lot for me. Museums want to borrow my pieces; collectors in the West have parties for me for managing to preserve these things. Princesses and countesses call me asking if I will buy their things—I am happy to. This collection I see as a legacy I will leave the world."

This poor woman, Sasha thought. *Her Fabergé is her ticket to the West, and she has no idea how much of it is fake.*

"So, what do you think?" she asked expectantly, gesturing to the room around them.

Sasha looked carefully at each piece. A few were real. A few were partially real. Most were audacious forgeries. What was it Géza von Habsburg had called them? *Fauxbergé?*

"It's quite something," Sasha said quietly. What disturbed him most was that she seemed to have no idea that her collection was so riddled with forgeries. He liked her and felt pity for her.

"Perhaps, one day, you might consider giving a lecture on the collection for me," she said. "We have become very friendly with some people at the Metropolitan in New York, and they are thinking of doing a large show of Russian Fabergé collections. Now that you are no longer with Leighton's, perhaps they might need you? I would be happy to ask the right people. Then again, you might want to open a shop of your own in New York. I know that we would be happy to help you—Dimitri is looking for a partner, and certainly New York could use a wonderful jewelry store that sold the best of Fabergé and exceptional Russian-made jewels. Can't you see it? "Prince Alexander's Fine Jewelry and Fabergé. New York, Saint Petersburg, Moscow, Palm Beach, Aspen, Beverly Hills . . ."

Sasha paled. So this was the Dikarinskys' plan. Sasha was to provide a noble front for the sale of their fakes. *"You needn't disturb yourself on my behalf,"* he said coolly. *"You are too kind to think of me in such a way,"* he said in Russian.

"Nonsense. We're pleased to help our friends. You *do* consider yourself our friend, don't you, Sasha?" she asked, looking over his shoulder at a servant who had moved into the doorway of the small exhibition room.

"Madame, your guests are arriving."

"Thank you, Katya. Send them into the salon. Alexander Kirillovitch and I will be in presently."

"Well, Sasha," she said cheerfully, "shall we go in?"

❖ ❖ ❖

Sasha moved through the lunch like a supernumerary in an opera. There were curators of every major museum in Moscow and Saint Petersburg. Sasha met dozens of Russian journalists and politicians invited by Madame Dikarinsky. There were at least ten of the wives of the richest men in Russia, several of whom curtsied to him when he kissed their hands in greeting, which both disturbed and amused him. Everyone in the room, it seemed, was drinking glasses of Cristal as if it were water. The women were covered in jewelry of a type Sasha had rarely seen outside of the display cases at Leighton's, and certainly never worn during the daytime. The room buzzed with discussions in Russian of the upcoming viewings of the sales at the Kremlin.

"And what of the Empress's necklace?" remarked one of the women. "Will it return to the capital, or vanish into the Middle East?"

"No one is sure that it actually was Alexandra Feodorovna's," said another young woman timidly.

"Of course it was. Christie's is an English firm, and beyond suspicion in their research. It is our Russian auction houses that are corrupt and terrible. Christie's? Sotheby's? They are above reproach, and so is Leighton's," said the hostess.

"Still," said the shy woman, "I couldn't wear it. It would be too awful."

"What do you think, Prince?" the first woman said, turning to Sasha. "Do you think the necklace was the Empress's?"

"I am afraid I simply do not have enough information. I would say it was an important necklace, but I certainly do not have enough proof to say it is anything other than that."

"Well said," remarked a man nearby. "At any rate," he continued, "if the Empress's jewelry is real, our specialists would be able to say so, and the pieces would be acquired by the Church as relics. As you know, the Empress is a holy martyr. . . ." Several of the women crossed themselves self-consciously. Piety was growing increasingly fashionable in Moscow.

"Nadezhda!" called out another one of the women, conspicuously attired in Versace and sapphires. "Will you add the Snow Maiden to your collection?"

"If God and the Central Bank are willing!" she replied. The women shrieked with laughter.

"Shall we go to the table?" Madame Dikarinsky asked grandly, gesturing with a plump hand to the dining room, where small round tables set with Fabergé silver and cymbidiums sat under the gaze of dozens of early Boyar portraits.

❖   ❖   ❖

That lunch was hellish, Sasha thought. There had been endless gossip from the women, silent horror from the curators, bullish manners from the politicians, and prying from the media about the figurine, about Sasha's opinion on Madame Dikarinsky's collection, and about Sasha's own family. French nouvelle cuisine was followed by a heavy Russian dessert. The women gorged themselves on the sweet, creamy pastries; after tea, Madame Dikarinsky rose.

"Thank you all so much for coming. I look forward to seeing you at my dinner when the sale is over in May. I hope that I will be able to show you something magnificent—the Snow Maiden!"

The women laughed appreciatively, and made their good-byes to him and to the other guests, donning their expensive furs, which in the case of one white snow leopard coat was endangered as well as expensive, and leaving through the great front door.

"What did you think?" Madame Dikarinsky asked Sasha. "I think it was a great success."

"I must agree," Sasha said. "Though if you don't mind, madam, I am very tired. Would it be rude if I was to lie down for a few hours before tonight's reception?"

"Not at all. You know how to find your room, I suppose? Ring if there is anything that you might need. Everything is available to you here. Moscow is heaven on earth these days, if you know the right people."

Sixteen

ᔕASHA RESTED, BUT FITFULLY. The room was so large, it made him uncomfortable. He was upset that he had accepted the Dikarin-skys' hospitality while still in New York. Had he not been at Leighton's, he never would have done so in the first place. It was amazing, Sasha thought to himself, what one would do for a job. Glancing at the fake Fabergé clock on his night table, he realized that he needed to get ready for the Leighton's reception at the Kremlin. He rang a small bell push next to his bed. Within minutes, a manservant arrived at his door.

"Sir?" the young man asked.

"Would you bring me a small glass of olive oil, some black bread with butter, a piece of cheese, and a small glass of milk?" Sasha asked.

The young man looked confused, but nodded and left.

Sasha entered the huge bathroom. After a quick sauna and steam (they were there, after all), Sasha showered, shaved, and returned to the bedroom. His evening clothes had been pressed and carefully laid out on the bed while he was in the bath, and the food he had requested was set on a small table by the window, from which he had a view of the Convent of Martha and Mary. Sasha dressed, put on his shoes, and looked through his suitcase for the small leather box that contained the dress set given to his great-grandfather by Alexander III. The cuff links were the Emperor's cypher in calibré-set sapphires with a diamond imperial crown above, the pale blue ribbons of the Order of St. Andrew entwined around the letter *A*.

The studs were cabochon sapphires surrounded by enameled ribbon borders. He reached into the case again and pulled out his great-grandfather's pocket watch. Heavy, and made of gold, it had been a gift from his classmates in the Corps des Pages on the twenty-fifth anniversary of their graduation. The front of the case featured a large "XXV" in diamonds; the back featured a white enamel Maltese cross. From the fob were suspended tiny enameled heraldic charms, each the coat of arms of one of the donors. It was an impressive sampling of the families of Russia: Dolgoruky, Cantacuzène-Spéransky, Cheremeteff, Troubetskoy, Woronzoff, Scherbatow, Demidoff, Stroganoff, and Yusupoff. With the charms stretched across the vest of his dinner clothes, Sasha felt fine. In fact, he felt armed.

He quickly drank the small glass of oil, ate the bread and the cheese, and drank the milk. Sasha's grandfather had taught him to do this when he was in college. It coated the stomach before a long night of drinking vodka toasts, and it ensured, he hoped, that he would not get drunk. He glanced in the mirror. He looked fine.

Sasha headed downstairs, and ran into a maid on his way.

"Mr. and Mrs. Dikarinsky will meet their guests in the salon in a little minute," she said. "Please go inside, have something to eat and drink, and introduce yourself to the other guests."

Sasha went into the same room where lunch had been served. The salon had been transformed by a large central table laden with food: bowls of both golden and beluga caviar on ice, rare mushrooms stuffed with herbs, meats and smoked fish in profusion, and an avalanche of orchids and hothouse flowers. Sasha looked around. There was, apparently, to be a large cocktail party before the viewing.

Dimitri stood in the center of the room, surrounded by Russian women. Not the same women as at lunch, but a coterie of incredibly tall, dark, and beautiful Muscovites, not one of whom could possibly have been over twenty-five. Around the room, some women he recognized from lunch stood by their husbands, chatting with officials in uniform. Also in the room, lost and alone, yet still strangely conscious of the fact that they were at the center of the gathering, were the cast of characters from Leighton's: Anne Holton, Lena Martin, and John and Elise Burnham.

Sasha entered, and as he did, Anne smiled and held out her hand to him. Lena stared at him with a grim expression she must have learned at law school, and John Burnham nodded politely, as if he didn't quite recognize him.

"Sasha, it is nice to see a familiar face," Anne said, leaning forward to give him a kiss on both cheeks.

"Hello, Anne. How nice to see you."

"I wish we were staying here," John Burnham said. "I am convinced that the Hotel Metropole is full of spies," he went on, oblivious to the embarrassment he was causing to the people nearby who could hear him.

"John, don't be unkind," Anne said with a warning tone. "The Metropole is very comfortable. The service is the equal of any European luxury hotel, and the days of foreigners being followed is long over."

Maybe where you're staying, Sasha thought.

"It's one of the most beautiful hotels I've ever visited," added Lena with genuine admiration in her voice.

"*To drink?*" asked a butler in Russian, as he sidled up to Sasha's elbow.

"*Vodka for the gentleman and for me. Champagne for the ladies,*" Sasha replied in kind.

"*Certainly, Your Highness.*"

"Why, Sasha, you're quite in your element!" John said. "What did he ask you?"

"He asked what we would like to drink, but it was a fairly superfluous question. One can only drink vodka with *zakouski*," Sasha replied. A polite smattering of applause spread throughout the room. Sasha looked up.

The Dikarinskys had arrived, and were being greeted with the deference once shown only to royalty.

Madame Dikarinsky was wearing Chanel, more appropriate for a runway than for a cocktail reception. Her rubies were vast. Mr. Dikarinsky was angrily muttering into a cell phone, following his wife through the crowd as he talked, a finger in his free ear.

"Who are they?" asked Mrs. Burnham.

"Our hosts," replied Anne under her breath, irritated.

"Ah!" said Madame Dikarinsky in recognition, walking over to them. "You have all found one another! Sasha, I thought that you would be pleased to see your colleagues here—that it would make you feel at home." She beamed, touching Sasha's shoulder.

"Your drinks, Prince," a servant said, offering the tray to the group.

"I was just saying to my colleagues," Sasha said, pausing deliberately, "that a gentleman only drinks vodka with *zakouski*."

"Very true," said Mr. Dikarinsky, taking a frozen glass from the tray. "Very true."

"Oh, no thank you," said John Burnham, a bit smug. "I'll just have some Champagne."

An awkward silence fell over the Russians. Mr. Dikarinsky looked at him incredulously.

"Champagne is for women!" he pressed. "Surely you would prefer vodka?"

"No, thank you. I'm not a big drinker." He smiled broadly.

Anne leaned over and whispered in his ear. His expression changed.

"Well, perhaps one," he said, lifting the glass from the tray.

"I don't trust a man who doesn't drink," insisted Mr. Dikarinsky.

"Who would?" Sasha said in Russian. He raised his glass. Mr. Dikarinsky followed.

"To friendship!" called out Mr. Dikarinsky.

"To friendship!" replied the crowd.

Sasha smiled at John and drained his glass in one gulp, setting it back on the tray. Mr. Dikarinsky did the same.

John Burnham looked at his glass and followed suit. He put the glass down, and Sasha could see the quick swallow had been rough on him. His eyes were watering a bit. The Dikarinskys smiled, and moved on through the crowd.

"Well, thank goodness that's over," John said, smiling at them.

"Over?" Sasha asked. "Hardly, Mr. Burnham. There will be toasts all night. I hope you have a head for vodka." Sasha smiled.

"Well, Sasha, I'll follow your lead. I'm quite a bit larger than you are," he said.

Yes, Sasha thought, *you are. But you will get smashed, and I won't.*

Sasha leaned over to Anne. "What did you say to him?"

Anne smiled. "I let him know in no uncertain terms that the issue of his masculinity was at stake here. I think he'll keep up from now on."

"Watch him," Sasha said, winking. "Well, if you'll all excuse me, I'd like to say hello to some people."

"Oh, Sasha," Anne said as he moved away, "go and say hello to Dimitri. He was asking for you back at the hotel."

Sasha made his way across the room to say hello to Dimitri, who was still surrounded by the Muscovite model corps.

"Hello, Dimitri," Sasha said, walking up to him and extending his hand. "It's good to see you. All well?"

"Everything is great," he agreed, wrapping his arm around the shoulder of one of the young women. "Are you ready for the preview?"

"Oh, I think so," he said brightly. "It should be beautiful. Is the reception in the Great Kremlin Palace?"

"Oh no," replied Dimitri. "It is in a room in the Armory Museum. Putting something commercial in the Great Kremlin Palace would be like having an auction in the Oval Office. Of all people, I would have thought that you would have known that."

"Well, anything seems to be possible in Moscow these days. See you at the reception."

"Sure. Listen, Sasha," he said in Russian, *"my friends and I are going to a new nightclub after the reception. Very exclusive. Very luxe."* He smiled. *"Perhaps you would like a taste of the new Moscow?"*

"Well, how can I decline an invitation like that?" Sasha smiled. Dimitri would certainly know the best nightclub in Moscow, and perhaps he could get more information about Dikarinsky and his business. He was grateful for Dimitri's trust.

Sasha walked away from Dimitri and headed toward the table of food, where an increasingly cheerful John Burnham was regaling the guests with his hopes for the figurine.

"We've had a great deal of interest," he said to the group gathered around him. "We are certain that we will break every record for a Fabergé figurine with this sale—it might even climb into the millions. We very much hope so."

"Isn't it true that the Ozerovskys are suing you, and that the sale might be stopped?" said a reporter from *Kommersant*.

"We are negotiating with the Ozerovskys and the von Kemp family trust, but I am not at liberty to say where we are in those discussions."

"Perhaps then Prince Ozerovsky would care to comment," the same reporter said to Sasha in Russian.

"I am not part of my family's suit," Sasha replied in English, so that the Leighton's employees would understand. "The Revolution is over. Though I am a Russian, I was born and raised in America. I believe that the piece may be sold by whoever owns it now. I don't feel entitled to it, or attached to it. I hope only that whoever buys it will remember that today, in Russia, a million dollars goes a long way. I would hope that they would make a similar contribution to a worthy cause here."

The room was silent for a while. There was murmuring as several people finished translating into Russian what Sasha had just said. People nodded approvingly. Several men slapped Sasha on the back as he moved across the room. A voice came from behind him, light, mocking, and very familiar.

"Now that, my darling, was a speech worth listening to."

Sasha turned around to find Victoria standing in front of him.

"Victoria!" he exclaimed, kissing her on both cheeks. "There you are. How did your search go for retail space?"

"I don't think that Moscow and my clothes are a particularly good fit," Victoria said as a young woman slithered by in a transparent dress through which her breasts were clearly visible. "Muscovite women seem to appreciate more *obvious* effects than I usually offer my clients."

"I'm glad you stayed for the reception."

"I stayed for you. You and this embroidered sable-trimmed St. Laurent jacket I can't wear anywhere in New York for fear of being spray-painted by one of those PETA nuts. I thought Moscow might be just the place."

"You're unbelievable."

"Thank you for noticing. What's happening?"

"Well, things are getting interesting. I have a lot to tell you." Sasha leaned over and whispered into her ear. "I think the figurine is a fake."

Victoria's eyes widened.

"Well, Mr. Expert, you have been busy. I don't want to discuss anything here, Sasha. Let's go back to your hotel and talk. There are simply too many people."

"I understand. But I'm not staying at a hotel. I'm staying here."

"Some digs. You had best come back to the National with me and stay in my room. I don't trust your hosts at all. I mean really, Sasha, look at their wallpaper."

"I can't, Victoria, it would be rude—"

"Oh, Sasha, you're impossible. I'm going to fix my face, and then you can show me around this Epcot version of old Moscow, and we can take in a night on the town. I want the Kremlin in the snow, the best caviar and vodka the city offers, and then the male corps de ballet of the Bolshoi in my hotel room. Right now, however, I want to use what is undoubtedly one hysterically overdecorated loo."

Victoria swayed off to the bathroom. As she moved through the crowd, the heads of the male guests swiveled to watch her go by.

❖   ❖   ❖

The cars proceeded slowly up to the Spassky Gate, which had been specially opened for the occasion. Blazing lights inside the Kremlin walls illuminated the falling snow, and the Palace of Congress was lit for the occasion.

"Is that where we're going?" Victoria asked. "It looks like Avery Fisher Hall, but run-down and ugly."

"Welcome to Soviet architecture of the 1960s."

"Ugh," Victoria said, reapplying her lipstick. "Perhaps we can run off and look at the Crown Jewels in the Armory instead."

"Actually, that's where we're going—the party is in the *Oruzheinaya Palata*, which is what they call the Armory in Russian, but if you try to break into the Diamond Fund, they'll shoot you, Victoria."

"And put a hole in this embroidery? Forget it."

The Armory was one of Sasha's favorite places in Moscow. Filled with the treasures of the tsars, the galleries were all open for the occasion and the guests walked through them open-mouthed at the sights that met their eyes. Persian weapons studded with jewels and wrought with inscriptions in gold. Sixteenth- and seventeenth-century English and Augsburg silver, examples of such rarity that nothing like them existed today in the countries where they originated. A hall of the thrones made for the Romanovs and the tsars who had preceded them; the ivory throne of Sophia Paleologus, brought from Byzantium—the diamond throne of Ivan the Terrible, and the dual throne of the twin tsars Ivan and Peter, with a seat behind for their sister, Regent Sophia, who would whisper instructions into her brothers' ears while hidden from the court's view. Coronation gowns and embroidered uniforms stood guard in glass cases in every corner.

"I can't believe this," Victoria said. "I've never seen anything like it."

Sasha looked around with interest. He had studied all these things for so long it was almost as if he couldn't even see them anymore. It was a pleasure to watch Victoria move from piece to piece, exclaiming over the beauty of the craftsmanship.

They moved into the rotunda and saw the collection of Fabergé Imperial Eggs.

"You know," Victoria said thoughtfully, "you see pictures of them over and over, but when you see them in person, they're so very different."

"What do you mean?" Sasha asked.

"Well," Victoria said thoughtfully as she looked at the Alexander Palace Egg of 1908, "you think that when you see these things, you'll be dazzled by the execution, and by the precious materials, and by the audacity of their expense. . . ."

"But?" Sasha asked.

"But, when I look at them, they make me so sad. We're not even supposed to be seeing them at all—they are so personal. I can see a husband, albeit an extremely rich husband, giving this to a wife whom he loves very much. Look at the sweet portraits of the children outside, and the model of their house on the inside. It's so . . . intimate. It gives me the creeps just to look at it at all."

Sasha smiled. "Welcome to my life. Everything I deal with has blood on it." He shrugged helplessly.

"I don't know how you sleep."

"I don't. Not these days, anyway."

They followed a long and worn red carpet with black borders past rows of unsmiling guards up a shallow staircase to the Hall of the Patriarchs, a medieval room restored in the nineteenth century to the old Slavic style. The walls were a deep crimson, and decorated with floral designs in gold leaf. The ornately carved moldings were polychromed in rich, saturated colors, and from the vaulted ceiling, portraits of the patriarchs of the Russian Orthodox Church looked down with grim expressions at the dazzling display.

The room was fitted with dozens of vitrines, all holding pieces from the Leighton's, Christie's, and Sotheby's sales. Around the room, specialists whom Sasha recognized chatted with Russian clients. Sotheby's had done well, Sasha noted, to hire four exceptionally beautiful girls, all Russian, who chatted easily with the clients and languorously drew pieces of jewelry out of the cases for them to inspect.

Sasha noted that Anne stood alone in the Leighton's section, trying to make do by handing out Russian translations of the printed materials. He felt sorry for her, but he knew that if they hadn't suspended him, he would be right there, drawing in clients for them.

"How much longer do we stay here?" Victoria asked, lifting a shot of vodka off a passing tray.

"Well, we need to look at everything, and we're meeting Gennady and Leonida here. After this, there is a buffet supper and dancing in one of the other rooms, and after that, Dimitri and his Russian Rhinemaidens have invited us to some nightclub," Sasha said.

"What fun," Victoria said without much enthusiasm.

Sasha shot her a warning look, and then the two moved around the room again. They looked at the Sotheby's offerings, and then went to Christie's jewelry.

"Now, that is something I'd like to have," Victoria said, pointing to the diamond collet necklace that had been the putative property of Empress Alexandra. Sasha looked at the piece in person for the first time.

The stones were round, large, and exceptionally clear. They were what had once been called "stones of the first water." Sasha looked at the clasp with curiosity. It was a pavé diamond coiled snake, twisted into a figure eight, biting its own tail. Tucked into the open parts of the serpent were two large pear-shaped diamonds.

"Eternity," Sasha said.

"Pardon?" said Victoria.

"The snake," Sasha replied, "twisted into the infinity symbol. It is a symbol of eternity. You see it everywhere in Russia."

"It's very pretty. Hadn't you noticed it before?"

"No. I'm surprised they didn't make more of it in the catalogue. Those diamonds must be ten carats apiece themselves."

"Subtle," Victoria agreed. "*J'adore*. It's too bad some of the stones are chipped."

Sasha looked closely. Victoria was right. Some of the diamonds had very small chips and scratches. It was to be expected—they had probably been through a lot, even if they hadn't belonged to the Empress. Sasha looked over the case. A curator from the Armory was engrossed in conversation with the director of the Diamond Fund, where the Crown Jewels were kept. Sasha didn't know either of them, and he wanted to hear what they were saying. He moved next to them and smiled politely.

"They're very beautiful, aren't they?" he asked in English, a bit too loudly.

"Yes, they are," said the Armory curator, equally politely, in heavily accented English, then turned to her colleague and they continued their conversation in Russian. "*. . . as I was saying, is there a chance of a positive identification from photographs?*" she asked.

"*In principle we could,*" replied her colleague, "*but in this case quite impossible. There were so many similar collet necklaces in the collections, it would be impossible to say exactly which one it was.*"

"*But the clasp, surely it is identifiable?*"

"*It would be in our interests to keep that information to ourselves. I found a drawing for something similar in the confiscation files at the state archives . . .*"

"*Which ones?*" the woman asked with interest.

"*The ones from the 1930s.*"

"*Have they been declassified?*"

"*They never were classified in the first place—they were open to all members of the Commission of Valuables. No one else would have known they were there. Many of the reports were assembled by torturing prisoners for information. They are not really reliable. . . .*"

Sasha was intrigued. He would have to remember to ask Gennady about the Commission of Valuables and their confiscation files.

The curator and director moved on. Sasha watched as people filled out absentee bidding forms for the pieces in the cases. It was getting hot. Looking around, Sasha saw John Burnham was red-faced and drunk, standing at the case in which Snegurochka revolved. Sasha was getting tired of looking at the figurine, which glittered mockingly from the case.

The crowd was growing, and the sound of music and the clinking of glasses came from the adjoining room. He wanted to leave, but he knew that to do so would only mean going back to the Dikarinskys.

Suddenly, in the corner by the door, Sasha caught sight of Gennady and Leonida.

"There they are," he said to Victoria. "Let's see if we can get to them before dinner."

Sasha and Victoria moved through the crowd, passing the cases full of jewels and Fabergé, and made their way to Gennady and Leonida's side.

"Gennady, Leonida, please meet my cousin, Victoria," Sasha said.

"*Ah, what a pleasure!*" Gennady said in Russian, extending his hand. "*I see that beauty is a family business.*"

Victoria smiled. "Sorry," she said. "I'll need the U.N. simultaneous translation for that one."

"*The other side of the family, Gennady—Victoria is an American,*" Sasha explained to Gennady.

"*Pity,*" Gennady said.

"He says that he's pleased to meet you, and that you are very beautiful."

"How kind. How do you say 'thank you'?"

"*Spasibo.*"

"Well, spasibo to you," she said, holding out her hand, which Gennady took and kissed.

Leonida tapped him on the shoulder. "Careful, my dear," she said in English for Victoria's benefit. "I packed a *knud.*"

They all laughed, and Sasha turned to Victoria.

"Untranslatable. It hurts when you get hit with it, though. It looks like dinner is starting. Shall we go in?"

The four walked into the next room. In one corner, a small Russian orchestra was positioned and getting ready to play. There were two *balalaika* players, a guitarist, a violin, an accordion, and a *dombra*, or standing bass *balalaika*. Two weary-looking singers in folk costume lounged nearby.

"Looks like the cheerful union is on strike," Victoria commented.

"They'll perk up," Sasha said. "They always do."

As if on cue, the musicians snapped to attention and began the lively "Kalinka." As the musicians played, the singers rhythmically swung their skirts in time to the music, grinning madly.

"Told you," Sasha said, turning his attention to the buffet.

"You would think at the Kremlin that we would get a better spread than this," Gennady said, gesturing with disgust at what Sasha thought was a fairly lavish buffet.

"It seems like more than enough for dinner to me," said Sasha.

"It's not even enough for *zakouski*."

"I think you're a very hard man, Gennady." Sasha smiled.

The four carefully filled their plates, and went and sat at a small skirted table by a leaded-glass window that looked out onto the interior of the Kremlin, where the snow fell softly.

"Kremlin in the snow," Victoria said, sticking her fork carefully into a stuffed pickled mushroom. "One down, three sights to go."

"I don't think that I can guarantee you the boys from the Bolshoi." Sasha smiled. "Listen, Victoria, I have to beg your pardon—I need to have a conversation with Gennady that will be hard to translate. I promise to fill you in later."

"*D'accord*," Victoria said. "Fire away, Slavic wonder."

Sasha smiled and turned back to Gennady. He began their conversation in Russian. "Gennady, I was hovering by the case with Alexandra Feodorovna's necklace, and I overheard two curators— one the director of the Diamond Fund—talking."

"Talking nonsense, most likely. The Diamond Fund is controlled by the Department of Finance, not the Department of Culture. Many of the people there are bureaucrats, not art historians."

"Nevertheless, he said something very interesting. At the archives, he mentioned the confiscation files of the Commission of Valuables. What are they?"

"Semilegendary," Gennady replied.

"Seriously, my friend. What are they?"

"Ostensibly, after the Revolution, the Commission of Valuables was set up to catalogue and evaluate the nationalized property left behind by the aristocrats. Lists were drawn up."

"So those are the confiscation files?"

"Not exactly. In the late 1930s, after the bloom was off the confiscatory rose, so to speak, Papa Stalin went a step further. He ordered the arrest of people who had been servants or minor members of important families before the war, and the KGB forced them to confess if they knew where objects of value owned by their former masters were."

Sasha shuddered.

"If there are such files, they are no doubt inaccurate. However, we can certainly ask for them if they aren't classified."

"According to the curator, they are not."

"Well, we'll ask Kirill Stepanovitch tomorrow when we go to the National Archives. Also, I still want you to meet Orlovsky. He knows everything."

"I look forward to it," Sasha said and smiled at him. As he noticed the Dikarinskys approaching their table, he rose.

"So, Alexander Kirillovitch," said Mr. Dikarinsky, after helping his wife into a small chair and taking a seat himself at the table. "What is your professional opinion of the sales? What are the best things—what should I buy?"

"Well," Sasha said uneasily as he sat back down, "I believe that Dimitri is your adviser, is he not?"

"Two opinions are always better than one."

"Well, the necklace is astonishing, but the provenance is unproven, in my opinion. I think actually my favorite piece is the imperial tea set. Beautifully made, exquisite condition, impeccably researched."

"And Snegurochka?"

"I'm afraid I cannot say anything about the piece while the case is on."

"I like a man who is true to his word," Dikarinsky said.

"Sasha . . ." Victoria interrupted.

"I appreciate your respect on this matter . . ." Sasha continued.

"Sasha . . ." Victoria said again, painfully squeezing his hand under the table.

"What?" Sasha asked, looking away from Mr. Dikarinsky toward where Victoria stared at the people entering the room. He saw a short grey-haired man chatting with a group of people. "Shit," he said under his breath. "It's Craig Tippett."

"Sasha," Victoria said, "look who he's with."

Sasha looked at the woman standing next to Tippett, her back toward Sasha. She was tall and dark, her red dress with a plunging back revealing a beautiful view of her pale skin. Craig Tippett said something and she laughed, turning her head to the side, and revealed her unmistakable profile.

It was Marina.

"I don't believe this," Sasha said to Victoria.

"I can," Victoria said as Marina caught sight of them from across the room and turned back to Craig Tippett. "I don't trust her."

"She is my cousin—I won't be rude," Sasha said, standing up again as Craig and Marina slowly began to make their way across the room.

"I thought you'd never ask," Victoria said, grabbing Sasha's hand and pulling him onto the dance floor. "This is my favorite song."

"Victoria, this is 'Moscow Nights.' Do you even know this song at all?" Sasha asked.

"I know it's a fox-trot, and I know that you need time to plan what you're going to say to her—lead."

"It will be fine," Sasha said, pulling away.

"Sasha, do you honestly think Marina has come from New York with a lawyer who also has a case against Leighton's just to ambush you in the middle of the Kremlin and wish you luck? She's sure she's got the advantage over you, and she's here to drop a bomb."

Sasha grabbed Victoria around the waist, and they stepped onto the dance floor.

"Slow, slow, quick, quick, slow, slow," he said in time to the music.

"That's better," Victoria whispered into his ear. "What are you going to do?"

"I'm simply not going to engage with her over the figurine."

"Not going to work, Sash. Plan B?"

"I have no idea." He sighed.

"I do." Victoria said.

"What?" he asked as they swept past Marina and Craig Tippet, also on the dance floor now.

"Tell her the truth," Victoria said.

"What do you mean?" Sasha asked.

"That you think the figurine isn't right. You said so. She's probably here because she's made some shady deal with that lawyer, and she thinks she's got you beat. If you tell her that the figurine might be a fake, you'll throw her off balance and you might even get her on your side. Trust me, if I know anything about Marina, it is that she will not want to be embarrassed. If you let her in on this, she'll roll over—I guarantee it."

The two continued dancing in silence, and soon the song ended.

"Into the lion's den?" Victoria asked.

"Let's go," Sasha said, and they moved through the dancers.

Noticing that they were leaving the floor, Marina positioned herself to meet them.

"Sasha, I'm so glad to find you here. I believe you know Craig Tippett."

"Of course. Nice to see you again."

"We have to stop meeting like this," Tippett said with a smile.

"I hope so," Sasha said without humor. "Marina, this is Victoria de Witt."

Marina raised her eyebrows. "We met in Paris. Sasha, this is really family business."

"Victoria is family, Marina," Sasha said. "You may say what you like in front of her."

"*Sasha,*" Marina switched to Russian, "*let's not have a scene. I want to speak to you with Mr. Tippett. We must have an important conversation.*"

"Fine," Sasha said in English. "Victoria and I were just on our way to Maxim's for a drink. Why don't you join us in, say, forty-five minutes?"

"Sasha, I—" Marina began.

"We'd love to," Tippett interjected. "I trust that you'll join us, Miss de Witt?"

"I wouldn't miss it for the world," she replied.

Craig nodded and, taking Marina by the arm before she could say anything else, moved back into the crowd.

"Now we really have to go," Sasha said to Victoria. "I hope that John Burnham didn't see me talking to them."

The two slipped out of the building and walked along the cobblestone square to where the cars were waiting.

Sasha opened the car door for Victoria, and soon they moved back out into Red Square.

"Back to the Dikarinskys', sir?" the driver asked.

"No," Sasha said. "First to Maxim's for a drink, and then I'm not sure of the next stop."

"Certainly, sir," the driver said as he steered them out of the Kremlin's grounds.

❖   ❖   ❖

Maxim's was quiet. The red upholstered walls shimmered in the low light, and the large windows looking out onto the Okhotny Ryad gave a beautiful view of the falling snow.

Sasha and Victoria settled into a small banquette and decided to order a light meal, having been deprived of finishing their food at the Kremlin.

"So?" Victoria asked. "What the hell was that?"

"I'm not sure myself, but we'll find out at ten, won't we?"

"I guess. It should be very interesting."

The waiter approached the table.

"Welcome to Maxim's. May I get you something to drink?" he asked in Russian.

"Vodka, a bottle of Taittinger, blini, and caviar—beluga," Victoria said. She turned to Sasha. "On me."

The waiter bowed slightly, and left the table.

"How on earth did you know what he said?" Sasha asked, marveling.

"What else would he have said?" Victoria asked. "It's the universal opening sentence. Have you noticed how much this place looks like Doubles? I feel right at home."

The waiter returned with their order, and Sasha and Victoria savored the delicious food he had brought. Shots of vodka were followed with glasses of the excellent Champagne.

"This is living," Victoria said. "Best caviar and vodka in the city. Two down, one to go."

"You're too funny, Victoria," Sasha said, laughing and not noticing as Marina and Craig entered the restaurant.

"Well," Marina said, approaching the table, "I see we're celebrating. I hope the mood remains so festive."

Sasha rose as Marina slid into the booth next to him, and Craig slipped in next to Victoria.

"Help yourselves," Victoria said, gesturing to the food and drinks. A nearby waiter immediately brought additional small plates.

"Thank you," Marina said icily. "Sasha, I'll get to the point. Mr.

Tippett and I had several conversations in New York, including one with your father and stepmother."

"So I've heard," Sasha said, glancing at Victoria.

"What Marina is trying to say, Sasha," Craig interjected, "is that the two halves of the suit have decided to join forces. Together, the Ozerovsky family association and the von Kemp family trust have a much greater chance of success in this suit. Marina and I are here to suggest that you join the association. Otherwise, the outcome of the suit could prove extremely embarrassing to you, and you will certainly lose your job."

"And I suggest," Sasha said deliberately, "that you drop your combined efforts."

"Oh, Sasha," Marina said, "we're asking you to do this for your own good—"

"Marina, I'm not sure what your real reasons are for pressing this suit, but I'm sure I would disagree with them under any circumstances." Sasha sighed. "However, I am telling you this to spare your embarrassment, and to prevent the family from getting caught up in a scandal. You see, Marina, I think the figurine might be a fake."

Marina began, "Nonsense, Sasha, you yourself—"

Craig Tippett interrupted. "Countess, I would like to hear what Sasha has to say. He isn't foolish enough to make up something this serious, and he is an expert in his field. I, for one, would like to hear more."

"In Saint Petersburg, at the archives, I was made aware of a series of thefts that have been plaguing the various archives around the country. Someone has been stealing original Fabergé drawings. Mysteriously, objects that match those illustrations then appear on the market. Some of those objects I saw in New York in a major private collection—"

"Gloria Greer," Tippet said, nodding his head. "I saw you looking at her collection very carefully. I wondered why."

"You're very observant," Sasha said.

"I'm a lawyer. Continue."

"Many of the pieces are in the Dikarinskys' house in Moscow. Perhaps two dozen or more. Finally, some of the stolen sketches were details of Snegurochka."

"Amazing," Victoria said sipping her drink. "Who's doing it?"

"I think it's Mr. Dikarinsky. I think he is using Dimitri and the rest of us. But I have no proof of that."

"Well, don't try to look for it in their home. I would advise you to get your things out of there and leave Moscow," Craig said.

"Sasha, you can't be serious?" Marina said. "Really?"

"Really, Marina. I'm sorry, but it's true."

Marina looked down at the table and fingered her glass of Champagne.

"I think that you're right. Sasha has to get out of the Dikarinskys' house. Sash, come stay with me at my hotel," Victoria said.

"I think I will."

"I don't believe it for a second. Sasha is making this up," Marina said.

"Well, Dimitri asked Victoria and me to join him at a new nightclub tonight."

"I'm going with you," Marina said.

"That was my suggestion," Sasha said. "I think you should come and see."

"I've spent a lot more time with Dimitri than you have, and I know all his friends from when I was here for work. I think I know him well enough to ferret out if he's even aware of what is going on. I want to know what he knows. If he had any idea about this, I'll kill him. I'd never make an introduction again. It would ruin me to be caught up in a scandal like this." She looked at Sasha, glowering. "If you're right, I'll drop this suit, but if you're toying with me, I'll ruin you—no one embarrasses me. *No one.*"

Seventeen

⌒

The car pulled up in front of a brick-and-granite facade on a street not too far from Red Square. There was a line of well-dressed men and women standing outside a brightly lit doorway. As the car joined the line to drop them off, Sasha checked his pocket again for the words he was supposed to whisper to the doorman for entrance to the club called the Twelve Chairs.

"What a weird name for a club," Victoria said, as the car crawled forward in line.

"It's the name of a novel by Ilf and Petrov, written in Moscow in the 1920s."

"What's it about?" Marina asked. "I slept through Soviet literature at the Sorbonne."

"It's complicated," Sasha said. "I'm not sure what it has to do with nightclubs."

"Isn't it also a Mel Brooks movie?" Victoria asked.

"I do not think we can hope this evening will be amusing," Marina said irritably, pulling her fur collar up farther around her neck and looking out the window with disgust. "I *hate* Moscow."

The car was crawling closer and closer to the door when Sasha noticed that, a few cars ahead, Dimitri and several of his friends were stepping onto the sidewalk.

"There they are," Sasha said to his cousins. "Shall we get out of the car and meet them?"

"Absolutely. Sasha, honestly, this is the most fun I've ever had. I feel like Nora Charles," Victoria replied.

"I'm glad you're so excited," Sasha said, putting his hand on the door.

"Don't worry, Sasha. Nothing will happen to us. We're Americans." Victoria patted him on the shoulder reassuringly as she got out.

Sasha didn't have the heart to tell her that nothing could save them if everything he feared about Mr. Dikarinsky was true. He hadn't read lately that organized crime cared about a victim's passport. Sasha squared his shoulders, took a deep breath, and opened the door, turning to help the ladies out once he had stepped up onto the curb. The three walked over to where Dimitri and his friends were gathering in front of the club.

"*Dimitri, thanks for the invite. We're very pleased to be here,*" Sasha said in Russian, shaking his hand.

"Marina! I'm surprised to see you here," Dimitri said with pleasure.

"The pleasure is entirely mine. Sasha, my lawyer, and I have had quite a productive chat together." She glowered at Sasha.

Dimitri reached out and kissed Marina on both cheeks. "That is the best news I've heard in weeks. Is there hope the suit might be dropped? Then this is a celebration! I'm pleased."

Sasha forced himself to smile. "Dimitri, this is my cousin Victoria. Victoria, this is Dimitri Durakov, a client."

"I hope I will someday hear you call me a friend, Sasha. Victoria, Sasha, please meet Roman, Tamara, Ivan, Kostia, Katia, and Larisa. Everyone, this is Victoria, from New York, and her cousin, Prince Alexander Ozerovsky. You all know Countess Shoutine already." Dimitri alternated between Russian and English.

The women all smiled at Sasha, and looked at Marina and Victoria's clothes carefully, patting their own expensive furs for reassurance. Though the men looked a bit rough around the edges, they were carefully groomed. They were certainly a well-dressed group.

Dimitri approached the bouncer at the door.

"*I am from Starograd, and am on my way to Georgia,*" Dimitri said in Russian.

The bouncer nodded, and let them all into a vestibule.

Sasha looked up as he entered the building. Though from the outside, the building looked industrial, Sasha realized as they entered that the bland facade hid what had once been quite a grand house. The marble steps led up to a dark vestibule, and the treads of the stairs were worn low. To the right, the former space once occupied by the *dvornik* had been turned into a ticket booth.

Sasha reached into his breast pocket for his wallet, but Dimitri held up his hand in protest.

"Sasha, please, I have this. I invite everyone here. You are my guests."

Sasha knew it was both fruitless and rude to argue. He thanked Dimitri for his hospitality and began to shrug off his coat. As he did so, he saw Dimitri peeling off 10,000 rouble notes. Sasha stared, aghast, as Dimitri put more and more roubles down on the tray of the cashier. Almost 300,000 roubles. At the current exchange rate, Sasha calculated, that was almost $10,000. The nightclub entrance fee was $1,000 a person. Sasha stared at the money as the cashier counted it again.

"What's the matter?" Victoria asked.

"The nightclub is a thousand dollars per person."

"Expensive town," Victoria said. "I'm glad we're not paying. Take off your coat and stay awhile. This looks outrageous."

Sasha slipped off his coat and gave it to Dimitri, who was laughing and gradually disappearing under a pile of furs.

A uniformed attendant arrived at Dimitri's side to take the coats, and received a large tip. The group moved into what once must have been a long picture gallery, dimly lit, and filled with lasers that traced eerie red and green patterns on the elaborately plastered ceiling. The electronic dance music was deafening.

The hall was full of small tables, where couples sat drinking and smoking. As they walked toward the far end of the room where the bar was, Sasha marveled at the enormous tank full of fish that formed the divider between the bar and the rooms beyond. As they approached, Sasha realized that the tank wasn't full of fish. It was full of naked women, floating around in the water as men who were gathered at the bar threw folded roubles and dollars at the walls of the tank. The bills bounced into a trough around the tank's base; periodically, one of the shirtless bartenders would gather up the bills and dump them into canvas bags located beneath the cash registers.

"*What do you think?*" Dimitri asked Sasha.

"Unbelievable," Sasha replied in English for Victoria's benefit.

"Now this," Victoria said, "is worth the trip. This erases everything in New York."

Dimitri smiled. "I told you that Moscow had changed, Sasha. There's something for everyone here at the Twelve Chairs."

At the bar, Dimitri ordered Cristal, and a waiter carrying a tray loaded with the distinctive bottles followed them around the aquarium to the huge doors that led to the dance floor. Nothing in his experience had quite prepared him for the sight of the new Moscow at play.

The dance floor was in what had once been an old theater or ballroom. A huge stage held the deejay, as well as statuesque topless showgirls, who wore enormous Las Vegas–style versions of Russian folk headdresses, G-strings, and high-heeled boots. Above their heads, the extraordinary nineteenth-century plasterwork made the proscenium and the ceiling appear to be writhing with naiads and dryads. In the center, the god Apollo leapt forth from the white plaster, extending his pale arms and golden lyre over the dancing crowds, his lips twisted in a slight smile and his eyes half closed.

Sasha, however, could not close his eyes. Hundreds of young people swarmed over the dance floor, some dressed like models and others barely dressed at all. Wigs and wild makeup were the norm, and on platforms around the dance floor, well-built men wore boots, tight hot pants, and Russian navy caps. Everyone danced madly. The music was largely western, but periodically, there was a mix into which the deejay dropped snatches of political speeches.

It was unnerving to hear a violent bass track of Caucasian drums overlaid with Madonna's "Material Girl" and the voice of Putin: Madonna sang, "'Cause we are living in a . . ." while Putin shouted back, "open society."

Sasha looked out across the room. Under spotlights sat twelve gilt ballroom chairs with upholstered backs and seats—no doubt the "twelve chairs" of the club's name.

The waiter carrying the Champagne moved in front of Sasha, Victoria, Marina, and Dimitri's entourage, placing the bottles on small tables near the edge of the dance floor.

"Please!" Dimitri shouted over the noise. *"To the table."*

Everyone sat down, and the Russians immediately began smoking. Dimitri offered Victoria a cigarette, which she took. Reaching into her evening bag, she pulled out a black enamel and gold cigarette holder. Sasha looked at her and raised his eyebrow.

"What?" she asked. "It was in the bag with a matching lighter. Sue me—I can't do this in New York anywhere."

Dimitri laughed, and lit the cigarette for her.

Sasha turned to Larisa, who sat to his right. "And how do you know Dimitri?" he asked.

"Who doesn't know Dimitri?" she said, smiling charmingly. "He knows everyone worth knowing in Moscow. He deals with all the Fabergé collectors, and he has sold lots of jewelry to my mother and aunt." Larisa smiled and tossed her hair, narrowing her black eyes at Sasha with interest and intent. "So," she said, smiling, "did your family get out of Russia with all of your fabulous jewels?"

Sasha recoiled. "Well, that's quite a question . . ." he said.

"Oh, I didn't mean to be rude," Larisa said quickly, to cover her gaffe. "Only because if you didn't, you might make your fortune tonight." She tossed her head back and blew her smoke into the air, turning her attention to the man on her other side. Sasha looked across the table at Victoria, who was evidently enjoying herself and had obviously forgotten that they were in danger. Marina was talking with Dimitri when he suddenly noticed Sasha looking around.

"Quite something, isn't it?" he asked. *"I never go out in Europe or the States anymore. Nothing compares."*

"You must be doing well here," Sasha said, smiling. *"Forgive me, but the entrance fee here is insane."*

Dimitri looked confused. *"I don't pay for entry here,"* he said.

"But at the door," Sasha protested. *"I saw you—"*

Dimitri laughed. *"That wasn't the entrance fee. That was for the game later. Have you ever read* The Twelve Chairs?*"*

"No," Marina admitted. *"I haven't read any Soviet fiction."*

"I'm not surprised," Dimitri said. *"The Twelve Chairs takes place in Moscow in the 1920s. A bourgeoise admits to her son that before the Revolution, she hid her collection of jewelry in the upholstery of some chairs that were in her dining room in Starograd. The son vows to find them, but the chairs have already been sold by someone who didn't know, so the son goes on a journey to locate the chairs and find the treasure—on the way he goes all over the Soviet Union and is faced with the many situations created by the conflict."*

"I see," Sasha said. *"What does that have to do with the chairs here?"*

"Ah," Dimitri said, smiling, *"I was just about to explain to Victoria and Marina."*

"The reason," he said, continuing in English, "that I paid so much money was to enter us in the lottery. Every ten minutes, the deejay will call out a number from the coat check tickets. Those numbers will correspond to a person who has paid the lottery fee. Everyone at these tables has done that. At two A.M., the twelve people who have been chosen climb on the stage and pick lots to choose a chair. They go to their places, and when the music stops, they rip open the upholstery of their chair."

"And?" asked Victoria.

"The lucky one will have a hundred thousand dollars worth of diamonds hidden in his chair."

"You can't be serious," Victoria said.

"I'm very serious," Dimitri said with a smile. "I have won twice."

"Well," Victoria said, her eyes sparkling. "I hope your guests are as lucky."

"I hope so, too," Dimitri said, taking Victoria's hand and kissing it.

I can't believe this is actually Russia, Sasha thought to himself, looking around. This was not even like the Palladium had been in the early 1990s, when he had actually gone to nightclubs in New York, or like the clubs in Ibiza or the south of France. There was a desperate quality to the way people were enjoying themselves—as if it all might be taken away tomorrow. *Then again*, Sasha thought, *it very well might*.

"Victoria," Sasha said, "why don't we take a look around?"

"You're on," Victoria said. "Dimitri, thanks for the briefing. If they call six fifty-seven, I'll never forgive you if you don't come get me, because I won't understand when they shout the number."

"You have my promise," he said, smiling.

"Shall we?" Victoria said, taking Sasha's arm.

"Yes, you two go ahead," Marina said, cozying up to Dimitri. "I'll keep Dimitri entertained while you're gone."

"I'll bet," Victoria whispered to Sasha as the two walked to the back of the dance floor. At the back of the room stood a dais on which stood the twelve spotlighted chairs. People crowded around, trying to guess which chair held the jewelry. A number of enormous bodyguards stood, arms akimbo, in front of the chairs.

"Perhaps I'll wait until they call my number," Victoria said. "What's through there?" she asked, pointing to a set of Moroccan-style doors set into the wall. Through colored isinglass panes, soft lights flickered.

"I don't know," Sasha said quickly. "But listen, Victoria. This is wild, but you *have* to focus. We are here for one reason only: to figure out Dikarinsky's angle. We need to find out if he's responsible for the archival thefts, and whether Dimitri knows anything about what we think is going on. Don't get sucked into the rest of this."

Victoria looked at Sasha. "You're right, I'm sorry. I hadn't thought about it. I think Marina will find out what we need, though."

The two moved toward the doors, and Sasha opened one. Victoria preceded him into the room.

It was very dark, but refreshingly cool and quiet after the tumult of the dance floor. The long, narrow room had elaborately tiled floors and plastered walls. It was as if the door they had just passed through separated the discotheque from an antechamber of the Alhambra. Sasha's eyes slowly adjusted to the dim light.

Along the walls of the room, overstuffed sofas and banquettes were lined with people, many groping and kissing each other frantically. Sasha was immediately embarrassed. Victoria was curious.

"Don't pull away," she said. "Stick close to me, and we'll go through to the other side—there's another door."

"Victoria," Sasha hissed. "This is disgusting."

"Oh, Sash," Victoria said wearily, "you're so repressed. Come on." She grabbed his hand, and the two of them forced their way through the writhing crowd.

Sasha smelled something. "What is that?" he asked.

"Hashish," Victoria said matter-of-factly, and pulled him through the second set of doors.

They were now in a grotto. Stalactites dripped from the ceiling and stalagmites rose from the floor. Palms grew in every corner, and a bevy of vines crawled up and down the cast-iron posts that supported the roof.

"This room is amazing," Victoria said. "What was it?"

"I don't know," Sasha said. "Probably a winter garden."

"Dig the blue ceiling."

"It's glass," Sasha said. "You're looking through the snow sitting on the roof."

Small tables full of well-dressed people were scattered around, and a deejay played Western and Russian disco. As they entered, the crowd was rising to its feet for a song from the 1970s by Boney M.

"*'Rasputin!'*" screamed the crowd.

"What is this?" Victoria asked. "I feel as if I've wandered into a Soviet bar mitzvah."

Sasha smiled. "It's 'Rasputin,'" he said.

"Here's the chorus," Sasha said. "Let's dance." He grabbed Victoria's hand, and the two ran onto the floor, joined by most of the people in the room who waved their hands in the air, singing at the top of their lungs. Sasha noted a number of people doing drugs openly, and he shook his head as he sang along with the crowd:

> *"Rah, Rah, RASPUTIN*
> *Lover of the Russian queen*
> *There was a cat that really was gone.*
> *Rah, Rah, RASPUTIN*
> *Russia's greatest love machine*
> *It was a shame how he carried on."*

"That's a scream, and thank you for the trip to 1978," Victoria said, pulling Sasha off the floor.

"Sorry," he said. "I love that song."

"So does Moscow, evidently. More doors ahead."

Walking out of the winter garden, they were confronted again by the enormous tank, which was now full of men. The women who had been in earlier were drying themselves in semiprivacy behind a curtain. One caught Sasha staring, and she pulled the curtain tight with an angry snap.

"I've always loved seafood," Victoria said, staring at the tank. One of the nude blonds swam around the tank, following Victoria as they returned to the bar. "I could get used to this place," she said.

"Maybe Marina is finished seducing Dimitri. We should go back," Sasha said, pulling her along with him.

The two moved through the front bar until Sasha saw Marina standing in a group surrounded by some of Dimitri's friends from the table. Larisa was regaling them with a story in Russian.

"And so, against my will, I am taken to this new sex club in Saint Petersburg—an S and M club. I tell you, I was fairly horrified."

"What was it like?" Marina asked, her voice dripping with disdain.

"Well, it's closed now. It wasn't very interesting. Lots of men and women skulking around in dark corners."

"No sex?" asked Dimitri, amused

"Of course not," Larisa replied, leaning forward to light her cigarette off of Dimitri's. *"You can imagine—a room full of Russians. Everyone was looking for someone else to beat them. Everyone went home disappointed."*

The crowd around Marina burst into laughter, and she looked over their heads at Sasha and Victoria.

"This place is ridiculous," Marina whispered to Sasha. "Is there someplace quiet where we can all talk?"

"Dimitri, is there a quiet place where Marina and I can go chat?" Sasha asked.

"I don't think so. The scene in the Moorish hall gets a little difficult. You might have to go outside," he replied.

"Nonsense," Larisa interjected. "Dimitri, you remember where we went last time we were here." Larisa gestured to the back of the nightclub with her head.

Dimitri's eyes brightened, and he gave Larisa's waist a lascivious squeeze. "I forgot. If you go back into the disco, there is a mirrored door behind the deejay booth. It sticks, but push it hard, and you'll get through—no one will stop you. Climb the stairs to the top, and there's a glassed-in section on the roof—it's where the manager's office is. No one will bother you."

"Great views," Larisa added.

"That's fine with me," Marina said. "We won't be gone that long. Take care of Victoria, will you, Dimitri?"

"My pleasure," he said, waving them on.

The two forced their way through the crowd, and they passed the tank, still full of naked men swimming.

The cousins made their way to the mirrored door in the disco, and Sasha forced it open with his shoulder. Behind the door was a worn wooden circular stair, the walls covered in chipped and peeling plaster painted an industrial green and covered with graffiti. It had evidently been a servants' staircase at one point.

"This is a bad idea," Marina said, shivering.

"We'll be fine," Sasha said, starting the climb and handing her his jacket.

They arrived at a large metal door at the staircase's end. Sasha opened it and let Marina through before anchoring it with a chipped cinder block evidently there for that purpose.

"Oh, Sasha!" Marina called from the darkened glass-enclosed roof. "Come and see!"

Sasha walked toward the sound of her voice, the loose copper panels of the roof creaking under his feet. He looked up.

The Slavic style towers of the GUM department store framed a view of Red Square ahead of them. The ancient red walls of the Kremlin were floodlighted, as were its cathedrals and towers. The red stars glowed dimly from the rooftops, and the tricolor flags of Russia snapped in the crisp winter wind. To the left, St. Basil's sat bathed in light; to the right, the history museum and the reconstructed cathedrals glittered, their domes frosted with ice. In the distance, the lights of the hills of Moscow twinkled in the unusually clear air.

"I can't believe it," Marina said. "It is so beautiful."

"It is, isn't it," Sasha agreed, moving closer to her and trying not to fall on the uneven flooring. Marina tore herself away from the view and turned to face Sasha.

"I'm not sure you're right," she said finally.

"About the figurine?" Sasha replied.

"About Dimitri. I started to chat with him about the club and the Mafia in a very stupid way to see if he would freeze up, or give me some kind of clue."

"Anything?"

"No. Cool as can be. Then I said I thought that Dikarinsky was very, um, *uncultured*," she said, using the Russian word, "and that it wouldn't surprise me if he were involved in any number of illegal activities."

"What then?"

"He agreed with me."

"So what makes you think I'm not right, then?"

Marina looked back over the view of Moscow. "Sasha, he *wants* us to believe Dikarinsky is behind everything. He was far too eager to agree with me. I got a flood of suspicions and information about oil deals and government officials and precious metals. It was too much information to come from someone who is normally so guarded. You've known tons of Russians, both émigrés and new Russians—when has any of them voluntarily given you information like that? We always play these things closer to the vest than that."

Sasha thought about what Marina had said. She was right. He needed to speak to Gennady and to get that research done quickly.

"Sasha, I didn't want you to be right about the figurine, and I'm not sure you are, but I am a very good judge of people, and Dimitri is more involved than you think he is. He's not an innocent, no matter what you think. Watch him."

"I see what you mean. We should all leave here together and go back to the hotel. I'll see what I can learn from Dikarinsky back at the house tomorrow, and I'll meet you and Victoria at the archives in the afternoon. I'll leave a note for you at the desk of the hotel with the time. I know how to find my way there. I'm concerned about going back to the Dikarinskys' house, though."

"I don't think you should go back there tonight. Why don't you stay at the hotel with Victoria?"

"It might be suspicious."

"It will be safer. Please, Sasha," Marina said, with what approached genuine concern in her voice.

Sasha realized she was right, and he was cold. "Let's go back inside."

The two walked back down the stairs and returned to the Twelve Chairs. As they walked through the Moroccan hallway, they saw it was strangely empty. Entering the main room of the club, they realized that the contest had begun. Sasha and Marina looked around for Dimitri and the rest of their group, but, blinded by the spotlights, they couldn't see anyone on the dance floor. Sasha walked out into the room and scanned the space for Victoria, and he eventually found her, standing on the dais at the far end of the room, behind one of the twelve gilt chairs.

"So, it seems your friend was chosen." Sasha turned. It was Larisa. "I myself had no such luck."

"I'm sorry," Sasha replied.

"I'm just glad you didn't miss this. This is always fun." Larisa turned away from Sasha and back toward the stage, where it appeared all the contestants were gathered. The announcer was the blond man from the tank in the bar, but he was now wearing a tuxedo.

"Dear guests! The Twelve Chairs is pleased to announce its weekly contest!"

The crowd roared.

"Guests, when the audience counts to twelve, open your chairs!"

The dancers on the floor began the countdown in Russian, and spotlights whirled around the room. Victoria had no idea what they were saying, but what was happening needed no simultaneous translation. The drum roll got louder and louder, as did the chanting of the crowd.

"Ten! Eleven! Twelve!" the crowd burst into cheers as the contestants struggled to rip open the loose seat cushions. It seemed that part of the fun was to watch them try to tear into them without benefit of knives or scissors. As they succeeded, one by one, the crowd let out expressions of disappointment when no diamonds were revealed. The applause continued until only Victoria and a small wiry man with a beard were still trying to open their cushions. Then, using the pin from her brooch, Victoria ripped the fab-

ric of her cushion. The crowd cheered at her ingenuity. But nothing was inside, and the crowd cried out in disappointment on her behalf.

The bearded man finally opened his chair with a pocketknife he got from somewhere, and he pulled out a red velvet pouch.

The crowd roared. The crowd hissed. The crowd, it seemed, was on Victoria's side.

The man with the beard looked at the crowd and shrugged his shoulders. He held up his hands like a prizefighter.

"Vik-to-ri-ya!" shouted Larisa, and the crowd around them picked it up. Soon, the room was chanting Victoria's name. The man pointed at Victoria and the crowd cheered. He shrugged, raised his eyebrows, and walked over to Victoria, handing her the red pouch.

The crowd cheered.

"That was very cultured of him," said Larisa. "Very sporting."

Sasha joined in the crowd's cheering and applause, as Victoria opened the bag, and poured a small stream of diamonds back into the man's hands, splitting the bag between them, to the cheers of the crowd. The music began again, and the crowd turned away from the dais and back to the dance floor.

Sasha forced his way through the crowd to get to Victoria, who was suddenly surrounded by unsavory-looking admirers.

"Can you believe it?" Victoria asked incredulously. "This was a scream, but I am certainly ready to leave if you are. You're not going back to the Dikarinskys', are you? Come back and stay with me at the hotel. Let's get out of here before these people try to mug me for the diamonds."

The three hurried back to the coat check, got their things, and ran outside to find their car. They dived into the car and leaned back against the seat, exhausted as the car pulled away.

"I have never seen anything like that," Victoria said.

"The diamonds?" Marina asked, turning to her.

"My God, no," Victoria replied. "I've got better stones of Gran's at home—I mean Dimitri!"

"What happened?" Sasha asked.

"Well, they had just called my number for the raffle, which I knew because everyone started pushing me and got very excited, when Dimitri came down the hall with this *look* on his face! I mean, Sash, people pulled back from him to give him room. Anyway, this was right after you and Marina walked away, and he said, 'Tell your cousin I'll see him tomorrow,' and left. Everyone else followed him except for Kostia and Katya, neither of whom speak English, of course, so they just shoved me on the stage, and you saw the rest." She sighed heavily and peered into the bag of diamonds.

Sasha looked at Marina, who shrugged. They would have to wait until the morning to see the outcome. Victoria looked at the two of them.

"Hey—don't be so gloomy. I need help." She shook the pouch. "These add up either to one very sad bracelet, or one pair of very fabulous earrings, I'm not sure which."

Sasha looked out the window as Marina and Victoria debated the possibilities. They were all exhausted. Too exhausted to notice that as their car surged toward the hotel, it was being followed by a nondescript black Lada.

Eighteen

Sasha woke, and rose from the upholstered sofa in Victoria's suite at the Metropole. He slipped into the bathroom, took a quick shower and shaved, then slipped back into his evening clothes from the night before. With his coat on, no one would notice, he was sure.

He knocked on Victoria's bedroom door.

"Sasha?" she called.

"Yes, may I come in?"

"Sure," she replied, and he opened the door. Victoria looked very small in the enormous, overly upholstered bed.

"Just for the record, the sex was amazing," she said, reaching for a glass of water.

Sasha laughed. "Listen. I'm going to call my father from here, because I know I can't talk with him on the phone at the Dikarinskys'."

"Good idea. I'll shower and pull myself together. Don't worry, you'll have privacy. I'm going to have breakfast with Marina and Craig Tippett. He actually seems kind of nice."

"You're a better man than I am, Gunga Din," Sasha quoted blithely. "Thanks. I'll go call."

Sasha dialed the hotel operator and asked to be put through to his father's number at home in New York. The phone rang a number of times, and finally Diane answered.

"Hello!" she said cheerfully.

"Diane, it's Sasha."

"Oh, Sasha, thank goodness you called—your father didn't know how to reach you in Russia, and he's been trying to find you since this morning. We've been calling everyone."

"Diane, I'm sorry to have worried both of you. Listen, I need to speak with Father. I'm hoping we can put some things to rest this morning. I have important news."

"Oh, so does he, Sasha. We are very proud of you. Big kiss. See you when you get back to New York. Hold on for your father." She put down the receiver, and he could hear her calling for Cyril.

"Hullo, boy," his father said, his voice warm and friendly.

"Hello, Father. Things are a bit crazier here than I had expected."

"We'll be happier when we get you home safe, Sashenka. Listen, I have a lot to say to you, starting with the suit. I'm going to drop it."

Sasha was silent, waiting.

"I've been thinking about what you said at dinner in New York. I've wanted only the best to come from this situation, but I think that I've been a little shortsighted. Getting all wrapped up in the figurine made me forget what your mother *really* would have wanted. She would have wanted you here with your family, and working at your passion. I let myself get carried away, and I apologize. Marina called last night and said you thought that the figurine was a fake. She suggested that we wait for a bit to see what is going on. I had my lawyer withdraw the claim this morning. The letters should have arrived at Leighton's in New York hours ago."

Sasha grinned. "But why?"

"Sasha, your mother taught you everything you know. If you say the piece is a fake, the piece is a fake. No questions asked—you'll be able to prove it soon enough, I'm sure," his father said.

"Well, well. What about Marina?"

"Like her mother, Marina is in this for Marina. She won't go out on a limb for anyone but herself, and she'll soon realize that it is in her interest to drop everything. What will you do next?"

Sasha took a deep breath. "I'm certain the figurine is a fake. We're going to the archives to try to prove it this afternoon."

"It sounds dangerous. Be careful." Cyril switched to Russian. *"Good-bye, son. I am very proud of you, and your mother would be, too. She loved you very much, and I hope you know that I love you, too."* With that, he hung up.

Sasha hung up the phone as well and smiled. He couldn't remember the last time he had heard his father speak in Russian. He stood up, and went back into Victoria's room.

"Listen—I'm going to run back to the Dikarinskys' house to see if I can get my things. I was supposed to stay through this weekend, and then go to their *dacha*. I'm going to have to get out of it, and I don't know how."

"Already taken care of."

"Pardon?"

"Craig just slipped a note under the door—your father dropped the suit, and so John Burnham is looking for you everywhere. He wants you moved out of the Dikarinskys' and into a suite in this hotel—something about conflict of interest. Craig also said that he told the von Kemps the piece might be a fake, and they're dropping the suit until it can be authenticated."

"I'll be damned," Sasha said. "That's luck."

"I'll say. See you at three. The faster we get out of here, the better. Now—important question: Can I wear Balenciaga to breakfast?"

❖   ❖   ❖

Sasha left after a few minutes, took the beautiful staircase to the lobby. He was passing the entrance to the restaurant when he heard a familiar voice call out: "Sasha! Join us!" It was John Burnham. Anne and Lena Martin were with him. "How are you, son?" John said, clapping his shoulder when he walked over to their table. "You are the tricky one! How did you manage it? We didn't even know. I'm very pleased. Very pleased indeed. I know that Anne has missed you."

Sasha looked at them incredulously. He noticed the bottle of Champagne on the table, despite the early morning hour. And he noted Anne's dull expression.

Lena spoke. "We just got the call from New York about the letter from your family's lawyer dropping the suit. I was so pleased, I called John to tell him immediately. We had a little meeting, then called Anne. We're very proud of you, Sasha. You've handled this extremely well. Leighton's values this a great deal." She handed him a plain paper fax, and waited while he read it.

Citing "family accord," which prompted the Ozerovskys to drop the suit entirely, there was a "common hope" that a portion of the funds from the sale of the figurine would be donated to the former Ozerovsky Children's Hospital in Saint Petersburg. If this could be arranged, the Ozerovsky family association would immediately drop its suit.

"The whole thing has fallen down like a house of cards. Sasha, it is obvious to us that this is all your doing. So we were trying to call you to invite you to give you the good news. First, that Dimitri has agreed to the terms of your family's agreement, and second—"

"Other good news?" Sasha asked, curious. "What is it?"

"Your new appointment," Anne said calmly.

"Yes, we are very pleased. Anne has been made international director of the Russian department and will move to the London office. You, Sasha, will be head of New York. Congratulations."

"And my suspension?" Sasha asked.

"Over as of this minute. Welcome back." John leaned back in his chair, and gave a large grin, downing his glass of Champagne.

Sasha looked at him, and at Anne's sad eyes and untouched Champagne. He could tell that she hadn't been consulted. London was an important promotion for her though—he hoped that she would grow used to it.

"So, I'm now the head of the department in New York," he asked steadily.

"Absolutely," John replied.

"Then I would very much like to get back to work and go to the archives this afternoon with Gennady Antropin. Also, I would like to make sure that all of this is okay with Anne."

Anne looked at him, and she gave him a small smile.

"Well, this is what you've always wanted, isn't it?" she asked, and raised her glass. "To Sasha, and good luck. Trust me, New York is no prize. You can meet Gennady at the archives at two P.M."

Sasha, Anne, Lena, and John Burnham all took a drink. It was apparent that no one but John was completely unworried.

"Well, then," John said cheerfully. "That's all settled."

❖　❖　❖

Sasha walked to the desk, and asked for two pieces of paper and two envelopes. On each sheet of paper, he wrote: "2." He placed them in the envelopes and addressed one to Victoria and the other to Marina. Then he passed the envelopes to the concierge.

Exiting the hotel, he decided to walk back to the Dikarinskys' house on the Bolshaya Ordynka.

Cars rushed past him, and the wet snow crunched beneath his shoes. Soon, the Moskva River sat brackish under the bridge, and the Moscow hills were muddy smudges against granite-colored skies, a stark contrast to the glittering views of the night before. Sasha shivered, and looked ahead toward the south side of the river, and the end of what he genuinely hoped would be his last trip to Moscow.

❖　❖　❖

Sasha climbed the steps to the Dikarinsky house, and when the doors opened, an anxious-looking servant he had never seen before took his coat.

"Highness, Mr. Dikarinsky is waiting for you in the library. There is an important message for you, and we had no idea where you were. Hurry, hurry."

The two of them moved down the hall to where Dikarinsky sat waiting.

He stood as Sasha entered the room. *"Well, son, you must have had quite a night!"* They continued in Russian.

"It was very pleasant, thank you. I hope you and Madame Dikarinsky were not disturbed by the fact that I did not return. It was very rude, and I hope you'll forgive me."

"Forgive you? Ha!" Dikarinsky laughed. "I didn't sleep here last night either." He moved around the edge of his malachite-veneered desk, indicating that Sasha should sit down. Sasha sat in the chair he was offered.

"It looks like we both had someplace better to go, no? The Kremlin, Maxim's, and then a suite at the Metropole? Looks like ninety years after the Revolution, you princes still have the same method. The American girl was quite a piece of skirt—that I'll give you! Class all the way. Forgive you? You may be U.S. born, but you're Russian. Just because a fly is born in a barn, doesn't make it a horse!"

Sasha was embarrassed by Dikarinsky's coarse assumption that he had slept with Victoria.

He cleared his throat. "Miss de Witt is my cousin, Mr. Dikarinsky."

"Aha!" Dikarinsky said, shaking his head and laughing "Decadent to the end! I was only concerned this morning when my bodyguards lost you. We followed you from the nightclub to the hotel, and we knew you had breakfast with the Leighton's staff, but when you left the hotel on foot, we got worried. It is impossible to protect you in Moscow if you walk—particularly in evening clothes. Quite stupid of you really. You're no idiot. You should have gone by taxi."

"You're right. I apologize."

"No need. Here. A fax arrived for you here last night. From Leighton's. Apparently business is to deprive us of your company. My wife will be most disappointed."

Sasha looked at the fax, the same one he had seen at the hotel. Attached was a note from John Burnham explaining that as Sasha was now head of the New York department, and with Dikarinsky a potential client, it was awkward for Sasha to continue to enjoy their hospitality when there was so much work to do.

Dikarinsky spoke. "I'm afraid you won't be able to join us at the *dacha* this weekend, and I am very sorry. Belovo is very pretty. But I am very pleased that your family has dropped the suit, as it will make it easier for us to add Snegurochka to our collection. It has been a pleasure having you, Sasha. I'll take care of your room at the hotel, and arrange an entertainment of some sort for you and your colleagues tonight. I'll see that your things are packed and moved, and that you are set up as you were in Saint Petersburg."

Complete with surveillance, Sasha thought. *Great*. He thanked the older man and turned to leave the library. Once back upstairs and in his room, Sasha found a note on his bed, along with a change of clothes. It was from Dimitri:

Dear Sasha,

I'm glad this is all finally taken care of. I really feel that you can be very helpful to me in New York. I look forward to a long and very successful relationship with Leighton's. I hope that we will have a chance to speak before you leave Moscow. I have an opportunity that I believe you would find very interesting. . . .

Sasha looked up from the letter and glanced around the room. His things had been packed while he had been talking to Mr. Dikarinsky, or perhaps earlier, upon receipt of the fax. He turned his attention back to the note.

As a token of my affection, and in hope that we will work together even more closely in the future, please accept this small gift in appreciation of all your help—I recently found it in a collection here in Moscow, but you should have it.
Sincerely,
Dimitri.

Sasha looked down at the bed and noticed a familiar holly wood box. He picked it up and opened it. Nestled in the white satin lining was a beautiful diamond brooch composed of a Maltese cross in diamonds, sitting on a crescent moon—the Ozerovsky coat of arms. Though it now had a brooch fitting on the back, it had two mounts that indicated it had once been a hair ornament.

Sasha turned the brooch over in his hands. It was lovely and well made, and all the right marks were on it. Something bothered him, though, but he couldn't quite put his finger on it. Covering the brooch with one hand, he studied his own signet ring, which also bore his family's coat of arms. He compared the image on the ring to the brooch.

The moon was facing in the wrong direction.

Fabergé would never have made such a mistake. But if Dimitri had had the brooch made, and had taken the coat of arms from an old engraving or a photographic negative that was accidentally reversed, he just might have.

It wasn't Mr. Dikarinsky after all. Marina was right. It was Dimitri.

But who could have made the brooch? It was of exquisite quality. Sasha racked his brain for a clue, and then it hit him. He would go to see the jeweler Gennady had mentioned at the Kremlin—

Vadim Orlovsky. Sasha knew he needed to see Orlovsky, and soon. But first, the archives.

Sasha changed into more casual clothes. Pushing the Fauxbergé bell push for the last time to summon the servant to get his bags, Sasha left the English bedroom, then walked slowly down the staircase and out the door of the house into the car that waited for him in the bitter Moscow midday.

Nineteen

~

SASHA'S CAR ARRIVED AT THE HOTEL, and he went in to speak to the desk clerk.

"Good afternoon. My name is Sasha Ozerovsky—"

"Ah, yes, sir. I just received the call from Mosdikoil. The bellhop here will take you to your suite. We'll send your luggage up right away."

"Thank you." Sasha reached to take the key. "Tell me, there were some messages left for Miss de Witt and Countess Shoutine. Have they been picked up?" The desk clerk looked at his computer screen.

"Yes, sir. They have."

"Thank you." Sasha followed the bellboy to his room, which was as luxurious as the one at the Astoria in Saint Petersburg. Sasha tipped the bellboy, then checked his phone messages. Nothing. On the desk, there were several notes on a tray. Sasha picked them up.

"*Sasha! How extravagant!*" one of them read. "*John and I would be pleased to join you for the ballet tonight. Let's get together for a drink beforehand. What fun! Best, Elise Burnham.*"

Sasha frowned in confusion and opened the next note.

"*Divine,*" it read. "*See you at two, and after, you can tell me what to wear tonight. XOXO Victoria.*"

The phone rang.

"Sir?" said a voice in Russian. "This is Masha from Mr. Dikarinsky's office. We met aboard the Eagle, remember?"

"Of course I do, Masha. How are you?"

"Busy, thank you. Mr. Dikarinsky asked that I arrange something special to celebrate your new appointment at Leighton's for this evening. There will be a small reception at your hotel, and then you will be escorted to the Bolshoi for tonight's production of *La Bayadère*. Afterward, dinner for all of you at Yar, which is a Russian restaurant and very amusing. I have taken the liberty of inviting Mr. and Mrs. Burnham, Mrs. Holton, Mrs. Martin, Miss de Witt, Countess Shoutine, and Mr. and Mrs. Antropin. With you, that will fill the ten seats in the presidential box."

Sasha did some quick math. "Actually, that makes nine, Masha."

"Ah yes, of course. Well, with the Dikarinskys away at their *dacha*, Mr. Durakov will be the tenth for the ballet and dinner."

"Of course," Sasha replied. "Masha, you think of everything. Thank you."

"I will see you beforehand, sir. Good-bye." She hung up.

❖   ❖   ❖

Sasha quickly straightened himself up, pulled on his coat, and headed back for the lobby, which he knew would be crowded. He reached into one pocket for a phone number and into another pocket for his cell phone. As he walked down the main stairs of the lobby behind a Japanese tour group, he dialed the number. The number rang and rang. Finally, a man answered.

"*I'm listening.*"

"Is this Mr. Orlovsky?" They spoke in Russian.

"Who wants to know?"

"My name is Sasha Ozerovsky, and I am a friend of Gennady Antropin's."

"Any friend of Gennady's is a friend of mine," replied Orlovsky. "How may I help you?"

"I have a friend who would like some diamonds set quickly as earrings." He paused. "I hear you do work for Dimitri Durakov."

Orlovsky laughed broadly. "Always in a hurry, that Dimitri. Yes, I do. Well, if the design isn't too complicated, and you don't want an elaborate setting, I can do it fast enough. My schedule isn't bad tomorrow, but today is impossible. In fact, I'm expecting Dimitri. I'm doing some restoration for him."

"Yes," Sasha said, "he mentioned that to me."

"I'll tell him you called then, and thank him for recommending me to you."

"Actually, I'd prefer it if you didn't. I believe he thinks I'll steal all his sources for restoration." Sasha laughed brightly. "You won't mention I called, will you?"

"Not at all," replied Orlovsky. "I can keep a secret, and frankly, I could use some more business. I live near the Arbat. Let me give you my address. Tomorrow morning around ten, then?"

Sasha agreed, and the two men made their arrangements as Sasha continued to walk around the lobby, insinuating himself within one tour group or another. There was no sign of guards, and no one eyed him suspiciously.

Sasha walked to the front desk, and the concierge pointed toward the middle of the lobby. Sasha looked—Gennady was sitting there on a sofa. Sasha smiled and approached him.

"How was your Moscow night?" Gennady asked.

"I'll tell you at the archives."

"That good?"

"Too much to say. My cousins are meeting us there."

"Are they trained researchers?"

"No, but between us we have seven or eight languages, and at this point, we all need to be working together. There is too much to be done."

"If you say so. We do have a lot of work. I've no idea if the files that you want are available. The archives we are going to contain the personal records of the Romanov family, and they are a labyrinth. We need to be as efficient as possible."

"I understand," Sasha said. "Our car is waiting outside. Let's go."

The two men walked through the security check at the hotel doors, then stepped into the waiting sedan.

The car pulled away, and drove through the streets of Moscow. Sasha and Gennady were both quiet for a long time. Sasha finally spoke.

"Gennady, I called Vadim Orlovsky."

"Why?"

"Dimitri gave me a diamond brooch that he purports belonged to my family. I noticed there was an error in the rendering of my family's coat of arms. I have a feeling Orlovsky made it for Dimitri."

"Well, he's very talented, but he would never create a fake."

"What makes you say that? Don't you think he could be the jeweler who made Snegurochka?"

"He is talented enough, yes. But he can't make purpurine, and he is the most honest and deeply Orthodox man I have ever met. He would no more create a forgery than kill a man."

"But could he be persuaded or intimidated?"

"No. He would put in a deliberate flaw, some kind of mistake that an expert would notice immediately."

"Such as a reversed coat of arms?"

"I don't know. Perhaps, or an inventory number out of sequence, or Odessa or Kiev marks on metalwork that only ever came from Moscow or Saint Petersburg. It is his goal to create a catalogue raisonné of Fabergé—a complete compilation of every legitimate piece ever made. He is, in my opinion, the greatest expert."

"Well, come with me tomorrow. The meeting should be very interesting."

❖　❖　❖

Their car rolled up to the Akademik Nauk archives, where the Romanov personal files were retained. Once out of the car and inside the door, they were met by a cheerful older man who greeted Gennady fondly.

"Sasha, this is my friend Kirill Stepanovitch. He is the one to ask about those files."

"Kirill Stepanovitch, forgive me for being blunt, but I need to find out something very important about a piece of Fabergé."

"Can't help you there. Those files are in Saint Petersburg."

"Well, what I need is something specific. I heard that the Committee of Valuables had a list of confiscations that was recently requested by the Diamond Fund."

"Young man," Kirill Stepanovitch said, "why don't you tell me exactly what you want to find, and I will tell you how to find it."

"I believe the piece in question might have been confiscated during the 1930s and then sold by Antikvariat, because it ended up in a collection in Germany."

"Not really enough information for me. There are so many ways to look."

"Then these confiscation files are no good to us?"

"You don't have enough information for him to know," said Gennady.

Sasha sighed, and turned to sit down in the vestibule to wait for Marina and Victoria to arrive. He stared at the steady stream of scholars who had come to do research in the archives.

"Wait," said Kirill Stepanovitch. "What did you say your name was?"

"Ozerovsky." Sasha turned to face him again. "Alexander Kirillovitch."

"Prince Ozerovsky?"

"Yes, once," Sasha replied.

"Well, then, I have an idea. Might a servant have known where the piece was?"

"Perhaps."

"Then it is simple. You need to go to the KGB."

"The what?" said a voice behind them. Sasha turned. It was Marina, and Victoria was with her.

"Apparently the information we have is too broad for the confiscation files to be of any use. We need to go to the KGB," Sasha told them in English.

"Why?" asked Victoria.

"Come with me," said Kirill Stepanovitch in Russian. "We can go in here." He led the group into a small office off the main hall. Everyone sat down, and Kirill Stepanovitch took the seat at the head of the table. "The confiscation lists won't work," he continued in Russian. "They are endless lists of objects that were taken from safety deposit boxes, from safes in homes, from warehouses, country estates, things like that. They are lists of objects. If you were looking for an imperial necklace, or the chalices from a specific church, you would go to the lists for that place, that bank, that palace; you would turn to such lists, which are often incomplete. But since you have a name, and a great name at that, you must turn to the KGB."

Sasha glanced over. Marina was softly translating for Victoria, who nodded as Marina finished her sentence.

"Why the KGB?" Victoria asked.

"KGB because," Kirill Stepanovitch said in heavily accented English, smiling at Victoria, then continuing again in Russian, "you see, in the 1930s, when the money ran thin, Stalin began a search for valuables. He and the NKVBD, the secret police, rounded up many people who had been associated with the great families, banks, jewelry firms. They questioned former servants and minor members of noble and merchant and academic families to find out what they knew, and where things were."

"And so?" Sasha asked.

"And so, if you go to the KGB archives, and tell them that you are Prince Ozerovsky, and that you want your family's file, you will get a folder, and it might have the names of any of your family's past associates, confidants, or servants who were questioned, what those interrogations revealed, and, sometimes, what happened to those people."

"But surely these files are confidential? I can't simply walk in and ask for it, can I?"

"Yes. You can. Sometimes it takes a long time. Since the fall of communism, these files can be made accessible, depending on the reason. I have friends in the archives there, as does Gennady. We can help you."

Sasha looked at Marina, who had translated for Victoria. "What do you want to do?" he asked. "We might find out if the figurine was really given by Cici to someone in the household, but even then, we can't be sure that what we have is a fake."

"I'll go and help you read them," Marina said. "With Gennady, we might be able to get through them fairly quickly."

"I'm happy to tag along, but since I can't read Russian, perhaps you'd rather I go back to the hotel?" Victoria asked.

"No," said Sasha. "While we're there, I want to check in with the people who handle art theft—they might have information about the Saint Petersburg archive thefts, and then we'll need someone just to go through pictures. Why don't we all go to the KGB files at Lubyanka." Sasha found that just saying those words was hard for him, they had such a resonance of misfortune and unhappiness.

❖   ❖   ❖

The car had driven into Lubyanka Square from Dzerzhinsky Street, then driven around the main facade of the KGB building, which looked to Sasha like an old Russian Palace on steroids.

They drove around the corner and pulled up in front of the door on the side of the larger building. Gennady turned around from the front seat: "I'll go in and ask about the files." He started to get out of the car, and then turned back. "If I don't come out again, tell my children I love them." He looked and Sasha and Marina's terrified and dumbstruck expressions.

"I'm sorry. Terrible joke." He got out of the car. Marina took Sasha's hands, and they sat in silence.

In about ten minutes, Gennady came out, a slight smile on his face, and he approached the car. "It is different than I expected, but then everything is. The agent inside is interested in the case, and would like you to come inside. My friend in the archives will release all the files to us without going through regular channels. Please come inside." He opened the door of the car, Sasha, Marina, and Victoria got out and climbed the stairs to the offices. Once inside, an agent guided Victoria and Gennady to the art fraud department, leaving Sasha and Marina behind to examine the Ozerovsky file.

The waiting area where Marina and Sasha remained was lit by too-bright fluorescent fixtures. Many armed and uniformed young agents walked purposefully up and down the halls. Sasha was sure that if he went to the FBI offices in Quantico, Virginia, it would look pretty much the same, but he felt as if he and Marina, in their expensive French and English clothes, were like ghosts. No one even met their eyes as they stood waiting.

A young agent approached them.

"I am Agent Kovalev. A pleasure."

"Agent," Sasha said, extending his hand. "I am Alexander Ozerovsky, and this is Marina Shoutine."

"Sir," the agent replied. He turned and kissed Marina's extended hand. "Countess, if you would follow me."

Marina smiled.

The young man took them up in an elevator and then to a very small room with one table and a few small folding chairs.

"Now, which files would you like?" the agent asked.

"Ozerovsky," Sasha replied.

"And Shoutine," Marina said. She turned to Sasha. "When will I ever get the chance again?" she said in English.

The two cousins sat for a while in the small room waiting. There was no discussion. There was nothing to say. Sasha couldn't imagine what Victoria was feeling, alone with Gennady, and no one with her who spoke English. He regretted leaving her.

After about twenty minutes the files arrived. Agent Kovalev put a small file in front of Sasha, and a larger one in front of Marina.

"The Ozerovsky file is quite small because the entire family fled, and many of their closest servants went with them. The Shoutine file is much bigger. The Shoutine family was large, and they had many estates all over central Russia. During the collectivization of the estates, many more people were investigated. If you have any questions, I'll be down the hall."

Sasha looked at Marina, and then at his file. He opened it and began reading.

> File: Andrei Karpov, Combine operator.
> Former butler to the Ozerovsky family.
>
> During interrogation of the subject, admitted knowing silver objects belonging to the family buried in garden, along with religious objects of precious metals of value.

Sasha looked down the page. It continued:

> Objects retrieved, and turned over to Department of Valuables.
>
> Value approximately 169 gold roubles.
>
> Subject expired in detention.

Expired in detention? Sasha wondered if he had been murdered, or if he had simply been detained for so long that by the time the valuables were discovered he had died.

Sasha continued reading. There wasn't much of relevance in the file. He went through page after page, but most simply said that the subjects didn't know anything. People who refused to cooperate frequently "expired in detention."

Sasha flipped through the pages, scanning them purely for information about the figurine. He saw nothing, however. One report toward the end did catch his eye.

> File: Elena Karlovna Zefirov
> Schoolteacher, Kursk District.
> Former "Sister" at Former Convent of Martha and Mary, Moscow.
>
> During interrogation of subject, admitted that while in service to the former Grand Duchess Elizabeth Feodorovna, sister to the former Empress, she was privy to a private meeting between the former Grand Duchess and the former Princess Ozerovsky (Fled Russia, 1918.) in which Ozerovsky tried to return a valuable jewel given to her by the Grand Duchess in 1905. Subject discovered that the blue diamond in the jewel virtually priceless.
>
> It is assumed the jewel left the country with Ozerovsky.

There was a later addition from 1936.

> Subject discovered teaching religion to her students, maintaining former Grand Duchess a saint.
>
> Executed on July 16, 1936, by order of Kursk Soviet.

Sasha couldn't believe it, and read the page over again. The brooch his great-grandmother was wearing in the picture his grandfather had taken. The brooch his father had given to Marina's mother for her wedding day. The brooch over which their mothers had stopped speaking to each other. It wasn't a sapphire. It was a blue diamond.

Sasha turned to Marina and was shocked to see she was rigid and pale, staring blankly at the pages in front of her. The papers from her pile were spread all over the desk and floor.

"I can't look at these anymore," she said quietly in Russian. "I didn't know; I never knew. Look at this—hundreds of them. Servants, peasants, Jews, teachers, clergymen. Innocent people. Whole villages. All of them dead because of their loyalty to the family. 'Wouldn't cooperate.' 'Refused to collectivize.' 'Refused to renounce decadent religion and social practice.' 'Expired in detention.' Why did they do nothing? Why didn't they say something? They just died, and it is all our fault."

"You did nothing," Sasha said. "It's not your fault, or your family's fault. They resisted, don't you see? They would not be bullied or allow themselves to compromise with tyranny. It's not about you. It's history."

"But, why?" she whispered, looking at the pages scattered around her, essentially the only tombstones the hundreds of people had.

❖   ❖   ❖

Sasha and Marina followed Agent Karpov to the place where Gennady and Victoria were going over the piles of photocopies and photographs.

"This is almost impossible," Victoria said dejectedly. "There are photographs of things dating back to the 1930s and Stalin's sales, up through the things stolen by the Nazis during the war, the illegally exported items in the 1970s, as well as the recent thefts. It could take days to sort through all of the material. I haven't worked so hard since I was at Parsons going through the files at the Costume Institute." She sighed and put down the photos in her hands, which Sasha could see were all medieval tapestries of no use to them.

Sasha and Gennady spoke at length with Agent Kovalev about the situation with Snegurochka.

Finally, the agent said, "Unless you have some kind of proof, something that will allow me to directly point a finger at forgers or people who are illegally exporting precious metals and stones from the Russian Federation, I'm afraid there is nothing I can do. Please take my card, and do not hesitate to contact us if you learn any more. The illegal export of valuables is a major problem both in Moscow and in Saint Petersburg, and we would be grateful for any assistance you might provide." Kovalev walked them back to the door.

"I'm afraid I have to get back to work—someone broke into the mineralogical institute several months ago, and we finally have a lead. Thank you for visiting." He glanced at Marina, who was still pale and shaken. "I hope that next time you receive better news here." He waited for them to get in their waiting car, then closed the car door. "Come again," he said, and nodded as they pulled away.

Sasha nodded to the agent and then turned to Gennady. "Gennady, I made an appointment to visit with Orlovsky tomorrow at ten. You will have to come with me. I have a feeling that he is going to be the only person who will be able to help us. Victoria, Marina, tonight, we are all going to the Bolshoi Ballet, and . . ."

"And?" Marina asked.

"And we are going to have to work very hard to convince Dimitri that I am fully prepared to accept his offer and go into business with him."

"Sasha, how?" she asked.

They spoke rapidly in Russian.

"I need to make him trust me. He gave me a fake Fabergé brooch—so when we show up tonight, I want you to wear the brooch; it will send him the signal that I believe him. The suit is dropped, and so all is well."

"English, please," Victoria said.

"Sorry," Sasha said. "We're trying to make certain that Dimitri still trusts us."

"Of course he trusts you. At the club last night, he was certain that he convinced Marina that Dikarinsky is behind all of this."

"Well, it's time for me to let him know that I know the truth—the figurine and the brooch are both fakes. But I also have to let him know that I don't mind, and that I want to be part of his scheme. That should throw him." Sasha looked out the window. It was going to be tough, but he'd bluffed with consignors and dealers at Leighton's before.

Twenty

~

THE DRINKS PARTY WAS AWKWARD. John and Elise Burnham had been very jolly and social, and Masha, in a clinging red gown, served as translator between the Burnhams and the Antropins. Anne Holton seemed distracted and slightly off kilter now that Sasha was the center of the attention. From this moment on, the sale was his, and her future was in London. Lena Martin exhibited a new joy and a vivacious pleasure in her surroundings. With the lawsuit dropped, she no longer had to maintain her legal reserve, and she was enjoying what was now a free and exciting trip to Moscow.

It was time for toasts, but since Marina, Victoria, and Dimitri hadn't arrived, the group was left suspended in false cheer. As Masha gave instructions to the waiters and waitresses to pour more Champagne, Dimitri finally arrived with Marina on his arm. She looked absolutely beautiful, in a long black satin gown with oyster grey bands at bust, ribs, and waist. At her ears were a pair of enormous black pearls and pinned to the bodice of her dress was the diamond Maltese cross and crescent moon brooch that he had given her earlier.

This is perfect, Sasha thought. *He's fallen for the whole thing—he looks pleased as can be.*

Dimitri approached, smiling, with Marina on his arm.

"Well, Sasha, I couldn't be happier," Dimitri said. "I'm glad you and your cousin are united."

"Well, blood is thicker than water, after all."

Marina smiled, leaned forward, and gave Sasha a kiss on the

cheek. "I should have listened to you when you said you knew what you were doing, and that you trusted Dimitri. And thanks for this gorgeous clip. It was sweet of you to give it to me."

"I didn't think I should keep it, given my connection to Leighton's, and I can't imagine a better person to have it than you." He smiled at her, and she winked.

"I'll leave you two to talk. I'll get us each a glass of Champagne." Marina lifted her skirt lightly, and swept to the bar.

"I'm glad this has all worked out," Dimitri said.

"I am too," replied Sasha. "Listen, Dimitri, you made me an offer in New York, which Madame Dikarinsky reiterated."

"I did," Dimitri said, his voice warming. Sasha switched to Russian so the Leighton's employees would not understand.

"When we get to the ballet, and the women and Leighton's people are busy with *La Bayadère*, what do you say we sit down and talk in one of the salons?"

"What will we talk about?" Dimitri asked.

"About your offer."

"I'm not sure it still stands," Dimitri said, feeling him out.

"That's a pity," Sasha said.

"And why is that?" Dimitri asked, raising an eyebrow.

"Because then you'll never know how I managed to incontrovertibly authenticate Snegurochka, stop the lawsuit, and continue with the sale . . . since you and I both know that she is a forgery."

"I'm listening," Dimitri said, smiling. "Why the interest now?"

"Let's just say that I learned during this process how disposable I am to Leighton's, while I realized that, to you, I am invaluable. You have a great plan and great jewelers. I have the expertise and the name to make it work. Together, we could become a very powerful team."

"I look forward to our discussion," Dimitri said. Sasha smiled, and the two shook hands. A light sprinkling of applause scattered through the room. Sasha turned and saw Victoria walk in. As usual, she stole the show.

Victoria was in a long, sweeping white gown of sparkling tulle, gathered like a fin-de-siècle ball gown with a bustled back.

"Now this, Sasha, is Dior," Victoria said, leaning forward for a kiss.

"Did you come with one hundred trunks?" Sasha asked. "I can't believe you had this here!"

"I plan ahead," she said simply.

"You're unbelievable."

"Why, yes, I am. Hi there, Dimitri. I guess we're all at peace now."

"Why, yes," he said, smiling. "One big happy family."

"I'm sure," Victoria purred, taking the glass of Champagne from Marina as she rejoined them.

"Well!" said John Burnham cheerfully. "I'd like to raise a glass to the Ozerovskys and the Shoutines for putting an end to all this silliness; to Sasha, who has made this all possible, and whose promotion means that much is in store for the Russian department; and to all the rest of you, for whatever it is you do here!" He took a big gulp of Champagne as Dimitri crossed to say hello to him and his wife.

"Your boss is charming, darling," Marina said. "I hope you learn to be so graceful when you toast people who've dropped a major lawsuit against you."

Masha interrupted the conversations.

"Please excuse me," she said in English. "The cars wait for you downstairs."

"Thank you, Masha," Sasha replied. "I guess we'll head to the ballet."

❖   ❖   ❖

Sasha thought entering the Bolshoi was one of the more amazing things one could do in Moscow. The group passed through the great columned portico beneath the bronze horses, which reminded Sasha of the horses of San Marco, or the team above the Brandenburg Gate. Moscow's first great theater had been the public theater of Prince Ouroussoff, but by the early nineteenth century, it had been decided to build the Bolshoi, or "great" theater of Moscow. Finished by Mikhailov in 1824, the theater was destroyed by fire twice; the current theater was the result of the 1854 restoration by the same architect who did the Mariinsky Theater in Saint Petersburg. Unlike the discreetly blue-and-gold Mariinsky, however, the Bolshoi was crimson and gold, with a vast parterre and tiers of boxes that held two thousand people.

The lobby was filled with marble, gilding, crystal, and Muscovites of every description. As the crowds presented their tickets, they were divided by seats, and thus by income. Those who moved toward the boxes were still, as they had been before the Revolution, Moscow's elite.

Sasha entered the box behind Mrs. Burnham, Lena Martin, Anne, Victoria, and Marina. They filed through the small salon that preceded the box, decorated with red silk damask and small crystal chandeliers; a table with *zakouski*, vodka, and Champagne was set up for them in the small antechamber. Sasha moved into the main section of the high-ceilinged box and helped the ladies into the gilded side chairs.

The vast theater was filling up, and Sasha turned to Victoria. "I hate to admit it, but even I am impressed. I've never been in this box before. This is incredible."

Victoria looked around the theater. The red velvet curtain had huge hammers and sickles embroidered at the corners, and the hammers and sickles appeared to be woven into the fabric as well. Over their heads, the hammer and sickle still sat in the cartouche that had once held the double-headed eagle. "Why still with the communism here?" she asked. "Everywhere else they've been changed."

"It was in this theater that the Bolsheviks split from the Mensheviks," Sasha replied. "The Soviet Union was really born in this room. I guess it's too important, particularly in Moscow, to keep the symbols here. I don't particularly care—it looks great, don't you think?"

"Spectacular," Victoria agreed.

Sasha admired the well-dressed and bejeweled women who filled the boxes to their right and left. One never saw jewelry like this in New York. Nowadays, there was an almost puritanical aversion to display in Manhattan. But in Moscow, it seemed, people reveled in a chance to show their power, their youth, and their indescribable wealth.

Soon everyone was seated, and the conductor entered to great applause. He noticed the group in the presidential box, and the orchestra burst into the National Anthem.

The theater rose to its feet for the hymn. Sasha looked around at the blank faces of the people in the theater. He turned to Dimitri. "Why is no one singing?"

"As of yet," Dimitri replied, "our anthem has no lyrics. They can't decide on them."

The lights of the great theater dimmed. The huge red curtain rose, and the orchestra and ballet leapt together into the beginning of *La Bayadère.*

Sasha's nerves returned. It had been thrilling and comforting to enter the Bolshoi, and to forget his situation for a moment, but it was now time for him to face Dimitri.

As soon as he was sure that his cousins and colleagues were paying rapt attention to the stage, Sasha rose quietly and stepped back through the curtains that separated the box from the antechamber; he noticed that Dimitri did the same.

The two left the box and strolled through the huge and empty halls of the theater. They walked in silence for a bit, and then Dimitri spoke: "I'd like to hear what you have to say."

He would have to weave truth and fiction in order to convince Dimitri. Sasha began. "I noticed something odd early on. The figurine was flawless." Sasha started. "Looking at the craftsmanship, I couldn't spot a single thing that was wrong with it. It was a perfect figurine. But when Lydia Crane came from London, she said something that unnerved me. She mentioned that the bow was different. She remembered it as being opaque red enamel, and the bow on the figurine was blue *guilloche* enamel."

"Things are reenameled from time to time. Why the suspicions?"

"When I went to the archives in Saint Petersburg, the only drawing of Snegurochka I found was of the braid. Not only was the enamel red, the whole configuration of the hairstyle was different. That and the fact that one of the archivists mentioned one of the other drawings that was missing: a lapis box surrounded by snakes. The box we saw together at Gloria Greer's."

Dimitri looked at him. "What else?"

"Only things that I can't reconcile: at the Dikarinskys, virtually everything is a fake. Some very obvious, some not. If you sold fakes to Gloria and the Dikarinskys, why are they so obvious, and why is Snegurochka perfect? I can't explain it."

Dimitri and Sasha continued in silence through the empty corridor.

"You've been promoted at Leighton's. Why leave now?"

"I wouldn't leave now. I would see Leighton's through the sale of Snegurochka. Let's let Leighton's pay for the tour, and we'll meet all the clients we need to set up our own business. We'll sell the piece for a record price, then use the publicity to open up our own business, and let the Dikarinskys pay for it. You provide pieces of the same quality, and I'll provide the cover and the clients to buy them."

Dimitri smiled and patted Sasha on the back. "We're in business," he said.

"That quick?" Sasha asked incredulously.

Dimitri reached into his pocket and pulled out a small tape

recorder. He pressed Rewind, then pressed Play. ". . . you provide pieces of the same quality, and I'll provide the cover and the clients to buy them," said Sasha's voice.

"Now, my friend, we are in business. Thanks to this, if you ever change your mind or get cold feet, I have proof that you knew Snegurochka was a fake, yet you sold her anyway. We're in this together now. Tomorrow afternoon, I want you to meet me at this address. We'll talk, and I'll explain everything. Let's shake on it."

Sasha and Dimitri shook hands, and Sasha forced himself to laugh cheerfully. "I think this calls for a toast," he said jovially.

Well, I'm in it, for better or for worse, Sasha thought. *I better figure this whole thing out by tomorrow afternoon, however, because now I'm in too deep to get out.*

Twenty-one

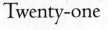

THE NEXT MORNING, Sasha woke and called Gennady on his cell phone. "I couldn't tell you last night, but I'm dancing with the devil."

"What do you mean?"

"I agreed to go into business with Dimitri. He didn't come outright and say it, but he indicated that Snegurochka and the pieces he sold to the Dikarinskys are fakes. I'm signed on to become his partner after the sale."

"In principle, this is very dangerous, but we're closer than we've been to knowing the truth. We'll meet in the lobby in one half hour, and we'll go to Orlovsky ourselves."

"Gennady, I'm terrified."

"It's bad, but not too bad. I'll see you downstairs. Oh, and Sasha?"

"Yes?"

"Make sure you buy a small tape recorder to wear at your meeting with him. I'll see you downstairs."

❖   ❖   ❖

Sasha crossed the lobby. He had his tiny recording device in his pocket. *Only in Moscow would they sell tape recorders in a hotel gift shop*, Sasha thought. He was ready to head to meet Orlovsky.

"You ready?" Gennady asked.

"I think so," Sasha said.

The two got into the waiting car and headed off to Orlovsky's studio. The ride wasn't very long, and soon they were pulling up to an old building in poor repair just off from the old area known as the Arbat, where artists sold their wares and young people gathered when it was warmer. Today, Sasha noted, it was damper than it had been since he arrived in Moscow, and the wind was bitingly cold.

Sasha paid the driver and the men rang the bell. An old woman soon opened the door and gestured for them to enter.

"And you want?" she said gruffly in Russian.

"Orlovsky, Vadim Apollarionovitch," Gennady replied.

"He's upstairs. Third floor." The woman shuffled away.

The interior stairwell was in poor condition, but it had once been a beautiful entry hall. They climbed the steps to the third floor.

Vadim Orlovsky was a happy bald man with a pot belly and thick glasses. Opening his door, he smiled at them and peered through his heavy frames, then looked confused.

"Mr. Ozerovsky? Gennady! What a surprise!"

"Vadim. May we come in?"

Orlovsky opened the door wider and let the two men enter.

"It's nice to see some friends and to have two at once!" he said. "Tea?"

Sasha smiled and nodded. He pulled the bag of diamonds Victoria had given him from his pocket and laid them on the table, spilling the stones across a piece of black paper, where Orlovsky could see them clearly and separate them.

Orlovsky shuffled around the studio, humming to himself as he prepared the three glasses of tea. Sasha looked around. The studio was far from modern, and it was filled with many old-fashioned jeweler's tools one never saw in the States. Hand-powered polishing machines, huge engraving devices for *guilloche*, a curved workbench like those seen in old photographs of the Fabergé workshops. Sasha idly picked up a small chisel for silver chasing, which sat on the table. It was delicately balanced, and the handle was worn by years of use. Sasha turned the handle over and saw a small plaque set into the handle. PROPERTY OF K. FABERGÉ AND CO., BOLSHAYA MORSKAYA, he read.

Sasha put down the chisel quickly. *Old tools from the workshops in Petersburg? Here?*

Orlovsky joined them at the table, and set down the tray of tea.

"Now then," he said, picking up his loupe to look at the stones. "Hm. Not the finest quality, but they seem to be cut well. You have a lot of marquise cuts here, also a lot of rose-cuts. Not desirable. Two pretty pear-shaped stones of approximately the same size. What are you thinking of? A necklace with a big center drop?"

"Earrings," Sasha said, his eyes restlessly scanning the workshop.

"Ah! Good idea. We can use the two largest stones as drops. I'll put them in a millegrain setting and surround them with the tiniest stones—visually they will appear the same size. . . ." Orlovsky stood up and went to a shelf on the far side of his studio, pulling down a large folder. "I keep these here from old projects; you never know what you might use later," he said as he began leafing through the pages. Gennady walked over and looked over his shoulder.

"Dima, old friend," he began haltingly, "where did you come across these?"

"I got a lot of them from Dimitri. He has a client who collects old Fabergé drawings. He gives me the copies. Aha. This will be pretty. It is an old clasp for a necklace, but reduced, it would make a pretty earring. What do you think?"

Sasha looked down at the page. The sketch was of a classical wreath bound with ribbons. Sasha could see he planned to use the marquise-cut stones as leaves. It would be pretty. The man was an artist.

"Charming," Sasha said, distracted. "Mr. Orlovsky, may I look around your studio?"

"Call me Dima, please. Go ahead—everything is for you to enjoy."

Sasha moved around the studio. He looked at every shelf, and at the pictures pinned to the walls. Finally, he came to a glass-fronted vitrine in the corner full of wax models for settings and stone carvings. His eyes ran over the pieces in the case until he noticed one item in particular. Smiling sweetly at him, and impaled on a black painted stand, was a wax model for Snegurochka's charmingly tilted head.

Sasha took a deep breath.

"Gennady," he said. "Come here, please."

When Gennady saw the head, he turned to his old friend. "Dima, how can you explain this?" he asked.

Sasha began. "Mr. Orlovsky, as I mentioned, my name is Sasha Ozerovsky. I work for a New York auction house, where a very important Fabergé figurine was recently consigned. A figurine of Snegurochka."

Orlovsky blinked.

"I have discovered that the figurine is a forgery, and I believe that Dimitri Durakov is responsible. Looking around, I have just found the model for her head here in your vitrine."

"Do you think I am responsible? I have nothing to do with forgeries—Gennady, old friend, tell this one that I—"

"I have already explained what a good man you are, Vadim. We are just curious how this model comes to be here, and if you know anything that can help us further."

Vadim took a deep breath. His elegant artist's hands trembled a little as he took a sip of tea. "Dimitri came to me about a year ago. He told me that he had recovered an important Fabergé figurine. The figurine of Snegurochka. He showed me a photograph of the figurine, and in it, the head was badly damaged. He said it had been partially ruined during the war. He told me he needed me to recarve the face from the original drawings from the archives in Petersburg. I was honored. It was a distinction to be chosen."

"Did you see the rest of the figurine?" Sasha asked.

"No. I was given a plaster mold of the section of the figurine to which the head was to be attached. A good stone carver can make the pieces match like a puzzle."

"I see," Sasha said.

Sasha looked at Gennady. "Could the piece be a pastiche, a combination of a real piece with false elements?"

"A restored original?" Gennady wondered aloud. "Perhaps, but I'm not certain."

Sasha looked at his watch and sighed. He needed to be at Dimitri's address later that evening, and it was quite a distance from Vadim's workshop. He needed time to himself, to think.

"I must go. Gennady, I have the tape recorder. Call me on my cell phone if you think that there might be more danger than I'm expecting. Here's the address."

Sasha bid Gennady and Vadim good-bye, then left the studio and got into a taxi. He had some time, and he needed time to calm himself. Where could he go that was peaceful? Someplace no one would look for him? He smiled. He knew exactly.

"Bolshaya Ordynka. The Convent of Martha and Mary," he told the driver.

The cab wound through the crooked Moscow streets past the apartment blocks, socialist office buildings, and new structures that seemed to be springing up like weeds.

The cab pulled up in front of the convent, and Sasha paid the driver and got out. He looked at the high walls in need of paint, and entered through the main gate. Sasha walked around the barren grounds, which evidently had been laid out as some kind of garden. Sasha wondered what the convent had looked like when Cici had visited the Grand Duchess in 1918. What else had passed between them that day besides the secret of the diamond brooch? They could not have possibly met simply to discuss jewelry; Russia was caught in revolution, and they certainly didn't know that Sister Elena, who had been there, would one day be executed for what she had heard, and for spreading the faith she had believed in strongly enough to take the veil.

"May I help you?" asked a female voice from behind him, in Russian.

"Thank you. I'm not sure. I just wanted to see the grounds."

"We are not in the best situation for tourists now, I'm afraid." The young woman before him wore plain clothes with a large olive wood cross around her neck. "We need a great deal of work. As you must know, the Grand Duchess was martyred in 1918. The convent was disbanded in 1926, and the sisters executed or dispersed. The communists used the church for a social hall, and destroyed or occupied many other buildings."

"I had heard," Sasha replied. "My great-grandmother knew the Abbess Elizabeth. I just wanted to look around."

"How interesting!" the young woman said, clasping her hands. "Imagine! To have known a saint. Come with me—have you seen the statue?" Sasha shook his head.

The young woman walked along the paths, chattering about the work the convent did now for the poor of Moscow, and how they hoped to rebuild the hospital and orphanage, as well as restore the chapels.

"Here she is," the woman said simply as they arrived in the courtyard of the convent.

Sasha looked at the tall white marble statue of the Grand Duchess as abbess of her order. Cool and elegant, she stood watch over the gardens, her hand outstretched in blessing. On the base was inscribed: "To the Grand Duchess Elizabeth. With repentance."

Sasha looked at the serene expression of the statue and it did help to calm him. *If I get out of this safely*, Sasha thought, *I will do whatever I can for this place.*

Moscow, 1918

Cici walked as quickly as she could down the Bolshaya Ordynka without attracting attention—the streets of Moscow were virtually lawless at this point, filled with looters and Bolsheviks attempting to impose order. Leaving Saint Petersburg had been difficult enough. The trains were checked regularly, and the exit through the Finnish border had become impassable. Leaving by sea was an impossibility, and so Cici had decided to escape in the most unlikely way possible. Karpov, the butler, and Nastasiya, the housekeeper, were disguised as her own children's parents, and she and her husband were dressed as servants. They had hidden as much jewelry and as many important things as they could among their luggage, but Cici's heart still ached at the thought of the rest of her jewels, which were in the vault of the Central Bank and could not be retrieved without attracting attention, as well as their silver, their Sèvres porcelain, and even her little figurine of Snegurochka, which was too bulky to hide and so had to be left behind. As soon as they had assembled their things, they quietly went down to the railway station and booked train tickets to Moscow. In Moscow, they hoped, there would still be enough confusion for them to secure exit visas, perhaps through the Ukraine or Poland.

It had not turned out to be easy in any way. Cici struggled to remember her native language so that she would appear a terrified German maid, and her husband was so much more innately dignified than Karpov, it was becoming more difficult to maintain the charade, the longer they stayed in Moscow.

In a last effort for intervention, Cici had decided to visit her friend, Grand Duchess Elizabeth, abbess of the Convent of Martha and Mary. Cici hoped that as a member of the Church, Elizabeth Feodorovna might still yet yield some influence with the local authorities—of all the members of the imperial family, she was the only one who had yet to be arrested. Cici took that as a sign that there was still hope.

She soon came upon the whitewashed walls of the convent and followed them toward the main gate. She glanced nervously across the street, where a group of police were nailing a sign to the door of the mansion of the merchant Diakunin which read: THIS HOUSE AND ITS CONTENTS ARE UNDER THE PROTECTION OF THE MOSCOW SOVIET. THE DIAKUNIN FAMILY HAS BEEN TAKEN TO A PLACE OF GREATER SECURITY. LONG LIVE THE REVOLUTION! Cici shuddered, wondering what had happened to their house on the Moika Canal in their absence.

She approached the locked gate and rang the bell. A small panel in the door behind an iron grille opened. There appeared to be no one on the other side.

"Who is there?" asked a nervous female voice from behind the gate.

Cici pressed her face to the grille.

"I am Citizen Cecile Ozerovsky, and I am here to see Mother Abbess Elizabeth."

The door opened, and Cecile slipped through, helping the sister shut and bolt the large and heavy gate. She turned and smiled at the petite young woman in a grey habit.

"Within these walls you are still Princess, Your Highness. I will show you to Mother Elizabeth. Please follow me." The girl gestured to a small path.

The interior of the convent was as tidy as its exterior. Within the court, there was a garden, which Cici thought was probably heaven in the spring. Despite the winter weather, she could see the neat flower beds; the roses and lilac bushes were carefully wrapped to protect them from the Moscow cold. There were several other buildings within the compound; a hospital for the poor, a beautiful church, and residences for the sisters and the abbess. All were not more than fifteen years old, but they had been inspired by medieval Muscovite architecture. Within the walls, all was calm, and the sisters went about their religious and civic duties protected from the chaos that had become Moscow.

Cici was shown to an administration building and ushered into a bright and comfortable sitting room. The nun seated there rose to greet her.

"Your Highness, what a pleasure to see you again," she said with warmth, extending her hand.

"Varvara Yakovlev?" asked Cici incredulously.

"Sister Varvara now, my dear," she said with a smile.

"I had no idea you had followed the Grand Duchess when she took the veil," Cici said.

"I could not leave my mistress," the woman said simply. "And life here is so peaceful, and so clear. It is a pleasure to be here rather than in the world. Particularly now."

"I agree," said Cici. "If I didn't have a family, I would join you in the cloister myself."

"Ah, we are not cloistered. Every day our sisters leave the convent and serve the poor of Moscow. Some choose not to leave the walls; other choose to do so. We are frightfully modern." She giggled at the thought of being modern, while behind medieval walls and wearing a pearl grey habit.

"It has been good to see you. I will let the abbess know you are here." She turned to leave, then stopped and turned back.

"Yes?" Cici asked.

Sister Varvara walked back to her and embraced her.

"Good-bye, Cici. May God bless and keep you. I can see it in your eyes—you will leave Russia, too. Others before you have come to say good-bye to Mother Elizabeth."

Cici looked down. Sister Varvara smiled again, and left.

Soon another door opened, and the small nun who had met her at the door gestured for her to follow.

Cici walked down a corridor, and entered an office painted sky blue.

Elizabeth Feodorovna stood to greet her. "My dear Cecile," said the Grand Duchess, holding out her arms to embrace her old friend.

Cici curtsied out of habit and then embraced the abbess, who smelled sweetly and pleasantly of honeysuckle and jasmine.

"No more curtsies, citizeness," said Elizabeth, suppressing a mischievous smile. "Now, please sit down. Sister Elena, will you please bring us tea, and the Princess and I will have a short chat. We have vespers at five so I have a bit of time. Cici, tell me how you came to us behind the walls."

Cici looked at the former Grand Duchess's serene and beautiful face, and she broke down. She told the story of the mobs, the violence, the looted houses of friends, the horrible breadlines, and the strikes. She told of their disguise and the escape, and how they were cowering in a rented hotel room near the train station.

Sister Elena brought the tea in to the Grand Duchess, who poured with great grace and nodded as Cici spoke. "The Lord never gives us more than we can bear, Cecile," she finally said. "What will you do?"

"I had hoped that you might have some influence with the authorities, Abbess."

"If I had, my dear, you can be certain that I would do all that I could for you, and for every person who came to me for help. Sadly, I am here at the mercy of God and the Moscow Soviet. Neither of them has yet seen fit to relieve me of my duties here, and I am afraid that it is of only the former that I may request help on your behalf. Do you have money?"

"We have what we need, and jewels besides. We should be all right. But the convent—I worry for you. In fact . . ." Cecile reached into her reticule and pulled out a red velvet box. "After your husband was . . . after . . ." she faltered.

"After 1905," the Grand Duchess said gently.

"Yes, after 1905," Cici said in relief at not having to discuss the Grand Duke's brutal assassination. "When you took your orders and the veil, you were kind enough to give me this most extraordinary jewel. Now, things like jewels seem very unimportant, and I thought I might return it to you—for the convent—in case there is, well, trouble."

"No, no. I will not hear of it. The brooch is yours, as I intended it to be so many years ago. I want nothing of the sort." The Grand Duchess paused. "We are well enough, thanks be to God. Unless . . . unless something terrible happens. I must ask you—are you planning to leave Russia?"

Cecile nodded.

"Then I ask you to do one thing for us," she said. "In the event that something unfortunate should happen to me—"

"No!" Cici interrupted, but she was stopped short by Elizabeth's contented expression.

"In the event something should happen to me, or to the trusts that supply funds to this convent, or should you ever hear abroad that the convent is in danger, please sell it, then do what you can to get the funds to the sisters here. If the revolution is a success, and Russia becomes the utopia these Bolsheviks promise, perhaps you will not need to do this. Unfortunately, I see more needy now than ever, and I believe there will be even more." She leaned back in her chair. "Please, for now, keep it."

Cici picked up the worn velvet box and opened it. The large sapphire brooch surrounded by diamonds sat inside.

Elizabeth Feodorovna took the box and looked again at the piece that had been hers for so many years. "When my great-aunt, the Princess of Hesse-Darmstadt, married Alexander II, he gave this to her as a gift. After she died, it was given to my late husband.

When we became engaged, he gave it to me, and he said that one Romanov had given it in love to his Hessian princess, and so again he gave it in love to his Hessian bride." Elizabeth smiled fondly at the memory, and she touched the brooch with affection.

"When I took the veil, I gave away or sold all my jewelry, save for a very few pieces of extraordinary sentimental value. This was the very last. It was my final vanity. Please keep it; hold it for me. If this revolution is a hiccup, and you return to Russia, I will remain pleased that it is in the family of one who has always been a friend, and who knew me when I was a child. But if . . ." her voice trailed off.

"It is a beautiful story, and I have enjoyed it these past years," Cici said. "The sapphire is very fine; why it must be over twenty carats."

The Grand Duchess looked startled. "Oh, no, Cici. Don't you see? The stone is a blue diamond. It is thirty-two carats, and almost without price."

Cici stared in awe at the stone. It was incomprehensibly valuable. With it, the Ozerovskys could buy their palace on the Moika four times over. She had never realized.

"I am sorry that I cannot help you further," Elizabeth said, rising, "but I pray that you will not have to do as I have asked you. The guards sometimes stop by in the late afternoons to make sure I haven't fled. I should leave now, were I you. Thank you for coming. I am afraid I must prepare for vespers, but Sister Elena and I will walk you to the gate."

Cici put the jewel in her bag, and she walked with the abbess through the wintry garden in silence, trailed by the tiny Sister Elena. With the Grand Duchess, Cici felt calm and at peace, as if everything would be all right after all.

"Good-bye, old friend," Elizabeth said, kissing her on both cheeks. "I pray that you and your family leave safely."

"And I pray for you and the sisters," Cici replied. She turned to leave.

"Oh, Cici," Elizabeth said suddenly. "The Dowager Empress Marie and some of the family are in the Crimea. Go south and leave with them, if you can. When you see them, tell them they are in my prayers."

Cici nodded. Yalta. The Black Sea. From there, they could book passage to Constantinople. The Whites were still in control there— it would be hard to cross, but perhaps. Cici realized that this was not simply a casual comment on the part of the Grand Duchess. She had just been given instructions on the only way she and her family were likely to escape.

She walked out the gate, which Sister Elena held open for her once again. Once she was through, she turned to wave good-bye. Elizabeth stood framed in the doorway. Standing there in her long grey habit and smiling serenely, she raised her hand in blessing, and the door of the convent closed quietly.

Cici would see that image in her dreams for years.

Twenty-two

~

SASHA RANG THE BELL at Dimitri's building late that evening. He was rung in quickly, and Sasha climbed the stairs nonchalantly, his mask in place.

"Up here, Sasha," called Dimitri.

Sasha came around the last landing and looked up to where Dimitri stood, casually leaning in a doorway smoking a cigarette. "Come on in," he said. "I want to show you our next two sales, my friend."

Sasha walked into the clean room. There was a fully equipped workroom, as well as jeweler's supplies. In contrast to Orlovsky's workshop, all of the most modern equipment was here. The windows were all shut and painted black so that no one on the outside could see in. Hoping that he was discreet, Sasha turned on the tape recorder in his jacket.

"So, here you are. Now I can explain." Gesturing to Sasha to take a chair, Dimitri sat down at one of the large worktables and pulled out two well-worn Fabergé boxes. He spoke in Russian. "You noticed the difference in the quality of the forgeries. When I started, I went to the best artists, and I started copying small hardstone figurines that are rarely signed, easy to copy, and fairly inexpensive to make. The results were fine, but they didn't fool anyone. After making some money selling those to stupid tourists who don't know better, I upgraded. I found one or two legitimate silver pieces and began making casts of them. Those were very successful—I sold a ton. E-bay is the greatest invention ever."

Sasha stared at him, fascinated.

"With the money from the silver, I had enough to move into enameling and gold work. You need very good jewelers and enamelers, but as you know, when the pieces are finished, they have no provenance. They are hard to sell in the West for real money, except to the uninitiated. For those pieces, I used those tourist shops that are all over New York—you know, the ones that are always going out of business?"

Sasha nodded as he began to catch on. "So that is where the Dikarinskys came in."

"Exactly. I met them and soon realized they would buy anything I sold them. The pieces I was making then suited them: flashy, covered in eagles, no subtlety. The Dikarinskys made more and more money, and I charged them to match. Eventually, I had enough money to hire the criminals."

"The criminals?" Sasha asked.

"Yes, the ones I used to start breaking into the archives to take the files. With those, I could copy lost original pieces and then sell them on the Western market, because these forgeries had something none of the others did—researchable provenance."

"Very clever."

"Thank you. I think so." He smiled. "So, I had a ton of cash, and I had to think how to take it to the next level. I realized that the flaw with my pieces was that they were too much alike. They were each created by individual artists, who did some things well, and other things not so well. . . ."

Sasha realized where this story was going. He remembered what his mother had said years before in London about the perfection of pieces that traveled through dozens of pairs of hands and past so many pairs of eyes in order to reach perfection.

"If you use one artist on a piece, well—he may be a master enameler, but his gold work might be iffy. Or his stone setting isn't perfect. That's when I looked at the structure of the Fabergé workshops. Each part of each piece was done by a different artist. What

I did was to tell many different artists that we were restoring a pre-existing piece. Each of them completed their own individual section with no knowledge that others were involved. Then I would have them assembled and finished here. The first result—"

"Was Snegurochka," Sasha finished.

"Exactly. Since then, I have been assembling pieces that will shake the art world once we sell Snegurochka. Look." He pushed one of the boxes toward Sasha, who opened it.

Inside was an exquisite spray of sweet peas on green gold stems that fit into a rock crystal vase carved to appear as if it were full of water. The fluted and ruffled blossoms were graduated flat enamel in shades of blushing pink and deep cream. It was a masterpiece. As a forgery, it was undetectable to him.

"Not bad, yes?" Dimitri smiled with pleasure. Sasha forced himself to smile and nod.

"But here is the triumph. This took most of last year." Dimitri opened the other box and pushed it across to Sasha.

Unbelievable. It was the Danish Jubilee Egg. Enameled in translucent blue and white, it was surmounted by the elephant with a *howdah*, the symbol of the Danish Crown. The egg was supported by griffons, representing the House of Romanov. Commissioned for the Dowager Empress in commemoration of her parents' jubilee, the piece had not been seen in public since before the Revolution.

According to Lydia Crane, it had been sold to the von Kemps in Berlin, and lost. Sasha understood. If Snegurochka were sold at auction, its provenance would be legitimized. If Snegurochka could have survived the war, so then could the Danish Jubilee Egg, and the Wheelbarrow Egg—each worth $10 million or more on the open market. Sasha was staggered by the audacity of the plan, and the perfection of these fakes that had passed through so many pairs of hands. Incredible.

There was a knock on the door.

"That is my chief workmaster," Dimitri said. "I asked him to come to explain how the pieces are assembled when no one ever works together. He can do it better than I. I'm no technician."

No sooner had Dimitri begun to approach the door than it was smashed in. The room was suddenly flooded with men in uniform, all waving guns and shouting in Russian. Sasha found himself pinned to the worktable, with his arm painfully twisted behind his back, his eyes centimeters from the base of the egg.

Those gold leaf-tip moldings are flawless, he thought in a surreal moment until the pain of his twisted arm blocked it out.

"In the name of the Russian Federation and its people, you, Dimitri Durakov, are under arrest. I am Agent Kovalev of the State Security Service. Release the other man; he is innocent."

Sasha was released and looked up. Dimitri was red with rage and struggling against the officers who were pulling him from the room. He turned back and gave Sasha a last twisted look, his eyes full of rage, blood dripping from his nose. He spat at Sasha as he was wrenched from the room and taken away. Gennady and Orlovsky entered after he was gone, ashen and concerned, with an excited Victoria behind them.

"I have it all on tape," Sasha said in Russian. "It was brilliant. Just look at these. He used dozens of skilled jewelers, none of whom knew that they were collaborating in the scam."

"I know," Gennady said. "We figured it out after you left."

"How?"

"Vadim began calling fellow restorers who might have done some work for Dimitri. In five calls, we found the artists who had manufactured Snegurochka's hands, *sarafan*, diamond overlays, and the green-gold grass. We realized what he had done, and all the jewelers promised to testify against him. Then a few hours later, Victoria called. She went back to the archives with Marina—they were reading inventory lists, and realized that only pieces made for the imperial family were in velvet boxes—Snegurochka's box was a fake. They called us, we told them what we'd learned, Marina translated, and that's how they got Agent Kovalev to come with his men. Remember how Kovalev mentioned a theft from the mineralogical institute? It was of a very large piece of purpurine—the piece used for Snegurochka. We made the connections, and we tried to find you so you wouldn't come here in the first place, but we couldn't. Where were you?"

"I went to the Convent of Martha and Mary," Sasha said.

"Well St. Elizabeth certainly looked after you," Orlovsky said, crossing himself.

She certainly did, Sasha thought. Smiling to himself he remembered his promise.

Twenty-three

ULTIMATELY, NEW YORK DECIDED that the Russian season had been a bit of a failure. At Park Avenue dinner parties, openings at galleries, and under the hairdryers at Kenneth, it was mutually agreed that the sales had not gone as well as might have been expected.

The sudden withdrawal of Snegurochka from Leighton's sale, combined with the uncertainty of the provenance of the diamond necklace at Christie's, made for uneasy bidders. Though Sasha's Fabergé tea table went for a record price, many pieces remained unsold. The Christie's and Sotheby's sales did no better, though Madame Dikarinsky paid a fortune for the necklace despite the bad press. Once again rumors swirled that one or more of the departments would close its doors.

Sasha, however, had no such worries for his own department. Though his sale had gone only relatively well, his discovery of the Durakov forgeries had taken Moscow by storm, and had earned him more than fifteen minutes of international attention. Back at Leighton's, Sasha had noticed a sudden deference from colleagues who had heretofore ignored him, and John Burnham made a point of addressing him by name and introducing him to their most important clients. Everyone wanted to hear the story from Sasha's own lips.

Newer, more interesting versions of his Moscow adventures began to be repeated around town. One involved a near-death escape from Lubyanka prison. Another in which Sasha wrestled a gun from

Dimitri's hands was a particular source of amusement for his grand-parents. Sasha's grandfather remarked dryly that were it true, he would have been the first Ozerovsky to wrestle, and Sasha's grand-mother noted that she had never seen anyone wrestle as much as Sasha—though it was usually with his conscience and not with a member of the Mafia.

Truth aside, Moscow had served Sasha well. His exploits drew in clients faster than anything he had ever done before, and his sale for the fall would be extraordinary. The Travis's salmon pink enamel clock was his now finally, and Madame Joubert's Fabergé Easter egg necklace had been consigned, though she hastened to add that her offer of a long weekend on the Riviera still stood.

In addition, and much to Sasha's surprise, Marina had called from Paris to ask him if he would accept the blue diamond brooch for sale. With everything she had learned about the history of the brooch, she felt that, though she regretted selling it, it was too valuable to sit in her jewelry box; besides, it would be better off if the families did what the Grand Duchess had originally planned. The brooch would be sold, fully documented, and 50 percent of the proceeds would go to the Convent of Martha and Mary in Moscow, the rest being re-tained by Marina to establish a Shchermanov family trust. Sasha wasn't altogether sure that Marina wouldn't be the trust's largest re-cipient, but it didn't really matter. They were friends, and the brooch would make his year. In fact, he was quite certain his father would buy it back to give to Diane.

Sasha was busy, and happy. He and Anne conferred a great deal by discussing ways to increase the importance of the Russian department. Working together, they increased efficiency by making London the center for Russian icons, paintings, sculpture, and porcelain, while concentrating the flashier jewelry, Fabergé, and sil-ver in New York. This micromarketing, they hoped, would increase the returns of their sales, without their competing with each other. They had returned to their respectful and easy relationship, and Sasha, for one, was glad.

Through an accident of the lunar calendar, Russian Easter had fallen early, and the Nobility Ball and his sale were only a day apart. Sasha was to meet Victoria that night in front of the Plaza. She refused to allow him to pick her up, and Sasha assumed it had something to do with whatever she had made for herself for that night.

❖   ❖   ❖

The Nobility Ball was Sasha's favorite event every year. Although it had once been described in *Pravda* as "the ball of ghosts," and although frequently the photographs that appeared in the society section of the *Times* were slightly mocking and less than flattering, the dance was sweet and intimate, attended by the same families and friends who had gone for decades. Sasha remembered how excited he had been as a child to see the large, heavy white envelope with the double-headed eagle arrive on the letter tray in the hall, and how much he enjoyed watching his parents leave for the dance: his father in white tie, his mother in a long gown. Even now, after going for ten years himself, he still felt a little excited each and every time the invitation arrived with his own name in careful calligraphy on the front.

Sasha stood outside the Plaza Hotel, carefully pressed and groomed, in the white tie that had been made in the 1930s in London for his grandfather's wedding. Sasha waited patiently, expecting a taxi or limousine to pull up any moment. Finally, a large moving truck pulled up in front of the hotel. The driver got out and ran around to the back, where he adjusted the forklift that automatically lowered items from the truck.

"You can't park here!" shouted the doorman, running down the stairs. "Go around the block—deliveries on Fifty-eighth Street only."

"I know, I know!" shouted the driver. "This is different." As the driver opened the back door of the truck, Sasha looked up and down the street for Victoria.

"Hey there, Your Highness!" Sasha heard Victoria say. "Nice night for a dance, no?"

Sasha turned to see Victoria step out of the back of the truck and onto the platform, which slowly descended, lowering her to the ground in front of the Plaza's red carpet.

She was wearing an unbelievable ball gown, which looked strangely familiar to Sasha. He suddenly realized that it was the dress worn by Audrey Hepburn in *Sabrina*. The gown had an enormous full skirt and was covered in embroidery.

"What an entrance," Sasha said.

"The dress is embroidered starched muslin. It wrinkles—Gran told me that in Paris in the 1950s she and her friends would rent trucks to take them to dances so they wouldn't crumple in taxis."

"So here's the truck."

"Here's the truck. And here's your date," she said, twirling to show him the dress.

"It looks suspiciously like Givenchy."

"Borrow from the best only," she said with a grin, linking her arm through his.

Sasha glanced at Victoria and noticed she was wearing the diamond earrings made from the stones she won at the Twelve Chairs. Beautifully copied from the Fabergé illustration in Orlovsky's studio, they were lovely, and hung glittering from her ears.

Borrow from the best only, indeed, he thought, smiling.

Sasha and Victoria walked through the lobby of the Plaza, eliciting admiring glances from people on their way to the various restaurants.

Passing the famous portrait of Eloise, Victoria grinned. "My role model," she said, pointing.

They climbed the staircase to the Grand Ballroom and entered the marble vestibule, a copy of one of the antechambers at Versailles. Passing through the ornate room, they went through the receiving line. Sasha first greeted the elderly and distinguished Prince Batushin, president of the Association. Prince Batushin had been involved in the nobility association for so long, to Sasha he seemed as permanent a part of New York's landscape as the Chrysler Building. Prince Batushin was the final arbiter on everything in New York's Russian community—what was *comme il faut*, and what was not; who was charming, and who was *déclassé*. Sasha introduced Victoria to him.

"Charming," Prince Batushin said, kissing Victoria's hand.

"That's a relief," Victoria whispered to Sasha as they moved down the line.

Sasha and Victoria greeted Prince and Princess Romanov, and then Sasha took his cousin Betsy's hand to kiss. As he did, he noticed her ring; a golden snake, twisted into a figure eight, with two pear-shaped diamonds set into the loops.

It was identical to the clasp on the necklace at Christie's.

He looked up, and his eyes met his cousin's. "That's a beautiful ring, Betsy," Sasha said, grinning.

"Let it be our little secret," she replied. "See you on the dance floor."

The ballroom was full, and Sasha could see the tables packed with people he knew. The Russian orchestra played vigorously. Victoria tugged at his arm. "What song is this?" she asked.

Sasha listened for a bit to the *balalaiki*.

"It's the *kahanochka*, a folk dance."

"Is it hard?" she asked.

"Not for you and me—come on."

They moved to the dance floor, and off on the side, Sasha demonstrated the steps and showed Victoria quickly how to hold her arms and when to clap her hands and stamp her feet.

"You learn fast," Sasha said. "Shall we?"

"Lead on," she said, following him toward the center of the dance floor. The two of them whirled around the floor.

Sasha took in the beautiful ballroom. He saw his father and Diane dancing, and his grandparents sitting at a table with Gloria Greer and Craig Tippet. With the Empress's diamonds clasped around her neck, Nadezhda Dikarinsky looked on, smiling at the dancers. Mrs. Dean sat with her family, her mother's grey Fabergé pearls with the diamond clasp around her neck.

Sasha and Victoria continued the dance to the end; when the orchestra finished and everyone burst into applause, he looked out over the crowd. *The whole evening is like an object of virtue,* he thought. *Every piece is perfect.*

ACKNOWLEDGMENTS

First, I thank Mark F. Darrel for reasons that are well known to him. I am grateful to my family for their help, especially my father, George Nicholson; my stepfather, Richard Locke; and my sisters, Sarah and Rebecca Locke. I also thank my wonderful agent, Charlotte Sheedy, a voice both nurturing and practical throughout this process. I thank my editor, Doris Cooper, for her early enthusiasm and her ability to help me see my characters for who they could become, and not just who they were.

The following is an alphabetical list of the many people who have helped me with the book, whether they know it or not. I thank in particular my former colleagues at Christie's, and also the members of the Russian community who have been especially kind to me over the years, and without whom *Object of Virtue* could never have been written. My deepest thanks go to: Bob Atchison and Rob Moshein, Alberto Barral, Anna Belorussova, Mrs. Nancy Biddle, Mario Buatta, Daron Builta and Steve Schaible, Jeanne Callanan, the late Prince Michel Cantacuzène-Spéransky, Count and Countess Nikita Cheremeteff, John Christensen, Dan Cochran and Greg Sutphin, Cynthia Coleman, Helen Cormack, Jim Downey and Jay McCrohon, Susan, Fréderic, and Lily Farcy, Mr. and Mrs. Wally Fekula, Haley Felchlin, Andrea Fiuczynski, Annabelle B. Fowlkes, Cynthia Frank, Prince and Princess Grigorii Galitzine, Princess Katia Galitzine, Prince Vladimir Galitzine, Regina George, the late Mme. Valentina Golod, Dr. Alexei Guzanov, Dr. Géza von Habsburg, Mr. Albert Hadley, Diane Hachtman, Patricia Hambrecht, Harry Heissman, Lucile Herbert, Michael Hughes, Alice

Ilich, Sandra Jordan, Karl Kemp, Frances Kiernan, Laura Laterman, Mrs. John Libby, Daphne Lingon, Gabriela Lobo, Robert Looker, Roberta Louckx, Francine Mallement, Leslie Mandel, Marina Miloradovitch, Geoffrey Munn, Mr. and Mrs. George Naryshkin, Evelyn Stefànson Nef, Marina Nudel, Mr. and Mrs. Ivan Obolensky, Anne Odom, Mr. and Mrs. Richard E. Oldenburg, Andrew H. L. Paneyko, Ed Parran and James Guidera, Susan Peacock, Natasha Pearl, Anthony Phillips, Faith Pleasanton, Dr. Stephanie A. Pollitz, Marc Porter, Lars Rachen, Shax Riegler, Tatiana Rodzianko and Anatoly Samochornov, HH Prince Nicholas Romanoff, HH Prince Nikita Romanoff, the late Prince Alexander Romanoff, Mr. and Mrs. Augustin San Filippo, the Messrs. and Dr. Mark A. Schaffer, the late Prince Alexis Scherbatow, Elena Siyanko, Dr. Valentin Skurlov, Jeanne Sloane, Justin Spring, the Hon. James Symington, Irina Tata, Alexis Tiesenhausen, Jill Trenchard, Dan Weiss and Amy Berkower, Genevieve Wheeler, Angus Wilkie, Richard Winger and Andrei Treyvas, John Wood and Randy Wilson, and Countess Marina Woronzoff-Dashkoff and Horacio Peña.

I am lucky enough to know some very Great Ladies, who must be thanked for their influence and their friendship. First, my mother, Wendy Nicholson Locke, and my grandmother, Shirley Webber, both of whom I admire greatly, and whose adult friendship I cherish. I also thank Lena Williams, who listened to my first stories. Jessica Jones and Casie Kesterson heard every version of this, and I thank these two Great-Ladies-in-Training for their friendship and patience. My gratitude also goes to Princess Michel (Pamela) Cantacuzène-Spéransky, Princess Vladimir (Tatiana) Galitzine, Mrs. Karl (Ludmila zu Schwarzenberg) Hess, Townsend Kemp, and Jan LaMaack Conklin. Thank you all for your friendship and example.

Finally, I must thank above all the late Lisa Turnure Oldenburg, who was responsible for my introduction to and interest in the decorative arts, a good friend to me for many years, and someone whom I miss every single day.

ABOUT THE AUTHOR

NICHOLAS B. A. NICHOLSON was a specialist in Russian Works of Art and Fabergé at Christie's, and in 1997 became the American Coordinating Curator of the exhibition: "Jewels of the Romanovs: Treasures from the Russian Imperial Court." He lives in New York City.

Touchstone Reading Group Guide
OBJECT OF VIRTUE

1. When we first encounter Sasha, he is a brilliant agent of his trade, making careful professional and ethical decisions that balance his service to Leighton's, his professional ambitions, and his responsibility to his birthright and his family's cultural legacy. Later in the novel, that sense of balance is disturbed and he recognizes, somewhat helplessly, that "Everything I deal with has blood on it." How does he ultimately reconcile these conflicting truths, and is he able to regain his earlier balance?

2. Fabergé, and Snegurochka, in particular, are seen by Sasha's father and others as symbols of all that was lost to war and revolution and forced exile. Each character wrestles with personal vanity and a sense of family entitlement while recognizing the importance of historical and cultural preservation. In the end, how are these internal conflicts reconciled?

3. Sasha is an expert on what is and isn't real, often seeing what even the most sophisticated eye allows to pass unremarked. And yet, his vantage on human character is often dangerously shortsighted. What do you make of this? What are Sasha's lessons ultimately?

4. Sasha has no control over or responsibility for his birthright, but he is determined to honor that heritage and do so on his own terms. How does he negotiate the seeming conflicts of a privileged family legacy and his own individualism?

5. As Sasha encounters the world of new Russian decadence, he loses more and more control of his mastery over what is real. What is the author suggesting about the moral and social conflicts of modern Russia and the people who are defined by it?

6. Sasha's mother has left behind a legacy of elegance, and is seen in idealized, even romanticized, terms—she is an "object of virtue" to those whose lives she has touched. How does she serve as a touchstone and guide as Sasha excavates both the history of Fabergé and of his family?

7. Sasha's father tells him that, like his mother, he is "dreamy and accomplished," "Russian *inside*," while he feels very American—Russian in title, or by heritage, or acculturation through his marriage. What is the author suggesting about the essential differences and the conflicts in the Russian native and émigré worlds?

8. What does Sasha's "Russian-ness," by his father's estimation, suggest about the kinds of longings and vanities in the world of New York Russian émigrés?

An Interview with Nicholas B. A. Nicholson

1. **You have become an acknowledged expert on Russian art, and Fabergé in particular. What attracted you to art, and to the world of art trade and preservation? It appears to be an interest you have had from an early age.**

I grew up in New York City, and am lucky to have a family that considers art important. Like Sasha, I was taken to museums and galleries and treated very much as an adult by my parents, who explained pieces to me and encouraged me to express my opinions about what we were seeing. I think my early exposure to art, and my familiarity with the collections at the Metropolitan Museum, the Frick Collection, and the Forbes Galleries, laid the groundwork for my professional career in art.

I became interested in Russian history and culture when I first read Tolstoy. During my senior year of high school, I went on a student trip to the Soviet Union, and that visit to Leningrad and Moscow really changed my life. I went on to major in art history and Russian studies in college.

2. **What gave you the impulse to translate this passion and expertise into literary expression?**

At first, I wanted to write a silly tell-all about the auction business. But as I wrote I realized that I cared too much about the objects and the people I had worked with to make fun of them. What was wonderful about Christie's was that I was able to work with some of the greatest experts in fine and decorative art, and to meet many important collectors and scholars.

I also made a number of friends in the Russian émigré community and was privileged to hear their family stories. The combination of these experiences turned into *Object of Virtue*.

3. Reading *Object of Virtue* is a truly sensuous experience. You take the reader inside the splendor of Fabergé and the material culture of Imperial Russia. The ability to *see* that culture, and convey it to a reading audience that is perhaps unfamiliar, is impressive. Can you comment on this?

I dealt with Russian objects and art on a daily basis for nearly ten years, and so it was very easy for me to describe the sensations of living with these things as a part of your everyday life. I also know many people who have intimate knowledge of Imperial Russia either because they have closely studied the period or because they or their parents had been there. I have read so many firsthand accounts of that time that I could imagine events in the past as if I had lived them. I am fortunate to have friends who are scholars of this period and were able to provide me with details I never could have known: that the car the Empress used in Saint Petersburg in 1913 was dark red, for example, or that the winter uniform of her chauffeur was cashmere.

4. Sasha comes from a family with tremendous wealth and social position, which he in no way eschews, and yet he lives a much simpler life than his parents, and he works. That may strike some readers as contradictory. Why did you choose to position Sasha in this way?

The children of the very rich whom I have known seem to live in one of two ways. Some acknowledge that their money is an advantage and they try to live a normal and productive life that includes working at something they enjoy. Others do nothing with their advantages, and coast along without direction. Sasha is very much the former. Also, I must note that Sasha's life is not so simple: the apartment he owns on the Upper East Side of Manhattan is certainly over half a million dollars, he can fly to Russia at the drop of a hat, and he stays in some of the world's most expensive hotels without thinking about it. In comparison to his parents he appears frugal, but it takes a great deal of money to live as "simply" as Sasha does.

5. Is Sasha a character who is familiar to you? Have you encountered peers like him in your travels through the world of Russian art trade? What part of you might be Sasha?

I know a lot of people who are like Sasha, and I like to think that there is quite a bit of him in me. Sasha admires and upholds tradition without being constricted by it, he is a loyal member of his family and a devoted friend to others, he is a consummate professional in his field, and he has great manners without being pretentious. I know many people of Russian descent like him, but I also know many Americans who share those qualities as well.

6. **The characters in *Object of Virtue* face enormous moral dilemmas as they grapple with the sale of Snegurochka. What is the position you are most sympathetic to—Sasha's? His father's? Marina's?**

I hope it is clear that I most admire Sasha's position. He believes that the figurine is, at best, a work of art he is vaguely sorry not to own, but to which he acknowledges he is not entitled. He understands that the object was created for his family at considerable cost to pre-revolutionary Russian society. Sasha's goal is always to preserve what was good about Russian culture (art, language, history, religion) while not perpetuating what was not (social and economic injustice, anti-Semitism, censorship, oppression), and his moral dilemma over the figurine's ownership is guided by those goals.

Sasha's father's reaction is interesting. He has always longed to have the same strong bond with Sasha as his late wife, and he sees the recovery of the figurine as a chance to do that. I think that Cyril's misguided attempt is, in the end, quite touching. He wants to impress and please both his father and his son, while honoring the memory of his late wife. In the end, by trusting Sasha and respecting his abilities, he does all of those things without the figurine.

I do, however, have pity for Marina and understand her dilemma: Marina is unable to distinguish between her own value and the value of the objects, which used to belong to her family and relatives. She feels a sense of entitlement to what was lost without a sense of obligation to the culture that produced them. You can see this in her callous comments to the curators struggling to preserve her family's furniture. Marina sees in a very dramatic way the effects of the old order, and the horrors of the Soviet system, when she finally understands what happened to the people who were left behind. This causes her to reevaluate her position and her opinion. I like to think that a little understanding and remorse are behind her sale of the brooch.

7. **Sasha's family, in the end, reconciles its terrible conflict over the sale of Snegurochka. That conflict, ultimately, is a projection of the difficult emotional and social negotiations of Russia's émigrés, exiles, and other citizens living between an evolving Russia and the West. Do you intend for this resolution to speak, in some way, to the larger social project of the Russian-American community?**

My experiences in the U.S. and in Russia that I drew upon to write this book are my own, and I never intended them to be either a lesson in history or a comment on the Russian-American community and how they should or should not react to their history.

It has been my privilege to know many different sorts of Russians: Russian Jews who left in the nineteenth century and have built new families, lives, and identities here in America; Russian noble émigrés who now live outside Russia but return regularly out of a sense of duty to restore its monuments and help its poor; recent Russian immigrants who have come here for a better chance for their children and are proud to be Russians; and finally, people who left Russia hoping never to see it again. I also know Russians who get up every day in Moscow and Petersburg, watching carefully to see what happens as their young government makes its way in a complicated world.

My book was never meant to be anything more than a fictional entertainment, but the people who inspired it and the situations in it are very real and very important to me. If readers come away from *Object of Virtue* with even a fraction of the respect and esteem in which I hold the Russian community, I will be very happy.